Straight Man Gay

Daniel Marion Culpepper

Straight Man Gay

© 2011 by Sherrie Yvonne Johnson
ISBN: 978-1-61170-046-6

Confession is by the author.
Welsh translations provided by the Welsh Language Board.
Professional proofreading services provided by WordSharp.net.

Please visit www.straightmangay.com for more information about this book, other publications, and to contact the author.

Printed in the USA and UK on acid free paper.

~Second Printing~

Robertson Publishing™
59 North Santa Cruz Avenue
Los Gatos, California 95030 USA
www.RobertsonPublishing.com

Dedication

To kind and gentle Patrick McAtee, who fills my mind with wonder and joy and expands my meager knowledge of a dynamic minority culture that is woefully misunderstood and to this day, still openly persecuted in so many violent ways by an ignorant society.

To my mother, who instilled in me the values, strength and perseverance that allowed me to believe I could accomplish this.

To the memory of
Roger Horwitz and Paul Landry Monette
and the millions who have died and are still dying.

Thanks

Although this book was written alone and without input regarding its content or subject matter, I embarked on this journey with the motivational input of well-wishers; those patient few who listened to my frustrations and knew I could overcome the countless hurdles. I want to thank Tina and Rina for their positive encouragement, Dave for kicking me in the ass, and Thanh for guiding me to the Billy DeFrank LGBT Community Center. I want to thank the Billy DeFrank Center for the use of their fabulous library and for allowing me to volunteer my time to support their vision of diversity and inclusiveness. I must thank those who read the manuscript and offered constructive feedback: Patrick, James, Liz, Edna, and Sioux. Ultimately, I give thanks to my wonderful sister Diane for her camaraderie and her numerous insights regarding my numerous oversights—and for obliterating my errant commas and self-doubt.

Confession

A burning love inflames my heart,
I cherish him as no one can.
Fate decrees we will not part,
The truth must out: I am a man.

Table of Contents

1
The Little Fool

Carol — January 10

My mother was an evil witch who carried her seething hatred of me to the grave. Her idea of parent-child bonding was to bung me in the street every time her current boyfriend felt up my knickers. And the only useful bit of wisdom she ever gave me was about money: If you can't make it, marry it. So I did. Twice. Okay, both assholes dumped me for a younger bint, but I've still got what it takes and I'm determined to use it to get what I want.

I lean forward and rap on the partition. "Will you turn that thing off? No, not down — *off*. I'm a paying customer and I don't want to hear that racket." I flop back into the seat and stare out at the rain. They're calling it moderate precipitation. Moderate, my ass. God has been pissing buckets on London for days. And when I say pissing, I don't mean that hesitant tinkle I let out in tiny spurts because there's some lingering cow in the next loo and I'm too shy to have a good, long pee. I mean that bladder-bursting torrent that splashes about the bowl with so much pressure I have to lift my bum off the seat for fear of a backsplash. This incessant rain is just amplifying my impatience with everything.

As we pull up to the address, I grab my umbrella and step out of the cab. Then I bend down to hand over the fare to this subservient creature. He stares at the money in his hand, looks up at me and frowns. Oh, no. This punter isn't getting a tip from me. Instead, I bless him with a few parting words: "Your cab stinks."

I cross the pavement, open the door, scope my surroundings... and truly regret saying I'd meet her here. It's a common dive full of common creatures living common lives with common thoughts rattling around in their common little brains. I rid myself of this existence years ago. I'm so much better than this now. And yet, here I am again, confronted with visions of nose rings, leggings, tattoos, and t-shirts with offensive slogans. I see skulls that are buzzed on the left, half-shorn up the back, and sporting one stringy lock on the right, dyed in a hideous day-glo hue. These are London's commoners; the dregs of society, the pale cretins I abhor and have worked so hard to leave behind. They are dead common, one step above street scum and only because they don't reek of urine. Laboratory mice produce more brainwave activity than this lot staring at my beauty with their dull, ignorant eyes. My understated elegance infuriates them. They know I don't belong here, a goddess among lepers. Their contempt (or is it simply jealousy?) bounces off my shield of superiority like the raindrops bouncing off the pavement.

I tug on my diamond-stud earring (a reassuring reminder of the Tiffany world I inhabit—a world I'm eager to return to) as the drone-waiter hovers near, hoping I'll grace him with an order. Whereas most cheap eateries present garish pictures of food, this down-market Petri dish believes encrusting the laminated cardstock they have the nerve to call a menu with bits of real food is more appealing to their undiscerning clientele. As if sticky gobs of canned marinara sauce and dried specimens of ricotta cheese would better sell the day-old calzones. Witnessing his lethargic swipe over the menu with a slimy gray rag—which only serves to smear the shit over the entire surface—makes the decision to say "no" an easy one. Drone-boy is lucky I've lowered myself to touch the water (bottled, thank God, but not even a recognizable brand).

I gaze out the window for a change of dismal scenery just in time to see a stretch limousine screech to a halt on the slick tarmac as a silly, little fool without an umbrella or mack darts across the street, trying to catch the bus. The tiny elf is prancing along on his tiptoes as if he were a show pony, sporting a pink bow in his wild, piss-yellow hair. I shake my head in disgust. He's just another commoner—and a faggy, little git.

2

I close my eyes and breathe deeply as I remind myself why I'm here. With only eleven months of maintenance left, I need another man, and he's got to be rich—very single and very rich. The hard part has been trying to find one without adult children clinging to his wallet. Those money-grabbing vultures can make a new stepmother's life a complete hell, sticking their big noses in everything, trying to sabotage a generous pre-nup or derail a revised will. The fact that I *did* find one shows my diligence and resourcefulness. Now I just have to snag him. And that's where she comes in. I've paid her a small fortune and I expect results. She had better come through for me.

I spy her as I open my eyes, just walking in, a moronic grin consuming the lower half of her fat face. With orange-glazed hair, pagoda earrings, and rhinestone-encrusted glasses she's just as bad as the rest, but older—a sad reject from the Cindy Lauper Fan Club. It's embarrassing to have this… creature approach me in public even if it is a shit-pit none of my contemporaries would ever frequent. She shuffles along with carrier bags and sacks and a plastic Gucci knock-off hanging from her shoulders, banging into everything she passes like a maced elephant charging through the jungle.

When she finally reaches the table, the look in my eyes clearly says, "It's about time!"

"Sorry, sorry. These half-day cabbie strikes are driving me mad. I was a little too long at the shops and by the time I did get one I had to share."

Smoldering anger seeps from my pores as I bite my tongue. I do not like to be kept waiting, especially by low-class people in low-class places. *What* is up with her hair? I've just realized it's one color in front and another in back… and the silly cow is chewing gum in my presence when I've asked her not to. I do my best to stay focused. Her antics are appalling, but I need answers. "Never mind that drivel. What did you find out?"

Her semi-bloated face entertains the look of amazement. "Hang on. Can I sit down first? Maybe you could treat me to a drink and a bit of nosh?"

Is she having a laugh? This ill bred, vile Patricia Thompson—a self-titled Informationist (a mere gossip)—is pushing her luck. With what

I've already paid, it wasn't my intention to slop the buggering sow, too… but she does have something I desperately need (and she knows it) so I relent. It takes her a few minutes to shed her cheap paraphernalia and shimmy-jerk her bulk into the booth. She orders a white wine, garlic cheese bread, deep-fried calamari, and fettuccini Alfredo off the plastic card while I stare in amazement. It's no wonder she's dripping with bad skin and cellulite.

As the waiter leaves, she jabs something in my face. "Before I forget, here's your invite. Now don't lose it. Without it you'll never get in." She spits her gum into a paper napkin and sets it on the table as if it were a delicate treasure.

I snatch the crumpled invitation and shove it in my purse.

"Uh, you wanna read that? See what it's about, what the fundraiser is for?"

"I don't care what it's for. You're sure he'll be there?"

"No, Carol," she exasperates, as if telling a retarded child something she's repeated a thousand times. "I told you before, I'm not sure of anything when it comes to him. He changes his mind at the drop of a hat. He says he'll go and then turns around and just mails a check instead. But the last I heard, he was still expected to show, okay?"

I slit my eyes, not liking the answer (or that bitchy attitude) one bit but not having any power to change it. "Okay."

As we wait for her three thousand calories to spew forth from the bowels of this fetid dump, Patricia's attempt at chitchat is a grating nuisance, like a lazy fly buzzing about my head. I'd eagerly smack it dead if I could only find a swatter. Why a lump of her nondescript upbringing would even think we had something in common, is beyond me. Her Cockney accent is rough, at best. Her language foul. Her mannerisms crude. Her appearance: haphazard, disheveled, disgraceful; yards of clingy, petroleum-based fibers encasing rolls of shameless, jiggling self-indulgence. I keep glancing at my watch. I feel as if I've reached my limit of exposure in this cesspool, and I want out. After twenty minutes, the first of her dishes finally hits the table, along with her wine. The second the waiter slinks away, I pounce. "Now, tell me everything."

She stabs several calamari rings and pops them in her mouth. She speaks as she chews: low class, typical, and gross. "Well, there's the obvious, right? Rich beyond belief, worth about four hundred million or more, only here in London for a few months, can't wait to get back to Scotland, and casually dating a couple of birds but no one in particular."

"Yes, yes. I know all that. Don't tell me that's what I paid you for."

The dirty glare flashed across the table could kill a horse. She adjusts her massive bulk and shovels more cholesterol into her gob. "All right, let's begin. He's got this thing about certain smells, so don't wear any perfume." My almost-beehive 'do' gets a critical stare. "And I'd lose that lacquer, too. He likes his birds tall and curvy so you're bang on, but those helium tits," she waves her fork at my breasts, "are really gonna turn him off. He can't stand fake knockers. I know you can't do anything about 'em and I'm sure they cost you a mint, but try not to shove those blimps in his face every five seconds, yeah? Just cover 'em up a bit, 'cuz right now they look like a great big arse stuck up under your chin. Christ, a turd could come flyin' outta that crack any second!"

My mouth drops open. How dare she insult my assets! My first ex paid a fortune for these triple-D, saline beauties.

She ruminates for a minute (in mind and in mouth) and swills her wine, oblivious to my shocked face and still staring at my breasts in a creepy, "Sure-wish-I-could-squeeze-'em" way.

Another thought finally breaks her spell. "He likes to shag early on but he'll always get a posh hotel room. He'll never take you back to his penthouse. As a matter of fact, you may never see his penthouse to begin with. That's off limits to everyone."

"Why?"

Her brow furrows and her loaded fork hovers in midair. "Not sure. All I know is you gotta have patience. And don't drop hints about wanting to see it—or his yacht—or anything else he owns." The fork resumes its mouthward journey.

"Right." I'm soaking up this stuff like the sun in Saint-Tropez. This is important information, and lack of information is where so many others have failed.

"Don't whinge on about weekend getaways or anything like that.

He'll drop you like a stone." She pauses as her plate of ghastly fettuccini arrives, slams some in her mouth, and continues. "And he doesn't wanna have dinner with your friends or family. He sees that as commitment, thinks you're tryin' to reel him in."

"I *am* trying to reel him in."

"Yeah, but discreetly, right?" Precious seconds are dedicated to emptying the contents of a saltshaker onto her food. "Now he's not into looks, so don't expect any compliments, but he remembers everything you say, so watch the lies if you have any. They could get you into trouble." Another dripping forkful approaches her gaping mouth like a jumbo jet on final approach. It's a wide load. She helps guide it into the landing strip with her fingers and then noisily licks each one. "He doesn't talk much. Sometimes he won't say a word for twenty minutes, so shut your trap if you notice him getting quiet and watch the questions. He can't stand lots of questions." She motions for the waiter to refill her wine glass. "He doesn't wanna take care of anyone. None of this 'poor little damsel in distress' crap. You need to deal with your own shit. He's not gonna rescue you, so you can't be needy."

I nod. "What about that gay comment he made a few years ago?"

"Huh? Oh, yeah. I looked into that. It didn't lead to anything. I'm not even sure why he said it. Although, the fag he was talking about—what's his name, John Kaiser—is a super-hot actor right now here in London, and he's gorgeous. Anyone would shag him. Hell, I'd shag him. But still, that's insignificant. No worries there."

"So you're sure he's not gay?"

She waves her hand dismissively. "Positive. He's straight, front door only, tits and clits. As a matter of fact, I found out a lot on that subject so listen up. At the hotel—if you get that far—never, *ever* jump his bones."

"What?"

"I mean it. Don't attack him and don't go for him. He can't stand that. Let him make all the moves, right? He wants to be in control."

"Are you sure? I know men *love* to be groped and seduced," I say with proud authority.

"Not this one. I'm serious, Carol. Believe me. One of my sources tried it, and she got a rude awakening and a cab lift home." Patricia stops talking abruptly, sits bolt upright, and stares at the diamond in my right earlobe as if possessed. Apparently, having scarfed her food too fast, she's now off-gassing; she tries to stifle a colossal belch—and doesn't succeed. The strong odor of cheap wine and garlic, accompanied by a disgusting, un-human sound, wafts across the table. Nausea and embarrassment engulf me as she rambles on. "Oh, and be prepared for a surprise in bed. And from what I've heard, I mean a seriously big surprise. This chap has an unbelievable pud!"

"Is that so?" I cringe at the crass slang. In my world, a penis is a penis—not a pud.

"Yup. You know that old saying about running the tartan up the flagpole to see who's gonna salute it?"

"Vaguely." I watch as she blots congealed Alfredo sauce with greasy garlic bread. "I suppose you're going to tell me I'll be saluting his... tartan all night long?" I make sure the tone of my voice conveys my upper-class disdain for her trash talk.

"No," she haughtily replies, as if I'm the one who's rolling around in a smut gutter. "I'm going to tell you: Forget the damned tartan; his pud is the flagpole!"

My face turns red. "Oh."

"Do you sweat during sex?"

"No."

"Do you snore?"

"I don't think so."

She shoots a doubtful look at me.

I sit up straighter in the booth. "No, I don't snore. I *never* snore."

"Good! That's champion." While she's been talking, Patricia has done a fantastic job of sucking up food like a Hoover and slamming back wine like a lush. Her plates are spotless—not a crumb left. She orders a third wine refill from the waiter, props her elbows on the table, and makes stupid faces and sucking noises as she tries to clear bits of food from between her teeth with her tongue. And then, because the tongue just isn't doing the job, she picks her teeth with her fingernails, carefully taking time to examine each morsel for its nutritional value once she's scraped it out. She finishes her command performance by unwrapping her gum (which now has bits of paper napkin stuck to it) and popping it back in her mouth. God, she's like a cheap tart with hairy armpits and a bad weave — dead common!

"Now, here's the most important thing I've got. This is what your money bought, okay?"

I eagerly nod and lean in across the table.

Her bulging eyes stare at me intensely as she mercilessly grinds her gum; a starving rat dead set on devouring a chunk of rancid bread. "Lose the emotions, Carol. He can't handle 'em and he doesn't want to deal with 'em. His world is calm and cool, no disruptions, no excitement. If you're nervous, shy, stressed, or angry, that's a turn off. He likes confident, strong birds who take everything in stride. Never panic. Never lose your temper. No tantrums, no begging, and above all, no crying — ever. I know you need the dosh soon, right?"

I nod. Patricia may be a lowlife, but she's got my number. She knows I'm desperate.

"Well, if you get emotional on this Scotsman or step one foot wrong, you can kiss his mega-rich, fine ass goodbye. Got it?"

I nod again, with just the slightest hint of humbleness.

Brian

I'm not a very visual person. I never have been. Looks don't interest me, and physical features are a blur five minutes after someone walks away. I'm more inclined to remember what someone said and the tone of their voice than whether they were wearing a black coat or a brown coat. Once they're out of sight, I wouldn't even remember if they were wearing a damned coat. I can't place a face in the crowd but let me hear a voice from years past and I'll remember everything we spoke of long ago. My keenest sense is my sense of smell, and as I grow older, I realize more smells — and scents — offend me. So, with the ability to remember things that were said and my acute sense of smell as my guide, I make most of my decisions in life that don't involve business dealings. My world usually chugs along at an even keel; well balanced, centered, and calm. I can't say that's the case right now.

I'm sitting across from Anna Kims, one of London's most beautiful women. She certainly wouldn't be mistaken for a particular Notre

Dame bell ringer, but as I said, looks are often wasted on me. Her age: forty-five. Her heritage: granddaughter of one London's most well-known clothiers. Her mission: land another millionaire. It's no secret. She's made that clear her whole life and has succeeded in dragging two (or is it three?) to the altar. Pity the poor buggers didn't last, but she did get a bit of maintenance out of each one. The money may be running out, though. I appear to be the next bugger. Am I shocked? Not really. I'm a big boy. I'm forty-one and I know the game. These days, it's easier for older, high-society women to make their intentions clear up front than waste time faking a silly romance to get their hands on decent money. They've got bills to pay like everyone else and, to them, marrying money is just like landing a job at Herbert Smith—only easier.

Anna is bright, witty, and decent company, but tonight she's also wearing a lot of perfume—way too much perfume. It smells as if she washed her hair with it, ate it, drank it, injected it, infused it, and then sat in a vat of it for three days (fully clothed) before putting just a dab behind each ear. And in the confines of the limo, my senses are being assaulted in the worst way. I'm getting headache and once I have headache, irritability and rudeness are not far behind. I'm an asshole in that way, and if I don't find relief from this pong soon she's going to find out just how big an asshole I can be.

She hasn't a clue I'm suffering as I stare into her face. She merrily drinks her wine and jabbers on about the inconvenience of the daily cab strikes. London's cab strikes don't interest me. Tonight, nothing interests me, especially Anna. Either that fact hasn't dawned on her and that's why she keeps talking, or (more likely) it *has* dawned on her and that's why she keeps talking—and drinking. I close my eyes. With every fiber of my being, I silently command her to spill wine down the front of her dress, but this chatterbox is a pro at pouring libations in moving vehicles, tipping the bottle gingerly and refilling her glass to the rim. I'm doomed. At this point, it would take an act of God to—

My thoughts are shattered as Jack crams on the brakes, the heavy limo screeches to a halt, and Anna—straight out of a classic Monty Python skit—hurls her full glass of wine into her face with a flourish. She's certainly not jabbering now. I'd be laughing myself stupid if I weren't so stunned by this incredible turn of events. I flip on the comm to discover the cause of this good omen. "Jack, is everything okay?"

"Yes, sir. Sorry about that. I just had a chap wearing a pink bow dash in front of the car."

A pink bow? "Is he okay?"

"Yeah, he's fine. Silly little fool was running for the bus. Didn't even look. He almost became your new hood ornament. Are you all right, sir?"

"Oh, yes. We're fine." I survey Anna, hair and dress drenched in red wine and a little bit still dripping from her chin. "We're just fine."

"We're *not* just fine! I can't go to dinner like this! I'm a mess!" she exclaims.

"No. You really can't, can you? And you certainly are a mess, aren't you? What a terrible blow." I try to feign sympathy and disappointment—but know damned well I sound like an asshole who doesn't give a shit. "Jack, it's unfortunate, but we'll have to take Miss Kims home and call off the dinner."

"Oh, my. That is *truly* unfortunate, sir. I'm *so* sorry. I'll cancel the reservations."

■ ■ ■

As I happily sip my scotch, riding alone back to the flat in a car that now reeks of nasty perfume and spilt wine and thanking God for the small miracle he just performed, I know what Mickey will think when he hears of tonight's incident. He'll assume I did something to ruin the evening, and normally his assumption would be right. I would have done something to ruin it because the evening would have been miserable. I would have made it miserable. I always do because I'm an asshole. Slogging through boring dates with beautiful, cash-starved women these past three years has left me as less-than-engaging company, even when I *can* tolerate their perfume.

Was the divorce hard? Oddly, no. We had an average marriage, but some people just can't stand each other after ten years. Moyra was doing her thing and I was doing mine. We looked at each other one day and realized we were strangers who couldn't satisfy each other's needs on any level. It was only a matter of time before one of us was suffering from multiple stab wounds and the other was being led away in cuffs. So she flew to Amsterdam and moved in with her lover—her best friend, Jane, from her college days (which shocked me just a little)—and I stayed on in the mansion outside Glasgow. I leap back and forth from Scotland to the flat here in London (a place I've always enjoyed) and life goes on.

"It's been a long time, Brian. The public wants you to start dating someone special," Mickey always says.

Mickey knows what the public wants. It's his job to know. I really like him, and I've always trusted him. He's never given me bad advice in the past, but dating for the public's sake is utter crap. I've ticked off every woman I've gone out with. Not a single one interests me. Not a single one understands me. And I know I drive him crazy every time I cock up a date he's arranged, but tonight I'm in the clear. Tonight, I have a little fool with a pink bow to thank for ending what would have been a miserable evening.

John — January 14

I'm a very visual person. I always have been. I love looking at things, especially beautiful things like a chic haircut, a sexy smile, a tight butt, or high quality shoes. I notice it all. You could say I drink in beauty and it wouldn't be a lie. And I love to touch things, to feel things—especially clothes. The style, the choice of fabrics, and the cut can make or break a look. When it comes to clothes, I think they're an opportunity to make a statement. And when I see something beautiful, I have to acknowledge it somehow, in some way. So, as I sit here squinting at myself in the mirror, humming *I Feel Pretty*, I have to acknowledge that... I am beautiful. I think. I lean in closer and squint harder. Contacts would help. How long has Mickey been telling me to get my eyes checked?

I'm a bit conceited. Some would say I'm very conceited and they're probably right. In my profession, I have to be. I need a lot of confidence and a big ego because I have to walk into each casting call with a hoard of good actors and believe I'm the best. When I do that, I always get the part—always. And because I'm good looking, I'm a bit cocky, too. Why shouldn't I be? Guys are always gawking at me and drooling over me. They get nervous and tongue-tied just trying to talk to me. They want to take pictures with me and date me. So do most women, even after I tell them I'm gay. It's the effect I have on people and I love it. Yes, just like Maria Nunez, I have the pretty face, the pretty smile, the pretty m—

"David looks hot! The public adores him! When you two step out, the press can't get enough. You're storybook!" Mickey proclaims, interrupting my *Westside Story* revelry.

"I know." I pat on more face powder and squint at my progress in the mirror. No. I should leave the make-up application to Linda the pro. It's important I look my best for the camera. I don't know what I'm doing and it shows.

"So what's the problem?"

Mickey is shocked and I don't blame him. He's tried so hard to keep our relationship going—five long years to be exact. David is a really good-looking guy and he can be sexy when he wants to be. There's no doubt he and I look great as a couple but I'm tired of the drama. He's unpredictable and volatile, and I want it to end. I turn around to look at him. "Mickey, he's changed. We don't have anything in common. You know he's not getting any work and that makes him angry and bitter. It's been hard on me. The relationship is such a sham now. I want out." As I see Linda approaching, I turn back to the mirror and study Mickey's reflection. He's going to have a bad reaction to what I've just said. He slumps back in his chair, emits a horrible groan, and mauls his face. Then he sighs and closes his eyes.

Mickey is a great guy. He's almost, but not quite, a bear. Born and raised in Los Angeles, his enjoyment of socializing comes through in his boisterous and good-natured demeanor. Hovering somewhere in his early forties, he's the proud owner of a booming voice and a magnetic personality that lights up a room long before he steps into it. A stocky build, bright red frizzy hair, countless freckles, and an overabundance of body hair that (I can only imagine) covers every square inch of his physique all pay homage to his Irish ancestry. If he weren't so damned hairy, I might have considered dating him when we first met, but the word 'waxing' never appeared in his lexicon so I kept my mouth shut. He also had the worst fashion sense I'd ever encountered in a gay man: drawstring, baggy-assed madras shorts and cheap, tire-soled burlap espadrilles — with bright white socks. In the end though, everything worked out for the best; he's my manager, we've become great friends, and I wouldn't want it any other way. If it weren't for Mickey, I wouldn't be sitting on the set of one of the most popular British detective dramas — as its star. He had to convince the stodgy producers they could have a hit with a (gasp!) real American actor and not just a familiar Brit faking the accent. He had to re-convince them when that real American actor turned out to be (double gasp!) gay.

He opens his eyes and ponders my reflection, weary and resigned. "I may be able to give him a kick start. No promises, mind you. There's an independent play by this new guy. I forget his name but the script is good. It's about a street hustler who gets framed for murder and then solves the crime himself. They've kept the casting call low key so there's sparse competition, and I have some history with the casting director, Andrew. I think I can get David an audition for one of the better parts — a speaking role, I hope. Again, no promises."

Linda takes one look at me and shakes her head at the damage I've done.

"If he smells charity he won't even consider it."

"I know, I know. I'll get Andrew to call him out of the blue, say he's heard some good things about him from a friend, wonders if he'd like to do a quick read — blah, blah, blah. I'll tell him to keep it casual."

He can see I'm still wary as Linda performs her magic to get me camera ready. Secretly arranging casting call opportunities for David hasn't worked in the past. A well-meaning production assistant usually tips him off that it was a favor, and then the dam breaks and a tsunami of wounded-pride shit (buoyed by plenty of alcohol) flows my way.

"I promise I'll keep myself out of the picture."

"Well, it might work if he just got a little role — anything, really. It might get him back on track. I don't know."

Mickey leans forward in his chair and practically bumps Linda's butt. "Look, I'm just asking you not to dump him yet, okay? Sometimes you just don't wanna be too hasty. You've got a lot of great things going on in your career right now, Johnny: the series, the musicals, the promotional appearances and the guest spots, all those endorsements. If the press gets wind of trouble in paradise.... Well, you've seen it. You've read about it. Look what happens when celebrities break up. The media always makes sure someone comes out looking like a shit." His hairy hand grabs my knee and gives it a strong squeeze. "Johnny, right now, with everything you've got going on, you can't afford to be the shit."

I close my eyes so Linda can apply translucent powder to my lids. Mickey is right about the media, especially the paparazzi. They snap a picture when David and I aren't holding hands and the next day there's a front-page headline screaming about which one of us caused our impending breakup. And if I did break up with David, he'd be so bitter. He'd have stories (true or not) to tell anyone who would listen, especially if they paid for an exclusive. I feel trapped. With my eyes still closed as Linda dabs concealer near the bridge of my nose and at my temples, I realize I don't have a choice. At least, not right now. "Okay, I'll stick it out for awhile."

2
Going Alone

John — January 14

My best friends are just like Ethel Merman's spectacular voice: tolerable at a low volume and in small doses, but only if I'm inebriated. I lovingly call them the nincompoops. Well... not to their faces. Together, the five of us have been through a lot since I've come to London: first calls, second calls, final cuts, demo tapes, modeling shoots, getting the part, not getting the part, elation, devastation. Some are employed and some aren't at the moment. They've listened to all my problems with David, and they're all gay, except Martin. Straight as a laser beam and married to Angie (we call her 'Angina'), their relationship is rocky. He insists he's not gay, but she won't believe him because he shuns underwear. I've told her gays don't hold the patent on going commando but it's no use. She's ignorant and homophobic, so I stay away from her—and her loony family. The poops and I try to meet at least once a week for lunch, dinner, or a night out on the town. It depends on our schedules, our finances, and our moods. Today, it's dinner and a trip to one of our regular clubs, a place where we all feel comfortable.

"Hey, Johnny! Where've you been, honey? We've already ordered," Jeff says.

"Greetings," Martin mumbles.

I sit down, grab a menu, and start scanning the salads. "Sorry. I had to discuss something with Mickey."

"Where's Prissy?" Ben demands.

"I don't know. Was I supposed to pick him up?"

He looks at each of us gravely. "Someone was supposed to. He had an audition. You know he lost his license."

We all know Prissy lost his license because of speeding, red-light running, and shitty driving in general. The little road terror has gotten more traffic tickets and has caused more accidents than anyone I know. We also know he's a pain in the butt as a passenger because he won't shut up about how badly everyone else is driving so no one ever wants to give him a ride. I flag down a waiter. "Well, if I was supposed to pick him up someone should've told me. I'll have a chicken salad and a diet soda, please." Head bobbing obediently, he scribbles on his notepad and ducks away.

"Salad and a diet soda?" Ben asks, looking up from his lasagna. Ben eats anything and everything. He's skinny, wiry, has no ass and puts away more food than a sumo wrestler in training.

I lower my voice. "I've been told I'm getting a little porky."

All three look at each other across the table and laugh.

"Yeah, yeah. Really funny."

Through a mouthful of prime rib, Martin asks, "Can they do that, man? Tell you to lose weight? They snap their fingers and you jump?"

"Of course they can." I pull out my phone and scroll to Prissy's number.

Jeff's confused gaze bores through me.

I roll my eyes and explain: "My weight can't fluctuate during the series. How's that gonna look on camera? I can't be thin in one scene and fat in the next." The waiter re-appears with my soda and I take a sip while Prissy's phone rings.

Still, Jeff stares.

"What?"

"But you're the star, honey. You're the moneymaker. I can't believe they can tell you to lose weight when you're the number one guy."

"It's not like that. I don't have the auth—Hey, Prissy! Where are you?"

"I'm on the bus."

I can't hear him with all the noise coming through the line. I thumb the volume and take another sip of soda. "What?"

"I'M ON THE BUS!" he screams.

Everyone at the table hears it. I nearly cough up my soda when I start laughing. We're all laughing. It's hard to imagine tiny Prissy suffering through a bus ride in London. He's still shouting up a storm after we've calmed down.

"...DAMNED BUS DRIVER CAN'T EVEN TURN A SINGLE *BLOODY* CORNER WITHOUT HITTING THE CURB AND THEY TAKE *MY* LICENSE AWAY?"

"So, I assume you're on your way?" My salad drifts down in front of my face. The pathetic thing looks as if it was pre-made and sitting in a cooler for hours—wilted, dehydrated, sapped of nutrients—but I'm too hungry to complain. I mouth, "Thank you," to the waiter.

"Yeah. I'll be there... whenever. Soon, I hope."

I shove the phone back in my pocket as Ben reaches across the table to skewer a piece of my chicken. "So what did you discuss with Mickey?"

I take a deep breath and say in a low voice, "I want to break up with David and he doesn't think I should, at least, not right now." I'm not insinuating I'm a great big celebrity, but I *am* a popular celebrity and reporters have been known to eavesdrop by taking up a close table. I've learned the hard way: You don't talk about personal things too loudly when you're famous, even if you're not mega-famous. All three exchange quick glances. It's the first time I've mentioned breaking up with David, and it's caught them by surprise.

Martin wags his little finger. "Is it because of his...?"

I shake my head. Martin, bless his ignorant soul, believes every gay breakup is instigated by the size of, look of, or working condition of a guy's penis. "He's just not the same. I don't feel... I don't know... respect for him anymore and there's no passion."

It's quiet as everyone concentrates on his food. Our little group doesn't handle extreme change well. When Jeff shaved off his wispy goatee, we couldn't look him in the face for a week even though we all agreed it *was* the right thing to do.

Ben finally puts down his fork and leans back. "You know, there's just no way around that." Then he leans forward over the table, pushes his glasses up higher on his nose, and whispers, "It's not like he can grow another one."

I roll my eyes and hiss back in a whisper, "It has nothing to do with his penis. His penis is fine."

Then Jeff leans in. "Isn't there something he can take? A pill or some of that gay spray?"

Ben perks up. "Gay spray? What the hell is that?"

"It grows your willy," Jeff proclaims.

"Really? How long?"

I glance at the diners near us. "Would you two shut up?"

"They've got these operations that... you know." Martin gestures with his knife. "But they never work. Damned thing always gets infected, turns green, shrivels up, and then just falls off."

Jeff scrunches up his face. "Eww."

"Look, would you guys be serious for once?" I plead, trying to get the vision of a shriveled, green penis out of my head as I attack a sausage-shaped clump of shriveled, green lettuce on my plate. "All I know is I'm tired of not feeling... not really enjoying...." I trail off as I look around the table at blank faces.

"Yeah, man." Martin wags his finger again. "That's not something you just ignore."

I give up. These guys are morons and it's just a joke to them.

Prissy finally shows up and collapses into a chair next to Ben. "Okay, what'd I miss?" His cheeks are flushed, his clothes are damp and his yellow hair, sporting his precious pink bow, is sticking up all over the place. He looks like a baby hedgehog that just fell out of a tumble dryer. He insists he wears the bow in honor of breast cancer awareness, which sounds commendable when people ask about it, but he really wears it because it's his favorite color and because Ben gave it to him.

I flag down a waiter. "Nothing important."

"Johnny's dumping David," Jeff whispers.

"Because he's got a small dick," Martin adds.

"And he can't feel anything," Ben chimes in.

Prissy looks at me with mock shock as he takes the menu. Again, I roll my eyes. If they're going to act like idiots, I'm going to ignore them — and sulk.

Ben finally pushes his half-finished plate forward and places his elbows on the table. "Okay, so let's say you're dumping him because of this... lack of respect thing. Then what?"

"What do you mean, 'Then what?'" I'm hunting down the last slivers of chicken in my sad salad.

"Well, all you do is give the tabloids a juicy story, David-The-Git makes you out to be a right bastard, and you end up going to bed alone."

"It has nothing to do with going to bed alone. I go to bed alone anyway, but I know what you're saying about the tabloids and David's reaction. Mickey said the same thing."

No one is eating. Everyone is searching my face for something more.

I set down my knife and fork. "Look, things were tolerable when he was in that summer review, right? But how long has it been—over two years now?" I glance at each of them. "Do you know what it's like to come home from the studio every night and hear the same old story of how he was late for the call, they didn't like him from the start, they rushed him through the reading, they said they'd call him back for a second look and never did? I've tried to be positive and supportive. I've tried to be understanding. I just can't do it anymore. He's moody, obnoxious, and rude." I lower my voice to a whisper. "He's drinking too much and he's been kind of violent."

Prissy flags down the waiter and points out his selection on the menu. He watches him retreat and then whispers, "Johnny, he hasn't hit you again, has he?"

Everyone leans in, waiting for my answer. The last time David punched me I hid the shiner under pancake makeup and behind sunglasses for a week. "No, he hasn't."

They're all relieved.

"But he's put some holes in the wall, broken a lot of stuff, and he's always passing out."

"Well, when are you going to dump him?" Jeff asks.

"I don't know. I want to do it before the Willowby event."

Again, all eyes are on me.

Martin laughs. "You're kidding. You'll dump him and then go to a function stag? Man, the tabs will have a field day with that."

"Why? It'll be okay. Other people are going alone. Mickey will be there and Rick and Sandy and...and Kyle."

Ben is amused. "No-Style-Kyle? He has to be the lumpiest anorak and the biggest gossip I've ever met. Just stand next to him and you'll probably sink your career. You mark my words." And with that, he pulls back his plate and shovels the remainder of his food.

Brian

"Brian!"

I pull the mobile away from my mouth. "Hey, Mickey." Just as quickly, I pull it back. "No, he didn't fix it. I know he was here last week. Christ, he was here for two hours, made a hell of a racket, and a big mess." I close the door and follow Mickey into the flat. He heads for the bar and pours a scotch and soda while I go into the living room and sink into a chair. "Look, I've said it before. I'll say it again. He's got to find a stud. The damned thing won't stay up unless he screws it into a stud." I'm rubbing my temple, ready to lose my temper. It's something I avoid at all costs but this situation has gone on forever. "Fine. Just get him out here on Thursday and tell him to find a stud this time." I toss the mobile on the table and rub my eyes. Mickey is now sitting across from me, looking amused.

"A stud?"

"In the dressing room—the long clothes rail. It's about to fall down again because he's not screwing the support bracket into a stud. I keep telling him: Find a stud, screw it into a stud. He doesn't listen." I loosen my tie and take a swig of scotch.

Mickey sighs wistfully. "Ah, Brian, we're all trying to find a stud to screw into. It's just not that easy."

I laugh. Mickey can brighten my mood on any day. "So what brings you here?"

"How was Monday night?"

I give him a roll of the eyes.

"Brian, Anna was perfect for you. I handpicked her. What did you do this time?"

"Nothing. She dumped wine on herself in the car."

He slits his eyes.

"I'm telling the truth. It wasn't my doing."

"Well, okay... if it honestly wasn't your fault. What about next Saturday? You're definitely going, right?"

"Of course. I said I would."

"Good! The word is out you're going to be there and that's got the press buzzing."

"Why?"

"They know you're going to make a hefty donation and then staying for the sit-down dinner — well, that's just icing on the cake. I'm not sure who you're sitting with yet. I haven't seen the seating chart. I don't think they'll be assholes."

I give him a cold look.

"I'll make *sure* they're not assholes. Lots of eyes will be on you, Brian." Mickey hesitates. "Will you bring Anna or maybe Vivian?"

"No, Mickey. I'm going alone."

"But Brian, why?"

"We've been over this a hundred times. I just want to go, force myself to chat with assholes, eat tasteless crap in a lumpy white sauce — God, it's always a lumpy white sauce — write a check, and leave."

"You could do that just as easily with a beautiful woman on your arm, couldn't you?"

"I could, but I won't."

"But what will the public think if — "

"Mickey, I don't care what the public thinks. This time, I'm going alone." I throw my tie on the table and finish off my scotch.

John

A cute shots boy shimmies by, balancing a full tray of kamikazes and Alabama Slammers above his head and swinging his little rhinestoned, micro-shorted tush from here to New York.

"Honey, it's been ages," Jeff shouts over the loud music as he watches that bouncing, sparkly ass disappear into the crowd.

I watch it, too. "Tell me about it."

"Okay, I will. The only friction I've been getting lately is from pulling my zipper up and down and let me tell you, I've been doing *a lot* of that!"

I laugh and shake my head. Jeff is beautiful. Unfortunately, he's also picky. He tries to accept flaws, but in the end, no one can ever measure up to his high standards and vision of perfection. A poorly-placed mole or a few lengthy nostril hairs just don't stand a chance, which is ironic considering he only has one testicle.

"You're gonna go to this thing alone?" Ben shouts as he sways a bit and spills his pint.

I nod, my eyes transfixed on all the men gyrating out on the dance floor. I love the music and I love coming to the clubs. I have an extensive fan base here and I live for the attention. I've started looking at guys again, even though I'm not ready for someone new. I may not be breaking up with David yet, but I want to see what's out there, what kind of man gets my juices flowing. I miss having a real relationship, one with a lot of sex. I'm someone who needs a lot of sex in a relationship.

I let my gaze (intermittently blinded by tiny strobe lights) wander around the crowded space. I see gorgeous guys with hot bodies, twisting and turning, pumping pelvises and swinging hips to the thumping beat. As conceited as it sounds, I know I could take my pick of anyone here. I'm that good looking. Specifically though, I'm searching for one particular guy. He's been here the last few times I've come: strawberry blond hair and brown eyes. I don't know his name but we always make eye contact—intense eye contact. I see him now, standing off to one side of the dance floor. The moment our eyes meet, he looks away. Then shyly, he looks back and holds my gaze for about three seconds before looking away again. There's a lot of tension between us, and I know he wants to talk. He wants to get to know me. If the nincompoops weren't here I'm sure he'd—

"Hey, why don't you ask that guy?" Prissy pipes up, invading my lustful thoughts.

I take my eyes off Strawberry Blond to look down at him. "What guy?"

Prissy is swaying a bit, too. He reaches up and clamps his hand on my shoulder to steady himself. "That guy, the rich one from the chat show. Why don't you ask him?"

"Who?"

"Prissy, what are you talking about?" Jeff slurs.

Ben stabs a knowing finger at Prissy. "Yeah, what's-his-name! Brian... something."

"Mallory," Prissy says, leaning—or more accurately, falling—toward him.

Ben laughs. "Yeah, yeah! Brian Mallory. You could ask him to be your date."

"I have no idea who you guys are talking about." These fools are too drunk to be taken seriously. I turn my attention back to the dance floor.

"He's this guy, right? He goes on this interview—"

"No, no. It's a chat show, Ben. He's on a *chat* show," Prissy shouts (and spits) up into my ear.

Ben giggles. "Yeah, that's right, a chat show, and he says he fancies you."

"'E's a *Scotsman*," Prissy proudly adds in the worst fake accent I've ever heard.

I shake my head. I've got hundreds of guys who have crushes on me and have said so in public. I get love letters from hundreds more. I even get nude shots from countless guys like Tate whom I've never met. He's the president of one of my 'official' fan clubs and keeps sending me pictures of his hairy butt and his less-than-impressive genitals. It's nothing new. I spy Martin making his way through the crowd with his pint and my half pint. Dozens of guys (including the shots boy) are checking out his ass, one of his best features and always prominently displayed in Levi's shrink-to-fit, 501 button flies—the only jeans he'll wear. "Big deal."

"Yeah, but Johnny, get this, okay? Listen to this!" Prissy's bony fingers are clamped hard on my shoulder. He's standing on his toes and almost kissing my ear at this point. "He's straight. He's totally straight!" He leans back, impressed with himself. "This mega-rich, married straight guy goes on the telly and says he fancies you!"

"Wha... huh?" I'm sure I didn't hear that right.

Ben giggles again. "I know. Weird guy, right?"

"Well, I mean, he was married when he said it. He's divorced now, but he's still straight," Prissy chatters, mostly to himself.

Martin hands over my half pint. "Who's still straight?"

"The Scottish guy who fancies Johnny. Said so on the telly, right on the telly. Said it to *everyone!*" Prissy waves his hand in a wide arc to include everyone at the club and spills his pint.

Martin, who never gets drunk, carefully takes the pint from him and sets it on the bar.

Jeff turns to Martin and says, "So these two yah-yahs think Johnny should ask him to the charity event." Then he belches loudly—right in Martin's face.

"I don't even know the guy. I've never heard of him. Why would I ask him?"

Ben turns to me. "It was just a thought. The tabs would have a field day with it: Gay Takes Straight Mate." With his silly giggles, he thinks he's just cracked the funniest joke.

I think he's a drunken ass.

He sees the look on my face. "Okay, okay. It was just a thought."

I turn back to the dance floor and sip my drink as I mull over what these two fools have just told me: A straight man has a crush on me.

Prissy fumbles with a button on his shirt with his free hand. "Well, he's gonna be there anyway."

I turn to him. "What?"

He clamps down harder on my shoulder to keep his balance. "The event. He'll be there anyway."

We're all looking at Prissy as if he's just become a cupcake. He's a bit baffling. Ever since we found out he likes to wear women's panties (backward) and can kiss his own elbows, we've decided he's a little... odd.

He rolls his eyes and almost falls over. He steadies himself on my shoulder again and continues. "I'm working it as a waiter. I saw the seating chart for the dinner."

We're still staring at him.

"My audition? The job I got? I'll be a waiter at the event."

Jeff looks a little shocked. "Honey, I thought you were auditioning for an acting job."

"So did I, but I caught the wrong bus." He's still fumbling with the button, which is now loose in his hand. "I was late and I missed the call. An agency rep down the hall said they needed waiters."

We're all smiling and just about ready to laugh.

Prissy pouts. "Hey, it's work and it pays."

He's right and now he's piqued my interest. "Marty, give me your phone."

He digs it out and I hand my half pint to Ben, who promptly starts drinking it. "What'ya want it for?"

"Information." Even though I have Internet access on my phone, I don't dare use it to look up anything questionable because David checks the history. And while some smartass might say, "Then just wipe out the history," they don't know David. Having no history at all would be ten times worse. I fumble around with the phone and turn so I can hold it away from the glare of the strobe lights. Prissy, hanging onto my shoulder and mesmerized by his own button, has to turn with me or fall on his face. "What's his last name again?"

He stretches up and carefully pronounces each syllable in my ear. "Mal...or...ee."

"Standard spelling?"

He pauses, deep in thought. "Two ells."

I spend a few minutes messing around with the phone. Martin stands close, watching my progress, while a drunken Jeff tries to convince an even drunker (and gullible) Ben that gay spray really does exist and will net him an extra inch with just two pumps. Prissy sleeps against my arm as he clutches his precious button. "Damn!"

"Wha...what?" Prissy is wide-awake.

"It's just a bunch of crap about his companies and his money. That's all these websites have."

"Well, yeah," Prissy slurs. "What'd you expect? He's a multi-millionaire. What else are they gonna write about?"

Brian — January 26

Today, I'm meeting Mickey for lunch. He wants to push another 'golden opportunity' under my nose. Lately, his golden opportunities have been a bit outlandish. It's because he's got his fingers in too many pies. He's made numerous stateside trips trying to play manager to new talent coming out of Los Angeles, and the jetlag has clouded his judgment. These opportunities usually just waste my time.

As our food arrives, he gives me his pep talk, the one he always gives. "Look, on Saturday night there may be a few guys who want to talk business. They'll want to see if you'll invest in their stuff. Don't get sucked into it, right? This is a charity event. You put on the charity image. You just look good, chitchat, and hand over some money. Someone might snap a few pictures, ask for a quick interview, or quote you on something. The last thing I need to see is you huddled in a corner, making a deal."

"I know, Mickey." I cut into my lasagna as he stares down, wide-eyed, at his plate. In one of London's finest restaurants, Mickey has asked the chef for a Kobe beef burger on a bap and he doesn't quite know how to attack the huge, dripping chunk of meat.

"I know you know, but you have a tendency to work business into everything and what we're trying to create — what we want the public to see — is a carefree Brian, a Brian who loves to socialize and schmooze and be a part of the arts."

I sip my wine. "But I don't love to socialize and schmooze."

"I know. God, I know. But just try, all right? On Saturday night promise me you're gonna try." Foregoing knife and fork, he grabs the burger with both hands and shoves way too much of it in his mouth. The sight is unappealing.

"Is this what you wanted to talk about? Saturday night? Because if it is — "

"No, no, no." He's trying to chew and spit out the words at the same time. "I've got a new business deal I want to pass by you — a really golden opportunity, Brian."

"Mickey…" I rest my fork on my plate and lean back in my chair.

"No, I mean it, Brian. This is a really good one. His name is Lars and — "

"Lars?" The golden opportunity is named *Lars?* That can only mean one thing: Mickey is after him. He's either another manager, an actor, a waiter, or a clothes designer. That's all Mickey ever hunts except for that one disastrous deviation when he was smitten with the overly affectionate rugby player who (amazingly) wasn't gay. That big mate knocked out two of Mickey's molars and fractured his cheekbone with one smack across the face after he tried to give him a victory snog, which isn't a big deal among men when it comes to rugby victories. But Mickey—unfortunately—tried to give it with tongue.

"Yeah, Lars. He's a clothes designer. Well, specifically, a swimwear designer. Oh, you should see his stuff, Brian! He's got real talent, real style, real vision."

I focus on a smear of greasy dressing that's proudly laid claim to his chin. "How long have you been after him?"

"After him? I'm not after him. What makes you think I'm after him?" His face is turning red and his eyes are darting back and forth. Mickey has never been able to lie to me. I resume eating and wait for the confession. "Okay, maybe I'm hoping something is there, you know? Maybe if we work together on some mutual collaboration and put in a few late nights to, uh...." Mickey's voice trails off as he waits, expecting me to say something.

At this point, I don't want to humor him. I just want to eat.

"Huh, Brian? What d'ya say? Will you come to see his work—his designs—if I set something up?"

"You know I'm very busy and I like to stick with real estate."

"I know, but this is *golden,* Brian. We'll take care of everything. We'll work it into your schedule. You come, you look, you go. No hassles. No gimmicks. No surprises. Okay?"

Knowing what deep money pits these opportunities usually turn out to be, I can't believe I'm going to agree to this, but Mickey is a good mate—and he's desperately on the prowl. "Okay. Set it up for next Thursday, late morning."

John — January 28

It's nearly midnight, raining hard, and I've just poured Ben and Prissy into a taxi after the grand opening of a new club. Wallowing in a drunken stupor with silly grins on their flushed faces, they're clutching each other like two rhesus monkeys—a mama and her baby. I've thrown more than enough money at the driver and given him Ben's address. There's no need to give him Prissy's. When they get this drunk, they always end up sleeping together. Prissy denies it, but Ben claims drunken sex with tiny Prissy is the best sex he's ever had. Martin will drive Jeff home, like he always does, and then catch hell from Angina for staying out late and running around with The Bent Boys — her not-so-endearing, homophobic label for us. I accept another hug (and photo opportunity) from the nightclub owner who was thrilled I made an appearance and climb into my Boxster. I love this sexy car. Three years ago, it was my extravagant present to myself for landing the series. I'll admit, getting a convertible was stupid. It always seems to be raining. But when we do have nice days I love to put the top down. Some of my best tabloid pictures have been snapped while I'm in this car with the top down. I rev the engine and drive off, ever mindful of keeping my butt on the left side of the road. My joy dissipates as I imagine the drama that awaits me at the brownstone I share with David.

I thought I was doing the right thing by letting Mickey put in a good word for him at the casting call. Mickey did more than that. Whatever he said to Andrew got David the lead. What a shocker! I was just hoping for a speaking role and Mickey went and amazed me. David was in the best mood after they called him. I even put the breakup on the back burner because things seemed better. But the call this morning from Mickey asking me to stop by the theater and speak with Andrew left a lump in my throat. I still remember that horrible meeting:

"Is he really that bad?"

"Just *look* at him, John. *Listen* to him. He thinks he's a prima donna," Andrew had said.

I listened and heard David complaining, even from the back of the dark theater where he couldn't see me. He was yelling for water. He was whining about the position of props. He was forgetting his lines and — worst of all — blaming everything on everyone around him.

"You know he wants his own dressing room and a chauffeured car?"

I cringed. Oh God, I didn't know he'd be like that. "Andrew, I'm so sorry." It was all I could say.

"*You're* sorry? I've wasted two weeks on this joker. I could kill Mickey for saddling me with this egotistical shithead." Andrew ran a shaky hand through his hair (well, what was left of it). Obviously, the frustration of dealing with someone as unprofessional as David had taken its toll on his nerves. He looked as if he hadn't slept in days. "We open in less than a week. I'm starting from zero here. I've got an understudy that's not even *allowed* on stage when Mister Prickhead is around. Every day it's something new, something else he finds unacceptable or intolerable. We can't get any work done. None of the acts are solid, not one—and he's been drinking." He fell silent as we watched David throw a juvenile, foot-stomping fit over a typo in the script. "I'm sorry, John. I've got to let him go—today."

■ ■ ■

I unlock the front door and step into the dark entry hall. The entire first floor is dark. I flip on the light. Disturbing silence. I walk into the living room. The smell of alcohol greets me before he does. He's sitting in a club chair with his back to me, facing the large bay windows. He turns his head. "'s that you?"

"Yeah."

"D'you have a good time with yer little friends?"

"We had a great time. Ben was doing this funky chicken dance and we laughed so hard. He was really serious about it, too, and then he—"

"I DON'T GIVE A DAMN! D'YA HEAR? HUH? *D'YA HEAR?*" There's a minute of silence. And then, in mock sweetness he says, "Know what I did t'day, Sweetie? Huh? Do... you... know... what I did t'day?"

I don't say a word.

"I got FIRED today. That's what I did. I went and got my ass FIRED!"

With difficulty, he stands up, stumbles around the chair, and faces me. As he reaches out to the back of the chair to steady himself, I see the bottle dangling from his other hand. It's whiskey, his preference when it comes to getting totally shit-faced and time is of the essence. Two inches shorter than me but a few pounds heavier and more muscular, he's always intimidated me in the worst way. His stringy brown hair has fallen into his eyes and his cheeks are sallow from dehydration. The gaunt, sickly appearance makes him look so much older than his thirty-three years.

"Aren't ya' proud of me, Johnny? Aren't ya' just fucking *proud* of yer Davie? He fucked up again, jus' like always." He swings the bottle and takes a sloppy bow. "At your service. I am... at... your service... to fuck up on command. So, ya' wanna give me one of yer famous pep talks? Huh? Ya' little fat ass! Wanna tell me how everything will be all right? How this jus' wasn't meant t' be? How I'll get the next one?"

He staggers toward me and instinct tells me to back away. I know doing so will only make him furious so I hold my ground, but I'm determined not to get hit again, so I watch his hands.

"Come on, Sweetie. Tell me it's gonna be all right. Tell me how great I am, how everyone *wants* me."

I catch him in my arms as he stumbles into me. Now he's crying. I've been here so many times, holding this drunken piece of misery while he cries and pities himself. It's the standard routine. I'm surprised he hasn't wet himself yet, but I'm sure it's coming. "David, the drinking. It doesn't help the sit—"

"What do *you* know?" He violently pushes away from me and looks me up and down with disgust. "You! You and your *series!* You and your contracts and your musicals! You and your stupid *fucking* FAN CLUBS! HUH, FAT ASS? *WHAT THE HELL DO YOU KNOW?*"

He hurls the bottle at the wall and I close my eyes as it shatters. A spray of glass and whiskey hits my face. Then, sobbing, he collapses to the floor and curls up in a fetal position. Without hesitation, I step over him and his mess, go upstairs to the bedroom, close the door behind me—and lock it. Even if I can't break up with this slob right now because Mickey thinks it's a bad career move, there's no way I'll take him to the charity event. I'm definitely going alone.

3
A Lavendery, Lusty Hue

Brian — January 29

Whenever I arrive at an event, especially a charitable event, I can tell within the first five seconds if it will be a one-scotch or a two-scotch night. I don't enjoy being social, and I don't enjoy the people I meet when I come to these events. Tonight will be a five-scotch night.

When I enter the hall, the likes of which resembles an airplane hangar decked in yards of blue fabric, sparkly lime-green lace that a hip, young designer mistakenly thought looked chic (but is actually quite revolting), and loads of stinky candles, I'm confronted by a colossal bouffant. This is no joke. The summit of a mountain of brownish tossed, teased, ratted, high-piled, and heavily lacquered hair is now in front of me. It has to be nearly half a meter tall and it's so diaphanous I can see straight through it. This monumental pyrotechnic incendiary is just begging for a match. God, I wish I had one. And below this monstrosity is… a woman—a rotund, beet-red faced, pissed-off-her-ass woman who smells of expensive perfume, stifling hair lacquer, and cheap gin. Her face is located across from my navel, and if I were to lift my knee, I would make contact with her gargantuan, saggy breast. I need scotch number one.

She grabs my left hand and shoves it down into her cleavage, causing me to bend forward in an awkward, uncomfortable pose. The feeling is oh, so bad. Then she brings it to her mouth and gives it a slobbery kiss. She won't release it. Now, when I'm at an event—any event—my left hand is my scotch hand, and this is important. Scotch helps me take the edge off the assholes I'm going to encounter, and it helps me become an asshole if the need arises. I do not hold anything in my left hand except scotch. The idea is to always keep it free to receive the scotch, to hold the scotch, and then to drink the scotch. So far, several trays of scotch have passed by and my left hand has been shoved back into the cleavage. I smile down at this portly drunk and she lights up like an artificial Christmas tree with little bulbs on the tips of each branch, displaying a wide, lipstick-smeared, toothy grin. "Hello, Mister Mallory! I am so *very* pleased you could come tonight," she giggles up at me.

This is Miss Ruth Willowby; Ruthie to her friends. She's a matronly patron of the arts, an absolute lush and—at this highly inebriated moment—swaying before me without a functioning brain cell in her head. But she's also so full of bubbly excitement every time I see her, I can't help but write out a big, fat check for whatever cause she's immersed herself in. I'm very fond of her, and my scotch hand seems to be the only thing sustaining her upright stance, but she really must let go of it... now.

"Ruthie, it's always a pleasure." I bend way down to kiss her pudgy cheek, which sends her into a fit of giggles. She gives my hand another slobbery kiss. This is not a good start to the evening.

She uneasily sways under her over-teased phallus. "I hope you've brought your checkbook tonight, as you've promised me a handsome donation for this wonderful, *wonderful* cause."

"Of course I did. I would never forget a promise to such an unforgettable sweetheart as you."

Again, a fit of uncontrollable giggles, and again, the left hand disappears into the creepy cleavage. That's it. I've had enough and I need a drink. I'm just about to yank my hand free, even if the move topples her, when I hear it—Mickey's familiar booming voice—right behind me.

"*Brian!*" With a slap on my back, he comes around to my side and sizes up the situation. "Right." He snaps his fingers at a nearby waiter and yells, "Scotch!" After rescuing my hand from its prison in the never-ending cleavage, he gently turns Ruthie around, carefully aims her, and launches her stout barge on its precarious maiden voyage into the thickening crowd, hoping another unsuspecting patron will eventually impede her tipsy forward momentum before she barrels bouffant-first into a statue, a pillar, a wall, or (Heaven forbid) a flaming candle. He slams a glass into my hand.

I sigh with relief as I stand upright again. "Thank you."

His voice becomes deviously low. "No problem. That's what I'm here for: to oust the drunken dwarf, grab the damned drink, and since you insist on going stag, to keep these lecherous leeches from clamping onto your filthy-rich backside."

I laugh and sip my asshole elixir.

John

Coming to this event alone was uncomfortable at first, but once I realized most of these people don't want to be with their respective hip bumpers, I felt much better. Keeping up appearances for the sake of maintaining sitcom ratings and pleasing PR managers takes its toll on any celebrity relationship, especially a floundering one—or worse, one that's been over for years but still has to be dragged (kicking and screaming) out of long-term storage and dusted off now and then for just such occasions. With fake smiles stretched from ear to ear (for the camera's sake) and small pleasantries sweetly gurgled at each other (for the reporter's sake), it's obvious these entertainers are just trying to get through the evening without ripping each other's faces off, and I know how *that* feels.

I meander around, offering a few "hellos," shaking hands, and doing my best to avoid answering the obvious question posed by the forever present, in-your-face media: Where's David? I skirt the issue by saying he's under the weather, which isn't a blatant lie. The last time I saw him, he was under something; the kitchen table, I think, happily clutching his therapeutic bottle of bliss. For the most part, I'm just idly and nervously waiting for *him* to appear: adjusting my tie, checking my hair in every reflective surface I find, wondering what my first words should be. And when I finally see him, all that first-meeting preparation dissolves, my brain turns to mush, and my dull life takes on a whole new hue—a lavendery, lusty hue.

No one has to announce Brian Mallory's arrival. No one has to tell me that's the straight guy who has a crush on me—who said so on primetime television. His presence is obvious. You can't miss it. It's not just the physical space he consumes, although his height *is* amazing. It's the aura surrounding him. It's what he projects and what he repels with every vague glance, every subtle gesture, every deliberate movement. It's the way all these people (including me) are reacting to him. It's his sublime radiance, and we all want to be hit by those fabulous beams.

I'm standing about thirty feet away, just watching the way he moves and what he does, getting a feel for his public persona. He lowers his eyes to look at people when they approach but rarely lowers his head. If someone stands too close, he steps back, as if a certain amount of airflow is always required between him and the interloper. He smiles easily but only a little. And when someone speaks to him, he looks away as if searching for an escape route. He doesn't want to be here.

The websites say he's forty-one. From where I'm standing (and with my poor vision) I can't discern his facial features, but he has a full head of thick brown hair, and he wears it a little long without gel or mousse. I check out the crowd around him. A lot of people are looking at him. Women are just gawking at him. As the main hall begins to fill with London's elite, I move to the left to get a better view. He's wearing a killer tuxedo. It's a captivating shade of deep blue and fits him perfectly. It has a firm cut across his broad shoulders and angles in at his waist. Italian and custom made, I'm sure. It must have been tailored as he wore it. It's the only way to get a tux to fit that well. And who is that standing with him? Wait a minute. Is that Mic—

"Hey, Johnny!"

"Wha...what?"

Kyle is chewing on a toothpick and looking up at me as if I'm covered in spots. "Close your mouth, man. You'll catch a fly." He gives me a jab with his elbow.

I don't say anything, but I do close my mouth. Then, I look down at him. I'm six-foot-one and he's five-foot-short—about the same height as Prissy—but Kyle Thompson is what you'd call 'geeky.' He tries to be cool but too much mega-hold hair gel and not enough mouthwash are his biggest problems. We've been in a few productions together, and he can't sing or dance to save his own life. He does his best work when he's cast as something odd, like bog fog or a stick. Last year, he snagged an award from the Bingham Amateur Theatrical Society for his riveting portrayal of mold in a wedge of bleu cheese. It figures; his mother is the chair.

"What's up?" He leans in a little. "You look like you've just been wanked."

Oh yes, and because he's so pathetically, sexually repressed, he makes a lot of tacky references to things found in and having to do with the pubic region. I lean in a little, too. Kyle is supposed to be a big gossip. If it's true, I might as well use this opportunity to put his talent to the test. I lower my voice and turn my gaze back to Brian. "You know that guy over there?"

He cranes his neck. "What guy?" Kyle's eyesight is worse than mine is. Even with his thick glasses, he has a hard time focusing on anything discreetly.

"Over there, with Mickey—the tall guy in the deep blue tuxedo. See? Now they're walking to the back of the hall."

"Oh, yeah. Brian Mallory, the pud stud. The lucky owner of every woman's dream crotch." Kyle turns to me and loudly pipes up, "What about him?"

I ask in my low voice, "Do you know anything about him?"

"Well, yeah. A little bit. Nothing much." Now he pulls away from me and sizes me up. "Why?"

I ignore his question. "Tell me everything you know." I continue to watch Brian and hear his voice—just faintly—as he's greeting people. It's a smooth, deep voice with a strong Scottish accent.

"Why?"

"Just tell me," I respond with the exasperation coming through in my words.

Kyle gives a little start. "Okay, okay. Don't work yourself into a bind!" He looks down, deep in concentration. He purses his lips around the toothpick, takes it out of his mouth, and begins. "Well, um, I know he's from Scotland, and he's got a shitload of money, and he owns a shitload of real estate, and he's divorced… and, um… he gives a shitload of money to charity, and he lives in a penthouse in one of those posh conversions on the river. So I guess that means it costs him a shitload of money." He looks up and smiles, very proud of his oratory.

I turn and look down at him, stunned. "That's it? That's all you know?"

"Well, I didn't say I knew a lot."

Brian's laugh drifts across the hall's expanse. It's a low, relaxed laugh.

"Yeah, but that's just crap you read in the tabloids and on the net."

He stares up at me. "Well, *excuse me*. What does it matter, anyway? Why do you need to know all about that tall pecker?"

"I just…. I do, that's all." And of course, right after I say it, I regret it.

"Wait a minute." Kyle's eyes narrow into slits and then grow huge. "Oh, you're not saying…. You don't mean…. You can't possibly have the hots for that guy. He's good looking and all, but Johnny, he's not even gay!"

God, Kyle. Do you have to say it so loud? "No, of course I don't have the hots for him. I don't even know him!" I blurt out in a strained, excited whisper. I calm myself down and continue more quietly. "He went on a talk show and said he had a crush on me and I just want to figure it all out."

"Well, why don't you ask Mickey?"

"Mickey?"

"Yeah. That redheaded pube has known him for years. They're really good mates." And with that, Kyle jams his toothpick back in his mouth, sticks his hands in his pockets, turns around, and marches off.

I'm dumbfounded. Mickey has known him for years? They're mates? How did I miss that one? I'm so nosey I thought I'd met all of Mickey's friends and associates. He'll have to introduce us. If he asks why, I'll say someone told me he was a fan of the series and wanted my autograph. Oh, no. That sounds too conceited, even for a fathead like me. I'll be honest and say I'd heard he was attracted to me. No, I can't do that. I can't show him up in front of people and make him uncomfortable. What do I say? What is my excuse to get over there and —

"Johnny, there you are!" Mickey booms, staring up into my face. "How's it going? Having a good time? Not too uncomfortable being on your own, right? Look, we've got a photo shoot lined up later so don't mess up your tux or your hair, and don't disappear on me even if you've spotted a cutie, okay?" He winks and puts his arm around my shoulders.

Here's my chance. "Mickey, I want you to introduce me to—"

"Fine. No problem. We'll do that later. But first, I want you to meet an old friend of mine. I've known him for years. I can't believe I haven't introduced you two, before. He might be interested in investing in that High Street show Danny's got in the works. Now he's not really into the arts as a patron, and he's not big on conversation. As a matter of fact, he may seem a little rude, okay? But he's a sharp businessman and he's open-minded when it comes to the smaller theatrical productions." Mickey abruptly stops talking and leans into my body. Then, he sniffs.

"What?"

"Nothing. I'm just trying to get an idea of how strong your cologne is."

I'm offended. "It's not that strong. I didn't use much. I put it on over an hour ago."

"Okay. That's fine. Don't ruffle your feathers. He's just got this thing about certain smells."

"What?"

"Nothing. Never mind. You're fine. You smell just fine. Okay! What'ya say, huh? Put on that million dollar smile and let's go dazzle him, all right?"

And with that, Mickey clamps his arm tighter around my shoulder and I find myself being propelled... exactly where I wanted to go.

Brian

I'm on scotch number two and I'm beginning to relax. During the first hour, I was able to avoid some obnoxious bastards like Roderick Steeleman and Felix Greenberg, but now I've wound up facing Erik.

Erik Hunt is a shitty little speck of nothing with a shitty little scent.

To call this wispy, Danish imbecile a man would draw attention to the fact his creator (whoever *that* was) buggered up in a big way. To call him a woman would be an insult to every female on the planet. The creature that best describes him seems to fall somewhere between an enflamed hemorrhoid, which would explain why he's such an irritating pain in the ass, and a nit, which would explain everyone's desire to get rid of him because he's so hygienically undesirable and embarrassingly parasitic. He's just a filthy bastard who sees himself as a major theatrical producer, but he couldn't produce his way out of a sock. He's raunchy and crass. Every vulgar statement that comes out of his mouth is sexist or racist. Whenever he gets someone to underwrite one of his productions, he buggers it up by over-spending on stupid crap or under-spending on important crap. He's never donated anything but abject misery to any worthy cause, so I have no idea why he's here tonight, and he will not shut up. He hasn't even noticed I haven't said one word to him—and I don't plan to. If it weren't for the check I still have to present, I'd be gone. I need scotch number three, and I need it now.

"Brian!"

There's no mistaking Mickey's bark over my shoulder. I turn away from Erik to face him and—

"Hi, Mister Mallory. I'm John."

He's right up in my face and breathing a little hard, as if he's just sprinted up a flight of stairs. So, this is Mickey's prized possession. He's standing a bit too close, I don't get the spiky hair, and his cologne is *way* too strong. I take a step back.

John

So, this is Brian Mallory. Now I understand why women gawk. He's not pretty boy, Please-Give-Me-Your-Number handsome. He's manly, Please-Screw-Me-Right-Now handsome. Being the consummate purveyor of beauty that I am, in a nano-second my brain cells sort the raw, straight-man data live-streaming through my pupils, convert it to a gay-friendly format, burn it into long-term memory, and classify him as an omnipotent demigod sent down from Mount Olympus to perform some heroic feat. Lucky for me (mere mortal that I am), Zeus forgot to summon him back. He's a real man's man. His thick brown hair, with just a touch of gray at each ear, has delicate streaks of gold. Either he's spent a fair amount of time in the sun or he's got a talented stylist. Mickey's voice drifts into my brain like thin elevator music, touting something about philandering… or philanthropy (whatever), as I stare at the palest green eyes this side of reality. But they're distant, unfocused—glazed over with a sadness that's probably been there for years. And I have a feeling the faint creases running from the corner of each eye out to his temples aren't from laughing. This man has felt pain—deep pain. Now Mickey is chattering on about chastity… or charity (I'm not sure and I'm not bothered). I'm more interested in Brian's height: about six-foot-six, taller than anyone here. If I were to press right up against him, my mouth would be just below his Adam's apple and he could plant a kiss on my forehead. He could whisper in my ear while I nuzzled his neck. I could nibble his—

Okay, snap out of it! We are *not* going there! Make-out strategies are not appropriate thoughts right now. I have to remember: This man isn't here to be drooled over—crush, or no crush. I tend to be too obvious when I see beautiful things and I need to keep my eyes in check, so I lower them. His tuxedo is truly distinctive with a faint aubergine sheen. I want to reach out and touch the fabric, feel its weight and texture between my fingers. I bet it's as soft as velvet. Broad shoulders, big hands, long legs. Everything about him is highly masculine, much too sexy, and begging to be groped. He smells faintly of… soap—just a mild aroma of soap. Oh, yes! I am definitely experiencing a lavendery, lusty hue!

Brian

"Hello, John. I'm Brian." I shake his hand. It's clammy, but he's got a firm grip and his scent is pleasant enough under that blanket of cologne. I pluck another scotch off a passing tray (irritated that it has a useless swizzle stick poking out of it), decide not to be an asshole, and let Mickey do all the talking.

"Brian—my good old mate—this is the guy I told you about. This is my absolute success story, my precious Johnny! He's the star of *TruthFinder Murphy*. You've seen it, right? Great show! Anyway, his career is just soaring right now. He's got a couple of musicals opening up soon, too. Right, Johnny?"

"Mickey, he prob—" John begins.

"This guy can sing, he can dance, and he can act. And just look at him, Brian. He's gorgeous!" Mickey lowers his voice and leans toward me. "And I don't mean flaming gorgeous, you understand? I mean straight-looking gorgeous. Do you know how many people just *won't* believe he's gay?"

"Mickey, I really—"

"Especially the women. They're all over him when he's out in public. How many propositions have you had, Johnny?"

"Mickey, it's not—" John, now red in the face and unable to finish a single sentence, is embarrassed by the non-stop boasting.

"Just look at those great lips and those serious eyes and that button nose! Do you know how many guys want to get up close and personal with all that? He was voted 'England's Sexiest and Most Desirable Gay Man.' He's got a fan base you wouldn't believe, Brian: men, women, girls, boys. There's not an age group that doesn't think this guy is hot! And who can blame them? He's beautiful! He was asked to do a *Playgirl* spread. Of course, that's not gonna happen. That's soft porn and just not his thing, is it Johnny? But it's a great compliment, huh?"

"Mickey," I interject, a little loudly to catch him off guard and dam his tidal wave of babbling, "can you find some better scotch? This stuff tastes like it came from the canal downstream of a bloke who's just pissed in it. It's giving me headache."

"Sure, Brian." Mickey, not at all offended by the interruption, troupes off to find better scotch. He knows when I say I'm getting headache it means I'm five minutes away from leaving, and he doesn't want that to happen—not tonight, when he promised the press I'd be here. So now, I'm left facing his precious John who's still standing a little too close.

He fidgets with his wine glass. "I'm...I'm sorry about that."

"It's okay."

"He just gets excited about things. It's hard to..."

"Shut him up?"

He smiles and nods. "How...how long have you known Mickey?" He wants to chat. He's just so uneasy right now; he's not having much luck with it.

"About eleven, maybe twelve years." I take out the swizzle stick and sip my scotch.

"Are you a business partner?"

"Sometimes, if it's worth investing. Mainly, we're just mates."

"Oh. Where did you meet?"

I think for a moment. "In a gay bar in Kensington."

Well, that's shocked him: mouth hanging open and eyes wide.

I take another sip of scotch and discard the glass on a passing tray, letting him stew before I explain. "My old driver had to take his blood pressure medicine. I went in to get him some water. At the time, in that area, it was the only place open late. Mickey started chatting me up right away."

John's eyes light up. "Really? He hit on you?"

"Aye. I had to tell him I wasn't interested." I smile as I see Mickey working his way back to us, an empty glass in one hand and a full bottle of Bowmore in the other. I look back at John. "He's really not my type: too short and too hairy." I give him a wink.

"Aha! Look what I found back in the kitchen. Oh, you oughtta see what they're gonna lay out for dinner," Mickey booms, his face flushed as he hands me the glass and opens the bottle. "And you oughtta see who's gonna be layin' it out—some fine-looking men back there. Tight uniforms, too. Very nice! So, Johnny, what d'ya think of Brian? He's okay, huh?"

John looks at me and blurts out, "I heard you were attracted to me."

Now it's my turn to be shocked and a little taken aback. "I beg your pardon?"

His face is flushed. "I heard you said it on a talk show—that you had a crush on me."

Ah, now I remember what he's referring to. "Oh, I'd almost forgotten about that." I watch Mickey pour scotch into my glass and then take a sip. "You know, I think Mickey can explain that a little better than I can."

Mickey nods. "Yeah, that was a while ago, wasn't it? What did they do, show a re-run?"

John's eyes dart between us. "I don't know. A couple of my friends said they saw it."

"Hmm, yeah. It must have come up as a re-run, probably because of this event right here. Well, I guess I should explain. You see, Johnny, Brian was in Sydney and agreed to do a satellite interview on this UK talk show to promote one of his Australian charities. It was right before the debut season of *TruthFinder Murphy* and I got this brilliant idea: Why not try to get in a plug for you and the new series? I passed it by the show's producers, and they thought it was fantastic. The host is lesbian and she likes to make a lot of lighthearted gay references. So they thought it might be a good lead in for Brian—who's straight—to say he had a crush on you. You know, break the ice. They flash your gorgeous face on the monitor, tell everyone you're the star of *Truth-Finder Murphy*, and Boom! Our first season has the highest-rated viewership of the year."

John looks like a bloke who's just seen a large sign along the motorway plastered with a photograph of his grandmother in a thong. "So... you weren't even here in England when you said it?"

I shake my head. "No. I was sitting in a hotel room seventeen thousand kilometers away."

"And... you don't... fancy me?"

"Sorry, no. I don't. I heard your name mentioned years earlier by Mickey, but I've never laid eyes on you until tonight. I guess you could say it was a small publicity stunt."

Now he looks like a bloke who was caught reversing on the motorway to go back for a second look at that thong. I'm feeling a bit embarrassed myself. Mickey should have told him about it three years ago. "Oh." He contemplates for a moment. "But didn't it bother you that people might think you were...?"

"What? Gay?" I smile and sip my scotch. "I really don't care what people think of me. I did it because Mickey thought it would help your career."

"And I gotta tell you, Brian, it most certainly did. *TruthFinder Mur-*

phy was just the start. The theater is biting at his heels. He's got a sensational musical review opening next Friday at The Altinda and an even bigger one after that." Mickey's eyes are sparkling. "He'll be doing some great dance numbers. That's why he's so fit. See?" He pats John's stomach a few times. "They're gonna be adding extra shows and more engagements throughout Europe, too. That's how good it is. That's how good *he* is."

"There're a lot of good performers in the—"

"Oh yeah, but they don't sing like you, Sweetie. They don't dance like you and they certainly don't *look* like you. Everyone knows that." Mickey turns to me as he sets the bottle down on the nearest table. "He's got top billing, you know?"

"Does he really? That's impressive." Top billing in a London production is no small feat. It takes a lot of ambition to want it and a lot of talent to get it.

"Who's got top billing? In what?" Of course it's Erik, butting in as usual.

Mickey faces him with apprehension. "Oh, hello Erik. I was just saying Johnny has top billing in his upcoming musicals."

Mickey and Erik don't get along. Erik has always made rude comments about Mickey's sexual orientation (at least Mickey *has* one), and even though he's strong enough to do it, Mickey doesn't have the nerve to punch him in the face. Over the years, they've worked on some of the same productions, and Mickey says they've had heated confrontations.

Erik sneers as he looks John up and down with disdain (or maybe that look is desire—with Erik, who can tell?). "So, John, you get top billing, again. You just seem to be on a winning streak, young man. What *is* your secret? Are you sleeping with the producers or something?" His smile is mocking.

"No, I'm not." John isn't amused, and his face is turning red yet again.

"Well let me tell you something, sonny. That's not going to work if she's a woman. Then, you're going to need a little talent."

Mickey steps in. "How dare you insinuate—"

"*Insinuate?* Come off it, Mickey. That's not insinuation. Everyone knows your lot blows rows and can't keep their peckers in their pants for a—"

Erik doesn't get the chance to finish his vile remark as my torso blocks his view of Mickey and John. He gives my dinner jacket a bewildered look, not realizing a brick wall has just sprung up in front of his face. I take another step forward and he stumbles back. This repulsive warthog is so short and I'm so close that I'm looking straight down on the pale dome he tries to hide with a greasy comb-over. I raise the (finally useful) swizzle stick I've been holding for the last fifteen minutes and run it under his wispy comb-over. I lift the stick and flip the caked clump off the top of his head, letting it flop down the side of his face. His shiny pate glows bright in the candlelight while the brittle locks hang down to his jowls. He's now a lop-sided freak. I place the scummy swizzle stick into his wine glass and give it a stir as I bend my head way down to his ear and speak quietly. "Mickey may not have the guts to rip off your puny balls and shove them down your throat, but believe me, I do. And I'll do it in front of everyone here. You are a disgusting ass boil and I want you out of my sight. Do you understand me?"

He's deathly white as he whispers, "Yes, Brian." He spins around, tucks his butt like a whipped dog, and shuffles off through the crowd. I turn back to Mickey and John.

Mickey sighs. "Thank you, Brian."

"You shouldn't tolerate it, Mickey. I keep telling you that. Just put him in his place. You know he's a slimy bastard and has no right to say those things."

"I know. I guess I'm a lover and not a fighter, huh?" Mickey gives me a big grin and then looks at his watch. "Oh, Johnny, we've got to take photos at the fountain. Brian, you wanna come and watch?"

"No, I have to check messages and make some calls."

"Hey, I said no business deals tonight," Mickey admonishes, disappointed in me.

"Sorry, but I have to. I'll see you later. Goodbye, John." I watch them walk off, pull out my mobile, and start checking messages as I sip my scotch. Thirty seconds later, I smell John's cologne again. He's come back for something.

John

I'm over the shock that this gorgeous man told the world he had a crush on me when he really didn't, but I can't believe he doesn't care that people might have thought he was gay when he said it. Any straight man I know would need a gun in his back before he'd say something like that—to anyone—even as a joke. Yet Brian said it on a talk show as a favor to Mickey to help my career, and he didn't even know me. What kind of man does that? "Excuse me. Brian?"

He impales me with those beautiful eyes. "Yes, John."

"You should come to a rehearsal next week at The Altinda if you get a chance. I think you'd like it."

He drops his gaze and fidgets with his phone. "I, um, have a lot of meetings during the day. I don't like to upset my schedule once it's set."

"I see. I understand." I shroud my disappointment and turn away. This man might have done me a favor three years ago concerning my career, but it's obvious he doesn't want any contact with me now. I could almost see 'Homophobic' flashing across his forehead in bright red let—

"You know what, John? I'll try. I'll try to stop by one day to watch a rehearsal if I have some time."

I whip around. "Great! That's great. You'll really like it. Goodbye, Brian."

"Goodbye, John."

With a silly grin, I giddily walk off to do the photo shoot and scold myself for making a false assumption. We didn't talk long and we didn't say much, but I'm thrilled I had the opportunity to meet such an interesting man. He's got a powerful personality, just like Mickey, but it's quieter and more intense. And unlike Mickey, he makes me feel uncomfortable and exhilarated. And there's something else about him. It's as though he's really sure of himself, confidently arrogant. I find that unsettling… and highly attractive.

■ ■ ■

The dinner is disappointing. With everyone shuttled off into three different halls, there's no way I can tell where Brian is sitting, let alone catch a glimpse of him. After half an hour, I finally lay eyes on Prissy who only scurries out of the kitchen long enough to tell me he's been relegated to scraping half-eaten food off everyone's plates because the event planners didn't want someone with yellow hair and a pink bow serving the meals. They also thought he was too scrawny to carry a loaded tray (which is probably true). He's happy though because the Afro-Caribbean chef has a great ass and bends over all the time to look into the ovens. I make him promise he won't try to grab it. I sit with Mickey and Kyle and four other people I've never seen before. And while they carry on with small talk and chow down on a dry chicken breast drowning in a lumpy white sauce and tasteless vegetables, I think of Brian Mallory and his pale green eyes.

Carol – February 1

There is no greater beauty nectar in the world than Botox. It was sent down to Earth from the heavens above as a gift to beautiful people like me so we can go on being beautiful forever. And while I also cherish that yellow, gelatinous stuff Maureen sucks out of my backside (I refuse to call it fat) and shoots into my lips, there is nothing (except possibly death) that will keep me from my Botox appointments. I never allow interruptions during my jabs either—except for today. My mobile is ringing and it's Patricia so this could be important. I raise my hand as the Queen would to her minion. "Wait with the needle, Maureen. I've got to take this call." I give her my 'You're dismissed for now but don't wander off' look, which tells her to get off her skinny ass and give me some privacy. Although slightly thick (the result of inbreeding, I'm sure), she takes the hint and leaves. "Hello?"

"Hey, Carol, it's Patricia. I've got a heads up for you."

It's obvious she's eating while she's talking on the phone. She knows I'm upper class, yet the distasteful cockroach shows me no respect, and that is *so* tacky. It only further serves to expand the chasm between our disparate worlds. I try to ignore her repugnant munching. "Really? What is it?"

"Remember that fag I told you about—John Kaiser?"

"Yes. I remember you said he was insignificant."

"Well, I still think he is, but I just thought I'd let you know he was at the Willowby charity event on Saturday night."

A charity event? This is why she calls me, why she interrupts my life? Why would I care if the gay boy was at a charity event on Saturday night? I add a hint of snideness to my response. "*So.*"

She adds a hint of it, too. "And *so* was Brian."

Momentarily frozen, a pang of jealousy passes over me and any residual snideness withers away. "And...?"

"I've got a reliable source telling me they chatted for about ten minutes and were talking alone—just the two of them—for a while."

"What did they say?"

"I have no idea. My source only observed from a distance and gave me a report. Still, I don't think it's a big deal—probably just a casual meeting."

The pang of jealousy intensifies. "I still don't like it. It sounds a little fishy to me." I'm concerned now. John Kaiser may be gay, but I've checked him out and Patricia is right: He's really good looking. I have to admit he's sexy, too—and young. The worst combination! If he got the idea in his little gay-boy brain to try to turn a straight, rich guy, how do I compete with a sexy, young queer?

"Well, they didn't hold hands or anything. They just chatted like people do when they go to these events and then went their separate ways. It's no big deal, okay?"

I'm hesitant. "It just feels like a bad omen."

"Look, I told you, Mallory is straight; they're not bum chums."

"Okay. You're probably right, but you let me know the minute you find out anything else, *especially* if it has to do with this...this John Kaiser, because I will *not* let a faggot get in my way."

Brian

"So you've just landed?" I say into my mobile, trying to mask my irritation, eyes on my watch. "No, that'll take you at least an hour, even if you can find a cab. They're on another half-day strike. You'll hit heavy traffic on the M-4 and there's ongoing construction in that area." I rub my temples to buffer rising headache. I don't handle the prospect of a tardy business associate well. A late arrival for one meeting screws up my whole schedule, which is carefully (okay, anally) planned down to the last minute, but I know this delay is unavoidable. "Look, give me a ring when you're near Hyde Park. I'll run errands and we'll meet at the flat. I'll order up lunch, and we can eat during the meeting. No, it's no problem. Okay. Goodbye, Viv." I end the call, hang my head, and contemplate my options. I need to center myself—to rebalance. "Jack, where are we right now?" I know I could look out the window and read the damned street signs myself, but he's paid well and I feel like being an asshole. Jack is used to chauffeuring an asshole.

"Shaftesbury Avenue, just passing Rupert Street, sir."

Again, I contemplate. Again, I rub my temples, working toward calmness. "Where's The Altinda? It's close, right?"

"Uh, Chaning Cross, on the right, I believe. It's coming up."

I didn't think I'd be able to catch one of John's rehearsals, but if Vivian's flight just landed, I have to kill this free time before I head back to the flat just so I can stay centered, so I can function normally and be in control. "All right. Let's make a quick stop there."

■ ■ ■

When we pull around to the back of the hulking theater, I tell Jack to give me about forty minutes and enter the ancient building through one of its rear doors.

A skinny, young bloke wielding a dirty mop and a bucket of smelly towels looks up. "Can I help you?"

"Yes. One of your performers said I should stop by to watch a rehearsal. Is that okay?"

"Sure. You want me to tell 'em you're here?"

"No, I'm not staying long. Can I just walk to the back of the theater?"

"You can sit in the seats if you want."

"No, I'd prefer to stand in the back."

"Okay, go through that door there on the left. And hey, watch your step, mate—the theater is pretty dark and if you fall, well... it's a long way down to the floor for you, isn't it?"

I sigh at the skinny smart ass. Lame jokes about my height are getting pretty old. "Yes, I guess it is. Thank you." I walk through the door on the left and up the side aisle of the theater. It's like a sauna in here and I'm glad I'm not staying long. In the dark, I nearly plow into Mickey as he comes in through a side door.

"Brian! What're you doing here?"

"Hey, Mickey. John suggested I come to see a rehearsal. I had a bit of time between meetings and was in the area."

"That's great! Sorry about the heat. The air conditioning is out but they're trying to fix it. It's an old theater. Wanna sit?"

"No, I've been sitting in meetings all morning and I've got another one in about an hour. I'll just stand in the back."

Mickey eagerly joins me so now I have the honor of listening to his commentary as we lean against the back wall under the mezzanine. "What d'ya think? Isn't he something? Stands out from the rest, doesn't he? I keep telling him, 'You're the best, Johnny,' and he just keeps showing me he truly is. He's gorgeous to watch, huh? Really graceful and sensuous with lots of rhythm, lots of emotion. He's great at jazz, too—and tap."

Mickey is in his element. This is what he loves to do: incessantly brag about his clients, sell them to the casual observer, casting directors, producers, and the media. The words of praise tumble from his mouth better than any written CV. I don't have to add much to the one-sided conversation. He's on a roll.

"In the beginning, he started out with ballet but that was too feminine for him, too prim and sterile. He has a lot of energy. He needs to move freely. He's six-foot-one, so he's a big dancer, and he's strong. He's a great leading man. He can lift women with no problem. He's got so much talent, so much ability and ambition." Mickey pauses, his eyes riveted on the smooth movements of his gifted, young protégé. "He's so different from David."

I continue to watch John and his contemporaries slog through their complicated routines in the stifling heat. "Who's David?"

"Oh, Johnny's louse of a boyfriend. He's just a joke and a headache at this point. He had so much potential; a beautiful face and a killer body, great for swimwear and underwear shoots. I don't know what happened. He got too conceited, got a big ego." Mickey shakes his head, but his eyes are still on John. "I've been trying to set him up with something—anything. For the life of me, I can't keep him employed for more than a week or two." He steps away from the wall and crosses his arms, gazing down at the stage with wonder. "But look at that, Brian. Look at that beauty I've got there; my precious Johnny! He's a star performer. He never argues, never complains. He's got endless energy, always studies his lines, and practices day and night if he has to. He's a manager's dream. He truly is—and he's all mine."

John

The rehearsals have been going well, up until today. The air conditioning isn't working. We're exhausted and sweaty and our timing is off. Marge has been stoically banging away on the piano (because her sister Marie broke her thumb) and we just can't get used to her rhythm. We really need the full orchestra here but (with the approval of their powerful union) they left, refusing to practice in this heat—and I don't blame them. We've got bits of crap falling down on us from the maintenance guys trying to fix the air conditioning units up in the rafters and not enough dry towels to soak up the sweat that's streaming off our bodies so Evan has to keep mopping up the floor; otherwise, we'll slip and break our necks. We're guzzling a ton of water and have to take numerous breaks as someone always has to run backstage to pee. I'm standing just off to one side of the curtain, head down, panting like a dog. My t-shirt and shorts are transparent and sticking to me like a second skin. By now, I smell quite ripe, like something that died about a week ago, and I'm watching a pool of sweat gradually become a lake on the floor. It's dripping off my chin, my nose, and my forehead. More sweat is trickling down my elbows from the leaky faucets in my armpits. I'm just baking in this disgusting heat.

Evan hands me a towel sopping wet with someone else's sweat. "So, you decided to bring in the Big Wig today, huh?"

I smell the towel, cringe, and hand it back, still panting. "What are you talking about?"

"In the back of the theater, watching the rehearsal. You decided you needed an impressive audience while everyone is sweating bullets up here?"

I pull my plastered shirt off my stomach with thumb and forefinger. "Who, Mickey? He's always here if he can make it. He's no Big Wig."

"No, I mean his mate, the really tall chap—Scottish, stinks of money. Is he a producer?"

I'm at the curtain, peering out into the theater before Evan can finish his words. If I squint hard, I can just make out two figures leaning against the far wall. *"Holy shit!"* How long has he been out there? Why did he have to come today of all days? I look terrible. I smell terrible. "Evan, get me a dry towel."

"We don't have any."

I look back at him just standing there, hunched in low self-esteem and chewing his gum. "Give me your shirt."

"What? No."

"Please? I just need it for a minute."

"You're not using my shirt to wipe your sweat. No way!"

Good old Evan, usually a pleasant and obliging puppy, can also be a real prick. So now I'm desperate. "Look, I'll give you a kiss."

His immature brain mulls over the offer. Barely out of the closet at nineteen and still a virgin, he's wanted a kiss for a while now, just a peck on the cheek to tell his friends, so I'm hopeful. It looks promising. I can't miss. "No. No way. No deal." He shakes his head.

Damn! I'm screwed. I scrutinize myself. There's no way I can go out there with my wet shorts and briefs suctioned so tightly against my crotch they're outlining my penis and testicles. I could do it in front of the other dancers and Mickey but not in front of Brian. I'm desperately searching for something on stage that's dry and absorbent. There's nothing except the curtains—but I'm not that tacky. I run to the backstage men's restroom. It's locked—in use. There's no time for shame. I bolt into the women's restroom, grab handfuls of paper towels, and jam them down the front of my briefs, hoping to soak up just a fraction of the sweat. I use another handful to violently blot my pelvis from the outside. Fifty-nine-year-old Marge walks through the door to find me pulverizing my crotch with a vengeance. "I'll just be a minute." My compromising state, coupled with a weak smile, does not bode well with her. She stares down at my ridiculous bulge, turns around, and pulls the door closed behind her.

Two minutes later, I take out the paper towels. It's not too bad. It looks pretty good. My shorts and briefs are still soaked but at least they're not letting the world know the size of my genitals. I emerge from the restroom to find Marge glaring with disapproval and folded arms. "Sorry about that," I mumble and scurry past her. She's always thought 'us gays' were peculiar and I'm sure I've just stoked the flaming fire.

I'm back at the curtain and I still see them standing out there. I can go out to talk to them; I just can't get too close. I might have dealt with the wetness but I still smell like the back end of something that should be yoked to a plow. I quickly walk down (as in, practically stumble down) the stage steps and finger comb my slimy hair. I need to slow my breathing. I don't want to pant in front of Brian. As I get closer, I hear Mickey talking up a storm and I see Brian is dead sexy in a smart chocolate brown business suit, a beige dress shirt, and a deep rust-colored tie. Pure class, like James Bond. I walk until I'm about five rows from them and then I stop. "Hi." It's unintelligent and uncool and the only stupid word I can think of as my cloak of nervousness envelopes me.

"Johnny, look who came to watch the rehearsal! Come on over here. Let us take a good look at you."

"No, Mickey. I'm kind of sweaty and... stuff." God, I stink so bad! I can't possibly come any closer.

"Oh, that's okay. Sweat is all right. Isn't it, Brian? I mean, it's not like perfume or cologne, right?"

"Sweat is fine, Mickey."

Hesitantly, I approach, trying to gauge just how close I can get without stenching him to death. I'm not panting anymore, but I still need to leave my mouth open to breath. If I close it, I'll probably make that horrible whistling sound through my nose. I've always been embarrassed by it, and three snout probes by London's finest ENTs haven't found the cause of it yet. "How are you?" Jesus, such a pathetic, weak voice!

"Fine, John. How are you?"

"Good. I'm good. Really good." I finger comb my hair again, trying to lift the plastered locks off my head, trying to coax a faint glimmer of my signature style from the damp mass, trying to look a little better than scummy vermin that's just crawled up a sewer pipe.

"I see you're very talented."

That was all Mickey needed. That was his cue to open the floodgates of eternal praise. He's complimenting me, left and right. He's boasting about my dancing, my singing, my acting, my looks. I've got a commanding presence on the stage. I'm one of the most expressive dancers he's ever seen. My voice is like a—God, he will *not* shut up! With his non-stop exaltation, he's morphed me into Fred Astaire, Julie Andrews, and Cyd Charisse, compacted my embarrassed ass into a dense cube and tied me off with a Gene Kelly bow. I feel so self-conscious and so stupid because right now I'm just a stinky, sweaty body with really flat hair and a creepy nasal whistle. I want to say something but I can't think of anything that will stop his motor mouth. Then Brian's phone buzzes. He pulls it out and looks at the screen. "I'm sorry. I have to go."

"Oh, so soon?" Mickey whines. "Can't you stay a little longer? They'll be starting up again in a minute."

"No. I have a meeting at the flat and it'll take me twenty minutes to get there." He puts away his cell and takes out his sunglasses.

That's it? He's leaving? I get five minutes of standing here attracting blowflies and mimicking a petrified dork while Mickey blabs his mouth off, and now Brian is leaving? "You live on the river, don't you?" The words are blurted out in desperation as I try to say something—anything—before he goes.

"Uh... yes, I do," he responds, a bit stunned by my outburst.

"Oh, you should see the place, Johnny. Beautiful views, just *beautiful* views. A real show stopper, huh, Brian?"

"I've always liked it. You should stop by when you're in the area, John."

"I...I will."

"I'll see you later. Good luck with the show. Goodbye, Mickey."

• • •

The rest of the afternoon flies by. I don't care about the heat or how tired I am or how much I reek. I don't care about the crap falling from the rafters or the smelly wet towels Evan still tries to shove in my face.

I even grab his ass and give him a kiss—a great big, fat juicy one—right on the lips that shocks the hell out of him. I'm over the moon because Brian came to watch the rehearsal, and I'm thrilled he said I could visit him at his penthouse.

4
Monkey Business

Carol – February 2

I don't know a damned thing about Burundi orphans, and frankly, I don't want to know a damned thing about Burundi orphans. I have a goal tonight, and it has nothing to do with giving my dwindling maintenance to abandoned Third World pygmies sporting distended bellies and moon-pie eyes swarming with flies. If that makes me an evil cow, then so be it. Life's a bitch, so suck it up.

I scope out the nondescript convention hall gussied up for the occasion in an understated tone of kitschy, opulent oppression; so discreetly fitting for the demeaning task of begging millionaires (dressed in two-thousand quid suits and gowns) to feed starving kids in an East African country they probably can't even find on a map. I certainly don't know where the hell it is—and I don't care. I make a beeline for a group of women standing just off to the side of the entrance. I smile sweetly and spew the usual crap about this being my first solo venture since the divorce, I don't know anyone here, do they mind if I chat with them for a bit—blah, blah, blah. These women have heard all the lies. It's nothing new. They're in the same boat I'm in and they're here for the same reason. They're not concerned about contaminated drinking water and the dietary deficiencies of pathetic orphans; they need a stinking-rich man.

I'm relieved to see none of them are my competition. Three are too old, one is way too young, and two are so hideously ugly I can't believe they're allowed out in public without burlap head sacks. These hippocrockapigs are a frightful sight. Their mothers should have strangled them at birth, put bullets through their heads (just to be sure), and buried them in unmarked graves in outer Siberia. The last one, the tall one in the prime position facing the entrance, has some potential in the looks department but her downfall is that she's hairy — extremely hairy. This woman has long sideburns and a hairline that starts about half an inch from her bushy uni-brow, leaving her with little to no forehead. And because she has no forehead, Botox would be wasted on her. Therefore, she can never be one of the beautiful people. She's almost attractive in an earthy, Frida Kahlo sort of way, but Patricia didn't say anything about Brian preferring monkey-women so I don't have to worry about her, and she's easily dismissed with the rest of the homely wenches. It is a pisser though that the mustachioed hominid is facing the entrance and I, the attractive newcomer, have my back to it. I'll just have to rely on her facial expression — and I know she'll have one — when my prey walks into the hall. In the meantime, I suffer through spurts of forced, uncomfortable chitchat amongst these wretched creatures, hoping he'll show up… soon.

■ ■ ■

I'm nursing my second glass of wine (at three-pound-fifty a pop!) when I finally see the look on Frida's face change dramatically. In fact, the near-drooling trance on all their faces tells me he's just made his entrance. Sipping my wine with an air of nonchalance, I turn around and catch my breath. Brian Mallory, two meters in height, handsome beyond words, and worth four hundred million pounds has finally arrived. According to Patricia, this heartthrob is hung like a Brahma bull and performs like a true blue Scottish Shag. He walks in behind a doddering, elderly couple and immediately angles to the left. He's moving along the far wall, avoiding the center of the hall, trying not to stand out. Fat chance. Everyone has seen him. Everyone is watching him. The women in my little clutch have dropped into silence as we all follow his progress. We are desperate, starving shrews and he is a chunk of raw, sexy meat. After a waiter hands him a drink (no charge, of course!), he stops now and then to field a greeting, give a faint smile, or bend for a peck on the cheek. He's cordial enough to those around him, but he has an agenda. It's clear he's only tolerating their fawning as he tries to get to the back of the hall, to a small group of men he spied the moment he walked in. They're probably his business assoc —

"Ahem!" Frida-The-Chimp clears her throat, and I turn to see her glaring at me with her hairy upper lip in a snarl. "Has someone caught your eye?"

I return the same glare but pair it up with the sweetest voice. "Yes. As a matter of fact, someone has."

"Well, let me tell you this, if it's Brian Mallory, you'd better put those buggy, little eyes right back in your head, darling."

"Really?" I smile at this despicable haute gibbon and sip my wine. It's going to be a pure pleasure bitch-slapping her hairy ass down.

"Look, I've been working on him for months. *You* need to find someone else."

"*I* don't need to find anyone else. If you can't handle a little competition…" I say with a "Come-off-it,-Bitch" smirk plastered across my face.

"Competition?" She eyes me up and down. "Honey, you are *not* my competition."

I sip my wine again and give her the look of pity I save for truly ugly people. "Honey, you are right. You are absolutely right. I'm *not* your competition. Your competition is in London Zoo, peeling a banana and dangling from a tree."

My words elicit gasps of horror from the other wallflowers.

"*How dare you!*" Her peach-fuzz face turns crimson as she seethes with outrage.

I smooth my slinky black dress and pat my perfectly coifed hair with my free hand. "Look, Frida — darling, if I were you, I'd spend less time trying to land a multi-millionaire you'll never get and more time trying to figure out how to get those lovely sideburns back to the corpse of Elvis, where they belong." I stare long and hard at that thick, black caterpillar quivering over her eyes. "Oh, and here's a word you may want to become more familiar with: E-lec-tro-ly-sis." Amid their gaping mouths, and with the confidence that exudes from a goddess who knows she's nothing less than hot shit served on a silver tray, I turn away from the pitiful slags and slink toward the group of men.

Brian

"Brian! You made it."

"Gabe. Craig. Vincent. Thomas, how's the back?" I shake everyone's hand. It's been about a month since we last met.

"Same as always. I'm living off pain killers now, trying to do anything to avoid having that damned surgery."

"Yeah, anything but lose the weight," Vincent quips.

Thomas gives him an evil scowl and hitches up his pants, but he knows Vincent is right. He's carried around a thirteen-month pregnancy for seven years now, and it's a solid mass he's determined to keep.

"So, did everyone have a chance to review the proposal?" Gabe asks.

We nod.

"Are we in?"

"I'm not sure," Craig says. "I have a few questions."

"Jesus, Craig, you always have questions. You had a month to review it for Christ's sake," Gabe admonishes.

Vincent glances around nervously. "Look, hold it down. If Gina finds out I'm having a business meeting at her fundraiser, she'll mince my balls. Now, we said we'd be ready to decide tonight. Craig, you've had enough time to get your questions answered. Are you in?"

Craig sheepishly glances at everyone and nods.

"Okay," Gabe says. "So we're all in at twenty percent?"

Thomas scratches his underbelly and hitches up his pants again. "I can't do twenty. I can only do fifteen. I took a hit in the market. I moved some stuff around but fifteen is all I can come up with. I really want in and that's my max."

"So, what does that mean?" Craig asks.

I sip my scotch and say, "It means the rest of us pick up one and a quarter percent or one of us puts up five percent or we drop the whole thing."

Vincent turns to me. "Which are you willing to do?"

"Either one but drop. It doesn't matter to me."

"You think it's that good?"

"I think it's that good."

58

"Are you sure?" Craig asks.

Vincent gives Craig a stern look. "Trust me. If he says it's good— it's good."

"Okay, the rest of us add in one and a quarter percent and we'll adjust the profits accordingly. Is that agreeable?" Gabe looks around and everyone nods. "Fine. I'll have Doug come up with a draft and get a copy to everybody. We'll meet once more to hash out any issues, all right?"

Again, everyone nods.

Vincent sighs with relief. "Bang on. I'm glad that's done. Now, what's everyone been up to? Brian, I hear you're looking for a mansion on some land here in England. Are you finally pulling up roots and moving here permanently?"

"No, I'm just working on an idea."

"Oh, yeah? Another business venture? Something I could get in on?"

"Not this time. There's no profit in it."

"Really? But wh—"

"Excuse me. I hope I'm not interrupting."

I look past Thomas's bulk to see a tall blonde.

"No, no. Not at all." He steps aside and shifts his rotund mass to let her into our group. "Always eager to include a beautiful lady in the mix."

"Thank you. I won't stay long. It's Brian Mallory, isn't it?"

"Yes." I can't say I've seen her before, but I've heard that voice before—years ago. She's not wearing perfume or hair lacquer so I'm wondering what she wants—and I'm wary.

"Hello. I'm Carol Lexington. I believe you've done some business with an old friend of mine, Angelica Flores. She's in Spain at the moment."

"Yes." Angelica Flores, a onetime business partner and brief lover, was a brilliant financial analyst but the most useless piece of emotional baggage I'd ever met. She truly had serious mental issues. I put up with several of her eccentricities, like her propensity to growl at prams and eat candle wax, but I packed it in when she pulled down her knickers and shat on the lobby floor of the Hôtel de Crillon because she couldn't find vodka in her mini-bar. That was my breaking point—and (apparently) hers, too. I'd also heard she was in Spain. I'd heard that's where her brother finally had her committed.

"Well, she spoke highly of you and suggested I introduce myself if we were ever at the same event. Someone pointed you out to me tonight, and here I am. I hope I'm not being too… forward?"

"No." I sip my scotch, wondering if that suggestion came while she was a guest in the same asylum or if (Heaven forbid!) Angelica recently had been released. And now that she's asked a question, I remember where I've heard her voice. She was the coat check attendant at my gentlemen's club in Oxford more than ten years ago.

"Excellent. Well then, maybe I could give you my card. I'd love to do lunch… or dinner, sometime."

"Fine." I take the card, quickly glance at it and slip it into my pocket. She's a hospital administrative consultant, which could explain her connection to Angelica in the best possible light. It's not bad. She's done well since Oxford. I might call her but I'd like her to leave now. My mates are uncomfortable because she's only zeroed in on me. I focus on a distant point just above her left shoulder.

She takes the hint. "Well, I look forward to your call."

I watch—we all watch—as she turns and walks away. Her bum is a bit on the hefty side and the chest is fake, but she's got good curves and she's tall.

Thomas scratches and hitches again. "Brian, I bet she's a steamy, hot lay."

I roll my eyes at him. He's always been classless when it comes to sharing his thoughts regarding women.

"Hmm. I've seen her around," Gabe says.

"What do you know about her?" Vincent asks.

"Not much. Married money, divorced, maintenance. Married money, divorced, maintenance."

Craig winks at me. "Hey, Brian. Just what you need, huh?"

Thomas is still leering after her much too long. "She's not bad. She's got class and knows she's hot." He grabs his crotch. "I'd shag her."

"Ah, jeez, Thomas. Come on," Vincent says.

"What? I'm only saying what we're all thinking."

"So, Brian. You gonna call her?" Craig asks.

I keep an eye on her and sip my scotch. "Might."

5
The Advantage Of Really Dark
Sunglasses

Brian — February 3

Jack has pulled up to the curb, adjacent to a long row of three- and four-story industrial warehouses in Park Royal. Most have been converted into studios, fabrication shops and pop-art galleries. I own about five or six of these buildings, including the one I'll be visiting today. I haven't seen it since the day I purchased it four years ago. I buy most warehouses as abandoned and then rent them out to starving artists and tinkering inventors who want to customize them to their own needs. I give them a few rules in the rental contract about what they can and can't do from a structural standpoint, try not to gouge them on the monthly payment because most of them are destitute, and then just let them have free reign.

Mickey is impatiently waiting on the pavement as I step out of the limo, highly cologned and strutting a unique form of haute couture I've never seen before—and hope *never* to see again. The tight beige pants (a bit see-through and bulging in all the wrong places) are not flattering and neither is the clingy, peach-hued polo shirt, sporting an open collar exploding with red chest hair. His shoes have heels—rather high heels. I believe women call them pumps. He's slicked his hair into a semi up-do with shiny goop that makes him look as if he's walking around with a duck's ass stuck on his head and he's wearing gold chains, an earring and several bracelets. His fingers are laden with rings. He looks like a nineteen-seventies pimp.

I watch Jack drive off to get the car washed and detailed. "So, what am I going to see today? What's his style?"

"Well, I'll admit his designs are a bit on the skimpy side, Brian, but everything is tastefully done. There's nothing tacky or raunchy," Mickey assures me, not realizing his own hilarious ensemble has already claimed rightful ownership of those two highly descriptive words.

The studio is bright and clean with tall, south-facing windows. It's apparent that on a limited budget, Lars has put substantial effort into creating an elevated and carpeted runway. He's brought in comfortable mismatched chairs, a low table and a bottle of expensive wine. There's soft jazz floating out of an old broken-down stereo in the corner. Mickey gushes like a schoolgirl when the designer appears from a back room, enthralled beyond words, as if the Queen had just made her grand entrance. He is utterly smitten — again.

Lars, a wiry Swede in his late thirties with a shock of cropped blond hair, is articulate and concise in his presentation, stammering just a little out of nervousness. He'll be the first to acknowledge he caters strictly to the young, openly gay community, but he hopes it's not a deterrent for me and that I see his vision coming through. He hands me his thick research portfolio, several spreadsheets with fabrication costs, pricing estimates and present orders. They're not sophisticated. They've been done by hand on grid paper, but the figures are clear and accurate. Nothing needs to be explained and I like that. He also hands me swatches of material so I can examine the fabrics he's used in his designs. Mickey and I get comfortable, he pours the wine into chipped (but clean) beakers and the fashion show begins. I remove a small pad of paper and pen from my coat pocket to take notes as he describes each design.

The young models he presents — five in all — showing me about thirty different swimsuits, are wearing very little; more than a G-string but much less than a brief. For a forty-one-year-old man who lives in boxers and surfs in long jams, I'd never be able to cram my big ass into one of them (not to mention the good-sized clarinet and jumbo maracas that front my particular band). And I'd never shave or wax the hell out of my hairy crotch the way these lads have, but if I set aside my own preferences and concentrate on what his clientele is looking for (which I should do as a good businessman), I can honestly say Lars has shrewd fashion sense.

Mickey leans toward me in his chair as I sip my wine and loudly whispers, "Does it make you uncomfortable, Brian?"

I peel my eyes off the approaching model to look at him. "Excuse me?"

"Seeing men like this?"

He can tell I'm confused.

"I mean, you know… parading around in skimpy swimwear?"

"No, Mickey. I don't have a problem with it." I turn my attention back to the model. I don't like interruptions when I'm conducting business.

"Well, I just…. I didn't want you to feel uneasy or anything."

As I watch the next model approach, I just wish he'd shut up. "I don't."

"I mean, I know it's not your style and—"

"No, Mickey. It's not my style. It's not supposed to be my style, is it?"

Mickey takes the hint and keeps his gob shut for the remainder of the show. The last of the models saunters down the runway, pauses briefly in a demure pose, turns and walks back.

Lars approaches me, rubbing his hands. "So, Brian, that was it. That's all I have. What did you think?"

I stand up. "It was a good presentation, professional in every way. They're excellent designs for your target market. You're very talented, and I'm impressed."

"Thank you. Thank you very much."

"I only have a problem with one thing and that's the quality of the fabric. Can you bring out the last model again?"

"Vidal!" Lars shouts over his shoulder. Out comes blond, lithe Vidal—a smaller version of Lars. He glides down the runway and poses near the edge, staring straight ahead with one delicate knee bent and his hand on his slender hip. Lars and I approach him. Mickey (with bracelets jangling, high heels clicking, and his pungent Old Spice aura smothering everything like an A-bomb mushroom cloud) comes along too, breathing hard and trying to stand as close to Lars's ass as he possibly can without actually humping it—although, I'm sure he would if he could.

"Excuse me, Vidal." I slip my hand into the waistband of his swimwear and stretch the fabric a bit with my fingers. "See, this really isn't good. As a swatch, it looks fine, but here—against the skin when it's stretched—you can see it's too thin. It'll tear at the seams within a few wearings."

Lars inspects the fabric and nods. "You're right, Brian. I see what you mean, but I can't go with a better quality right now…"

"Because you can't buy quantities large enough to net you an affordable price break."

"Exactly, exactly!"

I take my hand out of the model's waistband. "Thank you, Vidal." I turn to Lars. "We'll deal with that. I know money is an issue. I have a good contact. She can combine the order with other small orders for bulk pricing. I'll have her call you tomorrow." I hand him my pen and pad so he can write down his number. "She'll also help us find the right elastic. We need something that stands up to saltwater, UV and chlorine, as well as standard detergents."

Lars looks surprised. "So… you'll invest?"

"I'll invest upfront so you have working capital to put together a quality portfolio that incorporates all the designs you've shown me today. And we need to get you a small laptop. I want your spreadsheets in electronic format so you can send them to me. We'll review everything again in a few months to see where we stand, okay?"

"Okay. That sounds great! And what about the photo shoots and fashion shows in Hawaii and Milan?"

"I beg your pardon?" is my stunned response.

"I, um, didn't get around to telling you about that the other day," Mickey sputters up at me.

I don't even attempt to hide my irritation. "Well, let's get around to telling me about it now."

In the end, along with the portfolio and the laptop, I'll pay the airfare, food, and hotel expenses for Lars and six models for two weeks in Hawaii. I'll also temporarily freeze his rent on the warehouse. Lars has two other investors, including Mickey, who will cover paying the models, photographer, and equipment rental, and then airfare plus two weeks in Milan. If he can get the big orders — and he seems to be talented and motivated enough to get several — I should have a decent return on my investment within six to nine months.

"I'll have something drawn up and send it over, along with an initial check and the laptop."

"Thank you so much, Brian."

"You're welcome. And keep me informed of anything that comes up. I don't like surprises." I put away my pen and paper and pull out my sunglasses.

"I will. Goodbye, Brian."

"Goodbye, and thank your models for me." I discreetly toss a fifty-pound note on the table to cover the cost of the superb wine.

"Brian, I'll walk you out. Lars, I'll be right back." Mickey, in his skintight pants and chains, is chuffed pink as we leave the studio.

I'm waiting for Jack at the curb. He's five minutes out, Mickey is talking my ear off, and I'm barely listening to him. I have two meetings ahead of me, and I still need to prepare for them. I'm about four meters from the door we just exited, looking down the street for my limo. Mickey is standing in front of me with his back to oncoming traffic. As he's talking, I watch over the top of his head as another door opens farther down along the front of the warehouse and the five models stream out in their street clothes. Lars walks out behind them and talks with them for a few minutes as they stand on the pavement.

Mickey fidgets with his chains and says, "So, he's really something, huh?"

I watch Lars over Mickey's slicked head and from behind my sunglasses. "He's a good designer."

"Oh yeah, that, too. But you know what I mean, right?"

Oh, boy. Here we go. "Mickey, are you really going after this bloke?" I don't want to seem rude but even *I* can see that Lars isn't interested.

"Well, he's given me some signs, Brian. He truly has — some really strong signs. You saw how close he was standing to me in there. He's just a little shy. Most designers are shy."

I watch as the models walk toward an old battered estate car parked at the curb—a rust bucket on wheels. It's seen better days in a previous decade. I just can't tell if it was the last decade or the one before. Vidal lingers on the pavement a little longer than the others do. I continue watching with Mickey prattling on and on about shyness as Lars gives Vidal a passionate kiss, squeezes his small ass with both hands and sensuously grinds into his body. No shyness there at all.

"What do you think?"

I finally look down at Mickey as Jack drives up. "Excuse me?"

"I said I'm going to go back in there, help him finish off that bottle of wine, and ask him out. What do you think?"

Oh, I think not, my good old mate! "I think he needs to work on that portfolio without distraction, Mickey. This may not be the best time. Remember, you've got serious money invested in this, too. He's got an important deadline and he needs to produce."

"You're right. You're *absolutely* right, Brian. Business has to come first. Romance should wait, shouldn't it?"

"Um, yes, Mickey. In this case, I really think it should."

6
Welcome To The Biosphere

John — February 4

I'm squinting out the window, trying to get my bearings. It's raining so hard I can't see much of anything and what I can see doesn't look familiar. You'd think after five years I'd know most areas of London, but when I drive my car it's usually to go to a handful of familiar places (like nightclubs and restaurants) along the same route, and when I'm in a taxi or a limousine, I always zone out until I get to my destination. For anything out of my known realm, I need a Sherpa. "So, where are we?"

Sandy nudges me and tries to push the champagne bottle in my face. "Don't know."

I shake my head at her offering.

"Look, we're supposed to be celebrating. It was a great opening night. By the time we get there, we should be half-plastered, belching and silent-farting. What's wrong with you tonight?"

"Nothing. I just don't feel up to it." She's right, though. We had a fantastic opening night, the first reviews look great, and we're on our way to a gala party. A lot of big names will be there and so will the press. I wish I could say I don't know why I'm in a slump but I'd be lying. The dysfunctional situation with David has me stressed. What use is going to a great party if then I have to go home to him? He didn't make it to the show and I can't get him on his cell so that means he's either out with his obnoxious, unemployed friends getting drunk or he's sitting at home alone getting drunk. Neither scenario will have a good outcome.

"We must be near that industrial area along the Thames west of Southwark, judging from the buildings," Curtis offers with a smile. Curtis is great. He's a pleasant, easygoing guy with a powerful set of pipes that more than make up for his premature baldness and lazy left eye as far as the casting directors are concerned. He's keen on Sandy (my leading lady in several productions), but he's too afraid to say anything to her even though I've given him some pointers. They've spent the entire ride trying to cheer me up and I shouldn't be this glum.

I turn back to the window, wishing I were anywhere but here. My tux is stifling. Even with the air conditioning on, the limo is humid so I crack the window. We're passing towering brick buildings—old warehouses converted into opulent, multi-million dollar loft homes, penthouses, and specialty retail stores (better known as ridiculously overpriced designer boutiques) few working-class Londoners can afford to frequent. This must be the refurbished Docklands, east of Tower Bridge. The mega-rich live here. This is their posh, self-contained biosphere. They only have to leave this newly transformed paradise to attend celebrity functions, the theater and funerals. The rest of the world comes to their doorstep in delivery vans and catering trucks with just a concierge phone call, text message or click of a mouse.

The streets are dark, yet every wet surface reflects the headlights of passing cars. The piercing brightness is hurting my eyes and sending signals to my brain to initiate the first stages of a throbbing headache so I close them for a few minutes. I feel the limo gently turn a corner and as I open my eyes, we stop about fifteen cars back from a red light. My cheek is pressed against the cool glass of the window as I beg my brain cells to fight back the oncoming headache. I hear the rain splashing onto the sidewalk from a downspout that's too high off the ground. I turn to look at it. My eyes focus on a brass plaque screwed to the façade of a brick building. It's an engraved marker no more than eight or nine inches square. I can't read the small words at the bottom so I'm squinting, trying to focus on the large words in the center: MALLORY EIGHT. I sit up straight as I realize I must be right outside Brian's penthouse. My heartbeat has ramped up and a surge of adrenaline has kicked in. I reach for the door handle and before I know it, I've stepped out into the downpour.

Sandy's mouth drops open. "What the *hell* are you doing? Where are you *going?*"

I squint at her through the pouring rain and the open door. Farther up the street, the light has turned green and the cars ahead are moving. "I have to do something."

Curtis leans out past Sandy. "Are you *crazy?* You're in the middle of *nowhere!* Get back in here!"

"I'll be fine." I slam the door and make a dash for the lobby. Once inside, I hear horns honking. I look out through the glass door at two vaguely discernable, shocked faces staring back at me through the dark-tinted windows. More horns honk. Finally, the limousine drives off. I turn and gaze around the lobby. It's a considerably large space with a ceiling at least fourteen feet high. The carpeting is creamy white and the silk curtains are a deep burgundy with dull gold tiebacks. The walls are covered in beige rice paper and the furniture is dark brown leather. There's a towering fireplace in one corner, its gaping firebox stacked with a neat pile of logs. This place reminds me of a lobby in a swank hotel, except it's smaller, the lighting is dimmer, and it's quiet — a much more intimate setting. Along the far wall at the concierge counter, a smartly dressed woman is smiling and looking at me expectantly. As I cross the expanse of the room, I realize nothing echoes, not even the noise I make when I clear my throat out of nervousness. My phone rings. I pull it out and switch it off. I know it's Sandy or Curtis. I'll deal with them later. I slip it back in my coat pocket and keep walking.

"Good evening, sir. I'm Brenda. How may I help you?"

"Um, yes. Hello. Good evening, ma'am. I was.... I'm looking for.... Is Brian Mallory in?"

"Yes, he is. Is he expecting you, Mister...?"

"Kaiser. No. I was — I mean, he said I could stop by if I was in the area." Even though the words are true, I still sound like a liar — an unconvincing liar.

"Mister Kaiser, at the moment he's in a meeting, and he has another one scheduled for later, but since he told you to stop by, let me call Charles, his valet." She picks up a receiver.

I almost want to stop her. If he's in a meeting, then I should leave. I don't want to pester him. She's talking to Charles before I can open my mouth.

"Hey Charlie, how's it going up there? Still raining in the forest?" There's a pause and then she laughs. "Well, Mister Kaiser is here to see Brian." Another pause. "No, but he was told he could stop by if he was in the area, and it seems he's in the area." She smiles and winks at me. There's another pause and she pulls the receiver away from her mouth. "He's just off to ask Mister Mallory if you can come up."

I smile back stupidly and wait. And as I wait, a trickle of sweat runs down my spine.

Brian

This presentation is going nowhere. They've got a decent concept but no one is able to promote it. Why is it, they never invest money in a professional pitchman? Why do cocky upstarts always think they can sell what they've developed? They'll come here in three-hundred pound suits and print up glossy brochures that tell me nothing, but won't hire one brain-accessorized individual who can sell their idea. These five idiots have been at it for almost two hours now, and they've repeated the same facts and figures three times. Facts and figures that are inaccurate, flimsy, and based on —

"What do you think, Mister Mallory?" asks the one who, out of nervousness, keeps adjusting his tie, clearing his throat and wiping his runny nose with the palm of his hand. I must remember not to shake that snotty hand when this meeting is over.

I flip through the meaningless brochure again. "I'd really like to know how you came up with these growth projections and future sales figures. From what I see, the growth is based on condominium leases you hope to secure, not on leases you've got under your belt. Real estate investments, as I'm sure you're aware, are highly unstable right now."

"I understand your concern, Mister Mallory. Let me assure you we've studied the market research surveys put out by Finchleys for four years and we feel we've covered every contingency."

Finchleys? I rub my eyes and take a deep breath. I am so tired of this crap. "By reading a survey for the last four years, you feel you've covered every contingency as to projections of your growth and future sales of luxury condominiums in the present economy? You're basing those on a sponsor-funded *timeshare survey?*"

Nothing but silence and blank stares from the lot. God, these bastards are truly wasting my time. I pick up my pen and start tapping it on the table. I'm trying to exude patience while I think of a moderately polite way to tell them to piss off, but politeness is hard—especially for me. I'm relieved when Charles opens the door and pokes in his head. Right now, I could use a break. I beckon him, and he comes to my chair and bends down. "Excuse me, one moment," I say to the five wide-eyed morons cowering at the other end of the conference table. "Yes, Charles."

"I beg your pardon, sir. There's a Mister Kaiser to see you," he says in a low voice near my ear.

I nearly drop my pen. "What?"

"He's in the lobby, sir. He says you extended an invitation and—"

"He's downstairs? Now?"

"Yes, sir."

I'm dumbfounded. What the hell is *he* doing here? And why is he here now? It's not that it's late, but on a Friday night, in this weather? I'm not easily knocked off center but this is a surprise and it's upset the calm flow of things. I remember telling him to stop by, but I never thought he would. No one who knows me would have taken my invitation seriously. Everyone knows I can't stand having people in the flat. That's why I *never* have people in the flat.

Charles, still uncomfortably bent at the waist, is waiting patiently. "Shall I extend your apologies, sir?"

I rub my temples as I realize it was my own stupidity that brought him here. And even though I can be an asshole, it has never been my style to follow stupidity with rudeness. That just makes me look like a right bastard. "No. If he's in the lobby, you'd better have him come up. I should be finished with this lot in about twenty minutes."

John

My palms are sweating, and I'm fidgeting with a pen left on the counter. I'm beginning to think this wasn't the best idea. I shouldn't have bolted from the limousine so spontaneously. Things don't turn out well for me when I do them spontaneously. The invitation sounded genuine but maybe he didn't—

"Mister Kaiser?"

I nearly jump out of my skin at the sound of Brenda's voice.

"Mister Mallory would like you to come up. It's the dedicated lift just around the corner to your right."

At first, I don't move. I was expecting him to tell me to get lost. I smile awkwardly and approach the elevator. On the wall, there's a panel with one button. I raise my hand, but before I even touch it, the elevator doors glide open. I step inside and they close behind me. There aren't any buttons in the elevator. I don't hear or feel a thing as I'm propelled up six stories to the top floor. I only know I've arrived when the doors open. The sight takes my breath away.

I'm facing a forest of bamboo—thick stalks of it—soaring up into the darkness farther than I can see. The rain is pouring down, splashing close to my feet and making a horrendous noise. At first, I think I've accidentally ended up on the roof. Then, I realize I'm standing under a protective glass awning encircling a square atrium. An elderly, stooped man has come around the side of the atrium and beckoned me. With a good-natured smile, he holds out a frail, shaky hand. "Good evening, Mister Kaiser. I'm Charles. Please come this way. Quite a downpour we're having tonight, aren't we, sir? It should be letting up soon. Mister Mallory is currently in a meeting in the business wing; however, he hopes to wrap up things within the next half hour. In the meantime, he'd like you to make yourself at home in the flat."

We've now reached the opposite side of the atrium, our walk completed under the awning skirting the hole in the roof. Looking back, I can't even see a glimpse of the elevator doors through the bamboo stalks. Charles opens a substantial, thickly frosted glass door with little effort and ushers me inside. It's library-quiet when the door closes behind us, except for the faint sound of classical music: Delibes' *Notturno* from *Coppelia*. He takes my coat and presses a button on the wall. A panel glides open to reveal a closet and my coat joins a dozen others. Within seconds, the panel closes and the closet disappears. I follow him into the 'flat'—which is a gross understatement, like calling a class-one hurricane a slight breeze.

This penthouse is immense. I'm awed. A sea of white Berber carpet stretches as far as the gigantic sliding glass doors on the opposite side. Impressive modern paintings in bold, earthy colors hang on nearly every wall, each one spotlighted and labeled with a stainless steel plaque. The largest grand piano I've ever seen outside a concert hall squats near a commanding fireplace. Cream-hued leather couches, plush club chairs, and steel-framed glass tables and shelves are arranged in several conversational groupings. I see brushed-steel vases everywhere, full of fresh flowers and blooming branches that stretch to what must be twenty-foot ceilings dotted with recessed mini-lights and monumental skylights. But even with the flowers and artwork, the place has a sterile, austere feel to it—like a well-designed art gallery, not a home.

"Would you like a drink, sir?" Charles gestures toward a bar on my left, amply stocked with wine, liquor, and several amber-colored liquids in lead glass decanters sporting exotic shapes I've never seen before.

"No, thank you."

"Anything to eat, sir? We have a wonderful snap-up menu from any restaurant in Central London. I can have a full seven-course meal here in thirty minutes."

"No, I'm...I'm fine," I stammer, overwhelmed by it all.

"I see. Please feel free to look around or just sit—as you like. There's a library and media room down the back hallway and toilets around every corner." He smiles. "If you should need me, press any one of those buttons." He gestures to a small, illuminated button near one of the doorways. "You'll find them in every room."

"Thank you." I watch him disappear to who-knows-where. I'm left alone in this luxurious expanse not knowing what to do with myself. It's too intimidating. I feel miniscule, insignificant—and I'm too petrified to touch anything, even that small, illuminated button. I'm drawn to the view out the floor-to-ceiling glass sliders. Even in the rain (which is beginning to let up) it's spectacular. As I approach the doors, they glide open with a low hum, startling me so much I make an embarrassing noise and stumble back a few steps. God, I hope there aren't any surveillance cameras in here! I regain my composure and step out onto a covered balcony, protected from the weather by voluminous white awnings tethered to the building like horizontal sails. This warehouse sits on an inside curve of the Thames at a point where the river narrows. The view up and down the waterway is beautiful with magnificent Tower Bridge glowing in the distance. The buildings directly across the river are lit up like a waterfront cityscape. They've been converted into lofts, condos and retail spaces. As I stand at the railing, I look down to see the black sparkling river with a string of lights running along its length on both sides.

I step back inside the flat, and the doors close behind me. Aside from that faint sound of classical music (now Bach's *Air*), it's ominously quiet in here and, as in the lobby, nothing echoes, which surprises me because it's such a cavernous space. I give the piano a wide berth. It's a behemoth; a gigantic old Bösendorfer with shiny ebony and yellowed ivory keys and richly detailed legs. I bet it puts out a powerful sound, and it must be worth a fortune. Past the bar, the wide hallway beckons. Even with potential surveillance cameras tracking my every move, my nosiness and curiosity take over as I follow it around two corners. If my bearings are correct, I think I'm in the area behind the elevator shaft or even beyond it. On my self-guided tour, I'm working my way from the back of the penthouse to the front. I wander through two guest bedrooms with attached bathrooms (each one bigger than my first apartment); a professionally appointed gym with shower, three-lane lap pool, and sauna; a home theater that seats about two hundred; a second full kitchen; and a vast, two-story library housing thousands of leather-bound volumes and manuscripts. These rooms have fantastic city views out plate glass windows and automatic sliders that lead out onto decks and balconies. I make my way back to the main hallway and turn into the entrance of the master bedroom.

It's beautifully stark with cream-colored walls, steel blue bed linens on an enormous bed, and dark wood furniture. I gingerly touch the fabric on the bed, chairs, and chaise. It's all iridescent Dupioni silk and timeworn linen. The curtains are tufted, silver-threaded damask lined with yards of brocade. They must weigh a ton. Again, I encounter sliding doors that open and close at my approach and, once outside, more commanding views of the Thames. Back inside, there's a stately lowboy dresser along one wall below a substantial mirror. On top of the dresser sits a single silver tray with countless watches and cufflinks piled in it. I pick up a square platinum and diamond-encrusted cufflink and hold it up to the recessed light. Its brilliance is just exquisite. I put it back. I try on some of the watches: Louis Moinet, Vacheron, Patek Phillipe, Hublot. They're all expensive and they're all too big, dangling off my wrist like bangles. I wander into the bathroom. I'm stunned by the urinal on the far wall. Who the hell has a urinal in his home? I guess a really tall man with potent piss pressure who doesn't enjoy having pee splash around his toilet. There's a long, poured-concrete counter with two cobalt blue glass sinks. I open drawers under the counter, innocently looking for aspirin (actually looking for signs of an active sex life; condoms and lube). Nothing. It takes a minute to realize the bathroom is missing a tub, but the slate shower is beyond impressive with a plasma television, body jets everywhere, and a control panel that looks as if it could launch a space shuttle, steam a frothy cappuccino, and incubate a newborn—all at once.

I return to the bedroom and head for the dressing room. I gasp and my hand clutches at my heart. I've just stepped into Heaven. It's big—a clothes hog's dream come true. In the center, below a crystal chandelier, there's an imposing bureau with drawers on all four sides. I pull open a drawer to find nail files, clippers, sable hairbrushes, tie tacks, money clips and every grooming tool imaginable. Three walls of the room are outfitted with clothes rails, shoe compartments, tie racks and belt carousels. Separate areas house suits, slacks, shirts, coats, vests, hats, sweaters, jeans, umbrellas, and even a few kilts. It's like a men's boutique. I walk along the rails and racks, fingering the fabrics: pure silk, raw silk, merino wool, linen, mohair, Egyptian cotton, satin, cashmere, angora, charmeuse, pashmina, velvet—even a scrap of outdated velour. I know my fabrics. Several of the dress shirts have delicate, single gold threads running through them. I bet they're real gold.

I pull out jackets and coats and try them on in front of the full-length mirror spanning the fourth wall. I'm a munchkin with every sleeve hanging down to my fingertips and hems hitting me below mid-thigh, but it all feels so luxurious and I'm careful to put every piece back exactly where I find it. Then I spy it: the remarkable deep blue tuxedo Brian wore at the charity event. I'd know it anywhere. It was so unique. I remember wanting to touch the fabric the night he wore it. I lift the hanger off the rail. I hesitate. Did I hear an ominous creak? It must have been my imagination. I take down the suit and slip my arms into the silk-lined jacket. I love the feel of it. It's the softest lightweight wool I've ever touched. For some reason, wearing it here—in Brian's home—gives me chills. I sniff the collar and smell the faint aroma of his soap. Visions of his gestures, his mesmerizing eyes, the sound of his voice—it all drifts back to me like a wondrous dream. I quietly hum *Some Day My Prince Will Come* as I dance and twirl gracefully before the mirror, surveillance cameras be damned! I give my Snow White moment one final sublime, plié-pirouette combo and then reluctantly slip out of the jacket. I drape it back on its hanger and reach up to put it on the rail. And that's when I realize I should have paid more attention to the sound of that ominous creak.

The twenty foot length of clothes rail crashes to the floor, pulling out a lofty portion of the sheetrock from both end walls, the rear wall, and the ceiling where it had been (obviously, poorly) secured. Shirts, shoes, coats, suits, ties, hats—everything cascades and tumbles around my feet. The sound is horrific, and the chandelier is gently swaying. I'm in shock with my mouth hanging open and my arm still holding up the tuxedo on its hanger like the Statue of Liberty defiantly clutching her torch. I stare down at all of these beautiful clothes crumpled on the floor and covered in a fine layer of plaster dust and chunks of drywall. I barely notice Charles walk in. "I am... so sorry," I whisper as I continue to stare down at the devastation I've caused.

He calmly reaches up, lowers my arm, and applies his brute strength to pry the hanger out of my petrified fingers. For a frail, little man, he's pretty strong. "Don't worry, sir. We've had an issue with that particular rail for a while now. Would you like to come back into the living room? Mister Mallory is almost finished with his meeting."

Still in a state of shock and unable to move of my own free will, Charles pulls me out of the dressing room rubble and guides me out of the bedroom where he tosses the tuxedo on the bed as we pass by. He sits me down on the living room sectional, stands back to take a good look at my face, and decides to plant me in a chair outside on the balcony instead. Again, he scrutinizes me. Pursing his lips and furrowing his brow, it's obvious he still doesn't like what he sees and I'm in no condition to improve my appearance. "You look pale, sir. I think I'll get you a small glass of wine." He leaves and quickly returns with a large glass of red wine. I hold the glass by its bowl with two shaky hands and take a sip. It's wonderfully smooth and has a soaring alcohol content. I take another, longer sip. The wine leaves a lingering warmth in my throat as I swallow. I feel much better. I smile up at him and he smiles down at me. Then he turns. "Ah, here's Mister Mallory. I'll leave you in his hands now."

Brian's approach causes my heart to skip a beat and my chest to heave. He is a strikingly handsome man. He's wearing a charcoal gray business suit but his shirt isn't tucked in, and his burgundy tie is dangling loose around his neck. He takes off his jacket and throws it on one of the living room chairs. Charles, whimsically diminutive as he stands next to him, hands him a glass of scotch and a cell phone. He picks up the jacket and disappears down the hallway. Brian strides out onto the balcony, looks out at the last remnants of drizzle, and slumps into a chair across from me. With his head down, he starts scrolling menus on his phone. "Give me one minute, John. I've got to check these messages. I don't think they're important, but I never know."

I wait. I'm fidgety and nervous. I'm also sweating a bit. I sip my wine and stare down at his long legs, warning my eyes not to drift up toward his crotch.

"Good. No emergencies and no catastrophes." He lays the phone on the table, looks at me, and sips his scotch. "Now, how are you?"

"I'm sorry I broke your clothes rail," I nervously blurt out.

"Oh, yeah. I heard."

"Oh, my God! Was it that loud?"

"No, I mean Charles told me about it. Don't worry. I knew it was going to fall down. They've tried to fix it, twice. It's not a big deal.

How are you?"

"I'm...I'm okay." Jeez, I'm *not* okay. I'm a pile of nerves. I'm usually so cool and confident when I'm around people, especially attractive men. That's when I'm at my best, literally dazzling them and (figuratively) charming the pants off them. I take another sip of wine and, with a shaky hand on the stem, set the glass on the table.

Brian follows my movements with a concerned look. "You seem a bit nervous."

"Just a little... I guess."

"To be honest, John, you look like shit—like you're about to faint."

"Do I? I used to faint a lot when I was a kid. I'd have these panic attacks and—" Oh, God! Why did I just tell him that? What kind of butthead moron am I? "But I won't faint now," I quickly add.

Brian sips his scotch, studies me hard as if I was a new species of utter stupidity that just fell from the sky, and then stands up to move to the railing. "Come here."

I stand up and carefully walk over to join him. My knees feel as if they'll buckle any second so I hang onto the railing tightly.

He leans on the railing and points. "You see that building over there, directly across from us?"

I squint hard at the buildings across the river, trying to bring them into some form of fuzzy focus. "That one? The one with the arched windows?"

"Aye." He takes a sip of scotch. "That was the first warehouse I ever bought and converted. It took me two years. God, it was a nightmare. I didn't know what the hell I was doing. I thought I'd made the biggest mistake of my life."

I take my eyes off the warehouse and look at him gazing across the river. He's remembering the ordeal as I stare at his obscenely long eyelashes and his captivating profile: perfect forehead and brow, perfect nose (not shaped like a penis, thank God!), perfect cheekbone, sexy lips, perfect chin. "It's beautiful," I mumble, reluctant to peel my eyes off him and look back at the distant building.

"Aye, it is. When I finally finished, I leased all the units except that one right in the middle."

I squint again. "The one with the three big arches?"

"Aye. I kept that one. That one was mine. And you know what I did the first night I moved in, the very first night I was there?"

I look at him and shake my head. He's still gazing at the building.

"I stood there with a glass of scotch and I looked out that big window right in the center and said, 'Bugger all! I'd rather have that one over there.'"

I smile. "So you bought this building?"

He returns the smile. "Eventually, John. Eventually."

Brian

It's good to see him smile. When I first laid eyes on him, he looked so pale. From what Charles said, the falling clothes rail really shook him up. I just need him to relax a bit because I do much better around people who aren't nervous. His cologne isn't beating me over the head tonight and that's good. I should be able to tolerate him for about an hour. "So, why are you all dressed up?"

"Opening night of the show. I was on my way to a party."

"Really? I wish I could have attended opening night. How did it go?"

"Um, the early reviews look pretty good, but Mickey says the early reviews don't count. He says they're written by all the critics who slept with the director."

"And do you believe him — that the critics slept with the director?"

"No. The director is really ugly, and he's got bad breath. I wouldn't sleep with him." He smiles at me and I smile back. He's still a little nervous but he's trying hard to relax.

"So why aren't you at the party?"

"I'm not sure. I just didn't...." His voice trails off and his forehead wrinkles as he stares down into the river.

"Come on. Let's go inside." I grab my mobile and his wine glass off the table. I walk into the living room and flop down in one of the club chairs. I set my mobile on the coffee table, along with his wine. He sits down in a chair across from me and looks back out at the skyline through the sliders.

"Right now, it would be hard to go to a party and..."

"Try to act happy?"

He nods, picks up his wine, takes a sip, and pans the living room. I watch him as he takes in all the details. "You have a beautiful home."

"Thank you. I like it."

"Everything looks so expensive. I mean *really* expensive."

I take a look around myself. It's amazing how little has changed since I first renovated the place. It's depressing to acknowledge the monotonous life I've lived all these years; boring, tediously dull—and this room reflects that life. "There're only three things in here that are worth anything substantial. My ex-wife's piano, the Grecian urn behind it, and this table." I look down at one of my prized possessions: a custom-made, steel-framed coffee table with a thick slab of pale gray glass impregnated with lutetium dust and deeply reverse etched with the sea stacks of the Outer Hebrides. "Oh, and that big vase in the kitchen on top of the fridge. I'm not too fond of it, but an old friend gave it to me and I haven't the heart to get rid of it. She paid an unbelievable amount of money for it. Why? God only knows, but it's increased in value exponentially. The rest," I wave my hand, "is standard fare. You can get it anywhere."

"It just looks so nice and yet Mickey says you don't allow anyone to come up here."

I laugh a little and set my glass on the armrest. "Well... I guess that's true, at least regarding the flat. I have a lot of business meetings up here."

He sips his wine. "So your friends don't get to see this place but your business associates do?"

"No. Anyone I do business with comes up in a different lift and uses a separate entrance. Because of those curtains, they don't see the flat—ever."

"Oh." He thinks for a minute. "Why?"

"Why what?"

"Why don't you want your friends up here?"

"I guess I see it as an invasion of privacy. I don't like people in my personal space."

"Mickey says you don't like people at all."

I shrug. "He's probably right. I certainly don't make the effort. I find most people are either annoying, obnoxious, or a bloody pain in the ass."

"Mickey says you're difficult to get along with and really demanding."

I laugh again, sip my scotch, and narrow my eyes. "Do you get *all* your information about me from Mickey?"

"No, I just...." He's flustered and starts to fidget. I've made him uncomfortable. "I can't figure out why he'd say that. You don't seem difficult or demanding at all—to me."

"Let's just say I don't like most people, I'm really intolerant, and in my world I want things done my way. Okay?"

"Okay." He smiles, sips his wine, and leans back in the chair, comfortable again.

I study him. He's an interesting young bloke; not as cocky and conceited as I thought he'd be. He's awkward and unsure of himself. "You know what Mickey says about you?"

He's a bit surprised. "Me? No. What?"

"He says you're spoiled, and you'll do anything to get your way."

He takes the defensive. "I'm not saying I'm privileged or anything, but if I deserve something, I think I should get it."

"He says you throw tantrums and beg and badger people."

"Well, sometimes. If I need to, if I have to."

"So you don't deny it?" I'm really surprised he's admitting that.

"Let's just say I'll do what I need to do to get what I want if it should be mine and it's really important to me. Okay?"

I smile. "Okay." I like him. He's open and honest. I sip my scotch as Charles comes into the room and hands me a few slips of paper. They're phone messages taken at the concierge counter because I refuse to use the damned voicemail service. I had the system installed for the tenants but I think it's a bloody nuisance.

"If that's all, I'll be off now until your next meeting at one, sir."

"Aye. Thank you, Charles."

"You're welcome, sir. Goodnight, Mister Kaiser."

"Goodnight, um... Charles."

John watches him leave. The epitome of a quiet, obedient, nineteenth-century manservant, he's wondering if the old codger is for real.

I glance through the slips of paper and toss them on the table. "How long have you been in London, John?"

"Almost five years."

"The transition from America must have been hard."

"It was at first, but I've got some close friends. They're really special. We talk about everything, and we're always there for each other."

I sip my scotch and settle back into my chair. "Tell me about them."

"You don't want to hear about my friends." His embarrassment is obvious.

"Yes, I do. Tell me. What makes them so special?" I slouch down and stretch out my legs under the table. I enjoy listening to his voice because it's not grating or full of affectation. It relaxes me. That's probably due to his accent, which I don't often hear, except when Mickey is blabbering—and that's never relaxing.

He sips his wine before he begins. "Well, there's Ben. He's an actor and a model, but mostly he's a model because he's bone thin and clothes hang on him really well. The designers love him. He's skeptical of everyone, and he always looks serious because he wears dorky glasses. He thinks he knows how to do everything, but he really doesn't. Then there's tiny Prissy—"

"Prissy? That's his name?"

"No, his name is Presley-Louise Mortensen, but he can't stand it so we call him Prissy."

"And he prefers that?"

"Oh God, no. He hates Prissy more than Presley-Louise."

I smile. "Is he an actor or a model?"

"He's an actor—a classical actor. Most of the time, he prances around like a Pomeranian in heat and flirts a lot, with everyone. He likes to wear pink things or get naked, but on stage, he'll take your breath away. I mean, seriously, he's unbelievable. No one comes near him, and he never needs a script if it's Shakespeare. He's just amazing. He and Ben usually sleep together when they get drunk. They're like each other's security blanket or something. They fight like crazy, but they may be in love." The words roll out of his mouth quite fast. It's amazing how talkative he is with a little alcohol in him. "Then there's

Jeff. He's an actor, too. I guess he's got the limpest wrist, next to Prissy. He does a lot of commercials and voice-overs. You've probably heard him. He does the new Vauxhall Insignia commercial and a couple for Tesco and Uptown Corinthian. He had laryngitis for a week, and it shut down production on a dozen projects. He's paranoid about air quality—car fumes, pollution, smoke. He says his voice is his ticket to a retirement in the Bahamas, so he needs to baby it." He sips more wine before continuing. "And then there's Martin, my hairdresser at Shave. I tell him everything. He's probably the smartest person I know. He has so much common sense. I mean, he just knows right from wrong when everyone else doesn't. He reads people, knows exactly what's going on in their heads. He tolerates anything and everything. His wife is a pain when it comes to letting him hang out with us. She thinks gay rubs off if you get too close to it. I don't know." He stares down into his wine glass, deep in thought. "She's high strung because they've been trying to have a baby for years, and it's just not happening. She spends a lot of time in karaoke bars with her girlfriends, so as long as we pick a night when she's out singing, we're fine." He looks up at me, smiles, and sips his wine.

"They sound like great friends."

He nods and sips more wine. "They are. I'm lucky to have them."

I give him a minute before I ask the next question. "Who's David?"

Right away, I see I've hit a nerve. His expression changes and his face drains of color. He pulls his arms closer to his side as if he's suddenly felt a chill and looks back down into his wine glass.

"Mickey mentioned him when I came to your rehearsal," I explain as I stand up and go to the bar. I look back at him as I grab the wine bottle.

He's silent. Strangely, sitting there all closed up with his head down, he looks like a wee lad who's afraid to admit he's told a lie for fear of a spanking. I bring the bottle and pour more wine into his glass. I set the bottle on the table and return to my chair. When he speaks, his words are quiet and carefully chosen. "Right now... he's my... boyfriend."

"Are things okay with him?"

He shakes his head and still won't look up.

"Tell me about it." I have no idea why I'm prying into his personal life. I don't give a toss about anyone's personal life, except Simon's.

"He's going through a… rough time. Lately, he hasn't had much work, and that's created tension between us. He can't handle casting call rejections."

"You're doing really well in your career and he's not. That has to be a bad patch for him."

He nods. "He's bitter and resentful. It makes it hard. A lot of great things are happening for me, and he doesn't want to hear about them or be a part of them, like the show tonight and the party."

"Then it's good you have your friends."

A smile curves his lips. "Yeah. I don't think I could handle the situation without them."

"Do you love him?" Why am I asking this? Why do I even want to know this?

He thinks hard. "No. I don't think I've ever loved him. With Mickey's help, I thought I *could* love him if our careers took off, if we were both successful and happy. I mean, we look great together. Mickey always says we make a really hot couple. When I was younger, I thought that was enough, but all he does now is get drunk, call me 'Sweetie,' and hassle me about my weight."

There's a long silence but I know he wants to say more, so I give him time.

He scratches the side of his nose and leans forward, resting his elbows on his knees. "We came to London because of him, because of his career. I was a nobody. David had modeling and acting contracts coming out of his ears before our plane even landed. I started out bussing tables, measuring inseams, and scraping God-knows-what off park benches. Eventually, Mickey found small roles I could audition for. Most were cattle calls—just grueling and sometimes humiliating. David was so condescending, but I still took whatever I could get. When he started refusing to audition for small productions because he thought they were a waste of time, it upset Mickey so he gave the calls to me, and I kept getting better parts, bigger roles, more work, more recognition. Everything David rejected, I took. His reputation for nixing small roles got around and pretty soon no one offered him anything, even though he was a good actor."

"Why is that?"

"Good producers of small productions went on to larger productions. If an actor wasn't willing to be in a no-name show, why should a producer offer him something in a big one? My lucky break came with the audition for the series—and I suppose my instant popularity came with what you said on that talk show three years ago. Offers for theatrical roles hit me faster than I could respond. I started to soar and he started to sink."

"But there's more, isn't there?" I prod, acting on a nosiness impulse (that borders on outright meddling) I didn't know I had.

He looks up at me and whispers, "I don't think he's comfortable with who he is, with being gay. He's ashamed of our relationship and of himself. I'm sure he regrets coming out, and I think he blames me." He shakes his head. "Brian, you must think I'm so stupid."

"No, John. I don't think you're stupid." I feel sorry for him because his unhappiness is obvious. "Why don't you break up with him?" Great! Now I'm giving him advice. What the hell is wrong with me?

He sighs. "Mickey says it's a bad career move right now. David will throw a pity party, and I'll come out looking like a shithead. The tabloids.... Well, they'd have a field day." He looks at me with the saddest, deep blue eyes. "I just don't know what to do. What do you think I should do?"

"Me? God, I'm in no position to give advice on relationships. Right now, I'm the prime example of what *not* to do when it comes to relationships."

He seems surprised as he sits up straight. "Why?"

I set my elbow on the armrest and plant my chin in the palm of my hand. "I screw up everything, John. I mean everything. I'm an asshole—a bloody bastard. And you know what the worst part is?"

"What?"

"I do it on purpose."

Now he smiles. "Why?"

"God only knows. I go out with beautiful, intelligent women and within half an hour I've pissed them off."

"Don't you like women?"

"I love women. I think they're great. They're wonderful. I guess I do it because I just don't want to be with anyone right now. I want to be alone."

"Really? I don't ever want to be alone. I don't like how quiet it is when I'm alone."

"Really? I enjoy how quiet it is when I'm alone." We smile at each other, and I can tell he's very relaxed.

John

I don't know where Mickey gets his information. Brian isn't difficult or demanding. He's warm and kind and talkative. He's asking questions and listening to my answers. He's interested in what I have to say—and I've said a lot. I've just been yakking my head off—about everything. I'm sure it's the wine. I've almost forgotten about that stupid clothes rail and my troubles with David. I'm just enjoying my time spent with Brian. And as the hours tick away, I'm learning a lot about him, too. He's a vegetarian. He collects artwork—mostly paintings—but his real love is old books. He could easily do without air conditioning and voicemail. He walks to the local market every other day for fresh fruits and vegetables. He loves classical music and the smell of fresh flowers. He owns a ton of suits but only wears half of them, and he hasn't worn his kilts in years. He was in medical school for three years but dropped out (and pissed off his parents) when he bought his first piece of real estate and sold it at an unbelievable profit. His most favorite place in the world is the Scottish Highlands and his least favorite is Los Angeles. He suffers from insomnia (hence his 'round-the-clock' meetings), and he loves to cook, having learned how on his mother's old Aga when he was a boy. I'm devastated when Charles appears because I don't want my visit to end. I want this enchanted evening to go on forever. Brian glances at him and then his gaze turns back to me. "So, have I lived up to Mickey's description?"

"No, not at all. To be honest, he made you sound pretty offensive but tolerable. I think you're really nice."

"I'm glad to hear it. I've got a meeting in a few minutes."

"Of course." I carefully set my empty wine glass on the table. I stand up, just moderately drunk and swaying a little. "I liked talking with you."

He stands up, too. "Then come back again, John. We'll talk some more. I have to change. Charles will show you out. Goodnight."

And with that, he turns and walks out of the living room and down the hallway, taking the enchantment and my lusting heart with him.

■ ■ ■

I'm a little unsteady riding down in the elevator so I hold onto the handrail to make sure I'm upright when it stops. Once I'm in the lobby, I stupidly grin at Brenda, still standing behind the concierge counter, as I trundle by on my drunken flat feet. I whack into the glass lobby door, push on it a few times, and then finally take a step back and haul it open with a silly giggle. Outside, the air smells fresh after the downpour, and it's starting to sprinkle again. I want to wrap myself around a lamppost and belt out a Gene Kelly tune to the whole world. I want to stomp around in the puddles and loudly profess… something — anything — to the mailbox on the corner and the parking meters across the street and the still-noisy downspout. It's nearly one in the morning. Aside from somewhere near a bend in the Thames, I have no idea where I am. I don't know the name of the street. I don't have any transportation, and I'm pretty damned tipsy. I pull out my phone and turn it on. I've got nearly two-dozen messages but I'll check them later. Right now, I need a taxi and I hope it's not a strike day. I turn to the left to shed some streetlight illumination as I scroll through my numbers. I notice a large car advancing slowly. It's not in the lane. It's curb crawling with its lights off. As it draws closer, I see it's a stretch limousine with the ubiquitous tinted windows. I stand mesmerized (and swaying) as it pulls up next to me and the driver's window lowers. "Excuse me, Mister Kaiser. May I give you a lift?"

"Um… I don't—" I carefully bend over and squint into the window. As I feel myself falling forward, I reach out and place my hand on the car so I don't pitch head first through the window and into the driver's face, which is unfamiliar to me — very handsome, but unfamiliar.

"My name is Jack. Mister Mallory sent me around. He thought you might want to go to a party, sir."

My phone dangles loose from my fingers. "Oh. I was going to call a taxi."

He smiles up at me. "You're a few hours late, sir. People could be a little miffed. It might make a better impression to arrive in a limo than a cab, don't you think?"

I give him the jovial, demented grin of a lush. Yes, I'll go to the party. I'll be three hours late, pleasantly drunk (okay, pissed off my ass), and arrive in Brian Mallory's stretch limousine.

7
So Much For Sexy

Brian — February 7

"The Rolls or the limo tonight, sir?"

I adjust my tie at the mirror. "Limo, please, Charles."

"I'll let Jack know."

"Thank you." Tonight, I'm going out with Carol. I finally made the call. I guess I was attracted to her forwardness at the fundraiser and the fact she wasn't wearing perfume or lacquer. She's checked up on me. I don't know what source she used, but I can't complain. It would be nice to meet a woman who knows all my likes and dislikes from the start. I'll take her to The Wicksworth Mill and try not to sabotage the evening.

. . .

Even for someone who isn't very visual, as I watch her approach the limousine (escorted by Jack), I have to admit Carol is attractive: blonde hair, blue eyes, fantastic skin, and a voluptuous smile. She's also sexy—a little too sexy. She walks sexy, talks sexy, sits sexy, and keeps giving me sexy looks. I have a feeling this woman is going to eat sexy, too. Whatever source she used should have told her to lay off the sex, just a little. It makes her look desperate, and I don't like dating desperate women.

John

"Please, David. Do you have to?" I take a chance in quietly asking as the waiter leaves.

He chomps on his breadstick. "What?"

I lean over the table and lower my voice. "You've already had three."

He leans over the table too. "The minute I decide I need you to count my drinks, Sweetie; the first goddamned minute I decide that, I'll let you know. Okay?" He gives me a wicked grin. His speech might not yet be slurred, but his eyes are glassy and his words are cruel. He grabs another breadstick and waves it in front of my face as a warning. "We wouldn't want an ugly scene, would we—something that might embarrass the precious little superstar? No, I didn't think we'd want that. So you just smile like the famous piss-pipe queen you are and sit on your fat ass a little longer, and we'll get through this shitty anniversary dinner in one piece, okay?"

With tense jaw and clenched teeth, I look down at my folded hands resting in my lap. I want us out of this restaurant before more diners arrive.

"Hey!" he pipes up, tossing the breadstick onto my plate, "what d'ya say we *fuck* tonight, huh?"

My face drains of color when he says the word, and I raise my eyes to look at him. Oh God, I don't want him to talk like this—not here, not now.

A triumphant smile lights up his face. "What's the matter, Sweetie? Did I say something wrong?" He gasps and snaps his fingers as if he's just remembered a boiling pot left unattended on a burner at home. "That's right! You don't like it when I call it *fucking*, do you? It's too... distasteful for your virtuous ears." He leans back in his chair when the waiter brings his fourth whiskey, and stares at me with contempt. As the waiter leaves, he grabs a third breadstick, holds it up in front of his face, and examines it carefully as if looking for signs of weevil infestation. "Well, I've got news for you, little faggot: It's what we do," he says flatly, glaring at me past the breadstick.

"David, please. I don't want—"

"We *fuck*! We don't make love. We don't have sex. Hell, we don't even *screw!*"

A red heat is burning at the top of my cheeks. "David, don't—"

"We butt-fuck our brains out. Ask any respectable human being and he'll tell you faggots fuck ass like dirty dogs."

"Stop it!" I snap, with tears welling in my eyes.

"Stop what?" The question is asked with fake innocence and the smile returns as he basks in his glorious victory. His mood darkens again and the smile vanishes. He leans in across the table and sneers, "You're so *pathetic*. You think you're such hot shit. *You're not!* None of us are. We're weirdoes. *We're freaks!*" He downs his fourth whiskey in one gulp. "We're fucking abominations and society can't stand us, Sweetie, so get used to it."

As I sit at a linen-covered table in this upscale restaurant with luminous votive candles and creamy gardenias floating in porcelain fingerbowls, a lightning bolt of shame passes through me. Not because of who I am but because of who I'm with. I fight back the tears, determined not to give him more ammunition to torture me with. I remember the painful years I cowered alone—too confused to understand why I was different and when I finally did understand, too afraid to admit it to anyone. I remember the shame, and I rose above it. I rose above self-hatred and society's hatred. And I didn't conquer all of that—all of those years of suffering—to end up here, listening to venomous filth spewed at me by a damned bastard who's supposed to be my boyfriend.

Brian

Dinner goes well up until we finish the main course. She knows enough to stay away from taboo subjects like the flat, the mansion, and what I'm worth in today's market. She doesn't ask a lot of questions, shows a high interest in things I like, and quiets down when I've had enough of the small talk. She also shuns the meat dishes and orders a large broad bean and mixed vegetable casserole. If she's just doing that for my benefit she may regret it, especially if her digestive system isn't used to eating a plateful of oligosaccharides. This woman has done her research, trying to present herself as my perfect match, but it's as if I'm having dinner with myself, and I don't find myself that interesting.

"We're very compatible, Brian," she whispers across the table, her eyes half closed. Again, she's trying for sexy. Unfortunately, it looks and sounds as if she's popped a roofie and chased it with a double shot of vodka.

I watch the elderly waiter refill our water goblets. "Are we?"

"Oh, yes. Just look at the pleasant evening we're hav—DAMN IT! *Watch what you're doing!*" The words fly out of her mouth like machine-gun artillery fire when a miniscule drop of water splashes into her lap. The poor waiter almost has a heart attack and damn near dumps the whole carafe on her out of fright. I raise an eyebrow as the restaurant grows quiet and fellow diners glare. So, there's a crack in the perfect façade. Miss Sexy has a quick temper and little self-control. I'm not impressed and neither is anyone else. The rich *never* offend the wait staff because no one wants to end up with spit in his food. I'm waiting to see how graciously she recovers, and I'm definitely going to slip a twenty-pound note to that frazzled waiter.

"Oh, I'm sorry. I'm just.... It's just that this dress.... Well, the silk spots very easily."

"Does it, really?" I look on as she turns red and the low murmur of intimate conversation (most likely regarding her unbecoming outburst) returns to the surrounding tables.

"I...I have a high respect for wait staff, in general. I really think they do a fine job. He just caught me off guard. He gave me a little start."

"Yes. You frightened the bloody crap out of him, too."

Looking around self-consciously, she tries to compose herself. She smoothes her hair, takes a long sip of wine, and lowers her voice an octave. "Well, as I was saying," she continues, again in her roofie-like stupor, "we're highly, *highly* compatible—you and I—and of course, I hope we'll get to know each other better on a more... intimate level."

I tap my finger on the rim of my scotch glass. I think I know where this night is headed. I'm not opposed to it. I had a lot of meetings last week and missed a few of my workouts. I'm tense and I could use some sex. "Would you like to order dessert?"

"Oh no, Brian. I couldn't possibly eat another thing," she breathes heavily. "You know, there's an intimate piano bar in a charming hotel just around the corner. I'd love to buy you an after-dinner drink to show my... gratitude for such a splendid evening."

John

The evening was a complete disaster and a total embarrassment. Being asked to leave the restaurant—albeit discreetly—when David had the nerve to spit on the straight couple sitting next to us because he thought they were giving us a disgusted look couldn't compare to being thrown out of the nightclub one hour later because he made a derogatory comment about masturbation techniques to a double amputee. Who, in their right mind, would do such a thing? There'll be a write-up in the tabloids tomorrow, and I just pray a lawsuit doesn't follow. I'll have to give Mickey a heads up. He's used to dealing with a lot of damage control when it comes to David being out in public these days.

For now, he's passed out on the sofa. I paid the taxi driver twenty pounds to help me haul his drunken carcass into the brownstone like a sack of potatoes. At one point, my grip slipped and we accidentally whacked his head on the landing and then again on the doorjamb. Pity. I flop down into one of the chairs across from the sofa and stare at him as two distinct bruises begin to form on his forehead. He's snoring—loudly. His mouth is hanging open and a steady stream of drool is running down his chin. Slack-jawed and gray-pallored, with his lids half open and only the whites of his eyeballs showing, he looks like an old rag doll missing half its stuffing and tossed onto a garbage heap. How can my professional life be shooting up into the heavens when my personal life is sliding down into hell? This isn't the five-year anniversary I expected when I first met David. I wouldn't say things were great in the beginning with his superiority complex easily dominating my inferiority complex. On a daily basis, his lack-of-compassion persona never had patience in dealing with my lack-of-confidence ego. But I didn't think we'd end up here—like this. There's nothing I like about him now and, after those hurtful words in the restaurant and the scene at the club, nothing I respect. How long have I been taking care of him? Has it been two years or is it already three? I pay for everything, including the hefty mortgage and taxes. I clean up after him, cook for him, and continually apologize for him. There's been no affection. There's been no sex in ages. Not that I'd even want to have sex with him now, but I do miss sex. I *really* miss sex—a lot.

I tilt back my head and stare at the ceiling. I'm so tired of this nightmare. I want someone to take care of me for a change, to put me first and watch over me and protect me. I'm so lonely. I desperately want someone to love me. How many times have I sat down for an interview and been asked, "So, John, what project are you working on now?" Every time I've wanted to say, "Right now, I'm working on getting rid of my loser boyfriend and finding true love." If I could break up with him, I would. If I could kick him out, I would. David burps and smacks his lips. Two minutes later, he's snoring again. I get up and go into the kitchen. I bring out the waste can and set it on the floor next to his drooling head. I know from experience, after a few belches he always throws up, and tonight it will be our five-year anniversary dinner and seven shots of whiskey. It's something I don't want to see, hear, or smell. I trudge upstairs and go to bed.

Brian

I'm listening to various sounds. I hear faint street noise from the open window: a siren, a few drunken revelers, a passing lorry that desperately needs a new muffler, and not much else. The most hideous din is coming from the Blonde Amazonian Bedbeast on my left. Carol's snoring is atrocious. It's like that horrible racket a piece of plastic made when we'd put it in the spokes of our bicycle wheels as young lads and then pedal incessantly like maniacs in front of cottages of the elderly to piss them off. She's also been noisily and steadily farting her ass off. Apparently, broad beans and broccoli are not staples of her normal diet, and the small amount of air streaming in through the window isn't enough to neutralize the fetid fumes to a level my senses can tolerate. So much for sexy. I turn my head to study her; pale and bloated with arms and legs unflatteringly splayed out like an inflatable doll in the window display of a Brewer Street sex shop. Her mouth is gaping, showcasing an alarming amount of bridgework and dozens of filled cavities. It's obvious she experienced a bout of poor oral hygiene at some point in her life and made one particular orthodontist very rich. Her bulbous implants (showing signs of moderate capsular contraction, if I'm not mistaken) take on a laughable quality as she lies flat on her back: two raisin-nippled, yet forever-perky weapons of mass destruction, half rising out of subterranean missile silos, aimed straight at the ceiling and ready to blast off from a saggy, middle-aged chest that has no business sporting such unnatural-looking augmentations. I'll never get used to touching those damned things.

I close my eyes. The sex was okay. It relaxed me a little, but it didn't take my mind off work, and it didn't make me tired enough to sleep. Possessing a below-average libido and zero interest in foreplay, it's no wonder. Casanova, I am not. My motto is, "get in, get out, get going." I'll give it a few more minutes, but then I've got to leave. Hotel rooms are okay up to a point, but eventually the unfamiliar surroundings make me listless. If given the chance, if I ever do sleep tonight, I want to be in my flat, in my bed — alone.

I get up, find my coat, and dig out my mobile. I punch in a number and put it back in my coat. I quietly put on my clothes as Carol continues to snore and fart to her heart's content. I'll shower at home. Hotel showers, even at the priciest hotels, are notorious for transmitting athlete's foot so I avoid them at all costs. I leave the key in the room, hang the 'Do Not Disturb' sign on the door, and lock it behind me. In the lobby, I experience an overwhelming sense of security when I look out the doors and see my limo waiting at the curb. Safety. "Brian Mallory, room six-ten." The desk clerk hands me the bill. "The room is still occupied. The lady has the key. She'll need a cab to Earlsfield and may order room service before she leaves. Just add it to the final tally." I write a thirty-pound tip at the bottom of the bill, right above the blank total line, and hand it back to the clerk.

His eyes bug out when he sees it. "Thank you, sir. I'll make sure the lady is well accommodated."

"Thank you. Good night." I walk out of the lobby, cross the pavement, and duck into the limousine. Yes, safety. All in all, the evening wasn't bad compared to previous dates. She's pleasant enough company, and her downfalls are tolerable. The sex was okay, even with the fake breasts, the snoring, and the smelly flatulence — which is a pretty accurate indicator of my pathetic sex life. I'll probably call her again.

8
The Impact Of The Impact

Ben — February 8

I spy his child-like fingers out of the corner of my eye. "Knock it off!" *Slap.*

"Ow!"

"Prissy! Leave it alone! Damn, you!" *Slap. Slap.*

"What is your problem? It's only been your motor for five minutes. I can touch whatever I want."

I'm in a right sour mood on this unusually muggy day, and I don't need his lip. "Look, I just had that thing installed, and I don't want you to break it. Leave it alone!" *Slap.*

"Ow!"

"Would you two shut up? You're driving me spare," Jeff whines from the back seat. "I've got headache from you and all these damned fumes. I shouldn't be breathing this stuff." He dramatically sissy-coughs and clutches at his chest. "Me poor bronchioles! Can't we crank up the windows and turn on the air?"

I look down at the gauge. "No air. I'm already down half a tank." With petrol at nearly two pounds, I can't afford to worry about Jeff's lungs. Again, I reach out to slap Prissy's hand. Again, I miss. The little git is lucky he's got fast reflexes. I spend a moment trying to understand why I agreed to take him to this stupid audition. Then I glance over at his adorable profile and I know exactly why I agreed; because he's a squeaky little spitfire when it comes to sex and I'm dead keen on him. But we've been crawling along the M-4, nose to tail, for nearly an hour. My back is aching, Jeff is right about the fumes, and I'm starving.

Again, I try to slap him. "Jeff, tell this flea to keep his hands off my GPS!"

Prissy jabs at the screen with his bony finger. "Benny, it doesn't work. Look. Look how it jumps all over the place when I touch it."

"It jumps all over the place *because* you're touching it! Just leave it alone before you break it!" *Slap.*

"Ow! If you ask me, that thing's on the wonk," he declares.

"Well, I'm not asking you, am I? So belt up!"

Prissy is quiet for about ten seconds while his underdeveloped brain collars a new amusement that will annoy the hell out of me. He purses his lips and starts craning his scrawny, long neck around like an ostrich. This is the calm before the storm, and I just know he's getting ready to make a fuss about something. "Would you just *look* at this shit? If we don't drive past a bloody crash with a mangled body pretty soon, I'm gonna be pissed! I mean, *come on people, hit the pedal!* LET'S GO, MOVE IT!" he cries out in frustration. "Benny, I should have made you take the damned A-4!"

"Prissy, I should have made you take the damned bus!" This is why no one wants to give him a lift. If his big gob isn't yapping about your driving, it's yapping about everyone else's driving. He messes with—and breaks—every gadget in a motor. He complains about things no one can fix like slow traffic, articulated lorries and red signals. And to top it off, the prepubescent pixie insults you as often as he can.

"Benny, stop driving like a snail with piles and get in the right lane. It's moving faster."

I grip the steering wheel tight, striving for patience so I don't reach over and throttle him. "Don't tell me what to do. You're not me mum and you're not driving."

"You big *prick!*" he cries.

"You tiny *asshole!*" I shoot back.

"God, just *shut up!*" Jeff shouts.

Brian

I flip page after page of spreadsheets and hit the comm. "How are we doing for time, Jack?"

"Not bad, sir. I allowed for the construction and I'm sure this snarl will let up soon."

"Good." I'm not looking forward to this meeting. Poring over these documents one last time, I see blatant red flags in their ledgers. They certainly tried to make it look good but when you get right down to it, the numbers don't add up. Someone cooked these books and then prayed to the Accounting Gods I wouldn't look too closely. I just can't figure out how, where, or why they did it. I rub my eyes. As usual, they're itching from lack of sleep. I look out the window as we pass numerous cars, albeit at a snail's pace. They've got a great concept but someone at the top is cocking things up with dodgy money management. Now, they've come to me for an investment. Who wants to save a sinking ship when the captain and first mate won't even lift a hand to help bail? If Simon digs up what I think he's going to dig up, the deal is off. I don't like liars and I don't—

"Hey, Simon," I say into my mobile. "Really? A civil case in the states? So, he did file. What year? Yes, yes. That's sealed it. No, I won't. Hey, thanks a million. I owe you one. You will? When? Okay, call when you get here and we'll have dinner. Oh Simon, how is Robert? Okay. I understand. If you need anything.... Yes. Give him my best. Thanks, again."

So, they were involved in a lawsuit under a different name of course, and one of the (what did they call themselves?) 'key developers' filed Chapter 7 in California after three foreclosures. Great. Those are excellent financial failures to hide from someone you'd like to take for a one-point-two million pound investment. I sit back and smile as I gaze out the window. I may be dog-tired and stuck in traffic, but I'm looking forward to being an asshole today.

Ben

Telling Prissy to shut up is like telling a nipper with diarrhea not to mess his pants when you're at the shop sales. The shit's gonna come flying out anyway, there's gonna be a great big pong, and you're gonna wish you'd just left him at home with a child minder. "You really need to be in the right lane, Benny. It's moving loads faster than this one."

I ignore him and hunker down over the steering wheel like a determined lemming slogging toward the cliff's edge.

"Seriously, Benny. Look at 'em. They're all passing us."

We all look out the windows just as a beautiful stretch Rolls Royce Phantom floats by. I've seen a few Phantoms in my life, but I've never seen a stretch one up close. The damned car seems to go on forever. Smoky metallic silver-over-charcoal-gray paint and pitch-black tinted windows reflect our gaping mouths right back at us. From the envious looks on our pale faces, you'd think the world's largest penis just drove by. I am awestruck. "Man, that is fab."

"Can you imagine owning that?" Jeff gushes, his nose practically touching the window.

Prissy is leaning so far into me to get a better view I can feel his body heat. "None of us will ever own something like that. How much do you think it costs? Two hundred and fifty?"

"More than that, honey. It's a stretch—custom built."

Prissy excitedly paws at my arm. "Get in behind it, Benny. There's enough room."

I yank my arm away. I will *not* be pawed into submission by a git. "I said I'm not changing lanes."

"I think he's right, Benny Boy. It's moving a lot faster. Besides, we'll need to be in that lane in about fifteen kilometers anyway," Jeff says.

I don't like giving in to Prissy, especially after he's been a snotty little bugger, but Jeff is right. Eventually, we will need to be in the right lane. So I pull in behind the sexy Rolls. Damn! Even the boot looks hot. Too busy staring at my modest motor's reflection in its mirror-finish dark paint, I drift a little into the next lane. The driver of a mint-condition Xantia lightly taps his hooter to remind me he doesn't want to get that chummy with my beat-up wagon, and that's understandable. Prissy had so many accidents in this old banger, just the sight of its pockmarked carcass rattling down the motorway puts the fear of

God in fellow motorists. And with the seat-adjust mechanism busted in the forward-most position, I can't slide back the driver's seat either, so I'm quite the sight, hunched over the enormous steering wheel with it grazing my goolies, my knobby knees splayed out on either side of it, and my gooney face jammed up five centimeters from the wind-screen as I barrel down on everyone's ass. No one even wants to pull in next to this fine heap of shit at the car parks, which makes loading up after shopping a breeze. I smile, wave, and mouth a thank you to the concerned Citröen driver and inadvertently give Prissy the perfect opportunity to be an ass again.

"Benny, if you're too drunk to stay in your own lane, why don't you pull over and let Jeff drive?"

"Why don't you shut up?" I sneer at him.

"Why don't you both shut up?" Jeff pipes in, knowing he's just started a car war.

Prissy unhooks his seat belt and turns sideways to glare at him. "Who the hell is talking to you? I don't even remember *inviting* you!"

Uh-oh. This is *not* good and I cannot let this situation get out of control. "Prissy, turn around and buckle up. You're hitting the gear lever." Prissy loose in a motor (any motor: fast moving, slow moving, or immobile) is a bad omen; like having a wasp zoom in through the window when my free hand is clutching a cream-topped scone and my thighs are clamped on a cup of piping-hot java nestled in my crotch. I'm a bit worried.

"*Inviting me?* You jumped-up little asshole, *we* were going some-where. Ben and I had plans. You're the invader! You're the one who got us into this mess!"

"Yeah, right! Like *I* caused the pileup on the motorway." He's twisted around even more now, putting one knee on the seat.

"Prissy, just turn around and buckle up. There's not enough room for you to be messing about. Things are picking up. Everyone is mov-ing faster now. *Sit down!*"

Smart-mouthed Jeff continues to goad from the back seat. "Look, *Dickhead!* No one wants to ride with you because you can't shut your gob for three seconds."

"I can't shut my gob because jacked-up assholes like you and *Mo-*

ron Boy here can't drive!" Prissy is now leaning further into the back, propping himself up with both knees on the front seat. I try grabbing at his bony ass with my free hand because his unrestrained limbs and Jeff's sassy mouth are quickly turning me into a road hazard as I careen down the motorway.

"Oh yeah, Priss-Pussy?" Jeff teases.

"Don't you *even...*" Prissy threatens.

The flow of traffic has really picked up and I have a decent speed going. At this point, things happen pretty fast, almost simultaneously. They happen so fast, in fact, I really can't do anything to stop the inevitable outcome. Jeff dives into the corner behind my seat because Prissy has launched himself through the gap between the front seats with his butt sticking up in the air as he tries to hit him. Meanwhile, I'm shouting at the top of my lungs, calling them assholes and immature pricks and goddamned fairies (and whatever else I can think of) and the hulking Rolls has crammed on the brakes for stopped traffic ahead... at the precise moment Prissy braces his leg on my knee to take another lunge at Jeff. Unfortunately, my knee, by way of my calf and my ankle, is attached to my foot, and my foot is still hovering over the accelerator, not the brake. At least, it *was* hovering.

Brian

The impact is short and sweet. A few papers fall to the floor from the insignificant jolt, but for the most part, it isn't bad—a mere kiss on the steel-reinforced ass of my luxurious, two-point-seven-ton cocoon.

Jack's voice immediately comes over the comm. "Are you all right, sir?"

"I'm fine. You'd better pull over and see if the idiot behind us is okay."

"Yes, sir. I'll assess the damage, get his information, and we'll be on our way."

"Thank you, Jack." I lean forward and pick up the papers. I pull out my mobile and call the office to tell my secretary I may be late. With that call made, I'm trying to remember my insurance agent's name as I scroll through my business contacts. It's been a long time since I've talked to him and it's something that starts with a 'J.' Jacques. James. Johan. Jonas. Jonathan. Jonathan? I stop scrolling as my mind wanders to thoughts of John. I'm really surprised I enjoyed his visit. He was pleasant company once his nerves settled down. He stayed for almost three hours, but it seemed more like twenty minutes.

Ben

The impact is bone jarring. The exploding airbag slams my glasses up into my forehead. A bit dazed, it takes a minute before I let go of the steering wheel, reach up, pull the embedded metal rims out of my unbroken flesh, and put them back on the bridge of my nose. They're covered in powder and the frames are bent, but not broken. A pile of safety glass glistens in my crotch like uncut diamonds, and my legs are throbbing. I hear a hissing sound, a few 'pops,' and smell petrol and burnt rubber. I'm harboring a significant fear the gearbox may catch fire and go off like a bomb, but I'm still too stunned to move more than my hands and my eyeballs. The Citröen driver, whose lane I invaded a few miles back, creeps by and gives me a big smile and a thumbs up through the open window.

"Bang on, lad! Always best to smash a Rolls!" he shouts, his enthusiasm obvious.

Oh God, what have I done? I've just plowed into the Rolls Royce? Before I speak (for vanity's sake), I gingerly run my tongue over my teeth to make sure none are missing. "Is everyone okay?"

Prissy, who was half over the back of the passenger seat, trying to attack Jeff just before the impact, is now crumpled backward in the passenger seat. His tiny butt is stuck down into the floorboards where his feet should be, and his skinny legs are poking up in the air like little matchsticks. His pink, high-top trainers give a tentative wiggle near my face as a reassuring sign of life. "I've been better," he moans.

I sigh with relief. I'm guessing Jeff fared the best, securely buckled in the back seat.

"Shit," he whispers.

Concerned, I twist my stiff neck and look back at him to see where he's hurt. His ashen face is staring past me, out the gaping hole that used to be my windscreen, and over the crushed bonnet. He lifts his hand and points. I turn forward and squint through the smoke pluming up from the engine. A man is approaching from the Rolls, which has pulled off the motorway. He's in a dark suit, wearing sunglasses, and walking slowly. He must be the chauffeur, and he looks very big, very scary, and very pissed. "Bloody shitty hell."

Prissy, through grunts and groans, has somehow righted himself. He sees the chauffeur approaching, gives a low whistle and, priorities in order, folds down the visor mirror and starts primping like a whore on the pull. I yank the handle and my crumpled door falls from the chassis into the next lane of traffic. Even though other drivers have slowed down, I still hear someone honk and swerve to avoid hitting it. I climb out from behind the flaccid airbag and nearly land on my face. My legs are like udon noodles and won't support one ounce of my weight. Big Strapping Chauffeur Man catches me up under my pits before I hit the tarmac.

"Are you okay?" From his tone, he doesn't sound that scary or pissed. He sounds concerned—and he's quite dishy, too.

"I think so," I manage to spit out as I drape between his strong arms like a scrap of cloth.

He practically carries me to the side of the motorway and sits me down in the grass. Then he helps Jeff out of the back seat, walks him over, and sits him down beside me. Prissy hauls himself out of the passenger seat with all the grace of a drunken old slag falling off a bar stool at last call, picks his butt, grabs the chauffeur's bicep, and smiles up at him like a schoolgirl in love. Big Strapping Chauffeur Man gives his pink bow a puzzled look. He is not amused.

"Prissy! Let go of him and get my wallet and papers from the glove box."

He pinches up his impish face and throws me an evil glare, but just like with sex, he turns his tiny arse around and does what he's told.

Brian

As unfeeling as it seems, I haven't even turned around to see who hit me or what damage they've suffered. I'm extremely anti-social, especially when it comes to some bloody fool who's just slammed into the backside of my Rolls *and* messed up my afternoon appointments. I rely on Jack to tell me if there are injuries. He returns to the car and I lower the window. I adjust my watch to indicate absolute boredom and growing impatience with the whole ordeal. "How does it look?"

"She's okay, just a superficial scratch on her bumper. I'll have it buffed out while you're in the meeting."

"Good. And the other?"

Jack looks back, surveying the damage. "Well... it looks pretty much like it hit a brick wall. The engine is toast—nothing left, at all. The three lads are all right. A bit shaken, but no broken bones and no blood. They're going to call for a breakdown van and a lift. Here's the driver's information." He hands me a folded piece of paper and looks down at his watch. "I think we can just make the meeting, sir."

"All right, let's go." I hit Jonathan's number and unfold the paper as Jack climbs behind the wheel and starts the engine.

"Hello?" Jonathan says in my ear. "Hello, Brian? Brian...? Is that you?"

I can't speak for nearly half a minute as the car starts rolling forward on the verge. "Hey, Jonathan. Yeah, it's Brian. Um, let me call you back, okay?" I quickly flip on the comm. "Jack, what's with the two names on this paper?"

"Oh, yes, sir. I should have explained. The first one, Benjamin Taylor, is the driver. He says he just bought the car, but he doesn't know if the title has transferred yet, so he gave me the second one's name. That's the funny one below his."

I smile and, for once, don't give a damn that I'll be late for my meeting. "Presley-Louise Mortensen."

"Yes, sir."

Prissy

Benny is standing on the side of the motorway, mobile clamped to his ear, staring at what used to be my Volvo still blocking traffic. Well, technically it's his Volvo now, since he bought it from me three days ago. At this point, with it not going anywhere, I guess it doesn't matter if the wonky GPS system works. He's trying to get a tow and a lift. Jeff has his hand cupped over his mouth and nose, trying not to breathe in all the fumes. I'm trying to fix my bow and discreetly pick my knickers out of my butt crack.

"What do you mean, an hour?" Benny yells into the mobile. "I know we don't have injuries, but the wreck is sitting in the middle of the damned motorway!" He throws his hand up in the air — pure theatrical drama wasted on uncultured commuters. "Oh, this is unbelievable!"

As Jeff and I stand near him, we watch the Rolls drive off with that beefy, sexy chauffeur. I wonder what his name is. I bet it's something wicked-stud like Brock or Butch. Maybe it's Rufus. I'm sure Rufus is checking me out in his mirror right now. I turn sideways and throw out my hip to give him a better angle of my hot, sensuous body. He probably thinks I'm the cutest. I bet he'd like to —

Jeff suddenly lowers his hand from his face, and I suck my hip back in and stand up straight as we both stare at the big Rolls, which has applied the brakes and is now slowly reversing back in our direction along the verge. "Uh-oh."

"Hey, Benny?" I'm a little concerned as I reach out to tug his shirt.

With his back turned, he's busy yelling at the tow yard operator in his highly effective Snotty Bitch Queen voice. He distractedly slaps my hand away.

Jeff tries giving him a nudge as the backside of the Rolls keeps coming toward us. "Benny Boy, pay attention. Um, something's up and you really need to turn around — *now*."

Benny is on a roll. "Look, I don't care who else is broken down on the road. I don't care if it's the damned Queen *or* hung-like-a-horse Prince Charles!" He continues yelling into his mobile as he turns. "I've just had a *serious* crash and that should put me at the — "

Beefy Sexy Chauffeur steps out of the idling Rolls. He adjusts his jacket and approaches us. He smiles, ever so slightly. I wish he'd take off those sunglasses because I'd love to see the color of his eyes. "Mister Mallory would like to offer you a lift." His words are casual, matter-of-fact.

Benny is amazed. "Mister Mallory? *Brian Mallory?* That's *his* car...

and he's *in* it?"

"Yes, and yes."

"A lift? Really?" Jeff gushes, stepping forward.

Beefy Sexy Chauffeur slowly tilts his head, pulls down his sunglasses, and peers over the top rim. He's got some beautiful baby blues! "A lift. Really."

Brian

I look down at the piece of paper in my hand. Now I look up at the young blokes sitting across from me, lined up like three daft rock pigeons on a window ledge, wide-eyed and weak-bladdered, ready to piss out their innards and fly straight into the tempered glass at the slightest provocation. The skinny one in the middle, with bent glasses and red hair, is practically covered in fine white powder. He must be Ben. The tiny, yellow-haired one with the pink bow (a pink bow?), fidgeting and grinning at me like a depraved nymphomaniac with a vibrator shoved up his bum, has to be Prissy. I look at the third one. "Are you Martin or Jeff?"

Puzzled out of his skull, the words dribble out with difficulty. "Um... I'm...I'm Jeff, sir."

I recognize that voice from numerous irritating adverts touting the undeniable virtues of Weetabix, custard powder, and Thornton's Depilatory Cream: ("The silky miracle that helps you unhair... down there.") "Yes, so you are. I'm Brian."

"Mister Brian, sir. How...how do you...?"

"I'm a friend of John's. He's mentioned you—all of you." I look back at Prissy. "I recognized your name in particular."

He giggles, glances at my crotch, and bats his eyelashes at me. Jesus, he's on the pull!

Ben jabs him with his elbow and hisses, "Prissy! Cut the gay display."

Prissy stops flirting and sits up straight.

"Where were you going?"

"I have an audition, sir," Prissy proudly says.

"For Shakespeare?"

"Uh… yeah."

I look at Ben and Jeff. "And these two?"

"Well, I lost my license so I needed a lift. That's why Benny is here." Prissy lovingly smiles up at Ben and then rolls his eyes toward Jeff. "I have no idea why *he* had to come."

Jeff leans across Ben. "Ben and I were on a date, you little fairy-git. We were on our way to have lunch when you insisted he take you to this *stupid* audition."

Prissy now looks at Ben, confused and hurt. "A date?"

"Not exactly a date. It was more like an… outing." Ben's quiet voice trails off as he stares at the floorboards.

Jeff is outraged. *"An outing?* You make me sound like some old, incontinent granny you picked up at the old folks home for a day trip to Tesco!"

"Well, sometimes you do smell like pee," Prissy chides as he leans across Ben from the other side.

"*I* smell like pee? Who's the one who shat himself at Tony's party when—"

"Would you two just *shut up?*" Ben says through clenched teeth and with closed eyes.

There's a brief silence amongst the three as we cruise down the motorway. Their pungent colognes are battling each other, trying hard to win the 'Most Terribly Offensive' award, but their scents aren't bad. Ben opens his eyes and gives me a weak, apologetic smile.

Prissy holds his tiny pompous chin high. "What happened at Tony's party wasn't my fault."

Jeff leans across Ben. "Oh, really? So someone forced you to take four shots of jalapeño tequila and then drink two glasses of prune juice, did they?"

"Hey, Mister Mono-Nut! At least *I* didn't prance around in a G-string and then show everyone my nipple rings like I was—"

"PLEASE, *shut up!*" Ben pleads, embarrassed by the heated exchange of his love rivals. Again, he gives me a helpless smile that says, "I'm so sorry about these idiots."

I get a few more minutes of silence, but something about the pinched, pouty look on Prissy's face tells me this isn't over yet, and I'm finding it very entertaining. I'm glad I left the comm open so Jack can enjoy it, too.

Prissy folds his pencil-thin arms defiantly across his skinny, puffed-out chest. "Are you sleeping with him, Benny?"

"Look, I don't think this is the right place to be—"

"What's it to *you?*" Jeff challenges, leaning in.

"What's it to me?" Prissy's tiny voice is screeching now as he tries to stand up in the car. *"I'll tell you what's it to me! If you think—"*

"Oh, I think, honey! You wanna know what I think? I think—"

"FOR THE LOVE OF GOD! WILL YOU TWO FLAMING ASS-HOLES JUST SHUT UP?" Ben screams.

Prissy slams his butt back into the seat. He and Jeff both turn away from Ben in a huff and look out opposite windows, the lover's spat defused for now. I've got my arms crossed, and I'm smiling. I find this drama amazing. For a moment, I think they forgot I was even here. I like these blokes. From what I've heard, I like their personalities. They're a bit explosive, for sure, but interesting. I look out the window and see we're almost at my office building. "I have a meeting. At this point, I'm a bit late. After Jack drops me off, he'll take you to the audition and arrange a hired car. Jack?"

"Yes, sir?"

"His name is Jack!" Prissy whispers to no one in particular.

"What about their motor?"

"Taken care of, sir. It's being towed to Finnigan's."

"Good." I look at the lads with mild apprehension. "Um, Jack?"

"Yes, sir?"

"Please make sure that hired car is a bloody tank."

He gives a small laugh. "Yes, sir. I most definitely will. Office in one minute."

"Thank you."

Ben tentatively asks, "Mister Mallory—um, Brian, sir. You said you're a friend of Johnny's?"

"Yes. He stopped by my flat a few nights ago and we had a nice, long chat." I watch as their mouths fall open. "Didn't he tell you?"

John

"Where the *hell* have you been?" I'm staring at Jeff through the darkness and trying to whisper, but I'm so outraged I want to yell my ass off.

"Hey, Johnny. We had a—"

"Where's Prissy?" I demand as Jeff and Ben, both with their butts in my face, slide past me and fall into the two seats beside me.

"He's up on stage. Relax. We've had—"

"*Relax?* I've been waiting here for over an hour and I've been calling. Jeff, why haven't you answered your phone?"

He pats his pockets. "Uh, I don't think I...I must have left it in the car. Anyway, that's what—"

"And Ben, yours went to voicemail three times. How could you do this? How could you push it to the last minute? You know how impatient this director is. He's already seen some pretty good guys."

"Yeah, but—"

"Don't 'but' me. I personally asked Thaddeus to give Prissy extra time. He should have read an hour ago."

"Well, all's not lost, right? I mean, he's here, he's on stage, and he'll still get a crack. Look, I gotta tell you—"

I turn my attention to the stage. "Shh, I want to hear this guy."

Jeff whispers, "But Johnny, we—"

"Shut up a minute."

Ben tries from the other side of Jeff. "But we were—"

"Shh!" This guy is pretty good. His voice carries well. It sounds as if he's a singer. I look over at Thaddeus. He's impressed. I look back at the guy on stage. He's getting through the lines without a problem, but he can't take his eyes off the script for more than five seconds. That's good for Prissy. I look at Thaddeus again. He's standing up and he's walking. That's not good for Prissy. That means Thaddeus likes what he hears and now he wants to see how the guy looks from different angles. Will the audience think he's attractive? He's a bit bowlegged and stoop-shouldered, but he's got a great ass. You need that for Shakespeare. Every guy wears tights and every woman has her chest shoved up to her chin. Anyone bored with the play will still be interested if you've at least got a bunch of great asses and big boobs.

"Johnny, I really need—"

"Jeff, shut up. Whatever it is, I don't want to hear it until after—"

Thaddeus' voice booms across the empty theater. "Okay, next!"

I watch as tiny Prissy stumbles out onto center stage, wobbly-legged and pigeon-toed in his pink sneakers. At first he looks a little goofy, bumbling around as if he has no idea where he is or why he's there. Fellow actors snicker when he trips over his feet. Then, through the darkness, he spies us up in the seats, blows us a kiss, and waves.

"Name?"

"Presley-Louise Mortensen."

Thaddeus' boredom with these grueling auditions can't be masked as he stares at Prissy's unruly hair and that horrible bow. "Okay. I've been told you need a few minutes to... get into character. Is that right?"

"Yes, sir."

Prissy, I silently pray, please don't pick at your panties. Thaddeus drops into a seat next to his assistant, Hilda, while Prissy walks in a small circle, head down, one hand on his hip, and one hand holding the script at his side. He's got his toes pointing out like a little ballerina. God, give me strength! After three minutes, I start to worry. Thaddeus, visibly impatient and glancing at his watch, is concerned too. "He's taking too long," I whisper, staring at him on the stage.

"He'll be fine," Jeff whispers back, also staring at him on the stage.

Ben has absolute faith in his little fairy. "Don't worry, Johnny. He knows what he's doing."

Prissy stops walking, faces forward, and drops the script on the stage floor. *"No more light answers. Let our officers have notice what we purpose. I shall break the cause of our expedience to the Queen, and get her to leave to part."*

Thaddeus is alert. He's sitting upright in his seat.

"For not alone the death of Fulvia, with more urgent touches, do strongly speak to us; but the letters too of many our contriving friend in Rome petition us as home."

Now Thaddeus is standing with his hand on his chin, head down, eyes closed. He's listening hard to Prissy's voice, which is normally high pitched and squeaky. But when he's in character, it's different. It's deep and mesmerizing.

"Sextus Pompeius hath given the dare to Caesar, and commands the empire of the sea."

Now he's walking. He's looking at him from all angles. I'll admit, Prissy is tiny. If Thaddeus goes for him, he'll have to surround him with other miniscule actors and props, but he's got a good physique for his size and an angelic face. The audience would approve of him. Prissy's eyes are glassy and veiled as he recites. When he's in character, he doesn't notice anything around him so he doesn't turn toward Thaddeus — which is good. He's not supposed to play to the director as the director walks around. He's supposed to play to the audience, even if there isn't one.

"Our slippery people, whose love is never link'd to the deserver till his deserts are past, begin to throw Pompey the Great and all his dignities upon his son, who, high in name and power, higher than both in blood and life, stands up for the main soldier; whose quality, going on, the sides o' th' world may danger."

Thaddeus looks up at Prissy with admiration. "That's bang on. Give your number to Hilda." Then he shouts, "Okay, that's it! I've seen enough! Those who came late... I'm sorry. Maybe next time! Check the website." He yanks up his trousers and struts out of the theater as Hilda runs up to Prissy to write down his number and a dozen actors who didn't get a chance to read shuffle off behind the curtain to gather their backpacks and cell phones. I know what that's like — I've been there, myself. The theater lights come up and I sit back with a smug smile, confident Prissy has the part. He'll probably get the call tonight.

Jeff faces me. "Johnny, can we talk now?"

I turn to look at him just as Ben leans out of his seat to look around his shoulder. I'm stunned. He's covered in a light dusting of white powder and his glasses are perched lopsided on his nose. It looks like someone tried to blow him clean with a wimpy hairdryer after a bag of flour exploded in his face. Fine particles are stuck to his oily skin and embedded in the weave of his shirt. "What the hell happened to you?"

"We had an accident, Johnny! That's what we've been trying to tell you. It's from the air bag!"

"Wha—"

"We ran into someone," Jeff adds, who then turns to Ben and they giggle like adolescent schoolboys hearing a dirty joke about weenies and pee-pees.

"An accident? When?"

"Just now, right before we got here," Jeff says.

"That's why we were late," Ben explains.

"What the—" I'm now beyond stunned. I'm shocked. "Are you guys all right? *My God!* I had no idea! Did you go to the hospital? Are you okay?"

Jeff rolls his eyes and waves his hand. "Oh, we're fine, honey. We're just fine, but listen up. This is *so* wicked. Guess who—"

"Did ya' tell him? Did ya' tell him?" Prissy is breathless and flushed as he scurries from the stage up to our seats.

"That you guys had an accident? Yeah, they told me."

Ben leans out farther past Jeff. "No, that's not it, Johnny. That's not the fab part!"

"Tell him, Benny! Go on! Tell Johnny who we hit!" Prissy squeals, bouncing up and down with so much excitement he's practically jumping into my lap.

"Brian!" Ben proudly proclaims. "We hit Brian Mallory!"

At first, I feel like laughing. I mean, it has to be a joke, right? These dingbats can't be serious. Then, (when I realize it's *not* a joke) I feel like puking. I swallow hard as I look from one grinning face to the other. Please, God. Please tell me they did *not* just do this to me. "You... hit Brian's car?"

"Yup. Boom! Slammed right into his boot. The front of my car, all gone. His car, not a scratch." Ben is really happy with that outcome. He's quite proud.

"You... hit Brian's limousine." I feel numb and I truly am going to throw up.

"Oh no, it wasn't a limousine. It was a Rolls Royce."

"Yeah, Johnny—a stretch Phantom. Two-tone paint, metallic, glossy... just beautiful," Prissy coos. "Oh, and you should see his chauffeur. Phwoar!" He grabs his tiny crotch and I quickly look away. The sight of Prissy groping his insignificant package is only attractive to Ben.

"Wait a minute." I close my eyes, trying to recall my tipsy (okay, stinking drunk) ride to the party. It's vaguely memorable. I open my eyes again. "Brian has a stretch limousine, not a stretch Rolls. It must have been someone else."

Ben and Jeff stare at me as if a horn just sprouted from my forehead.

"Honey, it *was* his Rolls. He may have a limousine, but he also has a Rolls. A big one. A stretch one. We saw it. We hit it. And then... (Jeff beams) we *rode* in it."

"You... met... Brian?"

"Oh, yeah! God, he's good looking, isn't he?" Prissy chimes in, leaning hard on my shoulder with his pointy elbow. "Those eyes are to die for, and those long-ass legs..." He ponders a moment. "I wonder if he's got a great big—"

I frantically clutch Jeff's arm. "Oh God, tell me you didn't embarrass me! Please, tell me you didn't embarrass me! Did you say you knew me?"

"Hey! I take offense to that. How would we embarrass you?" demands Flour-Face Ben.

"Never mind him, Benny Boy. He's just stunned and a bit surprised," Jeff consoles as he gives me a slitty-eyed look and yanks his arm from my grasp. "No, Johnny. We didn't embarrass you, and we didn't tell him we knew you."

"Thank God for that." I slump back, relieved, into my seat.

"He already knew who we were."

I sit bolt upright again. *"What?"*

"It seems someone told *him* a bit about *us*," Prissy breathes into my ear.

Jeff is dejected. "He didn't know who I was, though. He asked if I was Martin. Why would he ask that? Who the hell would confuse me with Martin?"

"I don't know. I really don't—" I catch my breath. "Oh. I don't think I told him Martin was Jamaican."

Jeff folds his arms across his chest and glares at me. "Well then, that leads us to another question. Just when *did* you tell him about us?"

All three are staring at me, waiting for an answer. I can't lie and say it was at the Willowby event. They probably know the truth from Brian. I finally have to confess to my visit. I take a deep breath. "Last Friday. I went to see him last Friday at his penthouse."

"Okay, wa'ppun?" No one noticed Martin pop up behind us.

Jeff's eyes light up. "Oh, honey! Have we got a story to tell you!"

■ ■ ■

The drive to the restaurant induces a headache as Ben, Jeff, and Prissy spend the entire ride filling in Martin on all aspects of the accident. Each idiot has to give his opinion of how studly Jack was and how handsome and cool Brian was. Every minute detail is repeated over and over. I want to hear some of it, but not all of it and not half a dozen times. Ben is flying down the congested streets in this battleship-sized BMW sedan rental, compliments of Brian. I'm shittin' kittens in the passenger seat—way beyond paranoid—yelling at him to keep his eyes on the road so he doesn't crash this eighty thousand dollar car and trying to figure out if their bonehead encounter ruined my chances of ever seeing Brian again.

■ ■ ■

"What do you mean, 'Why didn't I tell you?' *This* is why I didn't tell you. Because I knew all you'd do is badger me with questions." I slouch in the booth and pick at my wilted lettuce. I am really tired of salads and today I ordered one without chicken or my beloved, salty bacon bits.

"Well, of course we're going to badger you," Prissy says and then leans over and slurps his soda. As usual, with any straw-appointed beverage, he's refusing to pick up the glass so he's got to sit on his knees in the booth just to reach the straw. It's like eating out with a five-year-old.

Jeff lowers his voice to avoid being overheard. "Damn, Johnny. You spend the night at a multi-millionaire's penthouse, and you don't think we're going to ask you about it?"

I sigh and shake my head. "I didn't spend the night. It was only a couple of hours. We talked. It wasn't a big deal."

Prissy wipes his mouth on his sleeve. "What's it like?"

"What's what like?"

"The penthouse. What do you think?"

Martin grates pungent parmesan cheese on his vermicelli with gusto. "I bet he's got a billiard table up there, doesn't he? He sounds like the kind of guy who'd have a billiard table."

Prissy's eyes light up. "Hey, does he have a swimming pool and a hot tub? Could we come over and go skinny dipping?" He loves the thought of potential nakedness and he'll take any chance he can get. Ben gives him a nudge to remind him to keep eating since he's always the last one to finish — again, just like a five-year-old.

I set down my fork and rub my forehead, trying to gather my thoughts. "Look, it was great, okay? The penthouse is fantastic. No billiard table, no swimming pool, and no hot tub. But it's an impressive home with an awesome view. You can see Tower Bridge from the balcony. The whole time I was there, it was.... I don't know, like a dream. All these things you hear about him, not liking people, being anti-social and difficult, no sense of humor; they're all lies. It's not him at all. He's funny. He's kind. He's quiet and patient and his eyes are *so* beautiful and intense. He's got this soft, deep voice. It kind of rumbles up from his chest. And when he smiles or laughs it just makes me so relaxed, so at ease. He listens to every word I say and — " I stop talking when I see four gaping mouths below four pairs of staring eyes. "What?"

Prissy is disappointed — and concerned. "I asked you about the penthouse. Don't you realize you just took off talking about him?"

Jeff leans across the table. "Shit, Johnny, you're not falling arse over tit for this guy, are you?"

"What? Of course not. I just think he's really nice."

Ben, with sharp knife poised above succulent steak, is studying me hard. "He's super good looking. I'll give you that. I'd climb up for a hide ride on that big Scotsman and shag his bones from here to New Zealand in a tick, but he's not gay, Johnny. You *know* he's not gay. He doesn't give off the slightest gay vibe — nothing. It's just not in him. Kinsey would slap a big, fat 'one' on his forehead."

"I told you, I just think he's nice." I'm trying to sound convincing as I stare down Ben's infamous skeptical gaze.

Martin shakes his head as he twirls pasta onto his fork. "You think he's more than nice. Sorry man, but I know you. It's in your voice. It's in your eyes." He pokes his loaded fork at me in accusation. "You're drooling this guy all down your chin. Your pupils are dilated, and you've got him rolling around in your head. You'd better not let anyone hear you talking about him like this outside of us."

"I'm not drooling him and...and he's not rolling around in my head. Can't I say that someone, who the general public thinks is really mean, is actually pretty nice?"

Jeff reaches for the pepper. "Yeah, you can say it, honey, but don't expect us to believe you."

"Remember what happened to Frankie with Long Dong?" Ben says. "That was right tragic."

I lean over the table and try to speak quietly but emphatically. "Oh, give me a break! This is *nothing* like what happened to Frankie." Franklin McNutt was a runway model who worked the circuit with Ben. He even spent time with us a few years back until he developed a heavy crush on another model named Donald Shore. Everyone knew Donald was straight, and because models often have to do quick changes out in the open, everyone also knew Donald was hung; hence the nickname, "Long Dong Don" which was shortened to "Long Dong" for convenience.

"Frankie was jonesing for that guy from day one," Martin says.

"And he was still jonesing for him at his stag party," Jeff adds.

"*And* as best man at his wedding," Ben says. He waits until a busboy refills our water glasses and then says, "And now what does he do? He minds their bloody nippers so Long Dong and his bird can have date nights and keep the romance alive."

Martin tries to get his point across in a semi-quiet voice. "He spends Saturday night changin' nappies, man! He's got nothin' but a life of shitty nappies, Johnny."

I feign calmness. "I'm nothing like Frankie and Brian is nothing like Long Dong."

Prissy giggles and gives a tiny body shiver. "Oh, I bet he's a *lot* like Long Dong!"

"Shut up!" I snap.

"So what're you gonna do?" Jeff asks.

"About what?"

They all look at each other.

Ben decides to speak up for everyone. "Haven't you been listening to us? You can't see him again and think he's gonna fall for you. It's not gonna happen. Read the psychobabble books. Crushes on straight guys are bad news. Real straight guys—and believe me, he's *real*—don't turn gay."

I muster up some fake confidence and real irritation. "Look, I'm his friend, okay? That's *all* I am. That's all I want to be. I know he's straight and I'm fine with that because I'm *not* interested in him. If you guys don't want to believe me, then fine." I pause for effect and then throw in a little catty attitude: "And girls, if I want to see him again—just as a friend—I will."

John – February 9

David is slouched in the club chair peering at Mickey through glassy eyes because he's already half blitzed off his ass, and it's not even noon. "What d'ya mean, it's a gold'n opportunity? Why would going to Hawaii and (semi-stifled belch, smack of lips) Milan be a gold'n opportunity?"

"David, Lars requested you specifically. He saw you in that French swimsuit portfolio and insisted I ask you to be one of the models." Mickey is doing his best trying not to push the patronizing button that sends him into a rage.

"But I'd have t' leave Johnny alone, and he doesn't want that, do ya', Sweetie?"

"I don't mind. I'll be okay for a few weeks." I keep my words unemotional as I hand a cup of coffee to Mickey.

"I'll keep an eye on him and make sure he doesn't get into any trouble."

David slits his eyes and glares at me. "Yeah... I don't know. He spends too much time with those idiots as it is."

I sit down on the sofa next to Mickey. "They're not idiots, David. They're my close friends."

"Hmm. Yeah, right." He turns his glazed eyes back to Mickey. "How much?"

"Twenty-five hundred for four weeks."

"Pfft! You're kidding. That's *nothing!* They paid me twice that t' do th' French shoot, an' I got a bonus at th' end."

"Well, David. Come on. That was three years ago and —"

"And let's rub it in, right? Let's rub it in that I haven't worked since then!" His voice is getting louder. He's going to explode if Mickey doesn't calm him down fast.

"Nonsense! You've worked. It's just a soft market right now, what with the economy and all." Mickey takes a sip of coffee. "No one is paying a lot, are they Johnny?"

I shake my head, not so much in agreement with him, but more to indicate it was the wrong thing to say and only succeeded in stirring up David's glowing embers.

"Oh, yes! Let's ask Johnny what someone should be paid for workin'! Let's ask th' *expert* who's never been unemployed a single day in his WHOLE FUCKIN' LIFE!" David raises his full glass of whiskey in a mock salute to me and then guzzles it down.

Mickey tries to get him back on track before he passes out. "Look, you get to travel, stay in great hotels, and work with some top people. You'll even get new portfolio shots and those could land you a hundred more jobs. You're the right one, David. You're the *only* one. You've got the look they want. No one else has it. What do you say?"

His bloodshot eyes are trained on Mickey as he lets out a long belch. His head is starting to loll, but he clearly gobbled up that undeserved praise like a starving dog devouring a wiener. I have to look away because the staged scene is so disgustingly pathetic. "Fine, I'll go. But I'd better get some perks while I'm there. If this guy wants me that badly he's gonna have t' come up with some really big perks."

9
The Impact Of Tarpaper On A Glass Dome

John — February 12

The sun is out, no rain clouds in sight, and I'm in a fabulous mood. My theme song for the day is *Oh, What A Beautiful Morning*, and I've been humming it and singing it since seven. David needs his passport to travel. He lost it to the authorities two years ago when he was found to be 'highly intoxicated and unruly toward professional flight staff' on a short hop from Lisbon to Madrid. The flight started out smoothly, but within ten minutes of reaching cruising altitude, David grabbed the crotch of one flight attendant and offered to blow a second one (demonstrating his willingness by pulling down the poor guy's pants as he was retrieving a pillow from the overhead compartment). Barajas Airport police cited him, fined him, locked him up in a drunk tank for eight hours, and confiscated his passport and two flasks of whiskey they'd found in his luggage. He was more upset about losing the whiskey than the passport. Now, to get the passport back, he has to sit through an eight-hour anger management course... and he has to do it today. It really is a beautiful morning and I'm positive it will turn into a beautiful day!

I've just pulled up outside Brian's building. Earlier this week, I thought Ben, Prissy, and Jeff's encounter with him was the worst thing that could have happened to me. But I soon realized it would give me the perfect opportunity to see him again. I could stop by to apologize for their ineptness and thank him for providing Ben's luxury rental. So, here I am, and just like Gordon MacRae, I do have the feeling that everything is going my way!

I spend a little time giving myself the once-over while I'm still in the car. I look damn fine but one last pre-flight check can't hurt. To the general population, the unzipped fly of a straight man is an unfortunate oversight. The unzipped fly of a gay man is the vulgar proposition of a horny bugger looking for a quickie, and I may be a horny bugger, but I am *not* looking for a quickie. I inspect my fingernails. They're trimmed and clean. I remembered deodorant, so I'm safe there. I run my hands over my face, knowing the extra time I took while shaving and moisturizing this morning paid off. My skin is as smooth as that fake stuff they sell as kidskin leather, and I know it's not kidskin leather so it freaks me out every time I touch it. But I can't stop touching it because it's so freaky, almost real. That's what my skin feels like: something freaky, almost real. I adjust the rear view mirror to check my teeth, and then I check my hair. I have a signature spike, but I went with a little less mousse to get a softer look. Who knows? He may want to run his fingers through it… for some reason.

I sit quietly, not humming or singing, with my eyes closed and my head down. I have butterflies in my stomach. I felt the same way just before my first date. I barely remember his name — Matt, I think — but I remember the date. He took me to a small Italian restaurant near Brighton Park. Our food was cold, service was slow, and I nearly choked to death on a garlic clove. After the exuberant waiter took a turn at slapping the hell out of my back, Matt applied the Heimlich maneuver, which worked — in a way. I did spit out the clove (shot it clear across the restaurant and into the homemade pizza dough), but a week later an x-ray revealed he also broke the costal cartilage of my ninth rib, and I had to wear an Ace bandage for six months. When we left the restaurant, he held my hand as we walked to his car and someone yelled out "faggots." He never returned my calls after that. Three months later, I heard he'd married a realtor's assistant and moved out of state. I cried for days. It's not one of my fonder memories, not a great time in my life. I still hear the names now and then and they're hard to ignore. But this is who I am, and I won't take the drastic steps Matt took just to avoid offensive names shouted at me by nasty, intolerant people. I refuse to live a lie or hide. So here I am again, me and my butterflies—sitting right outside Brian's building. I'm a minute or two away from seeing him. I keep reminding myself this isn't a date. This is just me stopping by to visit a new friend—a fascinating, tall, and handsome new friend.

I step out of the car and pop some coins into the meter. I have no idea how long I'll stay, so I put in the max—three hours. I cross the street and take a deep breath, trying to calm my jittery nerves before I step onto the stage—I mean, into the lobby. There's Brenda at the concierge counter with a friendly smile. I don't know if I should use her first name yet; it's only our second encounter. With the confidence that everything is going my way on this wonderful morning, and in my cheeriest, I-swear-I'm-not-desperate voice I say, "Hello there. Is Brian in?"

"Good morning, Mister Kaiser. I'm sorry, but you've just missed him by a few ticks. He's gone for the day. I'm afraid he won't be back for several hours."

"Oh. Okay." I'm trying not to look devastated as my face falls. I'm trying to look cool and in control, as if it's no big deal I spent two hours preening for this visit. Of course, he'd be out on a beautiful day like this. What made me think he'd be sitting in his penthouse doing nothing? I feel like a fool, getting myself all worked up over a guy who's out living his life, not sitting around waiting for a visit from me. He's probably forgotten all about me. I'm such an ass! Realizing I've been staring at Brenda just a little too long to seem normal and worried she's about to push a panic button secreted under the counter, I work up a small smile and take a step back. "Thank you. I'll try him another time."

Her phone rings. She picks up the receiver and puts her hand over the mouthpiece. "Do you want to leave a message, Mister Kaiser?"

"No, no. It's not important. Thank you. Goodbye." I turn to leave as she takes the call, but I stop when I hear her speak.

"Good Morning. How may I— Oh, Mister Mallory. I was just mentioning to Mister—Yes? He's coming today? Yes, of course I will. I'll let him in and make sure he knows. Yes, a stud. I'll be sure to tell him to screw into... a stud," Brenda says, a little perplexed as she scribbles the words on a notepad. "Excuse me? Oh, yes. I was mentioning to Mister Kaiser that he's just missed you. Pardon? Yes, he's still here. He's standing right in front of me." Small pause. "Okay, I'll ask him." She covers the mouthpiece and asks, "Do you have six hours?"

"Excuse me, do I what?"

"Brian wants to know if you have about six hours to spare."

"Yes. Sure." Well, *hell* yes! I've got six hours to spare.

She pulls her hand away from the mouthpiece. "Yes, Mister Mallory. He has six hours. Okay. Okay, I'll tell him. Yes. You, too. Good-bye." Her eyes are twinkling as she hangs up the receiver. "You're to wait just outside the lobby doors." She gives me a radiant smile. "He's coming back for you."

Coming back for me? Brian has already left but he's turning around and he's coming back... for *me*? This is great! This is fantastic! I get to go with Brian! I don't know where 'go' is, but who cares? He's coming back... just for me. In a stage production, this is where I would leap over the counter and give Brenda a big smooch. Then I'd leap back over and break out in euphoric song and dance among the lobby couches and chairs, wildly rejoicing in the simple act of a U-turn on a roundabout. Yes! On this beautiful day, everything *is* going my way! I really do feel like kissing Brenda, and her panic button, and her wonderful phone, and even that silly scribbled note that reminds someone to screw a stud! In reality, I gently thank her and practically skip outside to stand at the curb. I pace the sidewalk as I chew my thumbnail and gaze down the busy one-way street. I don't see his limousine. Then I remember he has a Rolls Royce, too. Well, I don't know exactly what it looks like (two-tone paint?), but I don't see anything resembling a Rolls, either. I quietly hum *I Could Have Danced All Night* as I check my hair again in the reflection of the lobby door and smooth out a small wrinkle in my shirt. Maybe I shouldn't have tucked it into my pants. It would have looked better un-tucked—more casual, more "Hey dude, what's up?" but then my butt wouldn't look as good, and I really want my butt to look good. He may be straight but I still want that prime asset in full view, just on the off chance. What gay man sporting a great ass doesn't? I discreetly check my breath. I look down at my watch. It's been about ten minutes. My palms are sweating and my delicate first-date butterflies are morphing into spastic moths whacking their brains out on a porch light, which is typical for me when I'm really looking forward to something that isn't happening as fast as I think it should. My humming is taking on a louder, more frantic (but not quite demented) tone. The next phase will have me throwing a small, bitchy tantrum accompanied by stomping feet and pouting puss, and that could be embarrassing for everyone involved so I hope he shows up soon.

I'm just getting ready to lean up against the building's brick façade (because my own pacing is starting to drive me up the wall) when I hear a low rumbling around the far corner. I hear it over all the other traffic in the street. It sounds like a truck—a monster truck. But it's not a truck. It's a Land Rover: a supped-up, olive green Defender One Ten and Brian is behind the wheel. It comes at me pretty fast, and I take a backward step for safety's sake as he pulls to the curb and stops on a dime right alongside me.

"Get in," he commands with a smile.

I run around to the passenger's side and, at the first break in traffic, haul open the door and slide into the leather seat. I pull the door closed and quickly survey him as he waits for another break in traffic: aviator sunglasses, leather driving gloves, and a long-sleeved khaki shirt. Worn, faded blue jeans (Levi's 501's, just like Martin's) loosely hug his long legs. The sun is dancing off his wind-blown hair and a toothpick is poking out of his mouth. Just add an Aussie wide brim and he could be on safari in the rugged bush. He looks *so* sexy!

"Belt."

I reach over and grab it. It's a lap belt and shoulder strap combo that I can't figure out how to secure, at first. But determined not to embarrass myself by asking for help, I finally click it into the mechanism and… we're off. Within seconds, I can tell Brian really loves to drive, and he really loves to drive *fast*. He's flying down the surface streets at speeds I wouldn't dare hit on the motorway, his right hand on the steering wheel, his left hand working the stick. I discreetly reach over to grip the door handle as my personal chicken bar and clamp my mouth shut. I don't want to disturb his concentration as we whiz by pedestrians, cars, busses, and trucks. After five years of living in England, it still tests my nerves to act the part of a calm front-seat passenger because I can't get used to the fact we're on the wrong side of the road, and my ass is in the wrong seat in the car. I distract my anxious self by examining the beautiful Rover. This is a grand car. It's old for sure, but it's been immaculately and expensively restored and upgraded. The cushy leather seats feel like velvet to the touch. The high-tech dashboard is filled with dozens of gauges, dials, buttons and knobs. Classical music is blasting out of a killer high-def sound system. Looking out over the hood, I can't see a single flaw in the paint job. In the back, there's room for — an elephant. I bet the seats fold down into a nice big bed. I would love to have fanatical sex in this awesome wagon. I see the hump of a canvas-covered spare tire out the rear window. This behemoth could use better shocks. The ride is a little rough. Well, no. It's *really* rough. Cushy seats aside, if we hit some ugly terrain, my fantastic asset is going to take a supreme beating.

Eventually we leave the city congestion and hit the main thoroughfare. Now, having forgotten about the apology that brought me to him, I feel more confident a question or two won't cause a loss of life. I release the door handle and relax a little. "Brian, where are we going?"

He doesn't take his eyes off the road. "Rittersby."

I have no idea where that is or what that is. "Why?"

Still eyeing the road, he reaches behind me and pulls a folder from the pocket on the back of my seat. He tosses it in my lap. As we bounce along on the rough asphalt, I open the folder and pull out numerous pages that resemble real estate brochures. One has a photograph of an imposing stone mansion. It's about five or six stories high and shorter left and right wings fan off the main house. The remaining pages list the features of the mansion: nearly sixty bedrooms and anterooms (whatever those are), countless parlors, libraries, sitting rooms, and dining halls. It sits on four hundred and ninety acres of farmed and forested land. The property has stables, barns, outbuildings, tractors, and other farm equipment. It even has a small chapel. The place is called (of all things) Gaylord Hall Estate. "Have you bought this?"

He shakes his head. "Might."

"As a home? Isn't it too big?" Staring down at these pages, I can't believe he'd want to leave his chic London penthouse for something this sprawling. I mean, it's awesome in a grand way, but what on earth would he do with all the space? He smiles, but it's a few minutes before he answers. I realize he's waiting until the end of Beethoven's *Minuet*, so I need to be patient. Everyone knows I'm not good at being patient.

"Not for me," he finally says.

His response only confuses me. "Not for me?" Does that mean he's not buying it as a home for himself or does that mean it's not too big for him? I take a moment to think about how I'll phrase my next question as Ponchielli's *Dance of the Hours* begins. "If you buy it, will you live there?"

He puts his head down, gives me a puzzled look over the top of his sunglasses, and turns down the music. The toothpick flips from one side of his mouth to the other. "No, John. Why would I live there?"

Visions of cartoon ostriches and hippos in tutus dance through my head. "Well, why are you buying it?"

"Haven't bought it. Haven't seen it."

I'm realizing the ability to convey useful information while listening to classical music is not one of Brian's strong points, so I'm going out on a limb to get to the bottom of this. "Okay, so if you do see it, and you do like it, and you do buy it, what will you do with it?"

Again, the toothpick flips sides. "Turn it into a retirement home."

He cranks up the volume and we drive on in silence. I want to ask more questions, but it's obvious he just wants to listen to the music, so I sit back and enjoy the ride. It's so pleasant being with Brian. He doesn't pick immature fights or bicker like the nincompoops. He doesn't berate me like David. He doesn't harp on me about upcoming publicity opportunities like Mickey. I'm convinced he just likes my company. He rarely takes his eyes off the road so I get to look over at his awesome profile, but I make it appear as if I'm looking out at the scenery on his side of the Rover as we now barrel along down country roads in an area far removed from the crowded streets of London. We're seeing tractors and combines and horses pulling carts filled with hay or wheat—or whatever it is they're filled with. Every time we encounter another moving object on the narrow road, Brian slows down, gives the right of way, and waves. Everyone, mostly farmers missing a few teeth, smiles and waves back. I guess it's a 'country' thing. You never get that in the city — the big smiles, the waves, or that many missing teeth. At one point, we're stuck behind a hunch-shouldered farmer perched on a dinky, wooden cart. He has a beefy black bull (not sure what kind) tethered to the back. Brian keeps the Rover about thirty feet away as we creep along, staring at the bull's meandering ass and swishing tail. And just as my eyes bring his massive, low-slung scrotum (majestically swaying to and fro) into sharp focus, Strauss's *The Blue Danube* begins to stream out of the Rover's speakers. So now, as I sit beside handsome Brian, I'm half mesmerized by a bull's ridiculously large testicles waltzing in perfect time to the lovely music. I'm actually getting a little horny from the oddity of the scene and the size of those enormous, shiny balls. "Brian?"

He turns down the music just a little. "Hmm?"

"Shouldn't he be pulling the cart?"

He smiles. "He's a stud."

"Pardon?"

"The farmer's got a donkey up front. The Aberdeen-Angus is used for studding. He was probably rented from a neighboring farm for a few days."

"Oh." The farmer guides his rickety caravan into a wide inlet, allowing us to pass. As we do, I take a good look at the bull. Even I can tell he's old but he looks healthy with a glossy blue-black coat and seems serenely content as he grazes from a wooden bucket slung off the back of the cart. "He looks happy for being such an old fart."

"Aye." Brian waves to the farmer and then turns up the music. "He's got pretty good rhythm, too."

I smile at Brian and he smiles back. Clearly, this multi-millionaire spent his boyhood days in the country, and seeing how well he relates to these kindly people, I'm sure it wasn't as the snobbish son of a wealthy landowner. He probably worked as a farmhand, shoveling hay and manure — getting all hot and sweaty. Yes, I can just picture him getting all hot and sweaty. I sigh deeply. After half an hour, Brian turns down the music and pulls out the toothpick.

"Okay, go ahead."

"Excuse me?"

"You have questions about the mansion. Go ahead."

I shift in my seat and rev myself up to hit him with a small barrage before my precious window of opportunity slams shut. "Why turn it into a retirement home?"

"A good mate of mine—Simon—suggested it. He thought this area needed something like that."

"Why?"

"Well, most people who live out here are poor. Even if they could afford to house their elderly in a home in the city—which they can't—they'd never be able to travel the distance to visit them often. It's not that far, but bus routes are scarce, and if you don't have a car or money for petrol, well.... People in retirement homes get lonely. They want visits from family. They need that contact. They don't want to be forgotten—and they shouldn't be."

"Is Simon an estate agent?"

"No. He was a police sergeant. Now he's a forensic accountant. His grandmother lived out here. She's the reason he thought of the idea. Unfortunately, she died in a car crash before I ever met Simon, but he still had the idea. When he told me about it, I thought it sounded pretty good. It's taken a while to find a decent place."

I look down at the photos in my lap. "And you think this might be the place?"

"Aye. It took a long time to come on the market."

I look up at him. "Does anyone live there now?"

He shakes his head.

"Has anyone lived there recently?"

He shakes his head again.

"Has it been maintained?"

He shakes his head a third time.

"Won't it take a lot of money to fix up?"

"Aye."

"And will you make money on it?"

Now he smiles. "No, John. Most likely, I'll lose money on it."

I'm perplexed. "Then why do it?"

He takes a long time to answer as he stares at the road and jams his toothpick back in his mouth. "It's not always about making money.

Sometimes, it just makes you feel better." He turns up the music.

I gaze at him as we bounce along the winding country road. I like him. I *really* like him, a lot.

■ ■ ■

It takes about an hour and a half to get to Gaylord Hall. It's a beautiful, stately place, and it's a whole lot bigger than it looks in the photograph. Some windows are broken, but most are intact. The landscaping, if you can still call it that, is wild and overgrown with rose bushes nearly covering the whole façade, but they're surprisingly lush from all the rain. There's a magnificent set of stone steps leading up to the entrance with secondary staircases on either side. The massive oak double doors are locked, so we're waiting for the estate agent; a woman named Wanda. I wonder what she looks like. God, I hope she's not pretty. The last thing I need right now is a pretty woman to ruin my perfect day with this beautiful man.

Brian is leaning up against the Rover, his long legs crossed at the ankles as he checks his phone for messages and whatnot. Because I'm trying not to bug him, I'm on the other side of the car about fifty feet away, picking up little stones and pitching them into the bushes along the wide gravel drive. I hear cows mooing in the distance, and the atmosphere is serene.

After a few minutes, Brian speaks without looking up from his phone. "John?"

"Yes, Brian?"

"Have you ever been to this part of the country before?"

"No. I went to Stratford once, and I've been to Cambridge a few times, but other than that, I've pretty much stuck to the city."

There's silence as I continue to pitch my stones. Then he speaks again. "John?"

"Yes, Brian?"

"Do you know what this particular area is known for?"

Well, this is nice. Apparently, I'm going to get a little history lesson about Rittersby. "No. What?"

Brian still doesn't look up from his phone. "Wild boar."

"Really?" I continue pitching my stones into the bushes. I know what a boar looks like (I think). I know it has tusks. It must look like a big fat pig with tusks. I still hear cows mooing. It sounds like one cow in particular is getting closer to us.

"John?" Brian says again, calmly and still engrossed in his phone.

"Yes, Brian?"

"Do you know what really pisses them off?"

"No." I keep pitching my stones into the bushes and wait for more of this fascinating history lesson on the wild boars of Rittersby. I love Brian's accent. His voice is so deep and soothing. I could listen to that voice all day long. It relaxes me.

"Pretty much exactly what you're doing."

My arm freezes in mid-pitch, relaxation gone.

Still with his head down and diligently scrolling screens on his phone, he calmly says, "I want you to walk back to the car very slowly. And if you see anything come out of those bushes, I want you to run—very fast."

For a few seconds, I'm frozen. I can't move an inch. I can't even breathe. I swallow hard and drop the stones. Haltingly, I drag my feet, one at a time. I'm walking backward with my eyes riveted on those bushes. For a moment, I think Brian is joking; he's trying to scare me so he can have a good laugh. That moment vanishes the instant I see the boar come barreling out of the bushes. It's terribly ugly, it's big, it's squealing—and that damned pig is FAST! I spin around and haul ass toward the Rover: head thrown back, arms pumping, legs flying. Thank God, I left the door open!

"SHIIIIIIIT!" I gracefully take air and dive, head first, into the car. I hear a loud BANG! as the boar hits the chassis a little to the left of the passenger seat. I scramble to pull my feet inside. I'm too afraid to reach over and yank the door closed so I just curl up as tight as I can across the front seats—a six-foot-one-inch man contorted into a three-foot ball, knees slammed into my chin. I'm breathing as if I've just run a marathon, and I'm so damned chicken-shit scared I think I'm about to faint. I don't see or hear the boar. Brian knocks on the window, and I nearly piss my pants out of fright.

He peers down at me through the glass. "It's gone. You okay?"

What the hell does he mean, "You okay?" Of course I'm not okay! Jesus Christ! I'm practically having a seizure here. Do I *look* okay? "I will be… in a… in a minute. It was just…just a little… unexpected." I slowly unfold my body.

Brian goes back to his phone, and I decide to lie in the car across the front seats and stare up at the roof until Wanda arrives. There's no sense in getting up until I have to, and I'm quite comfortable. I pop up my head a few minutes later when I hear a car pulling into the drive. It's a gold Mercedes Benz sedan. Brian opens the driver's side door of the Rover. I clumsily crawl out and almost land flat on my face in the gravel as I squeeze my body past the gearshift and the steering wheel.

"Brian! Sorry I'm late. I had a bit of trouble figuring out who had the damned keys!"

Wanda's personality reminds me of an English version of Mickey. Wanda's looks remind me of a SeaWorld walrus. She's probably pushing fifty (up a very steep hill). She's also short, round, flabby, and full of energy. Shirley Temple ringlets frame a wide, cherubic face. With an overbite so substantial it could devour her lower jaw in one chomp if she's not careful, and protruding chocolate-brown eyes that look off in different directions, she's very unattractive — and I'm very happy.

"Wanda, it's good to see you. This is John."

I shake her hand and, with the boar episode behind me, flash her my fantastic, confident smile. The one that asks the obvious question: "Am I hot, or what?" She recognizes me instantly.

"Hey, you're John Kaiser from *TruthFinder Murphy!* Wow! What a looker — dead sexy! Who'd have thought I'd meet a celebrity today, huh?" She looks up at Brian. "So, what's the occasion? They gonna film an episode here, too?"

"No. John is a friend. He came along for the ride."

"Bang on!" She eyes me up and down a few times and lets out a low whistle. It makes me a bit uncomfortable but — as always — it's flattering, too. She turns to Brian. "Oh, hey, there's something you gotta know, even before we go inside. This place is swarming with wild boar — haven't had a cull in years. They'll charge at anything and old folks in wheeled chairs and Zimmer frames can't outrun a boar — although it might be a wicked laugh to see 'em try. You'll need a strong perimeter fence. That's gonna be a big expense right off the top. Just wanna disclose that."

"Thanks. That's good to know." Brian looks at me and flips the toothpick.

God, I feel like such an ass.

"Okay, let's get in here, huh? Let's do this!" Wanda booms, clapping her pudgy hands. She marches her fat ass up the steps and pulls out a brass ring with nearly three-dozen keys on it. Of course, she has no idea which one opens the doors. After a few minutes and not showing an ounce of irritation, Brian steps up.

"Here, Wanda. Let me try." He takes the ring from her, removes his sunglasses, and examines all the keys. He picks one key—just one—and unlocks the doors.

Inside, the mansion is regal. Even with every horizontal surface covered in a thick layer of dust and grime, I still see how glorious it once was. The floors are probably Carrara marble. The walls are paneled in quarter-sawn red oak with ornate ebony and birch intarsia. The ceilings have original plaster moldings and splendid quartz crystal chandeliers draped in cobwebs. The doors are at least nine feet tall with leaded-glass transoms above, and tarnished solid brass hardware is everywhere I look: door handles, key holes, hinges, wall sconces, kick plates, and window latches. The formidable marble staircase rises up five stories in an elegant spiral.

Brian's eyes sweep the grand foyer. "Any looters?"

Wanda brushes low-hanging cobwebs from a doorway. "Nope. Too far out of the way for hoodlums to bother or remember it's here, and all the locals carry loaded Purdeys and Churchills. Everything's been left alone."

"Converted from gas?"

"Hmm. Back in the early sixties, but all the wiring is shot. I'm sure rats have done a number behind the walls. It'll need a redo to bring it up to current code."

My ears perk up at the mention of rats. I'm now on high alert for anything that might be furry or scurry. Neither word is acceptable to my twitchy nervous system.

Brian looks straight up the stairwell. "Is the glass dome intact?"

"As far as I know, or we'd be crunching it under our feet."

I stand next to Brian and look up into the stairwell. All I see is a big, black hole. "What glass dome?"

"That glass dome." He looks down at me and sees I'm confused. He smiles and pulls out the toothpick. "It's covered in tarpaper."

"Why?"

"For protection, most likely."

"Oh." I look up again. To me, it still looks like a big, black hole.

Brian and Wanda spend about forty-five minutes walking around the first floors of the main house and the two wings discussing things that need repair, replacement, alteration, or upgrading. I wander along behind them, hesitantly peeking into closets, cabinets, secret hallways, and back stairwells, fascinated by the sheer number of rooms and their cavernous size. In the kitchen, Wanda pulls out a mini-flashlight and they descend into the basement. From the top of the narrow stairs, it looks a little too eerie and dank for me so I'm staying on the first floor. I don't have a problem admitting I'm a thirty-year-old man who's petrified of little creepy crawlies, and if I see anything resembling a mouse, a rat, a spider, or a roach, I'll probably scream—like a sissy. I dust off an area of the marble kitchen countertop and sit there while I listen to fragments of what they're saying and look out at the beautiful scenery through grimy windows. I don't understand any of their gibberish; stuff about reinforcements for structural stability, retrofitting, soil analysis, and foundation underpinnings. Twenty minutes later, they're back.

I slide my butt off the counter and slap away the dust. "How does it look?" I don't know what questions to ask, but I want to join in as much as I can.

Wanda walks over to me. "Not good, John. She's got unstable areas and big holes in her foundation; there's a lot of settling. The amount of money it's going to take to fix her substructure is substantial." We follow Brian back to the foyer where he shoves his hands in his pockets and stares out the open doors. "As usual, I'm not sure what he thinks."

"Do you show Brian a lot of properties?"

"Oh, yeah, Sweetie. Tons of 'em—for various ventures, of course. But he never lets on. No emotions at all. I never know if he likes 'em or hates 'em—and I never ask."

Brian flicks his toothpick out the front door, turns, and heads up

136

the staircase. Wanda follows, huffing and puffing on her stumpy legs, and I bring up the rear. At each landing on every floor, Brian checks out the same area; a linen closet to the right of the top step.

"What's he doing?" I whisper to Wanda.

"Excuse me?"

"He's looked in the same closet on every floor. Why?"

"Lifts, Sweetie. He'll have to install them somewhere. He's looking for clear, vertical paths."

"Oh." It feels pretty good finally to understand something.

At the landing on the top floor just below the attic, Brian heads off into one of the bedrooms. I want to follow him and ask questions, but I realize checking out this mansion is serious business for him, and the last thing he needs is me under his feet. Wanda pulls down a rickety, telescoping ladder to access the attic. I cross my arms and watch in slack-jawed amazement, as she climbs—well, sort of crawls—up. Her head is down and her bulbous butt is sticking out as the strained ladder dangerously sags and cries out in protest under her enormous weight. She's certainly fearless, I'll give her that.

She calls back over her shoulder, "Come on, Sweetie."

"Yeah, right," I mumble under my breath. If she thinks Sweetie is gonna shimmy up that decrepit old thing behind her huge ass to stumble around like an imbecile in a spooky dark attic that's home to God-knows-what, then she's crazy. Sweetie is not an idiot. I decide to amuse myself by leaning on the banister and gazing way down the stairwell at the spiral staircase we just ascended. I'm imagining how elegant it looked in its heyday—a highly polished, thick mahogany railing and pristine white marble steps snaking all the way up five stories. It must have been spectacular to see London's high society out here at their country estate, promenading down these stairs in elaborate ball gowns and formal tuxedos with top hats and tails. Then I remember what Brian said when we were in the foyer about the glass dome being covered in tarpaper. I crane my neck to look up at it. Standing this close, I still don't see any glass up there, even when I squint. Off in the distance, somewhere overhead, I hear Wanda complaining about rat poop, spiders, and bats (scream-worthy flying mice, as far as I'm concerned). I turn around, brace my butt against the banister while I grip it with my hands, and arch my back out over the stairwell to see if I can get a better look at the dome. Being a dancer, I'm limber enough to lean out pretty far. Unfortunately, being a dancer (even a limber one) doesn't help me one damned bit when I hear the banister crack a fraction of a second before it gives way behind me.

I'm falling! I know I'm falling, but I can't seem to call out to anyone to tell them I'm falling. I raise my hands, hoping to grab onto—well, anything—even though there's nothing there. I sense that point where my body is almost horizontal. It's as if everything is happening in slow motion. I've had this feeling before in dreams, this sensation of falling from a great height, and then I wake up in a sweaty, violent spasm and feel so relieved. But this isn't a dream. I can't believe this is how I'm going to die. I'm going to die by falling five stories onto a dusty marble floor. I don't want my brains splattered all over th—

My neck snaps back as someone grabs the waistband of my pants and hauls me back onto the landing with one powerful, quick yank. As I slam hard against Brian's chest from the forward momentum, I clamp onto his shoulders with my fingers and take in a vast gulp of air as I try to catch my breath. My mouth is wide open, my eyes are wide open, and my heart is racing. The blood is pounding in my ears from fright. Brian's arms are around my waist, holding me against him. I'm shaking all over.

"Okay. It's okay. Look at me, John. Look at me, okay? You're all right. That's it. That's good. Just relax. That's right. Just keep looking at me. You'll be fine."

I'm wildly staring up into his eyes. I'm trying to stay focused on his voice and everything he's saying, even with my ears pounding from the rush of adrenaline. I'm trying to calm down and catch my breath. He still has me tightly around the waist. I still have my fingers clamped down hard on his shoulders, and my nails are digging into his flesh through his shirt. At first, I can't slow down my breathing, and I can't stop shaking. It seems impossible. Even though I'm inhaling really hard to the point where I'm wheezing up a storm, I'm not taking in any oxygen. I'm getting dizzy. Oh, God, I'm going to faint in his arms like a fairy maiden!

"Listen to me, John. Concentrate on my voice. I know you're

scared, but you need to relax. You're safe now, and you *have* to calm down. It's okay. You're safe. I won't let you go."

I try my hardest to listen to Brian's voice and ignore what my body is (and isn't) doing. After what seems like an eternity, I'm finally able to slow down my breathing and stop shaking, but I still can't close my mouth. I need it open to inhale and exhale, and every few seconds, I convulsively gasp and shiver. I close my eyes. Brian's chest is expanding and contracting against mine and somehow that profound sensation is reassuring and calming.

"Okay, that's better. That's much better. You're doing fine, John. You're doing great."

I finally loosen my grip on his shoulders, but I don't dare let go. Behind me, there's no banister. I don't even remember hearing it hit the floor five stories below. I swallow hard. My throat is parched. My breathing is slowing way down and so is my heart rate. The convulsions have stopped. Still, remembering my wonderful snoot flute, I keep my mouth open. My senses are coming back. I'm aware of all kinds of things. I'm aware of how beautifully quiet it is. Wanda must have traveled to another part of the attic and my ears aren't pounding anymore. I'm aware that this is the first time I've touched Brian since our handshake at the charity event, and he's still holding me around my waist with strong, muscular arms. I'm aware that, with my hands on his shoulders, my forearms are resting on his biceps, and we must look like two dancers waiting for the music to start. I'm aware of how our chests aren't rising and falling at the same pace. With his stomach pressing against the lowest part of my ribcage, I'm aware of the difference in our height. I'm aware of how close our faces are as I feel the warm air exhaled from his nostrils on my eyelids. I smell the faint scent of his soap. I open my eyes and I see my mouth is about three inches from his chin. I gaze at the soft skin on his neck and his Adam's apple. I raise my gaze and look up into those electrifying eyes. Without meaning to, I exhale with my mouth turned up toward his nose and his nostrils flair and quiver. I inhale and exhale again just to witness that curious effect once more, and it seems as if Brian moves his nose closer to my mouth by just a fraction of an inch. I don't think he's trying to kiss me. I think he's trying to smell my breath, which is odd. He abruptly pulls his face away from mine. "You okay?"

I open my mouth wider to say yes, but I don't hear any words come out, so I just nod. His body stiffens as he drops his arms from around my waist and takes half a step backward. I realize I have to let go of his shoulders so he can take another step. I don't want to, but I release my grip and drop my arms to my side. He takes another full step backward, and immediately I feel the loss of heat generated by his body. He motions me away from the edge of the landing. I cross over to the wall and lean against it. I close my eyes, trying to remember what every inch of him felt like as he held me just seconds earlier. After a moment, I open my eyes to see him standing next to the attic ladder, looking back at me. "I'm sorry. I wasn't thinking."

He shakes his head. "You gave me a hell of a fright, I'll tell you that. Are you sure you're okay?"

I nod. "Yes, just a bit worn out." I look up into the attic. "Are you going up there?"

He smiles. "Yeah, right. Wanda! Let's go! I've seen enough."

■ ■ ■

I'm sitting in the Rover, gazing out at Brian as he says goodbye to Wanda. I'm exhausted, sapped of energy. I'm still remembering what it felt like to be held by him. His body was so strong and unbelievably warm. With his arms wrapped around me, I felt safe and secure, like nothing could hurt me. I've never felt like that before—ever. Wanda comes to the passenger's side window as Brian climbs in behind the wheel. He pulls a fresh toothpick out of his breast pocket and sticks it in his mouth.

"Well, Sweetie, it was nice to meet you. You sure are dishy. You must have to beat the lads off with a stick all day long. Hey, are you okay? You look pale."

"I'm fine, Wanda. I'm just a little tired. It was really nice to meet you, too. I hope I see you again." We drive off as she squishes her bulky mass into her car. On the main road, I look back to see her turn in the opposite direction. I watch until the Mercedes disappears in a cloud of dust.

Brian looks at the road ahead. "Are you hungry?"

"Yes." I gaze at him with my head leaning back on the headrest.

"Brian?"

"Hmm?"

"I'm really sorry about what I did. It was stupid of me."

He smiles, but he doesn't take his eyes off the road. "You're still alive. That's all that matters. Let's forget it."

"But if you hadn't grabbed me—"

His smile fades, and he pulls the toothpick from his mouth. "But I did. This time... I could, so let's forget it."

■ ■ ■

We stop for a late lunch at a venerable English pub. My just-outside-death's-door energy surges back to life as we step inside and the aroma of all the wonderful food, pungent ale, and aged wine hits my nostrils. It's a lively place, full of laughter and shouting and fiddle music. The atmosphere reminds me of a rowdy renaissance faire—semi-restrained drunkenness and unrestrained good cheer. Brian is leading the way through the crowded main dining hall. Now and then, he has to squeeze between tight groups of revelers and duck under some of the low wood beams. The local patrons are awed by his height. I watch from behind as he reaches back, lifts his shirttail, and pulls his wallet from his back pocket. It's the first chance I've had to check out his ass. I don't get much of a look—just a fleeting glance—but a professional ass-gazer knows exactly what to look for, and the two-second eye feast I get is enough. He's got a spectacular ass! Usually, really tall men have no ass or a great big, boxy ass. Brian has a tight buttock, round ass that comes from running or squatting weights, and it looks hot in Levi's. It reminds me of Martin's ass—a beautiful, ripe peach. You just want to grab it, or bite it... or do something really sexy to it. As the crowd thins, I slow my pace to get more space between us. I want to see him walk. He has a really manly gait: long, slow strides, and just the slightest bounce off the balls of his feet at the end of each step, with a faint, unintentional sway in his hips. And then I see one of the sexiest things of all; his inner thighs rubbing together (just a little) which tells me he's got some massive quads. No skinny chicken legs are cowering in those jeans.

He picks a booth in the back, away from the raucous crowds and near the fireplace. He stands aside to let me slide in as if I were a woman and then sits down opposite me. Positioned way back here in the dark, I worry that he's afraid to be seen alone with a gay man. It makes me uneasy. I'm not blatantly gay. I'm not waving a rainbow flag or strutting around with my naked butt hanging out of leather ass chaps. People who don't know me can't even tell I'm gay. He shouldn't be worried. I'd never intentionally embarrass him. I slump down in the dark booth, feeling insecure and (I loathe to admit it) a bit ashamed. When the hefty server arrives, Brian orders a vegetable stew, and I meekly order a... green salad.

"You're having a laugh. That's all you're going to eat?"

"It's enough."

"It's a joke." He looks up at the server. "Two stews and a green salad, please. One house red and one strong Earl Grey: no milk, no cream, no lemon, no sugar. Thank you."

Brian stretches out his legs, leans back in the booth, and closes his eyes. I sit quietly, having no idea how to make myself look more straight. I glance around the splendid pub, taking in all the rustic architectural details. My wandering eyes fall on a husky, gruff man turned sideways in his chair and staring at me from a nearby table. I look away as fast as I can, but it's not fast enough. Within seconds, he's on his feet and slowly, drunkenly lumbering toward our booth. He has a bloated, ruddy face with a flat, wide nose that looks as if it's been busted twice. His belly is hanging low between the strained straps of his suspenders, and he has so much thick chest hair erupting from the collar of his flannel shirt, it looks as if a furry animal is desperately trying to scurry up his thick neck and seek refuge in his bushy, unkempt beard. Panicking a little, I look to Brian for reassurance. His eyes are still closed.

"*Fag?*" the man booms, leaning in closely and hitting me hard with sour beer breath.

"Um. I, um..." I know my face has gone white as I flash back to my date with Matt.

"*Fag!*" he barks again, proudly displaying the gap where a central and lateral incisor once resided as cozy neighbors in his big mouth.

I swallow hard. "Well, I—"

"Sorry, mate. We don't smoke." Brian, eyes now wide open, is looking up at the burly guy.

"Bugger! Aw' right, got it." He stomps back to his table.

Brian closes his eyes, settles back down, and smiles a little. I feel even more self-conscious and awkward as I cower in the booth and watch his relaxed face. After a while, as I stare at his eyelashes and serene demeanor, I think he's gone to sleep. Then, those sexy lips part and the toothpick moves back and forth. I've never been a fan of the lowly toothpick; modern man's simple (yet highly efficient) precursor to dental floss and the overrated Waterpik. I've always associated the pointy facial accessory with overalls and Kyle Thompson. But I must say, watching Brian's pink tongue deftly manipulate that three-inch sliver of wood between those smooth, thin lips is causing a disturbance my celibate crotch hasn't felt in ages. Damn! I wish I was that lucky toothpick.

"I can't think with all the noise, even sitting way back here," he mumbles.

Noise? We're sitting in the back because of noise? My insecurities are gone and I'm happy again. I sit up straight and give him a few more seconds of silence before I bombard him with questions. "Will you buy it?"

"Might."

"Even with all the work Wanda says it needs?"

There's a pause. "Aye."

"So what's holding up the decision?"

He opens his eyes, leans forward, and rests his elbows on the table. He looks right into my eyes when he speaks, and I feel supreme exhilaration. "It needs a lot of work, and it's going to take a lot of money. I don't have a problem with that. But it'll take up a lot of my time at the start. That means I'll have to stay in London longer than I'd planned."

The server returns with the wine and tea.

"And that's a bad thing?"

Brian pushes the wine toward me and pulls the tea toward him. "Thank you," he says to her. "I just don't like staying in London that long. I'd rather be home."

I sip my wine. "In Scotland."

"Aye." He takes out the toothpick and drops it on his teacup saucer.

"What's so great about Scotland?"

He forces a smile and that deep pain surfaces again in his melancholy eyes. "It's my home, John. It's where I belong."

"I was told you belong where your loved one is." It sounds corny and romantic, but someone did tell me that a long time ago. I just can't remember who it was.

The smile fades and his mind wanders briefly. "I love Scotland."

Well, that doesn't work for me. I don't want Brian in Scotland. I want him here, and I'm used to getting what I want, so I need to push the retirement home. I take a big sip of wine and think about how to approach this. "Well, Scotland isn't that far away. You could fly back now and then, still have your meetings in London during the week, and stay out here—somewhere—on the weekends. Maybe you could stay in the mansion."

"You've got to be kidding. Me, stay in that rat-infested dustbowl?"

"It could be cleaned up a bit. You could set traps, hang some curtains, throw down a few rugs, and haul in a sofa."

"John, that place doesn't even have electricity or running water."

"But eventually it will, right? I mean, what would be so terrible about spending a few nights there?"

"There's no bed."

"You throw a mattress on the floor."

"There's no bloody housekeeping service."

I roll my eyes. "You do your own cleaning. You make your own bed. You wake up every morning and think of all the great things you can do to the place. You can be full of inspiration. You can be full of ideas."

"And you can be full of crap. There's no way I'd stay there during construction. I like luxury. I'm used to luxury. I can't 'rough it.' Ever."

"So you're not going to buy it?"

"I don't know."

"But there's a chance you will?"

He sighs as our food arrives, a sure sign he's growing tired of my questions. "Maybe."

I am *so* hungry. The stew is thick, smells fantastic, and tastes like heaven in a bowl. It's hardier (and healthier) than anything I've eaten in the last four days and Brian was right: The salad wouldn't have done a thing for me. We eat in silence for a while as I shovel my stew, but I'm still not through with my questions. "What's the deciding factor, then? What will convince you to buy it or not buy it?"

He looks at me and lets out a small laugh.

"What?" I'm imagining there's embarrassing dribble hanging off my chin.

"Nothing. Look, you'll laugh if I tell you."

"No, I won't. I won't laugh. Tell me, please." I try my hardest to avoid whining those last three words.

He pushes aside his food and rests his elbows on the table. "Its scent."

I lean in a little. "Pardon?"

"Its... scent."

"You're basing your decision on how it smells? But that's not fair. It smells pretty bad right now. It's been neglected. You have to wait until it's cleaned up a bit."

"No, John, not smell — scent. I'll base my decision on its scent."

I give him a puzzled look. "But aren't they the same thing?"

"Not at all." He takes a sip of tea. Again, he looks right into my eyes, and again, I just feel so exhilarated by his piercing gaze. "Everyone and everything has a scent, an underlying aroma that rises above any other temporary smell it might have. It's like an essence that emanates from within. Most people don't notice it, but I do — with just about everyone and everything. That's what I'll base my decision on."

"Oh. I see." I'm thinking back to what Mickey said at the charity event about my cologne and how he checked with Brian if he'd be okay with my sweat at the rehearsal.

He looks at my blank face. "You think I'm a nutter."

"No...."

"Yes, you do. You think I'm a crazy bastard."

"No, I don't. I think.... I think you're fascinating."

I'm embarrassed by having said it aloud, but it's the truth. He does fascinate me, on so many different levels, and in so many different ways — like no one I've ever met. He pulls back his bowl and we finish our meal in silence. Of course, with every spoonful I take, I'm wondering what he thinks of my scent, but I'm too afraid to ask. The server comes to clear our dishes.

"So, what did you think of the mansion's scent?"

"I'm not sure. I had mixed feelings. It wasn't unpleasant but I may need to go back one more time."

"Can I come with you?" I blurt out, desperate for another chance to spend the whole day with him.

"You've got to be kidding me."

"No, why?" I'm afraid he's going to tell me he thinks my scent stinks.

"John, you bounced around for over an hour in an old car with horribly tight suspension and you'll have to do it again going home, you were charged by a boar, and you nearly killed yourself. You're telling me you'd come back here?"

"Oh, yes! I'd come back. I had a great time!"

He smiles and we sit quietly as I finish my wine and he has another cup of tea. Twenty minutes pass before he speaks. "Thank you."

"Hmm? For what?"

He pops his toothpick back in his mouth. "For not being a pest earlier today, for not bothering me at the mansion."

"Did you think I would?"

He nods. "You like to ask a lot of questions, and you like a lot of attention. You *need* a lot of attention. I think that's really important to you."

I'm a little uneasy. Of course, he's right, but I don't want to admit it. I look down into my wine glass. "I know you really don't care for people, and I don't want you to think I'm a pain in the ass." I look up at him.

He gives me a warm smile. "I don't."

■ ■ ■

The drive back to the city is great. Brian points out significant places along the way, including properties and businesses he owns or is thinking of buying. He tells me more about Simon—his best friend—and Wanda who gave him the expensive (but ugly) Baccarat vase. He talks longingly about Scotland. He asks me questions about my upcoming projects. He gives me his take on the accident with the nincompoops, which includes the campy bickering in the Rolls they certainly didn't tell me about. We pull up to the flat at about four-thirty. I don't want this day to end, but Charles has already called to remind him of a meeting scheduled at five and David's class will be over soon, too. I know I have to leave. I look over at my car and a headache starts pounding behind my eyes. I'm staring at a double-parked van and a fat man in coveralls, squatting down, preparing to clamp a neon yellow boot to the front tire of my Boxster. "Oh, great."

"That's not good."

I shake my head. "I only put in enough for three hours."

Brian pulls out his phone. "Jack, there's a boot being put on a black Boxster out here. I need it off. Right. Thank you."

I'm embarrassed to disclose what I have to disclose. "Brian?"

"Hmm," he mumbles, trying to gather up the real estate papers I've strewn all over the car.

"I have a couple of traffic violations." They're mostly parking tickets (and two for driving on the wrong side of the road), but I still shouldn't have neglected them.

"I know, more than two hundred pounds worth and you haven't bothered to pay them. That's why you're getting the boot and not another ticket. What is it about minor traffic violations that cause you to ignore the tickets they generate? It's just a matter of coughing up a little money."

It's a valid question. I just don't have a valid answer. "Um, I guess my reasoning is: If I ignore it, it'll just go away." I follow that lame sentence with a smile I hope comes across as charming.

Apparently, Brian doesn't absorb charming. He's still trying to lay a hand on all the papers. "Well, it boggles my mind why you would risk getting a boot."

"Yes, I can see where you'd be boggled. The problem is I don't think they'll take off the boot until I go down and pay the outstanding fines. I'll have to call a taxi."

Brian stops rifling around in the Rover, takes off his sunglasses, and gives me his own charming smile. "Really? You think so? You might just be surprised." He looks past me, out the window.

I turn to follow his gaze and watch as Jack, already across the street, has some words with the fat man. He nods his head a few times, picks up the boot, and takes it back to his van. Fifteen seconds later, he drives off. "Why did he...? How could he...? But I thought...." I'm amazed. I'm stunned. I'm really impressed. "How did you *do* that?"

Brian is watching Jack come back across the street and he's smiling. "A little money, John. I coughed up a little money."

John — February 16

"Damn!"

I sigh. "What now."

"My phone is dead. I need to use yours."

I give Mickey an exasperated look. He is really trying my patience today. First, he calls me at the set and asks me to drive out to pick him up at the airport because the taxi drivers are on another strike, and he's too high and mighty to ride the tube or take a bus. Then he insists airline personnel damaged his luggage and spends twenty-five minutes filling out a claim form because a gaudy, plastic Carmen Miranda zipper fob is missing from his garment bag. Now he has me fishing my phone out of my coat pocket as I drive. And I'll have a headache in a few minutes because Mickey, who has a big mouth to begin with, always breaks out in a bad case of cell yell when he's on a phone. No matter how clear the connection provided by modern, wireless telecommunication technology, Mickey still thinks he's clutching a soup can tethered to a string.

"Mickey, I've told you before: Keep your phone plugged into the charger."

"I know, I know. It's just been one of those days. Everything has gone wrong. I can't even find the damned charger." He looks at his watch. "And now I'm gonna be late. He can't stand it when anyone is late. It messes up everything else."

I finally pry the phone from my pocket. He takes it and punches in a few numbers. Then he closes his eyes. "Come on, Mickey. Come on, Mickey. You know this number by heart. You *know* this number."

"Whose number? Maybe I already have it."

"No, it's Brian's private number. Ah! I got it." He punches in the last digits and hits the speakerphone button because he's paranoid of germs.

I hear Brian's phone ringing. My heart is beating faster, and my palms are sweating. I'm excited! He's calling Brian on my phone! Brian's number will be in my call log! I grip the steering wheel tighter and my knuckles turn white. I'm trying to concentrate on driving so I don't breeze through a red light or alarm my fellow commuters by driving on the wrong side of the road, and I'm trying not to look nervous.

"Yup?"

"Hey, Brian! Mickey here!"

There's a long pause on Brian's end. "Mickey?"

"Yeah. Hey, I'm sorry, buddy, but I got a little tied up and I—"

"Where are you calling from?"

"Huh? Oh, it's Johnny's phone. Mine died. He had to give me a ride from the airport. They're striking, you know? All the taxis are on strike today. Watch the road, Johnny, and keep to the left. The last thing I need is a head on collision, okay? Brian?"

There's no response.

Mickey yells a little louder. "Hey, Brian—you there?"

"Yeah, Mickey. I'm here."

"Look, I'm gonna be about a half hour late. I know I said I'd be on time, but it's out of my hands. It's not my doing."

"That's fine. It's no problem."

"Really? Okay. Good. I'm glad to be back, though. Whew! I tell you, LA is a circus. Everyone's trying to pitch an angle. Times are tough and work is scarce. I couldn't wait to get out of there. Of course, I have to go back in a few weeks to deal with some more issues, but that's a whole other story!" Mickey pauses for dramatic effect. "And speaking of stories, I hear through the grapevine you've been seeing someone, huh? You've been getting in some extra-curricular activities while I've been away?"

My heart beats faster, my entire body heats up, and my hands are slippery with sweat. Oh, my God! Brian is seeing someone? How did I miss that? How long has he been seeing her, and who is she? Where were the signs? Why didn't he tell me? My head is filled with questions tumbling over each other as they race through my panicking brain. I feel nauseous and there's a lump the size of a walnut in my throat. I really have to concentrate on driving now, so we don't end up on morgue slabs.

Brian doesn't respond, so Mickey loudly prattles on. "See, it just goes to show me: I bug you and bug you and bug you, but the minute I leave you alone you go out and find yourself a nice woman."

"Mickey...." Brian's voice awkwardly trails off.

"And she's sexy, Brian; she's a real firecracker. I mean, I've seen photos: blonde hair, blue eyes, legs up to here, and cleavage out to there. Wow! You took your time and struck a pot of gold with that one! What's her name again?"

"Carol. Mickey, it's not—"

"That's right—Carol! Man, Brian! I'm *really* happy for you. Who knows; maybe she's the one, huh? From what I've heard, you two really turn some heads when you're out on the town. And I hear you've been renting hotel rooms, huh? That's gotta mean there's some heavy-duty booty going on, right? Way to go, tiger!"

Renting hotel rooms? Heavy-duty booty? Have I had my head stuck up my ass? Why didn't I know he's been seeing this...this Carol woman? Why didn't he say anything to me? Then again, why should he? I'm not his keeper and it's none of my business.

"Mickey, let's drop it, okay? It's not a big deal." Brian's voice is irritated and strained. He sounds uncomfortable with what's been said. Good. I'm not feeling so chipper, myself. Only Mickey seems to be a happy little son of a bitch with his damned soup can.

"Okay. You can fill me in on all the juicy details when I get there. Johnny is just gonna drop me off outside your building in about twenty minutes. He's got some place to go." He turns to look at me. "Meeting your friends, right Johnny? Gonna hit the queen scene and have some fun, huh?"

"Yeah." I force a smile because I'm just so happy he called it the 'queen scene' with Brian still on the phone. Oh, yeah, I'm gonna have some real fun tonight. Thanks, Mickey!

10
A Miserable And Frustrated Gay Bastard

John — February 16

The nightclub is nearing capacity. As usual, it's filled with gorgeous, sexy guys. The atmosphere is sizzling. The music is great. I feel like shit. It's just a perfect night!

An assortment of bodies parades by—some buffed, some not—in snug designer jeans and too-tight shirts (which not only flaunt pecs and biceps on those who have them, but emphasize the presence of nipple rings, too). Eye contact ranges from furtive glances gently tossed across the room by the shy and inexperienced to smoldering stares fast pitched right in front of my face by the bold and brazen, and testosterone levels are sky high as thumbs hook into pockets and fingers casually (yet blatantly) advertise potent packages ready for action. Truth, Oceans, Play, Polo Blue, and Brit hit my nostrils in dense waves as each pound of flesh glides by. A lanky, bleached blond lifts his shirt hem to flash a black G-string cutting hard into his hip. A swarthy gym rat whispers "bottom" as he brushes against my arm in passing. To my left, a wannabe Latin lover symbolically swallows the neck of his ale bottle and winks; the fellatious insinuation and open invitation too obvious to ignore, and too obvious to accept. In fact, none of the offers interest me as Mickey's words peal loudly in my brain: "One hustle could ruin your reputation." Keeping my fly zipped at times like this has garnered me a large, devoted and eclectic fan base too precious to lose and too cherished to disappoint. I turn away from it all, trying to clear my mind.

"What's with you?" Martin shouts over the booming beat.

I drink my ale. "Nothing."

"Don't give me that. I know you too well. I'm your hairdresser, remember?"

I flash a fake smile at him that says, "Up yours, asshole."

"No, seriously, Johnny — before the two buttheads and God's Little Git show up — what's wrong?"

I close my eyes and shake my head. "I don't know." I open my eyes, and they begin to water. It's not that I'm crying. I just feel the need to rinse a negative film off my pupils so I can enjoy the sexiness of this place as I have in the past. Martin gestures toward the back of the club with his ale bottle. Slowly, we work our way through the crowd with me stopping now and then to sign autographs on napkins and pose for cell phone pictures.

Martin sits down at an empty table and scopes the immediate area for reporters and anyone who looks as if they're listening in. "Now, spill it and don't dick around with a long, drawn-out story. You know they'll be here any minute, and you know they'll give you grief."

My eyes grow wide with surprise. "Why will they give me grief?"

"Because this is about Brian, isn't it? All this moping around and looking like soft shit smeared on a warm bulla. Which means you saw him again and something happened — something bad. So, come on. Tell me."

I take a deep breath. "I did see him again. I spent the whole day with him — just as a friend. It was perfect... like a fantasy. Then today Mickey had to call him from my phone. He had him on speakerphone so I heard their conversation." I pause because it's hard to say the words. "He's seeing someone, Marty. He's seeing a woman, and he didn't tell me. I don't even know who she is; Carol Something-or-other. I didn't get her last name, but she's got blonde hair, long legs and a big chest."

Martin is thinking hard, flipping through his mental rolodex of Who's Who in the city. "Hmm.... In his über-world, there're only a few single ones in London right now who fit that description that he'd go for." He sets down his ale and pulls out his phone. "I know her,

Johnny. I know who she is." He spends a minute poking at the screen before holding out the phone. "That's got to be her: Carol Lexington."

I set down my bottle and take the phone. I'm staring at a long-legged, beautiful blonde who's just stepped out of a sports car. She looks like a jetsetter—a high-class bombshell. I don't like this woman. I don't like this gorgeous, blonde-haired harpy staring back at me. She deserves a curse or a poisonous witch's brew or God's wrath—anything painfully lethal.

"Johnny?"

"Hmm…?" I mumble distractedly. I'm too busy wishing the black plague, decapitation by a dull saw or high-voltage electrocution on this stunning beast to pay attention to anyone or anything.

"I meant it when I said I know her."

I'm not distracted anymore. "What? From where?"

"She comes in to have her hair done by Lewys every few weeks."

I hand back his phone. I don't want to ask the question, but I have to know what Brian sees in her. "What's she like?"

Martin lifts his bottle, guzzles some ale and stifles a burp before he speaks. "She's a pretty nasty piece of work. Thinks her shit doesn't stink. Walks around like the Queen and expects to be waited on hand and foot. Really toffee-nosed. She looks at you as if she can't figure out why you even exist but to serve her. There's an evil mind in her head. She's a lousy tipper, too. Jumbo implants. Big ass. Flaky scalp."

My mouth drops open. I dread picturing any woman with Brian, but when I do, she's certainly not the type of woman I picture. Why would he be with someone like that? It doesn't make sense. "She's gotta be two-faced, Marty. She's gotta be putting on an act when she's with him. I can't imagine Brian would *talk* to someone like that let alone *date* someone like that. There's gotta be a reason why he's with her."

"Maybe it's great sex." Martin checks for my reaction.

My face is hot with jealousy, and I stare down at my bottle. "I don't want to even think that's the reason."

"Well, whatever it is, we'll discuss it later. They're here." And with that, Martin waves to Jeff, Ben and God's Little Git over my shoulder.

■ ■ ■

We've been at the club about an hour. Prissy, Ben and Jeff have wandered off somewhere. Either Prissy lost his bow and they're trying to track it down, or they've spotted that hunk Jeff swears looks like Will Smith, his idol. Martin and I are near the dance floor watching guys grind against each other to the loud music. A couple of (literally) tongue-tied babes are dancing so slowly and getting so gropey they should probably find a hotel room — or an alley — before the bouncer throws them out. If there's one thing these posh nightclub owners won't tolerate, it's blatant raunchiness. They run respectable establishments to attract prime clientele, not rent boys looking for a quickie. It's what distinguishes them from the sleazy gay bars.

To some, it may seem odd that Martin is here, but he's pretty sure if he went to a straight club, he'd meet a woman who blows Angina right out of the water and start up an affair without thinking twice. That's how bad their marriage is, and neither one wants to fix the stalemate status. The gay nightclubs are great for him. He gets to hang out with his friends, drink ale and listen to good music. Once in a while, when he's deep in his 'irie' mood, he'll dance — usually with Jeff (because, as he always says, Jeff oozes more reggae funk than the rest of us) — but just about anyone will do if he likes the song. And he's a really sexy dancer, so he's fun to watch. "You okay?"

I nod. "Yeah."

"You sure?"

"Hmm. It's good." I casually sweep the club. I see Strawberry Blond about fifteen feet away, and his presence surprises me. I've seen him at other nightclubs, but I didn't know he frequented this particular one. "It's a good crowd."

Martin looks around and swigs his ale. "There're a lot of good-looking guys here, Johnny. They all recognize you. You can take your pick, you know? You should talk to some of them." He looks at me for a response, but I just turn my eyes back to the dance floor. He's right, but I don't want to hear it, and he knows I don't want to hear it. "You need to meet guys. You need to meet *available* guys." He looks around us more discreetly. "They're all hovering at the shoreline, man, but no one is gonna dive in for the kill with me standing here. I'm gonna find Jeff, pry him off Will Smith, and see if he wants to dance, okay?"

"Okay."

I watch as Martin threads his way through the tight crowd. A lot of other guys watch him, too. Several follow him. He's tall, muscular and handsome, with an air of self-confidence I've always envied. He'll get several hits tonight like he always does, and they'll be crushed when he tells them he's not gay. I feel a lot of eyes on me, and while I'm usually pretty flattered by it—and comfortable with it—tonight, of all nights, I don't like the staring and the drooling. As I lose sight of Martin, I find myself wishing I were invisible. By the time I turn my gaze back to the dance floor, several guys have moved in closer. I sip my pint—and wait. Within a few minutes, Strawberry Blond approaches me with a shy smile. He's slender, about my age, and about my height. His name is Chris, and we awkwardly start talking. He has an easygoing personality and he could give anyone here a run for his money when it comes to attractiveness. He says he loves the series, thinks I'm hot, asks for my autograph and then asks someone to snap a picture of us with his phone. He buys me another bottle of ale and we talk for fifteen minutes or so about insignificant, mundane subjects. We drop into silence and gaze out at the dance floor for a while. Finally prepared for the pickup, he turns to me and leans in near my ear, trying to compete with the music. "So, John, I said it before, but I feel like I need to say it again: You're really hot. I mean, you're a super-sexy guy, you know? And damn! You're *so* good looking. Not just on your show, but right here—right now." He lowers his voice. "I'm feeling there's something pretty strong between us, something really intense going on. I'd like to get to know you a little better. Can we make that happen?"

I wait before answering, my eyes glued to the dance floor. A month ago, I wanted to hear something like that from him. A month ago, those words would have been perfect. I should be excited. My face should be flushed. There should be noticeable sexual tension between us and I should be flirting with him. Ultimately, I should be imagining us having wild sex. None of that is happening. All I hear is Brian's deep voice saying, "You're safe. I won't let you go." All I see are his pale eyes, the touch of gray in front of each ear, and (ironically) his toothpick. "I'm still with someone right now."

"I see. I understand."

We resume watching the men on the dance floor. Eventually, he moves in closer and stares down at my crotch for about ten long seconds. It makes me uncomfortable and I don't like the smell of his Armani Code. His eyes travel up to my face. "Mmm," he moans, trying to sound sexy. I'm sure he's just sprouted a hard-on, but I will not look down at his crotch. "You know, John, maybe when you're not with someone we could hook up."

I should give him a quick glance and a smile, but I still don't take my eyes off the dance floor. I want him to go away. "Yeah, maybe," is all he gets.

"Good." Undeterred, he digs in the back pocket of his tight jeans and pulls out a business card. "Look, here's my contact information. You take it and just see how it goes, okay?"

"Okay, I'll see how it goes." I look at the card and turn it over to find his cell phone number hand-written on the back. Jeez, he's got them ready to go in his pocket. Mister Prepared. I look up at him and flash my "Get lost, Bozo" smile, but he can't grasp the blatant hint. Since he won't leave, I will. "I'd better find my friends." I walk off without looking back.

■ ■ ■

Martin is flaunting a conspiratorial grin. "So?"

"So, what?"

"He seemed hot: good looks, nice body, decent ass."

"Yeah, he's nice." I look down at his card. "He's an antiques appraiser here in London; specializes in small firearms."

"Not bad, not bad. It sounds unique and artsy. He's wearing expensive clothes. I bet he makes some decent dosh. You gonna call him?"

I ignore the question. "He said I was really hot and super sexy."

"See? *See?* Johnny, look around you. Any of these guys—any one of them—would say the same thing. They'd kill to be with you. You're hot, man."

I roll my eyes. "God, you sound just like Mickey."

"You know what I mean."

"I know, but—"

"No 'buts!'" His serious tone and stern gaze startles me. "Stop fooling yourself. He's not interested in you. He's not into guys—period. Everyone here is. Everyone here wants you. These are the guys you need to meet. These are the guys who want to be with other guys."

"I know, but—"

"Look, has Brian ever said you were hot?"

"No."

"Has he ever said you were sexy or super sexy?"

"No."

"Has he ever said anything at all about the way you look?"

I lower my gaze. "No."

"Has he given you his phone number?"

I pep up. "I have it in my call log."

Martin gives me a pitying look. "Johnny…"

"All right, no. But he enjoys my company. He really likes to be with me. I can tell."

"Yeah, of course he does because that damned Scotsman thinks you're his bloody mate! That's all—just a really good mate, and nothing more. I'm sorry, man. He may be a grindsman, but he's a straight grindsman. He doesn't want to hug you, or kiss you… or screw you."

The words are thrown hard, and their impact stings. I drop my head and press into my temples. Martin steps closer and rubs my back. He's the only straight guy I know who has no problem showing simple honest affection to anyone when they really need it.

"Ease up, key. Talk to me. What's going on?"

I lift my head and pan the club as if seeing every lost soul clearly for the first time. "I understand what you're saying, but I don't want anyone here. I don't feel any attraction… to any of these guys. Not a single one. Nothing. I look at each one and all I do is compare him to Brian."

He sighs. "What is it about him? Why him?"

"I don't know. Believe me, if I did, I'd tell you. But I do know he's the right guy for me; he's the *only* guy for me." I try to put the way I feel into words: "I go through so many emotions when I'm with him. I'm nervous. I'm unsure of myself. I'm happy. I feel so incredibly safe with him, Marty. I think he excites me."

Martin carefully looks at me. "In what way?"

"In… that way."

He slits his eyes and stops rubbing my back. "Exactly how excited are we talking here?"

"Marty, I'd beg him for sex if I could." It's hard to admit because I have never wanted to beg *any* man for sex.

Martin takes a step back, holds his chin high and folds his arms across his chest. This is his reprimand pose: a superior stance he affects when one of us is just about to make an ass of himself or has just made an ass of himself. Prissy instigates this pose more often than any of us. "So, despite everything we said, you've fallen hard for this straight guy. Is that it?"

I nod with shame.

He scratches his head in frustration. "Well then, as the only one with a working brain in this pathetic lot, I've gotta think of a way to fix this shitty mess, don't I? Or you're gonna be one hell of a miserable and frustrated gay bastard."

"What are you going to do?"

"I don't know, but I'm sure it's gonna involve making a great big catastrophic mistake. I just don't know who's gonna make it—yet."

John — February 17

We're in the kitchen. I'm at the stove, cooking dinner as usual. He's leaning against the far wall, staring at me as usual. He hit the bottle early today (also, as usual), and I need to get food into his system to dampen his state of drunkenness. I'm counting the hours until he leaves for the photo shoot, and he has to be moderately sober to drag his sorry ass onto that plane.

"Where's the fucking meat?"

"Pardon?"

"Meat, Johnny. Meat! There's no goddamned meat!"

"I didn't have time to go to the store, so it's just vegetables and pasta. Sorry."

His sluggish brain is trying to figure out if I'm telling the truth. He'll either go ballistic or let it drop depending on how badly his head is pounding. After a minute, he decides to let it drop and instead turns to his favorite berating subject. "Have you put on weight?"

I grow tense. "No." He always harps about my weight when he runs out of everything else to criticize me about. It's his fallback option—one he knows will crush my self-esteem and self-worth. Thanks to his years of verbal abuse, the slightest hint of a love handle or belly fat poking over my waistband makes me feel unworthy of any man's affection.

"You sure? Your ass looks fat."

I close my eyes and bite my lip. "Yes, David. I'm sure."

"'Cuz I've told you before... I don't wanna be with a fat ass, you know?"

"I know."

"That just super disgusts me. It grosses me out t' see my guy with a big, ol' fat ass. It makes me not even wanna touch him."

"I know. I haven't gained any weight." I temper my simmering emotions and suffer through the next minute of silence, wondering what hurtful words he'll slap me with next.

"I'll miss your birthday, you know."

"That's okay. I'm sure Mickey will plan something."

"Oh, yeah! That's right! Good old Mickey will take care of it because he takes care of everything, doesn't he, Sweetie?"

I don't respond to his sarcasm.

And then the dreaded question: "Where's your phone?"

I don't want to turn around. I just keep stirring the vegetables. "Why?"

"I wanna look at it. Where *is* it?"

"David, I—"

"*Damn it!* Just...just give it t' me, okay... Sweetie? Davie's got a terrible headache and he doesn't wanna argue."

I turn, walk past him and go out to the entryway. I dig out my phone from my trench coat, come back and hand it to him. I go back to the stove. He's quiet (except for an occasional burp) as he checks up on my Internet site visits and scrolls through my call log and emails. He's been monitoring my cell phone activity for the last three years. At first, the invasion of privacy was only to see if I'd been hooking up with other men, but then he started checking my emails for casting call and audition announcements, paranoid I was getting notices that should have come to him. That pissed me off, so I retaliated by asking Mickey to only inform me of potential opportunities in person. It gave me a small sense of privacy and quashed the embarrassing nightmare of having him show up unannounced and uninvited at my auditions. But still, he hones in on the call log, desperate for accusation ammunition. "Who's this 'Brian M?'"

I'm determined to keep my voice even and calm. "I'm not sure."

"Okay. What's 'I'm not sure' doing on your phone?"

"I don't know. He might be someone Mickey knows. He used it the other day."

"You expect me to believe that?"

"It's the truth. Mickey used my phone when I picked him up from the airport." I reach over and check my boiling pasta.

"And he called this…this 'Brian M?'"

"I guess so. He called someone. I didn't pay attention."

"So, you didn't call him?"

"No."

"You're sure?"

"If I'd called a guy on my phone, wouldn't it be stupid of me to leave his name in my call log?"

His voice rises up a level because he's getting pissed. "Oh, because I check your phone? Are you trying t' tell me you've gotta problem with me checking your phone?"

"No, I'm just saying I could have deleted it if I'd made the call — if I'd wanted to keep it from you."

"Well, guess what? I'll delete it for you. Since you don't know him and you didn't call him, I'll just delete Mister Brian M. How's that?"

I muster as much boredom as I can. "Fine. I don't care." I don't care because I memorized Brian's number long ago.

Martin — February 18

"Marty, can you take one of Lewys's clients this morning? He called in sick, and she's already here," François says in his tired sing-song voice.

I have my back to him, checking my station for supplies and orderliness. "That's fine. I've got half an hour to kill."

"Excellent! Right this way, Miss Lexington. This is Marty. I know you're used to Lewys's technique, but Marty is an excellent stylist, has well-known clients and is in *very* high demand."

I turned the minute François said her name. Talk about sheer luck (or should I say shear luck!). Here she is: The whore of all whores, brushing him aside like the stench of sour milk and looking me up and down as if I was some brown repulsive thing that just backed up from the sewer into her loo. She does not like me, and now I have the pleasure of playing servant to this God-awful, ass wipe of a woman. She plops her hefty rear end in my chair with a 'fwump' before I can even ask her to sit down. I begin my routine: sheath around the neck (don't throttle her with it!), comb through the tresses (don't rip them from her scalp!), ask the client what style she's looking for (don't spit in her smug face!). "And what style were you looking for today, Ma'am?"

"What?" she snaps as if I'd just spewed Bantu Swahili in her face.

"I said, what style were—"

"I heard what you said. I *want* the style I always have. I want it perfect and I don't want small talk. Understood?"

"Of course, Ma'am." I have no idea what style she always has, and I'm too afraid to ask. All I know is I want her ass out of my chair as soon as possible. She is nasty! I grab my shears and combs and start snipping a little here and snipping a little there. I'm not accomplishing a damned thing but my actions are beyond impressive as I falsely attack her over-processed mane of straw. What I'd really like to do is give her a bowl cut. I just want to shear off about ten inches all the way around her fat skull and then stab out her putrid eyes. *Comb, snip, comb, snip.*

After ten minutes of glaring at me in the mirror she finally speaks. "Who's that?"

I jump at the sound of her cackling voice. "Who's who?"

She works her arm out from under the sheath and stabs a bony claw at Johnny's signed photo I have framed next to my mirror. *"Who is that?"*

I finally have a reason to smile. I have such a wicked mind, and it's come up with such a wicked idea. *"That* is John Kaiser — the American actor, star of *TruthFinder Murphy,* and the leading man in a musical that's opening tonight at The Skidmore. He comes in here all the time. He's my exclusive client." *Comb, snip, comb, snip.*

The near-sighted cow leans forward and squints hard, staring at the photograph. She's taking in every stunning feature: those dark blue eyes, the flawless skin, that mega-watt smile, and irresistible nose. She's seen him before and she is *not* pleased. Apparently, he's just backed up from the sewer, too. Her voice becomes sinister. "I've heard of him."

Oh, I know she's heard of him. I'm sure she knows all about Brian's gay crush comment, because as a gold digger she's scoured every source and memorized every bit of information she could get her grubby hands on. "He's really good looking, isn't he?" *Comb, snip, comb, snip.*

She unwillingly agrees. "He's okay." She *has* to agree. The bitch knows he's hot.

Comb, snip, comb, snip. And now, I set my ingenious trap. "He's been coming in a lot these past few weeks. He's got his eye on some- one special and *really* wants to look his best." *Comb, snip, comb, snip.*

She's glaring at me in the mirror again, wishing me deader than feathered mullets, but needing me alive — for the moment. "Do you know who?"

Ah, I've snared her! The hideous barracuda ravenously gulps down my poisoned bait! "I don't remember his name; a rich guy, a lit- tle older. He's got a penthouse on the river and a killer Rolls." I pause for effect and cock my head as I gaze at her reflection, eager to deliver my next three action-packed words: "Scottish, I think."

Her eyes become saucers as she works herself up into a small frenzy, something resembling a dangerously overfilled, helium bal- loon. *"That's* Brian Mallory, and he's *my* man," she says with powerful vehemence. "He's *not* gay."

Comb, snip, comb, snip. I shrug my shoulders, confident I've accom- plished my simple goal. "Well, I don't know anything. I just cut hair and listen to my clients' wishes." I remove the sheath and make an ex- aggerated effort to clean off any little clippings with my fan brush, wanting so desperately to whack her face with it.

"Well, let me tell you something, Marty." She snatches the brush out of my hand and seethes at my reflection with dagger eyes as her voice takes on a threatening tone. "Here's *my* wish: I want you to tell your little gay boy to stick to his own kind. Brian Mallory is one hundred percent *straight*, and Brian Mallory is one hundred percent *mine*. I've got him under my thumb and kissing the ground I walk on. So tell that damned faggot to *sod off!*"

She stands up, throws my fan brush to the floor, turns on her heel and stomps her fat ass out the door. No thank you, no payment, no tip. François's mouth is gaping as he watches her leave, but I'm grinning from ear to ear. Thanks to me, that evil bitch is paranoid, and because she's paranoid, she's going to mess up. And when she does, she's going to mess up good. I think I've just created the monster who's going to make that great big catastrophic mistake.

John

It's nine-thirty in the morning, raining as usual, and we're at Heathrow's terminal five. David's flight—first to New York, then Dallas, and on to Hawaii—is delayed because of a late connector. I've met Lars and the five models he'll be working with. They all seem competent and professional. They're excited to be trading in the never-ending rain and gray, foggy days of London for the tropical sunshine and warmth of Hawaii.

David, Mickey and I are standing off to the side, away from the others for a last minute chat. I watch as Mickey continuously glances over at Lars. Knowing him so well and having seen the signs before, it's obvious he's attracted to him. It's also obvious one of the models is Lars' boyfriend. Poor Mickey. He'd do a lot better if he set his sights on a guy who was available. Within seconds, I realize how stupid that thought is coming from me. I'm in no position to judge anyone.

"So," David murmurs from behind his sunglasses, "you gonna be okay with me getting up close and personal with those hot guys, Sweetie?" He has a massive hangover and talking must be painful for him.

I glance over at the models: handsome, young, bright-eyed, and gay as hell. God, if any of them wanted to take on this shitload of pathetic, self-pitying baggage I'd slap a great big bow on it and drag it, pull it, shove it across the concourse lounge with every last ounce of strength I had. "I trust you... completely."

Mickey reluctantly peels his eyes off Lars. "Okay now, David, remember you'll be shooting every day. Lars has to get in as much material as he can, so this is serious stuff. You have to be... to be..."

"Sober? Is that what you're trying to say? 'Cuz I can be sober... *if* I'm working."

"Good! That's good. You know you're a looker, David. You know you're hot. You saw the way the other models checked you out when we got here. You're their competition. You're the one they've got to measure up to. They're worried. They see your confidence. I see your confidence."

David is smiling and nodding in agreement. Mickey can really talk him up onto a pedestal when push comes to shove. I haven't the heart to tell him the full-blown alcoholic he's praising slammed two shots of whiskey this morning just to quell his body tremors. I know David is going to drink. My only hope is that with five other models and a busy schedule, he doesn't find enough 'alone time' to get piss-pants bombed. I pray he lasts the full four weeks, but I have serious doubts.

11

High Definition And A Very Dim Spotlight

John — February 18

Opening night of this musical is so important. *Drawbridge Down* was significant, too. We had great reviews throughout the run and landed two additional engagements early next year in Paris and Munich. But tonight's sold-out performance at The Skidmore is being scrutinized heavily by the press. They're expecting a lot from the show, and they're expecting a lot from me. I've got top billing. My name is on the marquee above the director's name, the producer's name and the title. To say I'm a bit nervous is a gross understatement. And unlike The Altinda, The Skidmore Theater is state of the art. It seats sixty-five hundred people on eight different levels. The stage is vast and the sets have hydraulics and motorized special effects, all controlled by computers. Half the props have computer chips in them. The Skidmore also has five high-definition video monitors. Everything is going to stand out in fine detail so everyone has to look perfect. Every time we go out on that stage, we're going to be checked and double-checked by makeup and wardrobe. No parsley between the teeth, no wax in the ears, and no weird stuff in the nostrils. If I can pull this off with a flawless performance, if I can live up to the name out there on the marquee, my theatrical career will skyrocket to the next level. And even though I'm still in a major funk over Brian, I'm in a positive mood about tonight, and I'm so glad David isn't here to spoil it.

• • •

"Johnny, that number was brilliant! Right on the money—just like Pauley wanted. He's gotta be pleased with that one," Mickey raves as I come off the stage, panting pretty hard.

"Mickey, this thing keeps poking me in the back. Can we get a piece of tape or something? It's rubbing me raw." I try to reach behind me to the mike packet stuck on the inside of my shirt as several makeup artists swarm over me to touch up my face.

"Sure, Johnny. Hang on." He runs off to find tape as I stand still for the makeup application. Wardrobe would sort out the mike packet, but when Mickey is around, he won't let them near me. He does it himself. Within a minute, he's back with a roll of tape. "Yes, sir. This opening night is really one of the best, huh? Packed house, lots of famous people out there." He lifts my shirt and fumbles with the packet. The makeup artists give me one final check and then scurry off to another performer. "Even Brian came."

"What?"

"Yeah, just showed up outta the blue five minutes before the curtain went up. That's a big deal, you know. If the press keeps seeing him at social events like this, he'll lose that reputation of his in no time. Hold still, Johnny." I twist around to peek through the curtains. I can't see a damned thing—too many faces and the theater is too dark. "And sitting out there with Carol. Well, that can only—"

"He brought *her?*"

"Well, of course. He's not gonna come to something like this alone, is he? He's gonna want a beautiful woman on his arm, right? I bet she got the tickets. I tell you, she's working on him hard, and he's right there lapping it up. She's gotta be something special, huh? I can't wait to meet her." Mickey lowers my shirt and gives the mike packet a pat. "There you go. You're all set. How does that feel?"

To be honest, right now it all pretty much feels like thick shit. "Fine, Mickey. Thanks."

"Now look, you're on a roll, right? You're hot tonight, Johnny. That crowd out there can't get enough of you, so you just keep doing what you're doing." He takes a good look at me and combs his fingers through my hair. "And remember, on that last number, that's when you really gotta blow them away, yeah? That's when you show them why you're the best. Pauley wants tears. He wants real tears just streaming down your face. We got some at rehearsal, but tonight I want you to think of something really sad, okay? I wanna see that beautiful face just dripping with tears. Remember, we've got the big monitors. That's what everyone's gonna be looking at. That's what I want them to see—your precious face just devastated and full of tears, right?"

All I can do is nod. With the way I'm feeling right now, I can guarantee Mickey is going to get a lot of tears. I can't believe this is happening to me. I can't believe he's out there with her—tonight. Once again, I feel sick. I still have the entire second half to get through and all I want to do is crawl into a hole, puke up my entrails, and die.

"Okay, Johnny. Your cue is coming up."

I watch in a daze as a dozen dancers pass by and run onto the stage. I don't want to do this. I don't even know if I *can* do this. I close my eyes and breathe in deeply. I turn my chin to the rafters and expand my diaphragm. I have to get through this. I have to go out there and be everything Mickey says I am. This is so important. My career is on the line. I can fall apart later. I can't fall apart now. I exhale as I lower my chin to stretch my spine. I open my eyes. I stand still, with my head cleared and my mind focused on nothing but the rest of my performance. I hear my cue and confidently step out onto the big stage.

■ ■ ■

The last number comes as an emotional release. It's a slow ballad—a quiet love song. I'm standing on the dark stage, alone, with one very dim spotlight on my face. As I begin to sing of the grief my character feels over never having won the affections of his true love, the love he pined for all those long years, I see them sitting there; dead center, five rows back from the orchestra pit. They're perfect seats, right in front of my devastated face. His arm is around her shoulders. My heavy heart just sinks in my chest and a burning heat envelopes my body. I watch as this beautiful woman reaches up to stroke his cheek the way I wish I could. I watch as she nuzzles his neck the way I've nuzzled his neck in my dreams. And then I watch as she leans over and tenderly kisses his jaw. And as I stare, mesmerized by this simple display of sensual affection, I begin to realize the awful truth: I've fallen hopelessly in love

with a straight man named Brian Mallory who will never love someone like me.

I sing my song to him from deep within my soul. I sing it with raw
passion and heart-wrenching pain. I sing it with that terrible despair
you feel when what you crave—what you desire more than life, itself—is unobtainable. Just as Mickey wanted, impressive tears cascade
down my face, yet my voice is strong and clear, and my eyes rarely
blink. The five-minute standing ovation and the four curtain calls that
follow are truly bittersweet. Every member of the cast and crew thinks
I'm crying tears of joy because the performance went so well. None of
them knows the painful truth. Afterward, I sit in my dressing room,
tired, emotionally empty, and numb to the world as dozens of people
stream in and out, bringing champagne, flowers, candy and unbelievable first reviews. They're the best reviews I've ever had on an opening
night and not a single pan from any critic, not even the homophobic
ones. I smile a little every time the door opens, holding out hope he'll
come backstage to see me—to congratulate me—but he never does.

When everyone leaves for the party, including Mickey, I lock the
door. I stare at my tear-stained, makeup-caked reflection in the mirror
and cry like I've never cried before. I feel so many emotions all at once:
anger, confusion, frustration, immense jealousy and hopelessness. I've
never ached like this, and I don't understand what's happening to me.
Through my tears, I look down at the powders, makeup bottles, con-
cealers and dozens of other tools of my trade covering the dressing table. I can't get the vision of them—sitting out there together, caressing
each other—out of my mind. They're probably having a quiet dinner
now, and then they'll go back to his penthouse and make love—wild,
passionate, heterosexual love—on his big bed. My emotions become
too much to bear and I erupt like a volcano. With one powerful sweep
of my arm, everything crashes to the floor. Some of the larger glass
bottles break, and I just sit and watch as creamy foundation oozes out.
Still crying, I stand up and hurl my costume rack to the floor. I kick at
the flamboyant clothes with a violence I've never experienced before;
the sequins, buttons and rhinestones fly across the room. I pick up a
pillow from the small sofa and rip it to shreds with my bare hands. The
damned pillow is me—and I hate who I am. I despise my disgusting

self. I grab another and another and yet another. I tear until I'm red-faced and sweaty, and some of my fingers are bleeding from where my nails have pulled away from the flesh. Then, in a state of pure exhaustion, I just collapse onto my knees. I bend forward and stay there—on my knees with my head on the floor and my butt in the air—a wretched mess stuck in a pile of spilled makeup, shredded pillows, and crumpled costumes, crying uncontrollably and still bitterly in love with him.

I finally make it to the party, but only after I've cleaned myself up and nearly downed an entire bottle of cheap, warm champagne. I last precisely one hour, act like an egotistical asshole in front of every member of the press (which, not surprisingly, is exactly what they expect from me), and throw up horrendously in the men's restroom. Then I crawl into the back of a taxi. At home, I just slide to the floor behind the front door and cry myself to sleep in the dark entryway, still wearing my tuxedo and my trench coat, and still remembering how softly that beautiful woman kissed him in the fifth row, dead center, behind the orchestra pit.

Brian — February 24

"He's in the lobby?"

Charles tops off my scotch. "Yes, sir. He'd like to know if he may come up."

It's a surprise, but it's a nice surprise. Without any meetings or other commitments, I'd planned to get in some reading and have an early night, but I enjoy his company. He's a pleasant distraction. I haven't seen him since the musical's opening night and that was only from across an orchestra pit. It'll be interesting to hear what he's been up to these past couple of weeks. "Sure he can, Charles."

"Good, sir. And will you need anything else tonight?"

"No. Thank you, and goodnight."

"Goodnight, sir."

I lay my book on the table next to my scotch and stand up. I'm a bit agitated, and I don't know why. I pace the floor a few times, not knowing what to do with myself. I run my fingers through my hair and look down at my clothes: faded jeans with a tear in the knee, a wrinkled blue dress shirt and brown socks on my big feet. Not even close to a fashion statement, but I could look worse. My mobile buzzes and I pick it up to look at the caller ID. Hallelujah, glory be, and joy of all joys — it's my ex-wife.

"Yup," I say into the phone as the front door opens. "Everything is fine." I smile at John and beckon him to come in as I prepare for the familiar dialogue Moyra and I are about to have. "I don't know. He still has to sort out getting a crane on the river and watch the weather forecasts." I motion John to have a seat as I go to the bar and take down a glass. "Look, he's your man. You picked him, Moyra. If he's not moving fast enough for you, then find someone else." I cradle the mobile with my shoulder while I open a bottle of red wine and pour it into the glass. "It doesn't matter to me. I'd have had it shipped out months ago if I could have." I walk over and hand the glass to John. "Fine. I'll let you know how it goes." I end the call and stare at the mobile for a minute.

"Ex-wife," I explain as John looks up at me. "Wants her piano — now. She hired a dolt who can't get his act together and then gets on my case about it." I smile down at him. Oddly, he doesn't smile back. He's not happy and that makes me uneasy. I feel uncentered. His scent is off, too. There's something different about it — something sad. "How are you, John?"

"I'm fine. Did I come at a bad time?"

"Not at all." I move to sit across from him with the big glass table between us.

"I was nervous about just showing up. You probably had plans."

I pick up my glass and gesture with it toward the book. "I was going to have a read. That's all."

He starts to stand up. "I could leave."

"You're fine, John. Please, sit."

He sits down again, sips his wine, and takes a closer look at the book. There's a puzzled look on his face. "What's the title?"

"*Brenin Gwych y Nos.* It's Welsh."

He's genuinely surprised. "You read Welsh?"

I nod.

"What's it about?"

I sip my scotch. "Well, so far, it's about a Celtic warrior in sixteenth century Wales who decides to enlist an army of country farmers to conquer a tyrannical king."

John sips his wine. "Does he conquer the king?"

"Aye, he does."

"And then what happens?"

"I don't know. I've only just started the book."

"Oh." He sits back and takes another sip of wine.

He sounds distressed tonight. He hasn't smiled since he walked through the door, and he's fidgeting in his chair. His mind seems —

"Why didn't you tell me you were coming to opening night?" he suddenly blurts out.

I'm caught off guard by the abrupt change in subject and the tone of his voice. I'm not sure what to say.

He continues, his face turning red as he speaks. "Mickey told me you were in the audience when I was offstage during one of the numbers."

I scramble for words. "You know, John, it was a last-minute thing. I didn't even know it was opening night. Carol suggested we go. I still don't know how she got those tickets so late." He winces when I mention Carol's name. I flash back to the awkward phone conversation I had with Mickey when he came back from Los Angeles.

"Carol. That's the blonde woman you're seeing?"

"Aye."

His cheeks are flushed. "I saw you. At the end, I saw you in the audience. Why didn't you come backstage after the show? Why didn't you come back to see me?"

Again, I'm scrambling for words. "We had late dinner reservations right after the show. There really wasn't time." He's obviously upset about this, and I can't understand why, but I want to appease him. "John, I'm so sorry. I really wasn't thinking. I should have come backstage. I should have told you how great the show was. It really was excellent. I thought *you* were fantastic." I take a large sip of scotch, hoping for the buzz I really need right now because I am definitely uncomfortable. "And...and I should have introduced you to Carol. She would have enjoyed meeting—"

He cuts me off. "She didn't want to meet me."

"What? I'm sure she would have—"

"No. She wouldn't."

"John, I'm sure she—"

"*No!*" he barks. Then he falls silent, eyes blinking rapidly, taken aback (just as I am) by his own outburst. He continues on more quietly. "She only brought you there because she wanted me to see you together."

"What? I don't—"

"She wanted to prove to me you're straight, Brian—that you're not gay, that there's no way you'd ever—" He stops, looks down at the floor, and gulps his wine.

I'm confused. I don't know what to say at this point. And it doesn't matter anyway, because he keeps cutting me off every time I open my mouth. I can't figure out what the hell he's talking about. Why would anyone, especially Carol, want to prove to *him* that I'm straight? He knows I'm straight. And even if she did want to, why would he care? Why would John care if I—Oh, dear mother of every god that ever lived! Don't tell me he fancies me! No! This bloke *cannot* fancy me! "Look, John, you know I'm straight. Carol has no reason to—"

"Are you dating her seriously?"

If Mickey had just posed that question, I'd tell him it was none of his business. John is different, though—especially tonight. He's overly sensitive, his emotions are running high and I'm not sure what's going to upset him. The last thing I need as I'm trying to enjoy a calm, relaxing evening is an hysterical bloke in my flat. "I've gone out with her a few times. I enjoy her company."

He sips his wine, deep in thought, his eyes transfixed on some invisible spot on the floor to the left of my chair. "Where did you go after dinner?"

"To The Harding Hotel."

"Why?"

Now this question I *really* shouldn't answer. It's none of his business and he knows it. He looks up with a hard-set jaw, daring me to answer him. I slouch down lower in my chair, trying to get comfortable. I stretch out my legs under the table and cross my ankles. I put my elbow on the low armrest and plant my chin in my open palm. I study his face, trying to understand his stubbornness and his intense emotions. I'm not used to being challenged and I'm not used to having my personal life invaded. No one has dared to do that before him. "To have sex, John. I went to The Harding with Carol just to have sex."

Again, he finds that spot on the floor. His eyelids quickly blink over his deep blue eyes. "Why didn't you bring her here?"

"Here?"

He looks up. "Yes, here. If you like her enough to have sex with her, why not bring her here? Why go to a hotel? Why not have sex here, in your flat, in your bed?"

His face has turned a deeper shade of red but he's obstinate, and he's determined to keep prying, and I'm determined he's not going to rattle me. It's a battle of wills. "It's casual sex. It's just two people having casual, meaningless sex. We're not exclusive, there's no commitment, and I don't want to deal with trying to get her ass out of here in the morning."

He opens his mouth and then slowly closes it, obviously shocked by my exploits. Then he says, "But what do you say?"

"I beg your pardon?"

"What do you say when you're having sex, if it's just casual?"

I smile. I almost want to laugh at his apparent innocence. "Well, I'm not a bloody speech writer, John, and I don't recite Keats or Shelley. I don't say much of anything. I usually just let my actions speak for themselves—and grunt. It's not very sophisticated, but that's my style."

"But surely you want to…to say things, to say passionate things and say what you're feeling right at the moment… and be open and vulnerable and talk about love."

My God! Is he for *real?* "John, I just want sex. It's a release for me. It relieves tension and helps me unwind after a long day, like jogging or lifting weights. It's never about saying passionate things, and it's certainly *never* about love. I wouldn't know love if I fell over it."

"So it's just hot, steamy sex—with a woman, any woman. That's all you're looking for?" His words are delivered with obvious anger and prudish disapproval.

"I can't even say it's hot and steamy. It's just basic, boring sex in a nice hotel room with a woman I'll be able to tolerate for a few hours. Then I leave. I come home—alone." I sip my scotch and watch his face. He's still shocked. Apparently, for the last few weeks he's had me stuck up on a damned pedestal as London's Most Virtuous Gentleman, which is silly considering I told him I was an asshole and a bastard.

"I couldn't do that. I could never do that."

"You mean to tell me you've *never* had casual sex?" I'm really surprised when he shakes his head.

"It's too important. It's everything. You're baring your soul to someone. You're letting them see every weakness, every flaw. You're telling them all your thoughts and all your fears. You reveal your innermost feelings...." His voice trails off as he stares at me with intense eyes. He's obviously someone who believes in true, undying love and everything that goes along with it. Unfortunately, I'm not and I don't, so I can't relate to him.

"It's not important to me. It's never been important to me."

The sliders are open for the evening breeze. Outside, there's lively activity down on the Thames. It's a passing barge, one of those dinner and dance cruises where some pissed bugger always falls overboard and drowns. They usually spy his body five days later, floating past a sightseeing barge. Tourists are always happy when they can take snapshots of Big Ben, Tower Bridge *and* a bloated, rotting carcass—great vacation memories. Inside, the flat is silent as we sit for a long time without talking—nearly half an hour. John is sipping his wine, staring at the floor. I'm sipping my scotch, staring at him, studying him. He's upset, and I don't know how to deal with it. It's a side of him I've never seen—a highly emotional side. I'm not used to emotional people. They make me uncomfortable, unbalanced. I avoid them at all costs. They're too unpredictable, too volatile and *way* too needy. I finally break the silence. "What are you thinking about?"

"Nothing."

"Are you angry, John?"

He shakes his head and whispers, "Right now, I don't really know what I am."

"Hey, look at me." He looks up and his eyes are glistening with tears. Jesus. Now this bloke is going to cry. It's another thing that catches me off guard. In my stoic world, crying has always been unacceptable—especially for men. It doesn't serve a useful purpose, and worse, it shows weakness.

"Brian, I could…. I could try to be like—"

I know where this is going and I quickly cut him off. I have no intention of letting a crying bloke embarrass himself further by telling me he'll try to act like a woman to gain my affection. It's just absurd and demeaning. "You're a very nice, highly talented young man, John. You really are. I'm amazed by your abilities and your drive." My words sound awkward and stupid. They sound trite.

He closes his eyes and shakes his head as the tears stream down his face. His lower lip starts to tremble, and he swallows hard.

I feel so bad this kind, sensitive bloke has to sit here and listen to a rotten bastard like me feed him a lame rejection, but I don't know what else to do. "I'm not attracted to men—not in the slightest way. They do nothing for me, psychologically or physically. If I have said or done anything to make you think otherwise, I sincerely apologize. It wasn't my intention to mislead. I'm very sorry, John, but I'm not gay." The words come out much harsher than I'd wanted them to.

He stands up, wipes his wet face with the back of his hand and places his wine glass on the table. "I know. I just really wish you were."

I stare at his empty glass as he walks to the door and leaves the flat. An hour later, not understanding what just happened, I'm still staring at it. God, I feel like an absolute shithead.

Brian — February 25

I am so bloody tired. I was up all night trying to figure out what to do about John and canceled two meetings this morning because of him. The ordeal shouldn't have me this rattled but I can't concentrate on business matters so I'm in the limo parked one block up from Shave. It's a busy styling salon with dozens of people coming and going. It's connected to an upstairs day spa, organic café and yoga studio as well. Whoever came up with that concept in this area was smart. They've got to be pulling in a tidy profit if their overhead is reasonable. Jack opens the door. I step out and put on my sunglasses. "Jack, I shouldn't be too long—maybe thirty-five or forty minutes at the most."

"Yes, sir."

I walk to the open door and step inside. There's a lot of activity going on in here with styling stations and hair-washing sinks in every available space. The owner should think about expanding into the vacant building next door and putting in better ventilation. I take off my sunglasses. The front counter stands abandoned. The music is loud, thumping hip-hop, which seems odd because the customers are in their thirties and forties. Maybe it's the kind of music salons are required to blast as those approaching middle age desperately claw at beauty regimens engineered to puff up their fading youth and thin their Louis Vuitton wallets. I have no idea what Martin looks like from John's description so I'm relying on him to recognize me.

It's amazing how, in a crowded place with numerous bodies moving about, your eye zeroes in on that one particular person who's standing completely still. That's how I find Martin. I'm looking at his reflection in the mirrored wall backing the front counter. He's behind me, about ten meters back, with shears in mid-snip in one hand, a lock of hair waiting to be cut in the other, and he's just staring at me. I take a seat, cross my leg, and open one of the tattered magazines. Luckily, I find the subject matter—yachts—mildly interesting. A frazzled, old impy thing darts around a far corner, scurries behind the counter, and leans out over it. His nasty cheap cologne (which still isn't strong enough to hide the fact he's just smoked a clove cigarette) initiates a gag reflex in my throat and causes my eyes to tear a bit. "I'm so sorry I wasn't here to greet you." He's out of breath as he dramatically fans himself with bejeweled fingers on a dainty hand. "I'm François. Do you have an appointment, sir?"

"That's okay. No, I don't. I just need to chat with Martin for a few minutes."

He looks over at Martin who gives a small gesture with his shears and smiles. "He's just finishing up. May I get you something cool and refreshing to drink? Today's special is the Good Morning, Please Murder Me Mango Margarita. It's very popular and quite fruity."

"Uh.... No, thank you. I'm fine." I turn back to the magazine and wait.

■ ■ ■

Martin is scrutinizing my reflection as I sit in his chair under a floral smock so hideously embarrassing he knows he has me at a disadvantage. The bright pink cape of shiny plastic has emasculated me. He, in effect, has hold of my balls. He's not like John's other friends; he's cautious and analytical, and he doesn't trust me—yet. He must be the protector. Ignoring all the other smells in here, his scent is... refreshing. It's clean, honest, and goes with his enviable dreadlocks. He's combing his fingers through my hair and massaging my scalp. It feels pretty damn fantastic. If I didn't have so much on my mind, and if the music wasn't so loud, I could fall asleep right now. Beside the mirror, there's a photograph of John smiling back at us. I keep my eyes off it. Right now, I need to focus solely on Martin.

"You know, staring at me like that isn't going to change the way he feels about you."

His first words aren't what I expected but they fit his scent and they set the tone. "I just don't understand why. Why does he...?"

"Think you leap out of bed every morning, throw on a cape, strap a bazooka over your shoulder and climb the highest mountain to shoot the damned sun into the sky? I don't know why. *He* doesn't know why. The fact is: He does."

"But I haven't done anything."

"Obviously, you have. You just don't know what it is." He reaches for his shears and comb. "From listening to Johnny, just seeing you blink turns him on."

I watch as he trims at my neckline. "But he's got a boyfriend."

He stares at my reflection, shears in mid-snip. "David the Dole Boy? Mister I-Get-So-Ratted-I-Piss-My-Pants? Do you honestly think he enjoys calling *that* a boyfriend?"

"So maybe he doesn't like me at all. Maybe he's looking for an escape... from David. Maybe he just needs to meet someone who's available."

Martin snorts, shakes his head and continues trimming. "Yeah, sure. And maybe if I plug my nose and blow really hard, I'll sprout flowers outta my ass." He finishes my trim and lays down his shears. He crosses his arms and looks hard at me. "He's got hundreds of sexy, available guys who'd give anything—and I mean *anything* you can imagine—to take his mind off David, and all he wants is you."

For a millisecond, I'm flattered by his words. That millisecond passes, and I swallow hard. "Well then, I've got a problem."

"You've got a big problem, Brian. It's one hundred percent gay, it's madly in love with you and it's called Johnny. What are you gonna do about it?"

"I don't know, but I cannot have him fancy me."

"Then stop seeing him." He picks up a brush and begins dusting me off.

"He just shows up."

"Then don't let him in."

"That's rude. Besides, I like his company. He's pleasant and easy to talk to."

Martin shakes his head. "You can't have the penny and the bun. It's not fair to him. For you, it's no big deal. You chum around with him during the day and wine and dine your bird at night. You're chuffed, man—all fruit's ripe. Johnny goes home to a stinking, self-centered lush." Martin leans in closely and speaks quietly. "He's an emotional wreck, Brian. He dreams about you. It's really hurting him. It's messing up his head and making him question a lot of things about himself, about his life—things that were fine before you came along. Just leave him alone, okay? Just don't see him." He takes off the smock, hands back my balls, and I stand up. As imposing as my height is to some, Martin isn't intimidated. "Look, I'll talk to him. I'll tell him to stop coming to your penthouse, but you need to do your part, too. If he does show up, don't let him in. He acts all innocent and harmless, but he's super manipulative. He's cunning. Believe me, I know him. If he really wants something, he'll do whatever it takes to get it. He'll work you over and you won't even realize it until it's too late. And avoid him in public, too."

We walk to the front of the salon. "Well, that won't be too hard. We don't exactly run in the same circles."

"Yeah, well.... Your bird might try something."

I place a hundred pound note on the counter in front of François. "Carol?"

"I don't trust her."

I shake my head at François as he tries to hand me change. "I take offense to that. She's a good person. Why would she do something?"

Martin levels his gaze. "She's not as nicey-nicey as you think, Brian."

"What's that supposed to mean?"

"Just keep an eye on her, okay? You watch her moves, and I'll watch Johnny's."

Carol

"Carol! I'm so pleased to finally meet you! Of course, I caught a glimpse of you at The Skidmore, but I was wondering when Brian would properly introduce us."

So this is Mickey: short, loud, hairy, and gay. Nice package — a real charmer. What an honor it is to meet such a distasteful muff. Well, if he's one of Brian's good friends, I'm going to coat him with honey. Right now, I have a keen interest in making any friend of Brian's my dearest and closest chum. I can always tell this joker to pound sand once I have that ring on my finger and my butt in that grand mansion. "Mickey, I've heard so much about you." I grab his outstretched freckled hand and offer him my cheek. "I was beginning to wonder if you really existed." I wink at Brian, who is the only reason I will suffer through this God-forsaken lunch.

On a positive note, it's a good sign he's introducing me to his friends. It tells me our relationship has advanced beyond late-night dinner and hotel sex to something more serious. Soon, the press should be calling us "an item" and I should officially be his girlfriend. I must have patience. It's going to be a hard job dragging this one to the altar. With his countless business meetings, the fact that I *still* haven't been invited to his penthouse and that damned faggot that has me on edge, it's been frustrating. But in the end, it will be worth it. It will be four hundred million pounds worth it.

The lunch is just as nightmarish as I imagined it would be with Mickey jabbering on about the most mundane subjects. He has no clue he's a boring loudmouth. If he weren't so obviously gay, I'd introduce him to Patricia. I'm the perfect audience, "ohhing" and "ahhing" at every word, asking appropriate questions and laughing at his feeble jokes. All the while, I'm stroking Brian's leg under the table and sneaking flirtatious glances at him. It's important he knows I can be a prim and proper lady above the table and a sex kitten below it. We'll get a room tonight, and the anticipation of sex is enough to keep a fake smile on my face as I beam at this disgusting, redheaded troll. Halfway into the meal, Brian excuses himself to spend a penny, and I'm left alone with the motor mouth. Since he's determined to talk, I need to get him on a subject that requires the least input from me. "So, Mickey, tell me all about LA."

"Well, Carol. The thing about LA is you never want to let your guard down because—" His mobile rings. "Oh, I beg your pardon. Excuse me, just one moment." He pulls it out and proceeds to yell into it. "Yes? Did you get them? Fabulous! Thank you, Julia, from the bottom of my heart! You're a doll, an absolute doll! Yes, yes—I'll pick them up at will call! Got it! Love you and kisses, too! Bye! I'm so sorry about that, but I've been trying to get opening night tickets to *Madame Butterfly* for Johnny's birthday and that was a friend who finally came through for me."

"Oh, how *wonderful*. And who is Johnny?" I gush the words with fake enthusiasm, expecting him to tell me all about his fat, trolly little boyfriend.

"Oh, I'm so sorry. He's John Kaiser. Maybe you've heard of him?"

I feel my face drain of color and I'm hardly able to keep my fake smile from turning into a wicked sneer. "Yes. Oh yes, I've heard of him." God! Just the sound of his disgusting name makes my heart palpitate and gets me so angry I want to scream my head off. If this faggot is so insignificant (according to Patricia), then why does he keep popping up, and how the *hell* do I get rid of him?

"I'm his manager, and I forgot to plan a party for his birthday this year. I blame all these trips to LA. My schedule has been so chaotic it just slipped my mind. But he loves *Madame Butterfly* and opening night is on his birthday. Well, you can't beat that, can you?"

As I start to answer, my cunning brain cranks out a devious plan. "No.... No, you can't beat that. Maybe I'll get tickets too and surprise Brian."

"Oh, my God! That would be *fabulous,* Carol! What a treat! Now remember, it's an early show. We could —"

"Oh, here he comes, Mickey. Let's keep the whole thing our little secret, okay? We'll make it a *big* surprise." I give him a wink.

"So what did I miss?" Brian asks as he sits down.

"Well, Mickey was telling me all about LA." And while Mickey regales us, nonstop, with his insufferable monologue on the sights and sounds of Los Angeles, I sit back and sip my wine, confident this lunch date was *not* a waste of time. I'll have the perfect opportunity to finally put that meddling faggot in his place — in person and on his birthday. That ought to be a present he'll remember for a long time. I'll show him what he's up against, and I'll do whatever it takes to make him feel embarrassed, miserable and inadequate. He will not ruin this for me. I've sunk too much time and money into this game just to stand back and let a queer walk off with my hard-earned prize. I'll get two opening-night tickets to that stupid show, even if I have to spend every last quid of this month's maintenance to do it. By the time Madame Butterfly kills herself, that insignificant gay boy will have no doubt Brian Mallory — the handsome and straight multi-millionaire — is all mine.

12
How Stupid Can You Be?

John — March 2

It's my birthday. I always have a big party on my birthday and spend a long night out on the town with dozens of friends. Mickey arranges it. He does it because he cares, but he also does it to make sure the paparazzi show up at the right place, the right time, and get the right shots. His mind is always on publicity and promotion. This year, Mickey forgot my birthday. It's understandable. He's been juggling new clients, and he's had more work going on in the states. He's flown to LA numerous times to—what does he like to say?—smooth some ruffled feathers. Of course, he's embarrassed because *Madame Butterfly* was the best he could do on such short notice (I'm sure someone gave him free tickets), but it's one of my favorite operas, it's opening night, and the seats are excellent. I'm not in the mood for a party, anyway. I've been on such an emotional roller coaster this past month; just sitting in a dark theater for a few hours will give my confused and tortured mind a rest.

• • •

I love when the show lets out for intermission and everyone is milling around. I usually run into two or three people I know—and several I don't—who want to get my autograph, snap a picture with me, and tell me how much they love the series. Tonight, Mickey and I have struck up a conversation with one of his former clients and her husband. She's an amazing actress who walked away from a lucrative career to fight a serious bout of breast cancer. She's asking Mickey what he thinks her chances are of a comeback. "Absolutely positive, Marisa!

You left the stage as a phenomenal star! The public will welcome you back with open arms. They've been *waiting* for you, Sweetheart!"

Excited by his words, she squeezes her husband's hand.

"The key is to put you in the right setting. We've got to package you perfectly! The first role we find has to be heroic—and I mean 'Joan of Arc' *heroic!* It's got to project *you!* Give me your number, darling. We'll talk, okay?"

I feel a light tug on my tux, followed by a timid voice. "Excuse me."

I turn to face two excited young girls, one holding a camera. "I just *knew* it was you! I *knew* it! See, I told you it was him! It's really *him!* May we snap a picture with you? We think you're *ever* so smashing in *TruthFinder Murphy!* We watch every episode," the older one gushes with wide eyes as the younger one giggles.

"Now, now girls, he may not be too keen. We could be interrupting his evening. Even big stars have private lives," a plump, flush-faced woman (who's obviously their harried mother) admonishes.

I flash them the killer smile that's paid the bills for the last ten years. "No, it's not a problem at all. I'd love to take a picture with three gorgeous ladies." Now, they both giggle and their mother smiles.

I decide to pose for four pictures: one with the girls, one with each girl separately, and one with the mother and the girls. Mickey, manning the camera, is orchestrating our photo shoot like a flamboyant gay director: telling us where to look, to turn a little to the left, and move in a bit closer. The last picture is taking forever. He's overdoing it with his instructions but the girls are lapping up the attention. And then, as my face plays host to a tired smile that wouldn't even pay for a postage stamp, waiting for him to snap the final pose, I watch him react to something he spies on the camera's screen—something in the background, behind us.

"Brian!"

Snap! My shocked face is forever captured on the last picture. Mother and daughters hug me and thank me. I'm grateful for their extended show of gratitude because it gives me an extra moment to collect myself before I turn around to face him. When I do, I can't believe how exhilarated and how uncomfortable I am. My heart is leaping out of my chest, my knees are weak and my pits are damp. Brian looks like a high-fashion runway model in a charcoal gray, double-breasted tuxedo, crisp silk shirt in the softest shade of ivory, and a creamy ivory carnation to match in his lapel. For just a touch of bling, he's wearing the platinum and diamond cufflinks I saw on his dressing table. They're throwing off a dazzling array of tiny sparkles every time his hands move. His leather wingtips have the softest sheen as if they were buffed for hours with pure cotton. His thick hair—with its gold highlights—shimmers under the recessed lighting. As I gaze at him, my mind flashes back to the last time I saw him—to that night at the flat when I revealed how I truly felt about him. I'm embarrassed about it and ashamed of my behavior. I showed up unannounced, pried into his personal life, and was extremely emotional. I even cried. Everything I said that night—every single word, especially at the end—was humiliating and inexcusable. And now my mind flashes back to Martin telling me to stay away from him for my own good. He meant well when he said it, but it was so painful to hear. Brian had gone to him— had asked him to tell me to leave him alone. I cried for hours and couldn't stomach food for days, suffering the worst rejection of my life. Now I'm wondering how Brian will react to me—what he'll say, or if he'll even speak to me. He must think I'm an emotionally unstable fool.

Mickey shakes his hand and slaps him on the back. "What the hell are you doing here, my good old mate?"

"I could ask you the same thing," comes the familiar deep voice. "Hello, John. How are you?"

"I'm great." I smile a fake smile, unable to look at his face. Instead, I stare at the knot of his tie and hope my palm isn't as sweaty as I imagine it is when we shake hands.

"I'm an idiot, all right? That's all I can say. I'm a failure as a manager and a friend. I forgot Johnny's birthday! Normally, I get all his buddies together for a big party at a restaurant, but this," Mickey spreads his arms, "is the best I could do."

"It's your birthday? Well, happy birthday, John."

The words are genuine and warm, but I still can't meet his gaze so I continue to converse with the tie. "Thank you." Then I turn to

Mickey. "Mickey, the opera was a really great—"

"Whose birthday is it?" interjects a tall, voluptuous woman as she sidles up to Brian.

I watch, not yet comprehending the significance of what I'm witnessing, as she entwines her hands around his arm and leans against his bicep. Then I feel the impact of being punched in the stomach. My God! This is Carol—in the flesh—right in front of me! Of course, he wouldn't be here alone! Of course, he'd be here with her! How stupid could I be? Mickey isn't the idiot. *I'm* the idiot! I'm the moron who never thought something this tragic could ever happen. I stand here trying to compose myself—trying to keep my face from turning red, and to keep from throwing up as Brian introduces this...this gorgeous, curvaceous and extremely busty woman to me.

"John, I'd like you to meet Carol Lexington. Carol, this is John Kaiser, and you remember Mickey from lunch, right?"

Lunch? Mickey went to lunch with them? A betrayal has taken place behind my back.

"Of course I do. Mickey, it's so *wonderful* to see you again," she purrs in a sickening, sweet voice.

"I guess if Mickey is one of my oldest friends, then John is... one of my newest." Brian gives me a warm smile.

I wish he wouldn't do that. I wish he wouldn't be so nice. We both know what an ass I've been. I still can't look at him and my discomfort is obvious.

"Well, John, happy birthday. And as they say, any friend of Brian's..." The words are said as she extends her hand. She expects me to kiss it. Well, I won't! She's not the Queen. She's not royalty. When I touch her skin, it feels cold and dry. She has slender fingers but they're bony and her nails remind me of a vulture's claws. Her rings are big and tacky. She may have beautiful features and thick blonde hair, but that fat-injected smile is fake, plastered onto her face with gobs of contempt—for me. Her eyes are a clear light blue, but they're heavily ringed with liner. And even though her skin is flawless and her Botoxed forehead never has to reveal worry lines over five o'clock shadow or razor burn, I swear I can smell her thick foundation (Remember, I'm an actor; I *know* the smell of foundation). She's the epitome of a woman. As I stare at her, I'm hit with every feminine feature Brian would be attracted to—everything that would arouse him. And every feature is a painful reminder of how he could never be attracted to a man—to me. I don't like her. I *really* don't like her. Of course, Mickey fawns over her.

"Carol, Carol, Carol. I am *so* happy to see you again! What a coincidence, huh? You look *marvelous* tonight, just *ravishing!* You're the most gorgeous woman here!" He kisses her hand half a dozen times. Just watching him slobber like this makes me ill.

"And you are just a peach." She bends over to pinch his chubby cheek as if he were a garden gnome.

Oh, God. I truly want to hurl. This merry scene isn't a coincidence. She planned this. Somehow, she knew we'd be here. She found out from Mickey. Idle chitchat passes between them for the next few minutes. I don't know or care what they're talking about. My discomfort is like a chokehold. I can't think of anything to say—not to this…this creature hanging on Brian's arm. And she *is* hanging on it, like a piece of slime. She's just a nasty piece of huge-breasted, feminine slime, glaring me down with her slitty eyes. They're silently telling me she's his sexy girlfriend and I'm a worthless pile of gay garbage. She's the winner and I'm the biggest loser on the planet. The lights dim, and I welcome the relief of escaping this nightmare and heading back to our seats.

Just as we begin to walk away, Mickey turns back. "Hey, what are you two doing after the show? Care to join us for a late dinner?"

Oh no, Mickey, no! *Do not* do this to me. Do not make this horrific night go on any longer than it has to. Don't force me to sit across from her and watch her fondle him through an entire meal.

She gushes up at him, "Oh, Brian, isn't that a *wonderful* idea?"

"Um, that would be great, Mickey. We'd love to. Let me pick the restaurant, okay?"

"Excellent!" Mickey is thrilled. "We'll meet right here when it's over. Ciao for now!"

I spend the next hour agonizing, biting my nails during the second half. I can't enjoy the performance because I'm too busy worrying about the dinner. How can I sit through a meal while that woman hangs on the man I love? She'll stroke his hair and make condescending remarks to me. I know she will. She'll nuzzle his neck and kiss him, and I'll have to watch. My mind goes crazy with questions and theories: Why did Brian say yes? Is he trying to torture me? He *knows* how I feel about him. Why would he be so cruel and vindictive? Why would he put me through this? Why on earth would he do this to me? Maybe he's trying to prove his point—to put me in my place, once and for all. Maybe they're both trying to. Maybe they planned this together. Maybe all three of them planned it over lunch—a conspiracy! My stomach is churning like a boiling cauldron. My appetite is gone. My mouth is dry, throat parched. I'm clenching my jaw so tightly I'm giving myself a headache. When Cio-Cio-San finally hands over the kid and prepares to impale herself, it takes a shitload of willpower to keep my ass glued to my seat and not pelt down the main aisle to join her onstage in an act of double suicide—one fake, one real (for everyone's viewing pleasure and fantastic opening-night reviews). Before I know it, the final curtain call is over and we're back in the main lobby, facing Mickey's tiger and the she-devil. I'm waiting for a bomb to explode as I sweat out of my tux, just a pile of raw nerves. I'm trying not to let my highly emotional state show.

"I recognize you from that series, don't I?" she whines in a syrupy-sweet voice.

I nod once, not wanting to say a single word to her. I notice Mickey has caught someone's eye. He's waving to a guy in the corner while he digs out his business cards. Oh, no! Don't go over there, Mickey. Don't leave me alone with Brian and the shrew.

"Guys, I'll be back in a flash. This will just take a second. I see a guy I've been trying to sign for two years. I hope I can reel him in this time. Wish me luck!"

Mickey is off on the chase, and I'm by myself—miserable.

"So, as I was saying, I recognize you from that drama series. You're just a *wonderful* actor."

Brian has disengaged his arm from her grip, pulled out his phone, and is—you've got to be kidding me—texting! He's texting while I deal with this nasty witch-hag.

She lays her claw on my arm and leans into me. "No, I *truly* mean that. I can't *imagine* what it must be like for you, what you have to go through on a daily basis to convince the fans of the show."

I stare down at her white, skeletal fingers on my sleeve and then look up at her smirking face with those bulbous lips. "Excuse me?" It's the first time I've spoken to her and I'm not sure what she's trying to say.

"Your female fans.... It must be so hard to convince them—well, I personally don't have a problem with that sort of... man-on-man thing like the *rest* of society. You know, if that's how you choose to live your life. But it must be *so* awkward for you. I mean, you have to hug and kiss women on the show, don't you? And you have to make it look like there's real passion there. You can't be enjoying that *at all*. It must make you *sick* to your stomach—just physically ill—*especially* when you prefer men, when you *obviously* wish you were with one of your own kind. I mean, how do you get through the scenes? Close your eyes, ignore the tits, and just pretend you're giving deep tongue to a guy?" She smiles a truly wicked, puffy-lipped smile and gives me a wink.

Well, *now* I know her game, now that she's made it so obvious. She wants me to feel uncomfortable and ashamed, and as the winner of Brian's affections, she's confident enough to say these cruel things in front of him. She really is a skank! Brian is still engrossed in texting. I glance over at Mickey. Now he's messing with his phone, too. Neither one is paying attention to what's happening to me. My face is burning as I try to quell my discomfort. I want to yell at her, to scream in her face that I can't stand her and even though Brian doesn't want me, she certainly doesn't deserve him.

She raises her whiney voice, causing nearby heads to turn. "Oh dear, have I embarrassed you?"

My fists are clenched, I know my face is glowing red, and Brian is still texting. I try to steady my shaky words. "I'm not embarrassed."

Again, her voice gets louder. "Of course I have. I've embarrassed you. I mean, emotional queers like you are so easily embarrassed. Just look at your pretty little face getting all red and blotchy." She's grinning broadly now, relishing her victory lap as more people are looking at me.

"I'm not embarrassed."

"Look, I know what I've said is embarrassing, and it's okay. Any faggot would find it embarrassing." Her words are said even louder as she tries to draw as much attention as she can to this scene of complete humiliation.

I'm determined not to lose my temper in front of everyone now staring at me as if I were a freak. I pull in a deep breath to calm myself before I speak. "What you've said isn't embarrassing. It's...it's—"

"It's rude." Brian is looking down at her now, his phone put away and his hands in his pockets.

"I... Excuse me—"

"I said it's rude." Brian's eyes are on fire.

"I didn't mean to.... I wasn't trying to—"

"You meant to be rude. You were trying to insult him. He's not embarrassed. He has no reason to be embarrassed. He's angry. He's furious. And I'm surprised he hasn't hauled out and smacked your smug face beyond senseless. You know who's embarrassed?" Brian's deep voice is calm and even, but his eyes are sizzling with anger. His gaze is frightening as he turns to stand directly in front her. "*I'm* embarrassed. I'm embarrassed to be anywhere near you. I'm embarrassed to have brought you here tonight, and I'm embarrassed to have introduced such a nasty, *evil cow* to my good friends." Her face is drained of color, she's frozen stiff as Brian continues, and theater patrons look on with intense interest. "If you weren't a lady—and I use that term in the broadest sense your thick brain could ever imagine—I'd knock those capped teeth out of that hideous mouth of yours and kick your flatulating fat ass all the way to Scotland." Barely stifled snickers rise up from the gathered crowd.

Carol sways a little, fluttering eyelids, stuttering words. "Brian, I...I..." A forced smile takes control of her pillow lips. "I am truly sorry for any.... It was never my intention to—"

"Leave."

"What?"

"I've ordered a cab. Get out of here." He leans into her for emphasis and then lowers his voice to a bone-chilling growl that sends a shiver up my spine. "You are a loathsome bitch. Do not ever...*ever* come near me again." He turns to me. "John, let's go." And with that, he calmly walks away, parting the substantial crowd she had so proudly attracted, like Moses.

I can't believe she did that! It was unnecessary. I wasn't her competition. He didn't want me. How stupid can she be? She *had* him! She had him *right* in the palm of her hand. I feel so bad for her, standing here like a clown amid these staring, judgmental strangers. She has that dumbstruck look you get right after someone slaps you hard across the face. She's trying to say something to me. Her fleshy lips are moving, trembling ferociously, but words aren't passing them. I almost want to tell her I'm sorry because for once she doesn't look like a nasty witch. Instead, I bite my lower lip, shake my head, and turn to follow Brian.

"Mickey, let's go."

"Sure, sure. Hey, where's ah… Carol?"

"Felt sick. Went home. Pity, I know. Let's go."

And with that, we leave.

Brian

Mickey makes the ride to the restaurant a real pleasure with daft jokes and funny stories of his poor business decisions when he was just starting out as a manager. It eases the strain between John and me, slackens some of the tension—and there's a lot of tension. He won't even look at me.

"Hey, Brian. Remember our first deal?"

"How could I forget? It was the worst financial decision of my life. I wanted to tan your freckled hide over that one."

"I know, and you probably should have!" He leans toward John as he recounts the fiasco. "I convince Brian, who I just met a couple of days before in a bar, to invest in this brilliant play. Get this: I've got Jeremy Coulter lined up as the lead. He's a little before your time, Johnny, but you know the guy, right?"

John nods, engrossed in Mickey's story. "I've seen his acting. He's fabulous."

"Right! That's *exactly* what I tell Brian: 'You'll love this guy! He's fabulous! The press calls him Mister Romantic. He'll rake in the dough.' I've hooked him. Brian goes full bore and finances the lot. Well, of course he does! I've promised him this great return, right?" Mickey starts to giggle. "So Jeremy wants his wife to have a small part. You know, nothing special—just a little speaking role. I agree. I mean, what do I care? She's not bad looking and her voice is okay." More giggling.

"Now, get this: opening night, place is packed, sold out show, everyone is there. Jeremy is all set, and I'm giving him a pep talk as I'm walking him to the stage, right? Well..." Mickey can barely control the giggles. "He hears this commotion behind one of the doors. It's a broom closet or something. Anyway, he yanks it open and what does he see? His wife, spread-eagle on a mop bucket, screwin' a prop boy!"

Mickey buckles over with laughter and John laughs a little, too. Remembering my staggering financial loss, I can only muster a smile at the memory.

"That was it," he manages through his fit of laughter. "No show. Nothing. I had to give back all the ticket sales. Brian lost a fortune—an absolute fortune!—and well, Jeremy went through a bad tabloid divorce. The press just raked him through the coals. They made a big deal of how Mister Romantic must have been so terrible in bed his wife had to be bonked by a stagehand." He calms down. "I really blew you out of the water on that one, didn't I, Brian?"

"You really did, Mickey."

"Oh, and remember when I bought that gun? That silly piece of shit?"

"Aye. It was a thirty-eight caliber and sounded like a cheap firecracker going off in a tin can."

"My God, Brian! You're right! It did! Listen to this, Johnny. I flat-out steal a client from another manager, a beautiful kid named Conrad Bigelow. I'll admit it was a really low thing to do, but the manager threatens me. Says he's gonna have a hit put on me! I need some protection, right? So, I buy a gun from this no-name hustler. God, it was so pathetic—old, rusty. I didn't even register the damned thing. Brian comes out to Los Angeles for a few days of business meetings right before Christmas and I'm showing it to him one night. I wipe my nose as I'm holding it and BAM! I shoot him in the leg." Mickey convulses into another fit of laughter, slapping his thighs with glee. John is shocked at first, but then gives a weak smile. "God, I'm so sorry about that, Brian. I really am. I know that hurt like a son of a bitch. But look at us now — the best of friends, some good deals behind us, and lots of trust, right?"

I rub my thigh. Sometimes it still hurts like a son of a bitch. "It really has been good, Mickey."

He goes on with more amusing stories and I'm grateful he's taking John's mind off the earlier situation at the theater. What Carol said was despicable, and I can't believe I let her continue with the whole diatribe. Martin was right. He tried to tell me she was evil, but how did he know? I just hope the dinner makes up for my thoughtlessness tonight.

John

This restaurant must be in Manchester. We've been driving forever, but with Mickey telling stories I'm more relaxed than I thought I would be sitting across from Brian. I haven't looked at him because I'm still so embarrassed, but I've forgiven both of them for not coming to my rescue right away at the theater. I console myself with the thought that had Mickey been next to me he would have said something immediately, and with the thought that it took Brian so long to react because he was... texting.

As we finally pull up to the restaurant, I realize I'm famished. As we climb out of the Rolls, I also realize this place is at the top of Mickey's price range, and mine. The name is unpronounceable French. The façade is bland and unassuming. There's a doorman protecting the entrance against common riff-raff and his face is impassive until he lays eyes on Brian's tall frame unfolding from the Rolls. The change in his demeanor is like night and day. The moment he sees Brian he's smiling, chatting, and grabbing our hands. He ushers us inside with arms around our shoulders as if we were old buddies attending his backyard barbeque. I'm half expecting him to slam a beer in my hand, whack me on the ass and tell me to grab a wiener off the grill.

These are aristocratic faces I've never seen before, the mega-rich.

Everyone is dressed to the nines, women are dripping with jewels and the haze of tremendous wealth is so thick in the air you could stick out your tongue and lick it like a salt block. I'm uncomfortable—out of place, even though I see dozens of smiling faces that recognize me and would ask for my autograph if given the chance. Prissy would never be able to sit on his knees and slurp his soda in here. The wait staff gingerly peel off our coats.

Brian guides us past the staring eyes. "I've booked a small table in a back room."

I hope he's not ushering us into the back because he's embarrassed by us. Hell, we're wearing Neil Allyn tuxedoes! Surely, these people can tolerate a couple of gay men while they eat. Why bring us here if he doesn't want to be seen with us? I'm uneasy about this dinner. I don't want someone to push me into a back room because I'm—"

"*SURPRISE!*"

My heart entertains a brief arrhythmia as the shock hits me hard. No color in my face; ghost white, I'm sure. Dozens of camera flashes explode, blinding me. Once I can see again, I'm relieved. The nincompoops are here, and a lot of other people are here, too. Linda, Sandy, Curtis and more than three dozen other friends, several from the musicals and the series, are gearing up to celebrate. Even Kyle is here, sans toothpick. Mickey is hugging me and kissing my cheek.

"I don't belie—" I don't get the chance to finish my sentence as I'm grabbed by Ben, slammed into a chair, and a glass of champagne is shoved into my hand by Prissy who plasters a slobbery smooch on my lips and starts dancing around me like a ballerina, emphasized by the pink tutu he's wearing over his pants—another present from Ben. Obviously, he's been drinking a lot. We'll have to watch him. If we're not careful, we'll end up with a tiny, naked ballerina in less than two hours. The long table is beautiful, featuring a stunning candelabra in the center. Cut crystal, polished silver, and dreamy white silk is everywhere. A sea of metallic silver balloons covers the floor, hundreds of glittery silver streamers hang from the ceiling and a large-scale 'Happy Birthday Johnny' banner is draped across the far wall.

"I bet you're wondering how we did it—how we got all these idiots here." Mickey's freckled face is glowing pink with joy.

"I'm wondering wh...*when* you did it."

Everyone laughs.

"At the theater, tonight—just now."

I'm dumbfounded.

As everyone fills their glasses with more champagne, Mickey explains: "I go off to talk to this guy about a contract, right? Well, as I'm trying to hook him, I get a text message from Brian: eight-eight-eight."

I'm still dumbfounded.

"It's our code to pay attention. You know, stop what you're doing, I've got something important or urgent."

I nod to show I understand as I sip my champagne.

"He's texting me to call one of your friends to get the ball rolling, so I called Linda and she called Benny."

"And then I called everyone else," Ben pipes in, raising his glass of champagne.

Jeff comes up and squeezes my shoulders. "In a flash, we've got this scruffy lot heading to the restaurant just for you, honey."

Mickey tops off a few glasses of champagne as he speaks. "Brian picked this place so everyone had a chance to get here before us. He called the restaurant during the second half of the show so they could decorate a bit, and—well, you'll see later. Hey everybody! Are we ready to eat?"

Everyone cheers, a champagne cork pops and the party mood is set in motion when classic Motown (selected by Jeff and Martin) starts streaming from the sound system.

The dinner is remarkable—a never-ending feast of delicious food. Course after course and dish after dish keep appearing out of nowhere: Hot platters, cold platters, flaming platters, soufflés, soups, salads, puddings, tapas-style finger foods and trays of cheeses and tropical fruit cover every inch of the table and two buffets along the far wall. We're dancing and drinking and eating like pigs. The food and music, coupled with all these happy, good-spirited people—some I've known a few years now—take away the misery I felt earlier tonight. I'm laughing and joking, and I'm at ease. Mickey and Brian are sitting at the opposite end of the table, talking between themselves throughout the dinner. It's hard to see either one clearly because of the candelabra and my not-so-great vision. At one point, I notice Martin standing behind Brian, bending down to whisper in his ear. I have no idea what he's saying but I imagine it's not pleasant and I'm sure it's about me. I'll ask Martin about it later. The rest of us continue celebrating with dancing and food and laughter. We also keep drinking bottle after bottle of Perrier-Jouet. It seems when one bottle is emptied, a full one magically appears to take its place. The wait staff hovers in each corner of the room and keeps a watchful eye on every aspect of the meal, jumping in whenever something is needed and then discreetly fading away again. A few wear headsets and keep the kitchen apprised of items that need replenishment. I've never seen an event so well orchestrated. By the time the two-tiered, chocolate ganache cake arrives — which must have been what Mickey was trying not to tell me about earlier — with my name in silver icing and thirty-one candles, everyone is stuffed and drunk. Prissy is naked as predicted (except for his tutu), and I get a wonderfully harmonized (albeit slurred) version of *Happy Birthday*. That's followed by hugs and sloppy kisses from everyone, except Brian. Mickey says he's gone off to settle the bill, personally thank the chefs and tip each member of the wait staff. I would have loved a birthday kiss from him. Still, if I think back to the way he dumped Carol and sent her packing, it's been the best birthday I've ever had and I'll never forget it.

13
He Deserves A Bickie

Brian — March 2

"Are you okay, Mickey?"

"Don't worry so much, my good old mate. I promise I won't break my ne—" Mickey cuts himself off and freezes on the drafty stairway. "I'm sorry, Brian. I wasn't thinking."

A sharp pain cleaves my chest, but it quickly passes. "Don't worry. It's okay. Are you sure you'll be all right?"

"Of course. This is nothing. I'm not even close to being pissed. I'll be fine." He resumes swaying up the stairs. "And Brian," he adds, carefully looking back over his shoulder, "it was a lovely gift—a fabulous surprise for Johnny. Thank you."

"You're welcome, Mickey. Goodnight." I make sure he gets through the front door of his condo and head back down the stairs into the chilly night air. I gaze at the dark clouds. It's going to rain hard tonight and it's going to be bitterly cold. Now I have to deal with John. Mickey was easy. He was drunk. John isn't drunk and John isn't Mickey. I climb into the Rolls. "So, John, you're next. Where do you live? We'll have you home in no time." I try to say it lightly but the words sound as strained and uneasy as I feel.

"I'd like to talk." He's looking down at the floorboards.

"John, it's late. I think—"

"Please, Brian. I just…. I need to get some things straight in my head. Please."

I look out the window and sigh. Then I hit the comm. "Jack, head back to the flat, please."

"Yes, sir."

We make the long ride in silence—sitting across from each other but not looking at each other. We're trying to figure out what we want to say, and what we need to say. I take a moment to text Charles, letting him know he can leave for the night and then stare out the window until we arrive. The walk through the lobby, past Brenda (ending her shift for the night) and the lift ride are just as silent. I need to convince him this infatuation is pointless—that there's no way he can go on wishing I were gay. Martin made it clear at the restaurant: He appreciated the surprise dinner and my tolerance for Prissy's harmless antics (even after he twice streaked through the main dining hall warbling *We Are The Champions* with three stunned waiters frantically chasing his tiny naked ass), but he expected me to let John know it was a friendly gesture and nothing more. Of course, he also warned me not to let him into the flat again. But what harm can one last visit do? John isn't a serial killer. He's a nice young bloke who's just a bit confused. I open the door, walk in after him and turn on the lights. I wait while he takes off his coat and hang it up, along with mine, in the closet. I gesture him into the living room, follow him and veer off toward the bar. I pour a scotch. "Drink?"

"No, thank you."

"Sit down, John."

He takes off his dinner jacket and drapes it over the back of his usual chair. I watch the red carnation fall from his buttonhole to the floor. He sits. I take off my dinner jacket, throw it on the sectional and peel off my silk cummerbund, which felt like a tourniquet all night long. Cummerbunds are one of the most uncomfortable things I've ever had the pleasure of wearing. I pull out my shirttail and, as usual, sit across from him on the other side of the glass table. With neither of us speaking, it starts out uncomfortable as I sip my scotch.

He's found his invisible spot on the floor, still determined to avoid looking at me. "Thank you for the dinner. I know it cost you a fortune. It was an impressive and thoughtful surprise." The words come out stilted, as if he's reading (badly) from a script.

"You're welcome. I enjoyed doing it."

"I'm sorry about Prissy's little burlesque. Sometimes he gets carried away."

"Don't be. He got a standing ovation the second time around. Everyone enjoyed it."

He's quiet for another few minutes and then says, "Brian, I want to apologize for the other night. My emotions were immature and things I said were invasive of your personal life and inappropriate. I know there's no chance…. I mean, I know…." He closes his eyes and takes a deep breath. "I know you're not gay. I'd just like to be your friend, if you'll let me." He opens his eyes and looks at me for the first time tonight.

"I'd like that, John. I would really like to be your friend." I give him a smile and he smiles back. Again, we drop into silence for a few minutes.

"Brian?"

"Hmm?"

"What did you see in her?"

I think about the question. "Obviously not what I should have seen."

"To me, she didn't seem like your type."

"And what is my type?"

"I don't know — but not her, not that."

I give him a wink. "I promise I'll pick a better one next time."

Again, we have a few more minutes of silence. Then I speak. "I'm sorry, John — for tonight, at the theater. It was unacceptable behavior."

"That's okay. You don't have to apologize for her."

"I wasn't. I was apologizing for me. My actions or my lack of actions were inexcusable. I'm sorry. I hope you will forgive me."

He's a little uneasy in answering. "Of course. You stood up for me in the end. That's what mattered and what was important. Besides, if you hadn't let her say those things, you wouldn't have known what she was really like."

I nod. He's right. That bitch's true colors came out in her words. More of the tension and uneasiness dissolves with each fragment of conversation, and I'm feeling comfortable again. I lean back in my chair and sip my scotch.

"Brian?"

"Hmm?"

"If you were gay—I know you're not—but if you were, would you find me attractive?"

At first, I hesitate to answer, remembering Martin's warning of how cunning John can be. But at this point, since we've cleared the air, the question seems harmless. "Well, uh, you're a bit young. I prefer women—excuse me—people my own age or a little older than myself. But, um, I guess so. Maybe. Probably. If I were gay, but I'm not."

"I know, but if you were...." His voice trails off.

"But I'm *definitely* not." I look at him intently to emphasize my point. But my look is wasted because he's not looking back at me. He's staring at his spot on the floor and biting his lower lip. His mind is working on something. He's latched onto an idea. What it is, I don't know, but he's determined to come up with a plan. He's like a four-year-old trying to figure a way to convince his mum he deserves a bickie before supper.

"Brian, have you ever kissed a guy?"

"No." I sip my scotch.

He looks up. "Why not?"

"Excuse me?"

"Well, you've done all this thrill-seeking stuff, like skydiving and mountain climbing. I'm surprised you haven't kissed a guy."

"I don't think kissing a guy rates up there as thrill-seeking stuff, do you?"

"Well, no, but if you do those daring things, you wouldn't be afraid to kiss a guy, right?"

Okay. Here we go. Here's his angle. He's going for fear. I sip more scotch. "I'm not afraid to kiss a guy, John. I just don't want to kiss a guy, and I'm not going to kiss a guy."

"Kissing a guy doesn't make you gay. You could kiss a guy and it wouldn't mean a thing."

"I could kiss a guy, and you're right, it wouldn't make me gay and it wouldn't mean a thing, but I'm not going to kiss a guy."

"You *could* kiss a guy, though. You could kiss me, if you want."

"I don't want to kiss a guy and I don't want to kiss you."

He's undeterred. "But if you *did* want to kiss a guy; I'm just saying you could kiss me. I wouldn't be offended or anything."

"Thank you. I'm glad you wouldn't be offended—or anything. I'll keep that in mind. I really will, but I still don't want to kiss a guy and I still don't want to kiss you." I sip more scotch.

"Kissing me isn't much different than kissing a woman, you know."

"Okay."

Now his cheeks are red. "I bet if you kissed me you'd think you were kissing a woman."

"Oh… I bet I wouldn't."

"I bet you would because I can kiss like a woman."

"I'm really happy for you but I still don't think I'd think I was kissing a woman."

He's still undeterred and his cheeks are even redder. "I bet I could kiss you better than a woman."

"Well, we're not going to find out whether that's true or not."

He leans forward with a glint in his eye. "We could. We could find out if it's true."

"We could, but we won't."

"Why not?"

"Because I don't want to kiss you, John."

"You could kiss me for my birthday, as a present."

"I could, but I won't."

"But if you wanted to… as a present to me."

"If I wanted to, but I don't want to."

"It would be a nice present. I mean, if you wanted to give me a kiss as a present it would be a really nice present."

"But I don't want to give you a kiss as a present."

"A lot of people give a kiss as a present."

"I know they do, but I don't want to."

"But why not? What are you afraid of, Brian?" He looks at me earnestly. "Are you afraid of me because I'm gay?"

I ponder his question. I'll admit I've been afraid of a few things in my life (necrophiles come to mind, getting kicked in the balls by a horse, and the ingredients of SPAM), but I have never been afraid of a gay man. "No, John, not at all."

"Then, kiss me. Please, for my birthday."

I shake my head and rub my temple. I need a break from his badgering because I've got pounding headache. I stand up and go to the kitchen. I open the freezer and put ice cubes in my glass—something I never do. I walk over to the bar and pour scotch over the ice. I gulp it down and pour more scotch over the ice. I walk back to the kitchen. I loosen my tie because it's strangling me and toss it on the counter. I should have taken it off long ago. I sip my scotch. I look at him sitting in the living room, watching every move I make. I gulp the rest of my scotch and walk back to the bar to pour another three ounces over the ice. I gulp half of it down and refill the glass to the rim. I walk back to the kitchen and look at him again, from behind the counter. If I'm going to kiss this bloke, I want to be drunk; I think I *need* to be drunk. "Fine, John. You want your birthday kiss, you can have it."

14
The Element Of Surprise...
And Not Much Else

John — March 3

"Where? *Here?*"

"Aye. Here."

"You've *got* to be kidding me."

"Nope."

"But—"

"Here," Brian says in his deep voice. It's final. The decision is made. No discussion.

I look around me in disappointment. "Here."

Brian has picked the most unromantic place on the face of this earth for my birthday kiss. His kitchen. His stainless steel applianced, high-gloss cabineted, hewn granite counter-topped, recessed fluorescent task-lighted, gourmet Poggenpohl kitchen. Every single surface is sterile, hard, shiny and cold. Good, old German ingenuity. This place may be perfect for chopping carrots and performing brain surgery, but it sucks for romance. And that's exactly why he picked it. I spy the dimmers at the end wall and take one step.

"Nope. Lights on."

I give him a pleading look.

His voice is ominously low as he says, "Lights... on."

There's no way I'll get an ounce of passion out of this operating theater, and he knows it. He's not looking forward to this, and he wants to make damned sure I know it. Well, fine. I'm a performer. I'm an actor. If this is my stage, then so be it. I can work with this and I can make this work. Now, positioning. I chew my thumbnail as I assess the space. The kitchen is long and narrow compared to the rest of the flat. Brian is propped up along the prep sink counter across from the fridge. His long legs, ankles crossed, are sticking out so far he's taking up more than half the aisle. His arms are folded across his chest, he's lowered his chin and leveled his gaze at me. In terms of body language, he has assumed the 'closed' position. From where I'm standing, I see his scotch glass on the counter to his left. Obviously, I should be against the fridge facing him. So that's where I position myself; up against the fridge, awkwardly ramrod straight, while he's casually leaning against the counter. Now he's starting to smile. He's finding this amusing. I ignore him as I work out how to deal with his protruding legs. I could straddle them, but that would only make me shorter, and I'm already at a height disadvantage. I decide to test-walk forward to see how close I can get before my feet touch his, when Brian suddenly stands up straight. Well, that's a good thing and that's a bad thing. I can get closer, but now he's also a full five inches taller. I'll just have to work with it by standing on my toes at the crucial moment. I move back to my starting position and lock my eyes on his. This is serious business now. This is my moment of glory. I lick my lips, take a deep breath, and move closer... and closer... and closer... and I'm just about to stand on my toes, lean over his folded arms, and plant a big, juicy wet one when—

His phone buzzes. It's sitting on the counter to his right, and I hadn't noticed it until now. Without hesitation, he picks it up. "Yup."

Standing this close to him, my lips all puckered up and ready to smooch, I hear a tinny, middle-eastern voice on the other end of the line launch into a barrage of business jargon: "...the merger's not going well... incomplete paperwork... substantial loss of time and resources... presentation was lacking in key issues that should have been addressed long ago...." It's a legitimate, poorly timed business call. I don't think it was a set up and Brian is fully immersed in it, trying to slow down the excited caller so he can understand what's going on. I slump back against the big fridge and assess this pathetic situation. Can I salvage any of it? Brian, with his phone in his right hand, has now picked up his scotch in his left hand. Great! Now he's talking *and* drinking, making the situation even worse; however, this does mean his arms are unfolded. He's revealed a weak link in his line of defense. He's left his torso wide open to a full-on frontal attack. He's turned a little to the left, and with his right hand raised to his ear, that puts me just out of his line of sight. I spontaneously decide to make my strategic move against the opposition while it's on the phone. In battle, they call this the element of surprise. Yes, this should *definitely* come as a surprise. I swallow hard, take a deep breath and launch myself across the kitchen aisle like a surface-to-air missile.

With one hand, I push the phone away from his face. It clatters to the ground near my feet. With my other hand, I grab him by the neck, haul his head down to mine and clamp my mouth over his. Now, his mouth was open because he had been talking on the phone, and he was in the middle of saying, "What you need...," so I shove my tongue in his mouth, and—not meaning to—cram it straight down his throat. He reacts by dropping his glass and it shatters on the marble floor. The smell of fine expensive scotch is coming up pretty strong. Now that he's dropped his phone and his glass, I realize his hands (just like enemy weapons) are free to launch a counterattack, so with my free arm I clamp onto his upper body in a bear hug as tightly as I can, dig in my fingernails, and hang on.

The kitchen is quiet, except for the tinny voice still audible through the phone on the floor: "Hello, hello? Brian, are you there? Brian? Hello...?"

I'm clamped onto Brian's mouth like that thing in *Alien* with my eyes tightly closed, my tongue rammed down his throat, and my nose smashed against his face. Interestingly, due to the spontaneous nature of my assault, I hadn't thought about what I'd do beyond this initial engagement so every tactical maneuver that follows comes as a surprise. Brian tries to pry me off his body with his big hands. He's strong, but with me locked in my bear hug he can't work his fingers between our torsos to gain any leverage, so he drops his arms. Slowly, he turns his head to the left. I read this as the beginning of a defensive strike and clamp down even harder with my fingernails, until I feel his breath on my cheek and realize he's only trying to free his nose so he can breathe. All right, I'll allow that. I'll let him breathe. Suffocation is not in my game plan. A few more seconds pass without movement—just the tinny voice, now shouting loudly from the phone: *"Brian? Hey, are you still there? I need answers! Should I call back? Hey.... Hello?"*

With nothing of significance happening on the front lines, I decide it's time to assess the strength of the opposition. I loosen my talon-like grip and that's when...

Brian, sensing the implied weakness, body-slams me into the fridge with a brute force I've never felt before. The back of my skull crunches into the stainless steel front panel. I hear a dull *"ka-thunk"* and realize the Baccarat vase has toppled off the fridge and landed unevenly on a neatly folded dishtowel on the counter—a good two-and-a-half-foot drop. Thank God, that horrendously expensive masterpiece of hideousness didn't break. But now I hear an ominous rolling sound. We both freeze as the ugly, lead-crystal vase lazily rolls away down the long counter. I hear it bump the rim of the farmhouse sink. I imagine it teetering precariously on the knife-edge of the counter and then I hear it crash to the floor. It explodes into a million pieces. I feel faint and sick, and I'm sweating—a lot. The back of my head is on fire. Bright spots are dancing on the inside of my eyelids, and I taste blood in my mouth. The body slam nearly knocked the wind out of me. If Brian's crush weren't plastering me up against the fridge, and if I weren't hanging onto him, I'd probably crumple to the floor. As the battle commences, he's now trying to push my tongue out of his mouth with his tongue. I engage him in a wild flurry of papillae combat and dig in deeper with my talons. Since he's supporting my weight anyway, I lift my feet off the floor, wrap my legs around his thighs like a girdle and yank down harder on his neck. I'm determined to keep my tongue in his mouth. It's a small victory and the only one I've achieved in this ill-planned skirmish, so I'm determined not to lose it.

Brian pauses. I don't know what he's doing because I haven't opened my eyes since the initial attack, but he's obviously strategizing. He lets out an enormous "I surrender" sigh, but I'm not taking the bait. The victorious tongue stays. And then I feel a strange sensation: Brian isn't trying to push my tongue out of his mouth anymore; he's just trying to move it out of the way. Having a determined tongue wedged down his throat for nearly a minute cannot be comfortable. I dig in deeper with my nails so he knows I'm not waving a white flag, and release my tongue — just a little.

And that turns out to be a pretty good strategic concession, because now Brian's tongue is moving against mine, caressing it. I tentatively mimic his caress but I'm worried it might be a booby trap. There's a good chance he'll bite off my tongue, but he doesn't. He just keeps stroking it. Hesitantly, I let him slide his tongue inside my mouth. Now he's exploring my gums and the roof of my mouth, pulsing his tongue in a rhythmic motion. I sigh and work my tongue back into his mouth, matching his rhythm, wanting to devour him as I taste his scotch. His big hands are on my cheeks, gently positioning my face at different angles. He's turning his head from side to side, intently poking his tongue everywhere he can — tasting every minute crevice of my mouth, and there's a low rumbling down in his chest. At times, our teeth are touching because we're digging into each other so deeply. With my hand still on his neck, I pull his head down harder to meet my mouth with more force. Once I feel he's pressing against my lips with all the strength he has, I move my hand up into his thick hair and massage his scalp. His chest is heaving and his body temperature has shot way up. Or maybe mine has shot way up. It's hard to tell at this point. It seems to be a mutual heat. My torso is drenched in sweat and my face is covered in sweat, saliva and blood (probably from the body slam).

I release my bear hug by pulling out my talons and when I do, it feels as though I've punctured his silk shirt, and there may be some blood there, too. I have no idea because my eyes are still closed tightly. I continue running my fingers through his hair as I let my legs drop to the floor, releasing my grip on his thighs. I step on something hard. I try kicking it out of the way but I can't, so I just put my full weight on it, trying to hold my own against Brian's strength and make myself a little taller as he bears down on me. I hear a crunching sound. For a full three seconds, neither of us moves. I think I can safely say the tinny voice will not be getting any answers. Again, I feel just a little sick but I keep kissing and caressing and pressing hard against him. I am so into this amazing moment! I am so into this amazing man! I can't believe how muscular his body feels. He must have some glorious ripped muscles beneath this shirt and I want to tear it off his body, but it's pure silk and I really respect pure silk. The moaning is getting louder. It may be coming from me. Yes, I'm sure that high-pitched, girly sound is emanating from me. Brian's chest is heaving fast. The sweat is running down my face and my neck. Fresh sweat is on my chest, in my pits, and streaming down my back. I've never sweated this much outside a grueling rehearsal, and it's unusual. I grab at his hips and his fantastic, rock-hard ass, yanking his pelvis against me so I can grind on him, and that's when I feel the most wonderful sensation: his super-duper erection.

I have no idea when it started. Initially, I was too busy trying to hang onto him for dear life to realize anything was happening in his lower regions, but there's no mistaking the massive, heat-seeking missile—or ignoring it. With my own erection uselessly crushed against his thigh, he's starting up a rhythm, hitting me so forcefully his penis is impaling my stomach like a fist through our clothes. If I were a woman, I'd be skewered like a rotisserie chicken, for sure. He's working faster now, furiously humping the hell out of my gut, thrusting away like there's no tomorrow—and I'm encouraging his fruitless actions by rhythmically yanking on his butt cheeks as hard as I can. The scene is a bit ludicrous—like trudging up the down escalator at Harrods with a dozen shopping bags; embarrassingly futile and exhaustive. Still, he keeps humping. I can't get enough of him and at this point, I just wish I were taller—and facing the other way—because his penis is a soldier on a mission, and I *so* want that determined soldier to complete his mission. I want it so badly my only thought right now is: sex! And that becomes the spoiling moment. The minute I pull away, open my eyes and reach up under his shirt for his zipper, Brian springs back. For the first time, I see the look on his face, and I know it's over. My wonderful, hot, steamy birthday kiss is over.

Brian is panting hard and wiping his mouth on his sleeve. I see a lot of my blood smeared on both. He's looking at me with a wild, almost frightened stare, as if he'd just encountered an armed intruder in his home. The shoulder of his beautiful silk shirt has rows of tiny holes, spotted in red, from where my nails pierced through the fabric and drew blood. His hair is wildly tousled, with one lock falling onto his forehead, but it still looks fantastic. He has a pained expression on his face. He closes his eyes and puts his head back. I stare at his neck, watching his Adam's apple bob up and down. I don't know what to say. I don't know what to do. My chest is heaving and I can barely catch my breath. I run my fingers through my hair and feel heavy sweat on my scalp. My eyes are burning, my head is pounding and my shirt is drenched in sweat and sticking to me. I feel the blood caked on my face. Under this fantastic fluorescent lighting, I must look like complete and utter shit. I glance around the kitchen. It's not bad, until you see the floor. There's a ton of glass, amber scotch, some blood, and a crushed cell phone. Some of the scotch has run around my feet and under the fridge. All in all, the battlefield is not a pretty sight. It's not a good outcome. When I finally catch my breath, I start slowly. "Brian, I—"

"Leave," he whispers.

"But, Brian—"

He raises his voice. "Leave." He pulls his head down to look at me. His beautiful pale eyes are filled with pain—a confused and distressed pain. It's a pain I've caused. "Please, John, just go." He closes his eyes and hangs his head. He's miserable and he doesn't want me here.

I gingerly step through the broken glass, blood, and scotch, tracking it from the kitchen floor onto his pristine white carpet. Not a good move, but I'm determined to do something right before I go. I cross to the bar and take down a glass with a shaky hand. I open the bottle and pour his scotch until the glass is half full. I turn back to the kitchen. I see Brian, motionless, his back toward me, still with his head hanging down. Over his shoulder, under the glare of that energy-efficient overhead lighting, I see a deep, circular dent in the panel on his big fridge. I turn back and fill the glass to the rim. I put the bottle down, pick up the glass and walk back to the kitchen. I stand at the counter, right behind him, and push the glass across the countertop toward his left hand. Then I grab my tux and head to the entryway for my coat.

And that's when I see just how terrific I look in the entryway mirror. I am a lovely sight. My eyes are red and puffy, my hair is sticking up in the back and plastered to my forehead in the front. My lower lip is busted open, hugely swollen, and starting to turn blue. I've got so much blood smeared across my face I look like a one-year-old who was left alone with a bowl of raspberry jelly. I take one of Brian's silk handkerchiefs out of the silver box on the entryway table, spit into it and wipe the caked crap off my face. It takes a lot of spit and a lot of wiping, but I won't go back to use the bathroom. I put the handkerchief in my pocket. Somehow, I don't think he'd want it back. I feel robotic as I take my coat out of the closet, put it on and open the front door. I step out into the chilly atrium and pull the door closed behind me. The rain is pouring down as I walk to the elevator. The doors open and I step inside. The doors close and the elevator descends to the deserted lobby. There's no smiling Brenda to see my disheveled state or my combat wounds — thank God.

It feels good to stand outside, even in this heavy downpour and freezing cold. I raise my face, close my eyes and breathe in the chilly air. No uplifting Gene Kelly tune is on the tip of my tongue tonight. I let the rain wash away the last remnants of spit, sweat and blood. Five minutes pass and now I do feel how cold it really is and I start to shiver. I hang my head and begin walking down the street to who-knows-where just as a big car approaches with its lights off. It pulls up alongside and the driver's window lowers to reveal a friendly face. "Hello, sir."

I smile as the rain drips off my chin. "Hello, Jack."

"May I take you home?"

"Did Brian send you?"

"No."

"Then maybe not. I'll call for a taxi."

"Mister Kaiser, get in. You need a lift. There's no need to wait for a cab and with the strike, you might not get one for hours. I'm sure he won't mind and if he does, I'll deal with it. I can handle him. Besides, you'll catch terrible cold."

What the hell? At this point, how could it possibly make things worse? Besides, I'm freezing to death and the shivering is seriously bad. I tell Jack my address and climb into the back of the Rolls, sinking into the luxurious upholstery. It's quiet and warm. The smell of leather is comforting. As we drive off, it's as if the heavy car is gliding along on a cloud. I stretch out my legs and stare down at my wet Balmorals. The silent ride gives me time to reflect on the night's fiasco. Concerning the birthday kiss, nothing went right. I shouldn't have attacked him. It was too spontaneous and the wrong thing to do. Thinking back on the shattered vase, the crushed phone, the dented fridge and the stained carpet, I caused extensive monetary damage—all in the span of about five minutes. "A real bang-up job," as Ben would say. There's nothing I can do about it now, so I lean my aching head back on the headrest, close my eyes and relive the flood of passion, the taste of Brian's scotch, and the crush of his powerful, humping body.

Brian

I don't know what just happened. I'm still trying to figure out if it really *did* happen. I'm so dizzy, I can't focus on anything. My mind is all over the place, my vision is blurry and the room won't stop spinning. It's the first time I've ever experienced vertigo. I close my eyes and grip the edge of the counter to maintain my balance. When I finally open them, I'm staring at a big mess on the kitchen floor. I'd move if I could, but I've got to wait until this erection subsides. Oh God, an erection! I look down at the precum stain on my shirt, compliments of my hyperactively lubricating schlong. What is wrong with me? Why did I kiss him back? I remember trying to get him off me, trying to break his grip on me. And then I couldn't help myself. It was something about his scent, his taste and the clean smell of his sweat. I couldn't stop my actions—no matter how hard I tried. In the end, I don't even think I was trying. I unzip my fly to relieve some of the pressure and discomfort.

Eventually, preceded by an erection poking out of my pants that's long enough to serve as a cane for the blind, I haltingly make my way to the bathroom and peel off my clothes. I step into the shower and stand under the cool spray. I need to clear my brain of that ordeal and get back to a point of calmness. Martin will kill me if he finds out about this. He told me to stay away from him. He warned me not to let him into the flat because he knew something like this would happen. I look down. I *still* can't shake this damned monolith; I just can't get rid of it. I close my eyes again, desperately trying to find the calm, centered state I'm so used to. "Jesus, John. What the hell have you done to me?" I stumble out of the shower and the bathroom, and lay down on the bed, staring up at the skylight. I don't understand what happened tonight, but I can't *ever* let it happen again. I need to stay away from him until I can get back to Scotland… and I need to get back to Scotland as soon as I can.

Carol

Drunk as a miserable old cow, I peel my mouth away from the near-empty vodka bottle to lean across the bed and look down at my ringing mobile. My puffy eyes focus on the name, and I just want to commit murder. This clueless bitch cannot be serious! How dare she call me at a time like this! I answer the phone and take in a lungful of air to help spew my fury.

"Hey Carol, Patricia here," comes her chirpy, putrid voice. "I've got an update on—"

"JUST FUCKING PISS OFF!"

15
Two Eighty Nine A One

John – March 7

Four days ago it was freezing. Now it's hot and humid. The weather, on top of this fever and the medication, has left me groggy and sick. It was standing in the icy rain outside Brian's flat that got me to this point. I should call Ben or Jeff to have them spend the night just to keep an eye on me, but I'm too achy to reach for the phone. I close my eyes and ignore my churning stomach. Of course, my mind wanders to Brian, which is a bad idea. I open my eyes and stare at the ceiling. There must be something I can do to help me fall asleep, but no matter what I think of, I always come back to Brian. I turn onto my left side, hoping it will quell my stomachache. It doesn't. I roll onto my right side. It feels better so I close my eyes and hope for sleep. The fever is getting worse and I'm sweating buckets. I push the sheet off and eventually fall into a deep sleep, despite my stomachache. I dream of Brian….

A hand brushes a wisp of hair off my forehead. I open my eyes to see Brian kneeling beside the bed. Jack gave him my address and he came to check on me. His facial features are fuzzy, but I can tell he's smiling. I smile back. I want to whisper his name, but it's as if my mouth is sewn shut. He stands up and leaves my view so I roll onto my back to follow his progress. Now he's undressing at the foot of the bed. He's not as tall as I remember. He takes off his shirt and throws it on the bed, up near my face. It smells of stale body odor. He drops his pants and his briefs. I want to look at him. Obviously, I want to check out his crotch, but his features are still fuzzy no matter how hard I try to focus on them. It's as if he's behind a slab of textured glass. He's climbing onto the bed now, coming closer to my face. Yet the closer he gets, the fuzzier his features become, and I smell the body odor even stronger. I'd never noticed that smell on him before, as if he hadn't washed in several days. Previously, he'd always smelled so clean. I turn my head away because the foul odor makes me feel even sicker.

"Johnny."

I hear his voice. It's familiar but not as deep or as soothing as I re-member, and it's the first time he's ever called me Johnny. His breath smells of liquor and sour bile. He's recently puked. I turn my head fur-ther to the side, trying to get away from that horrible stench so I don't throw up myself. He places his palm, cold and clammy, on my fore-head and roughly turns my face up to meet his. His kiss is sloppy, half on my mouth and half on my cheek. He climbs on top of me and his cold hand fumbles and gropes between my legs, squeezing and twist-ing my genitals hard—way too hard. I wince from the pain and finally find my voice. "No, Brian, please!"

I reach down and yank his hand away, but that just makes him an-gry. He pulls himself up off my body, smacks me hard across the face and hurls me onto my stomach. His body weight, transferred through his knee, is along my spine, and his hands are on the back of my head, pressing my face into the pillow. I can't breathe. I'm trying to lift my head by pushing down on the mattress with my hands. I can't do it with his knee in my back so I struggle to turn my head to the side, just to take a few shallow breaths. With his hands still pressing down hard on my skull, the pressure is almost unbearable, as if he's trying to crush it. He finally lifts his hands and removes his knee from my spine, but now he's gripping my neck with one hand, choking me hard with his fingers buried down in my neck muscles, and he's still using his body weight to press me down into the pillow. As I'm prone on my stomach, and with his hand firmly clamped on my neck like a vise, he savagely penetrates me. He's using his fingers and something else. I can't tell what it is but it hurts beyond belief—beyond any physical pain I've ever experienced. It feels as if he's tearing me apart with a butcher knife, and the abuse goes on for an eternity. I'm crying and trying to scream out. I can't. His chokehold has cut off my windpipe.

All I can do is wheeze and gasp, struggling to take in just a fraction of oxygen to maintain consciousness. Afterward, when he's finished brutalizing me, he leans down to my face. I'm in too much pain and too exhausted to move. Again, the stench of liquor and vomit hits me hard and his features finally come into focus. Through my tears, I finally see it's David. He yanks my head off the pillow by my hair and hisses in my ear, "Who the *hell* is Brian, Johnny?"

I want to speak. I want to say something that will lessen his fury, but the first blow to the back of my head stuns me senseless. The second one sends a blinding flash of light behind my eye sockets. I don't know what he hit me with, but it wasn't his fist. It was something much harder than a fist. He hauls me onto my back. He's straddling me now, breathing hard and looking down on me with wild eyes. *"Well, who is he, Johnny? WHO THE FUCK IS BRIAN?"*

Again, I want to speak. With the whiskey bottle in his hand, he slugs me across the face. The blow busts my lip wide open and snaps my head to the left. I taste blood in my mouth and see it spray across the wall five feet from the bed. For a third time I try to speak, but the blows to my stomach and my ribcage are too much. They just keep coming as I choke on my own blood and feebly try to raise my hands in self-defense. Thankfully, even though he's still pulverizing me, the pain finally fades away when I pass out.

Brian

"God, Mickey! Do we have to go over it again?" I'm rubbing my temples, trying to maintain patience. We've been at this for three hours now. Mickey's insignificant nightclub deal is becoming my biggest pain in the ass. I'm cramming two months of meetings into four weeks just so I can get the hell out of here, and he can't stop badgering me about the wording of a simple franchise contract.

"Look, I just need a sense of how you want it to read."

"I've told you what to write a dozen times and I've given you examples. Just get it down on paper. I'll look it over and sign it. How hard can it be?"

"Well, for you it's not a big deal. But for me, it's complicated,

Brian. Why are you getting so upset? I don't do this every day and I just need— Oh, excuse me one minute."

He pulls out his mobile and I brace myself, preparing for his inevitable yelling and the headache it's going to give me. Oddly, though, he doesn't yell.

"Hi Lars. How are you? Oh, really? Oh… really? What happened? I see. Oh…. I see. No, no—I understand. Yes, of course, you had to. How long ago was that? Really? No, no. I understand. Yes. I'll be sure to let him know. No. You don't have to call him. Um, look, I have to go. Yes. You, too—and Lars, I'm…I'm so terribly sorry. Goodbye."

I watch as Mickey lowers his mobile. He stares at his watch for a few seconds, deep in thought. Then he stands up. "Brian, I have to go. There's something I have to do. You're right about the contract. I'll draft up the wording and bring it over before you leave."

I'm a bit surprised. The phone call from Lars instigated something—something he doesn't want to tell me. "Okay. Is everything all right?"

"Hmm? Oh, yeah. I just…. There's something I have to do. Right now. It can't wait."

"Fine. Then I'll see you later." He quickly leaves the flat, and I wonder what the phone call was about. Something is up. Something regarding Lars has disturbed him. If I didn't have so much other stuff on my mind I might give it more attention, but right now, I don't have the time. If it's a problem regarding the business deal, I'm sure Lars will call me. Of course, I don't have a mobile right now thanks to John so it would be a wasted call. I'll just have to wait and see. It probably wasn't that important.

John — March 8

Familiar voices drift in and out of my brain. At first, the words all run together as meaningless, comforting noise. Little by little, the words become distinct, the voices are recognized more clearly and my comfort level increases.

"I don't want him to stay here," Martin says.

"No, he won't. He'll stay with me," Mickey says.

"We have to get him out of here as soon as we can," Jeff adds.

"Agreed, but until the doctor lets us move him, we stay with him. We don't leave him alone for one second, and we keep the press away," Ben says.

I'm lying on my side on the bed in the guest bedroom. I hear them discussing me as Prissy sits behind me, stroking my hair and rubbing my back. Now and then, he leans over and kisses my forehead. If I'd open my eyes I'm sure I could see them, too—but I don't want to open my eyes. They'll just fuss over me if they know I'm awake. I remember Mickey finding me: beaten, bloody from head to foot, floating in and out of consciousness. I remember the police officers coming to take a report and the doctor coming to examine me. I remember being carried into the spare bedroom and the unbelievable pain I felt when they moved me. I remember the wonderful sedative.

Jeff whispers, "What the hell did he use?"

"They think it was a broken whiskey bottle. They took it as evidence. He's vicious. He's just sick and vicious—a damned monster," Martin says in a low voice.

"Have they found him yet?" Prissy asks.

"No, but they will. Don't you worry," Mickey says. "He's got no money and nowhere to go. And in his state, he'll stand out like a sore thumb."

■ ■ ■

Over the next few days, I temporarily move into Mickey's spare bedroom and Prissy and Ben (who finally admit they're in love) move into the brownstone after the locks are changed. A solicitor contacted by David, who's gone into deep hiding thanks to his creepy friends, makes an offer: David will return to Los Angeles, keep his mouth shut and never bother me again if I promise not to file charges. As much as I want to see him punished for what he's done and as much as the authorities want to prosecute him for what he's done, I can't allow sordid publicity like this to get out—and he knows that. With my professional career going so well, I can't let the entire United Kingdom find out I was raped and sodomized with a whiskey bottle by my alcoholic ex-boyfriend. I agree to the offer. It takes an unbelievable amount of pleading with the authorities to keep them from pursuing the case but finally, understanding my unique situation, they relent under protest. Mickey pays for David's ticket to Los Angeles, I take a hiatus from the series and the musical for an acute case of laryngitis due to an aggressive throat infection, and everyone swears they'll never tell anyone what happened to me.

16
This "Ass" Thing

Brian — March 8

It's always good to see Simon. Not only is he my best mate, but he's also five centimeters taller than I am, so I don't feel so conspicuous when he's around. It's been a year since we were in London at the same time. He lives his life with Robert in Germany, and we've only communicated by phone for the last twelve months. It wasn't where they'd hoped to end up. The goal was a small village in southern Italy or a cliff-perched villa on Santorini, but Robert's diagnosis obliterated those dreams. I guess it was to be expected, but it still shocked the hell out of me when I heard the news, and the 'self-inflicted' stigma has been hard for them to deal with. Robert's medical needs and care are the priority now. Since Simon can do most of his work from a laptop, his days spent at hospital are productive and he's kept the bills paid. Even so, I've given him full access to one of my accounts, just in case the supplemental insurance starts rejecting Robert's claims.

This particular trip was made to see a specialist in West Ealing. Robert, too weak to travel but an avid reader of any research associated with possible treatment, relies on Simon to look into new laboratory studies all over Europe and the UK that show promise—even the faintest glimmer of hope.

We survey our meal after the waitress leaves. "How did it go?"

"Not so good. I don't think it's a feasible option. The drugs they want to inject are the same ones Robert couldn't handle the last time and they want to use higher doses. We've already had to come up with a new cocktail for the pain, and we finally stopped the diarrhea and vomiting. He can't go through that again, and neither can I."

"It's still that bad?"

"Brian, it's worse. He's continuously moaning unless he's drugged to the point of virtual incoherence."

"My offer still stands, you know?"

Simon shakes his head. "At this point, I don't even think he could make the trip."

"They deal with that, Simon. They know how to prepare patients for the flight. They won't stick him on a commercial airline, strap him in a seat and give him a packet of nuts. It's a dedicated, nonstop medical transport. He'd be the only passenger with a full medical contingency."

Simon sighs. "He's stubborn. He thinks it's charity."

I smile. "Still? Look, I know he's got excellent care where he is, but Consada Memorial has a reputation that's unmatched. If we could get him there before...."

"I'll talk to him again. I'll try to convince him."

"Good." We eat our food in silence. Simon is thinking about Robert. I'm thinking about John. We're just two blokes thinking about two blokes.

He finally says, "So tell me about the mansion."

"Hmm?"

"The mansion in Rittersby."

"Oh, right. It's pretty decent, not too bad."

"I was concerned with it being vacant for so long. Are there a lot of maintenance issues? How's the plumbing?"

"Hmm? Oh, um… not great. We'd have to replace everything with copper, but it's all readily accessible, except for one or two areas."

"And the roofs? They're slate, right? Replacing those could cost a small fortune. What's their condition?"

I'm pushing the thin strips of courgette around on my plate, making them form a spiral like the spiral staircase at the mansion, and I'm remembering John's scent.

"Brian?"

"Hmm?"

"The roof. The condition of the slate."

"Oh, yes. We would need to replace some of it, but it's held up pretty well considering the age of the place and lack of upkeep." I spend the next half hour fielding more questions about the state of the mansion and discussing the contract options and timeframes should I decide to buy it and renovate it. It all seems moot really, since I'm going back to Scotland early. I doubt any of it will happen. I just don't know how to tell him that after we've finally found the perfect place, his dream is a bust.

We watch as the waitress clears the table and refills our water glasses. As she leaves, Simon relaxes back into the booth. "So, what's this other thing you wanted to talk about?"

"Hmm? What other thing?" I'm puzzled. As far as I remember, we were only going to discuss Robert and the mansion.

"This thing that you haven't mentioned yet but has you so distracted."

"Have I been distracted? I hadn't noticed."

He smiles. "Brian, you've lost your train of thought about twenty times. You're a man who can remember anything anyone says, but right now, you couldn't repeat the last sentence *you* just said if your life depended on it. So what's up? What's on your mind and what's going on?"

The waitress returns to refill our scotch glasses. I wait until I'm sure she's out of earshot before I begin. It's a difficult story to tell, even to Simon. "I had a friend at the flat the other night—a bloke."

Simon sips his scotch. "Okay. And?"

"He kissed me."

Simon slowly sits upright. "He what?"

I take a deep breath. "He kissed me."

There's a pause. "When you say 'kissed,' you mean…?"

"Yes, that's what I mean." I'm looking at him intently so he knows I'm not joking. The last thing I need right now is to have him laugh about it.

He sinks back into the booth. "Okay. All right, then." A few minutes of silence pass while we sip our scotch. "Was it a surprise?"

"Hmm?"

"Did it come as a shock?"

I think back to how John attacked me in the kitchen. "Aye. Quite a bit of a shock."

"So, what did you do?"

I look around to make sure no one is near. "At first, I tried like crazy to get him off me, but I couldn't. Then I kissed him back."

Again, Simon sits upright. "Really? Hmm. So a bloke kissed you... and you kissed him back." He cocks his head. "Is he gay?"

"Aye."

"I'm assuming this is the first time you've ever...?"

I nod vigorously.

"What did it feel like?"

"What?"

"Well, did you like it, did you hate it?"

I'm embarrassed as I remind him, "Simon, I said I kissed him back."

"Okay, okay." He sinks back into the booth, stares at his water glass and sips his scotch. He starts to say something, then stops and takes another sip of scotch. Again, he sits upright. "All right, let's see. You're dating this woman now—Carol, right?"

"Well, no. Not anymore. It was just casual."

"Okay, but when you were dating her, you kissed her."

"Well, obviously."

"Rate her."

"Excuse me?"

"On a scale of one to ten, rate her kiss."

I stare at him in amazement. "You've got to be having a laugh."

"No, I'm serious. Rate her."

I think for a moment, trying hard not to taint her suck-face skills with the offensive scene at the theater. "Three and a half to a four."

"Okay. That's not bad—for you—for casual dating. That's not bad, at all. Now rate him."

This is just ridiculous. "Oh Simon, I can't!"

He leans across the table and looks at me hard. "Yes, you can. Close your eyes. Just think about it for a minute. Remember how it felt. Remember all the emotions and all the sensations. Okay?"

I close my eyes. It's certainly not hard to remember how it felt. I've been remembering how it felt every minute of every day since it happened. And I've been tenting the sheets every morning with a lovely replica of Big Ben, too. I open my eyes.

"Now, rate him."

I look him dead in the eye. "About a ninety-seven."

Simon, still leaning across the table, is flabbergasted. "Wow. He must be some guy."

"He's...he's pretty unsettling."

"Unsettling? Well, yeah. Judging from the way you look, I'd say he's knocked you off your feet. Your face has turned completely white." He flashes a devilish smile. "I guess I don't need to ask where the blood has just gone, do I?"

I lower my eyes and shake my head. I'm embarrassed, and I don't see the humor in his comment. Raging erections aren't something I've ever had to worry about before, and sprouting a super-sized Howdy-Doody every time I think about one particular bloke is starting to wear on me.

"What happened next?"

"Nothing."

"Nothing?"

"I told him to leave."

Simon sits upright. "So the shock factor kicked in pretty fast, then?"

I nod.

"Have you seen him since?"

I shake my head.

"Have you *talked* to him?"

I shake my head again.

Simon is appalled. "Well, don't you think that *might* be a good idea?"

"I don't know." I stare down at my water glass. For a while, we sit quietly—just drinking and thinking. The waitress comes to fill our glasses again. I watch her head back toward the main dining hall. "Simon?"

"Hmm?"

I lean in across the table. "Does this mean I'm kind of gay?" It's the question I've wanted to ask him since we sat down.

His eyebrows arch. "What?"

"Well, I mean.... I know I'm attracted to women, but when I.... The fact that it.... The way he...."

He gives me a fatherly smile. "Brian, it takes a lot more than one fantastic kiss to turn a straight man gay." He can see I'm not convinced. "All right, we'll analyze this *very* unscientifically. Answer some questions for me, okay?"

"Okay."

"What color are his eyes?"

"Deep blue."

"Right. What color is his hair?"

"Um... brownish-black, I think."

"You think?"

"I'm sure. I'm sure it's, um... brownish-black."

"How big are his hands?"

"His hands? I don't know... but he's got some bloody sharp fingernails, I'll tell you that. They're like little razorblades. They cut straight through fabric. They draw blood! I don't know how he—" I stop myself when I see Simon's blank face and open mouth.

"Fingernails? You noticed his fingernails? Okay...." Simon shakes his head as if to clear his mind of nonsense. "How tall is he?"

"I don't know. Um, wait a minute. Mickey said he was six-foot-one."

"So someone else told you how tall he was?"

"Yes, why?"

"It doesn't matter. Is he beefy?"

"What?"

"How's his build? Is he muscular? Is he slender?"

"I...I really don't know. He's strong, so I guess he might be muscular."

"You guess he *might* be? Does he wear tight shirts?"

"No."

"How's his ass?"

"What?"

"His ass. What's it look like?"

I'm baffled to the core. "Well how the *hell* should I know?"

"He doesn't wear tight pants?"

"No."

"Not ever?"

I shake my head. John, in tight pants? I don't even want to picture that.

Simon isn't impressed. "Brian, have you *ever* checked out a guy's ass?"

"Of course not! Why the bloody hell would I care what a bloke's ass looks like?"

He sighs. "You wouldn't, Brian, because you're not gay."

"I'm not?"

"No. You're not attracted to men, at all. You don't even notice the most obvious masculine attributes of men—attributes that gay men notice and really like. You only know the color of this guy's eyes, you guessed the color of his hair and someone else told you his height. I don't even *know* how to categorize that 'fingernail' thing."

I'm perplexed and frustrated. "Well, then what the hell am I?"

Simon takes a sip from his glass, rubs his hand over his face and gives me a tired look of pity. "Just a poor, pathetic straight sod who's fallen in love with someone who happens to be a guy... *and* who happens to be gay."

My mouth drops open and I shake my head in disbelief. "Oh, no, I am *not* in love with this bloke."

"Really? You, Brian Mallory, rate a kiss—*one* kiss—a ninety-seven and you're *this* bent out of shape over it. And now you want to sit here, look me in the face and tell me you're not in love with him? Don't take me for a fool and don't make yourself look like an ass. You're in love with him. He could be a damned rutabaga or a clump of dryer lint and you'd *still* be in love with him." He pauses, sinks back into the booth and sips his scotch before continuing. "Look, it might not be that bad. You hook up with this guy and hop back to Scotland, right? Sure, they'll probably make a stink at first, but then that blows over and you two just live your quiet little life together, rattling around in the mansion. It's not like you're in the public eye that much anyway."

"No. You're right. I'm not."

"There, you see? Everything works out fine." He lifts his glass in a small toast to himself for solving my dilemma.

"But he is," I say before he can take the sip.

He lowers his glass. "Really? What is he, a politician? Oh Jesus. Please don't tell me you've fallen for a goddamned politician."

"He's not a politician, Simon."

"One of those investment bankers? They're bad news, Brian. They lie just as much as politicians, they hide their assets, and they're all into hardcore porn and weird fetishes."

"Simon...."

"I mean it, Brian. He'll want you to make a kinky sex tape and pee on him."

I roll my eyes. "He's not an investment banker. He's an actor."

"An actor? A luvvie?" Simon sits upright, full of interest. "What? Stage, film, television?"

"Stage and television."

"Really?" He's intrigued, and I wonder if telling him this part about John is a big mistake. "Hmm. A gay English actor of stage and television. That's a good one. There're so many." He's looking at me for more information.

"He's not English."

"Not English? What is he?"

"American."

"A gay American actor of stage and television here in London. Hmm." His head is back and his eyes are closed as he thinks hard. "Give me more."

I reluctantly and quietly spill the beans. "His name is John."

"John...John." Simon shakes his head. "Nope. I can't think of any-one named John. My mind is a blank." Then, after a few seconds he says, "The only gay American actor named John I've even heard of is that gorgeous, young hunk from *TruthFinder Murphy*." He opens his eyes and beams across the table. "I swear he is a gay man's dream come true! You should *see* this guy, Brian. Honestly, he'll take your breath away. He takes everyone's breath away. He's so good looking and so damned sexy. He's a bit conceited — vain as hell, really — but if there's one gay man who could turn a straight man, then he's... the one… to…."

I don't think I've ever seen Simon's eyes grow so wide or his face turn so pale so fast. His mouth is moving but nothing is coming out. He picks up his water glass and gulps the lot. I watch as some of it dribbles down his chin and lands on the table. Beads of perspiration appear at his temples. "You've *got* to be kidding me! You *cannot* be serious! He's not the guy who…" He leans across the table and stares. "Brian, tell me he's *not* the guy who kissed you. Oh, my God! *Oh, my God!* What the *hell* are you doing with…? How could you…? When did you…? How did you even *meet* this guy?"

"Through Mickey, his manager. He's an old mate. He introduced us at an event one night and—"

"And what? You just happened to invite him back to your flat, and he just happened to snog you?"

"No, it's a bit more complicated than that. I made a silly comment on a chat show about three years ago and—"

"Wait a minute!" Simon blurts out, gripped by a revelation. His hands clench the edges of the table as if to keep it from levitating. "You mean to tell me you've *never* checked out his ass? You had John Kaiser in your flat, you kissed him—passionately—and not once did you check out his amazingly beautiful *ass?*"

I shake my head, thoroughly embarrassed, like I've just wet myself. It's clear Simon is disappointed in me, but I really don't understand this 'ass' thing.

"Damn, Brian!" He hangs his head and releases the table to rub his sweaty temples, trying to make sense of it all. "Do you *know* how many men would kill to be in your shoes? Do you *know* how many want to…? How hard some have tried to…? What they'd give to…?" He trails off and raises his head to give me a look of utter amazement. And for a fleeting moment—just as with Martin's words—I feel flattered and kind of special. Apparently, I am the chosen one. Simon sighs and sinks back into the booth, exhausted. "Well, that certainly explains the ninety-seven rating and your proud third leg. So what are you gonna do about it?"

"I've decided to wrap things up in the next few weeks and go home. I can't stay here. It seems as if my whole world is tilted on its axis. It feels awkward — like everything is leaning. I'm unbalanced and uncentered. I can't stand up straight anymore."

Simon smiles. "Well, maybe at this point in your life you're not supposed to stand up straight. Maybe you're supposed to lean a little."

He was trying for a lighthearted joke, but I'm not in the mood. The problem is too serious. "I need to put some distance between us and clear my head. It'll probably all blow over in a few months, right?"

"It might. It might not if he's serious about you. A gay man in love is hard to get rid of — like gum on your shoe, eczema, or a lousy time-share. I think you should talk to him and discuss your feelings."

"Oh, no. That is *not* going to happen. You know I don't discuss feelings. I only talk to you. No one else needs to know what goes on in my head."

"So you're just going to ignore what happened, leave England for good and hope it all goes away?"

"Aye. I think so. I think it's for the best."

"Well, I don't think ignoring it is the right move. I think that'll backfire on you."

"How?"

He sits up straight and gives me a long, serious look — a look filled with genuine concern. "I don't know, but for the record, Brian, and spoken as your best friend, I *honestly* think it will. That move will backfire on you, big time."

John – April 9

I'm in my super-unattractive, ratty old sweats, stretched out on Mickey's sofa. I've just finished watching a BBC documentary on the plight of the dwindling honeybee: *Nature's Amazing Creator of Natural Sweetness*, and now I'm poised to hear all about bhut jolokai: *The World's Hottest Pepper and its Many Culinary Uses*. I haven't shaved in days and I look like a bum you'd find smeared across a park bench, swigging from a bottle of cheap wine in a brown paper bag and making lewd comments to passersby. The front door opens.

"Hiya, Johnny! It's only me!"

"Hey, Mickey."

He shuffles in with two bags of food. "You all right?" He's giving me his 'truly concerned' look.

"I'm fine, Mickey. Really, I'm fine."

"Okay, okay. I can't help it if I'm a bit of a mother hen." He walks through to the kitchen and sets his bags on the counter. "Hey, I got some more of that pesto you liked so much last week. Remember? The one with all the pine nuts and loads of garlic? And I picked up more onions and those portabella mushroom ravioli, too. I didn't get the big ones that keep falling apart when I boil 'em. I got the small ones this time." He's busy shoving the food into the refrigerator and the freezer.

I stare at the television screen from my over-stuffed horizontal throne, bored out of my mind. "The big ones fall apart because you don't turn down the gas."

"What?"

"Nothing. It's not important."

He pokes his head into the living room. "Look, I've put a lot of this stuff in the freezer. It should be more than enough to tide you over until I get back."

"I can go shopping, Mickey. You didn't have to get all that stuff. Besides, you'll only be gone until Tuesday."

He comes out of the kitchen, wiping his hands on a dishtowel. "I know you can, but I don't want you going out if you don't want to."

"I appreciate that but it's been a month. Really, I'm okay."

"Good! I'm relieved to hear it." He flashes a big smile. "All right, my flight leaves at about seven and it's three now. Will you be okay if I take off?"

"Sure. Where are you going?"

He gathers his luggage, which consists of his fobless garment bag, a suitcase and a carry-on. "Well, I need to get a quick haircut and Marty says he can squeeze me in if I get there before three-thirty. Then I've got to see Brian about that nightclub franchise."

I cringe when he mentions Brian. The memory of David's brutal beating is almost gone. The memory of that fantastic kiss and Brian's rejection will never go away.

"If he's going to invest, he needs to sign the contract before he leaves. Oh, and I've got to get my tuxedo at the dry cleaners. I hope it fits in my garment bag. I've already stuffed so much in there, but I don't want to rent another one like last time. They're just crap, Johnny. I sweat up a storm because of those nasty, synthetic fibers."

"Mickey, why do you do this? Why do you always leave everything until the last minute and then run around like a crazy man?"

He grins. "I don't know. It gets worse with every trip I make out there, doesn't it?" It's clear he likes having a chaotic mess to deal with. "Okay, I'm going to leave a copy of my itinerary here on the counter, and I've emailed it to you as well. You have all my contact information. I only have one connector flight so I should be there in about twelve hours. Now, when I'm staying at The Montgomery they may upgrade my room if —"

"What did you say about Brian?"

"Hmm?"

"You said you had to get him to sign something before he leaves."

"Yeah, if he's in on it. He's got to sign the contract before he goes back." Mickey is fumbling with his wallet, de-bulking it before he shoves it back in his pants.

"Goes back where?"

He gives me a surprised look. "To Scotland, of course. It's about a month early, but he usually goes home around this time of year. He leaves tomorrow, so if I want his signature I've got to get it before I plant my ass on that plane. Okay. Have I got everything?" His eyes dart around the room, searching for that ever-elusive important item he won't remember he's forgotten until he boards the plane. "Yes, I think so. Now, give me a hug."

I stand up so Mickey can grab me in a bear hug and maul me while the revelation of Brian going back to Scotland sinks in.

"You be good. If you need anything — anything at all — you call me, okay? Keep the door locked and no wild parties. Don't forget you've got a meeting with Christie on Thursday. I'll be back before then, but you're the leading man. She wants your input on the costume designs and I want you to think of some good concepts before you see her. Okay? 'Bye, Johnny!"

I stand in front of the sofa with the television blaring as Mickey slams the door behind him. I'm numb and devastated. Brian is going home. Mickey says it's his normal routine, but what if I'm the reason he's leaving? I spend the rest of the evening stressing over it. I field calls from Prissy and Ben asking me to come out for a drink, but I want to be alone in my misery. I'm thinking of seeing him before he leaves. I want to apologize for what I've done, even though I probably shouldn't. Even though one last visit could make things worse.

17
Going Home

Brian — April 10

Considering the circumstances, I'm in a good mood. This day is going well. I've wrapped up most of my business in London, and I should be in Glasgow by six for a meeting with my top VPs. I've got Joe in the dressing room fixing the clothes rail. With half the sheetrock ripped off the walls and ceiling from the last time it fell, he can finally *see* the studs. Charles is rummaging through the basement storage rooms, looking for the crate to pack up the urn. I'll take it with me on the plane. Since it's priceless and very important, there's no way I'll run the risk of damage by having it shipped. I've got the movers preparing the Bösendorfer so the bloody thing can finally be craned out of here. I'll be glad to see that monstrosity gone. My world is returning to its normal state: calm, boring, and balanced. I like it.

"Now, Mister Mallory, we must be careful around the piano because I've unscrewed the leg bracings. If someone bumps it…"

"Don't worry, Hector. Charles already knows, and I'll tell Joe right now." I go into the dressing room to tell Joe to stay away from the piano. I come back to the living room and, for safety's sake, move the urn from the pedestal behind the piano to the plate-glass coffee table. My mobile buzzes. It's my bank manager. "Hello, Sophia. Yes? I didn't sign those? No, you're right. They have to be signed before I leave. That's not necessary. I'll walk over now. No, really. It's not a problem. They're about to move the piano and it would be better if I were out of their way. I'll be there in about ten minutes. Okay, goodbye." I decide to walk down to the bank, which is only a few blocks away, and leave

Hector to do whatever it takes to get that piano out over the balcony. "Hector, I need to run an errand. I should be gone for about twenty minutes. Will you be okay with the piano?"

"Sure, Mister Mallory. We're all set. Abe has the crane coming up the river. I'm just going to get the padding, lift and hoist cables from the van. Can I leave the door open?"

"Of course. If you need me, call me on my mobile. I'll see you in a bit." Once in the lobby, I let Brenda know where I'm going and head off down the pavement and around the corner. The weather is fantastic: semi-hot and sunny. Meteorologists say a major heat wave will roll in later tonight, but by then I won't even be here. I'll be far away from London and, more importantly, far away from John—for good.

John

I can't remember when I decided to get Brian a card. I was so tired of tossing and turning I finally got up at two-thirty and just watched television. I never did get any sleep, but I learned how to install ceramic tile around my bathtub, replace a sink trap and hang a tension-wire curtain rod using a laser level. There's nothing like pre-dawn DIY to numb a sleepless brain. I'm exhausted and I look like the walking dead with dark, puffy circles hammocking my bloodshot eyes. Thank God for wrap-around sunglasses. It takes a long time and three different shops to pick out the right card because I don't want one with a greeting inside. The one I finally choose has a black and white photograph of an old spiral staircase on it. Inside, I write, "Dear Brian, I'm sorry for everything I've done. Please forgive me." I decide not to sign my name. He'll know who it's from. I park a block away from his building, feed the meter for just fifteen minutes and walk to the lobby. I approach Brenda at the concierge counter with a weak smile. She's been on duty every time I've come to the building. It's as though she lives there. I guess I can finally greet her by name. "Hi, Brenda."

"Hello, Mister Kaiser. I'm sorry, but Mister Mallory isn't in at the moment."

"That's okay. I just want to leave this card for him at the counter."

She takes the card. "Are you sure you want to leave it here? You could pop up to the penthouse and leave it there."

"No, I'd better not."

"Are you sure, John?"

It strikes me as odd that she's using my first name. Not that I mind because I finally used hers, but it still seems strange. Then I realize what she's trying to tell me. If I leave the card at the counter, she'll have to hand it to Brian. He'll ask her who it's from, and when she says it's from me, he may not accept it. She knows we're not on good terms.

"He should be out for at least fifteen minutes, and I'll keep Charles busy in the basement." She hands back the card. "The penthouse is open. Just quickly pop up, leave the card and come back down."

I ponder her suggestion for a mere second. Although it's a bit spontaneous, the plan seems harmless. "Okay. I will." I walk to the elevator and ride up to the sixth floor for the last time. And even though I know he won't be there, I'm still nervous and I'm still sweating.

Brian

It's great having a bank three blocks from your flat. It's even better having a bank manager who meets you halfway on the pavement with your signing papers. "Sophia."

"Brian, I couldn't let you walk all the way. Besides, I wanted to get some fresh air. It's not often we have beautiful days this time of year. Here." She places the documents on a litterbin and hands me a pen. "It's a shame you're leaving London so soon. I hope it's not anything urgent calling you back."

"No, I'm just a little homesick and some things need my attention there." I sign the documents and hand them to her, along with the pen.

She flashes a big smile. "Well, have a pleasant flight and come back soon."

"Thank you, Sophia. I will." With my hands shoved in my pockets, I watch her walk away and then head back to the flat. She doesn't need to know I'm not coming back to London and that I've decided to lease out the flat, long-term; something I said I would never do. I pass the concierge counter without seeing Brenda. She probably went down to the storage rooms to help Charles look for the crate. I ride up in the lift, wondering if I'll still see that piano sitting there. I'm sure I will. I wasn't gone as long as I thought I'd be.

John

Where do I leave the card? I want Brian to see it but I don't want anyone else to just thoughtlessly pick it up. First, I try the kitchen counter. Lingering bad memories and the deep dent still in the refrigerator door cause me to scrap that idea. I try the plate-glass table next, but my measly little card can't compete with the magnificent Grecian urn sitting on it. I finally turn to the remarkable grand piano. He'll definitely see it there. The stark white envelope will stand out like an egret in a flock of crows. Carefully, I place the envelope on the piano. It's the closest I've ever been to this costly instrument and I'm uneasy. I've caused so much damage already; I would just die if I scratched this majestic piece. I take a backward step to appraise my handiwork. Yes, the envelope looks perfect. There's no way he'll miss it. I'm satisfied and I turn to leave. I stop dead in my tracks when I see Brian staring at me from the open front door.

18
The Impact Of Joe

John – April 10

When I was five, my mother and I took the train to Chicago. I can't remember why. It was probably to visit one of my aunts or uncles or one of her old college friends who had moved there after graduating. We were going to ride in one of the newer cars where some of the seats faced each other across the aisle. I knew the train would be crowded, as everyone on the platform seemed to have business in Chicago. The minute we boarded, I ran to claim two of those seats. It was a new way to ride, and I wanted to make sure I experienced it. I was really excited.

Fifteen minutes into the train ride, my excitement was long gone. What was so exciting about staring at another passenger across the aisle? And the one I had to stare at was horrible. She was (at the time) the largest woman I'd ever seen. I stared at her scuffed white shoes that were three sizes too small for her puffy feet. Then I stared at her ankles: each one horribly swollen with flesh creased over on itself as if her fat had dripped down and puddled there in hanging sacks because it had nowhere else to go. My gaze moved up to her calves, bulging like sausages in casings of shiny, sub-mucosa stockings in a sickening shade of brownish-pink. The color clashed nicely with the bright red dress she had stuffed herself into. It was bursting at the seams as she sat, resting her folded arms on humongous breasts. She didn't have a neck, so I bypassed her three hairy chins and went straight to her bloated face. It was almost the color of tomato soup with blue veins in fleshy cheeks so bulbous they invaded her eye sockets. She looked like a gaudy piñata, ripe for whacking with a big stick, or a great big—

"Johnny! Don't stare!" my mother hissed.

But it was so hard not to. And she was staring right back at me. What were these seats meant for anyway, if it wasn't to stare at other passengers? I see her glaring at me now—that obese woman on the train—in her white shoes and red dress. She's hovering over me, staring down with those bulging veined cheeks trying to squish her eyes out of their sockets. She's floating closely to me and I can't get away from her. Her eyes finally pop out and roll down onto her shoes. And then she expands outward and morphs into a… bus—a double-decker bus. Her scuffed shoes have become the pristine white grill of a bright red double-decker bus and her eyes are the headlights. My mind is a little foggy as I bring the bus into focus. It's not moving. It's not moving because it's a painting hanging up on a wall that's across from me. Where the hell am I?

I hear a deep voice speaking in quiet tones. It's a familiar voice and a comforting voice. It's Brian's voice. I want to look at him but I can barely move my head. I roll my eyes upward and the pain is blinding. There's nothing but brightness everywhere and I have an instant headache pounding behind my eye sockets. I lower my gaze and eventually Brian comes into focus. I see him, pacing near the painting of the bus and talking on his phone. He's looking at me. I watch as he walks over to a wall and reaches out to something, or for something. I can't tell what it is. Instantly, the blinding brightness is gone and the headache recedes to a dull, throbbing pain. My head spins and everything goes black.

■ ■ ■

I'm groggy, as if I've just woken up after a really kick-ass night on the town—still in a drunken stupor, laced with the onset of a killer hangover. I remember dreaming about a red bus, some white shoes and Brian's face hovering over me. It was a strange dream and I still see Brian's face hovering over me. Maybe I'm still dreaming. No, this pain seems real. I don't think this is a— "Brian?"

He's looking down at me with his hands shoved in his pockets, forehead wrinkled and face full of concern. "Hey."

"Hey." I'm bewildered. I don't know what's going on. I don't know where I am. There's some silence mixed with awkwardness, and I'm confused. "Where am I?"

He's still looking concerned. "My flat."

"What am I doing here?"

"Resting."

I'm a bit worried now. "Resting? Why? What happened?"

"Mishap."

Okay, he's not giving me much to work with. I need more than one-word answers. What the hell is "mishap" supposed to mean? Who even uses that word anymore? "What *happened?*"

"You had an accident. You just need to rest a bit."

I had an accident? I turn my head and feel a burning sensation in my right cheek. I wince at the pain.

"Try not to move. You need to keep still." His voice is calm. He takes his hands out of his pockets and sits down beside me on the…the sectional, I think. Yes, I'm lying on the left chaise of the big sectional in the living room. The painting of the bus threw off my bearings. It must be a new art piece.

I lift my hand and touch my cheek. Again, I feel the searing pain and gasp in astonishment. "Did you hit me?"

He smiles and the forehead wrinkles disappear. "No." He moves my hand away from my cheek and places it back by my side. "How do you feel?"

I give the question some serious contemplation because, dazed or not, I'm alert enough to know my answer will directly influence the amount of attention I'll get, and I want to milk this moment. "Terrible. My head hurts, a lot. I'm groggy. It's hard to focus on things."

He nods. "The doctor gave you something. You'll feel lightheaded for a wh—"

"*The doctor?*" Now I *really* want to know what happened. I'm worried. "I need to know what happened. Why did I need a doctor? How did I get here? What am I *doing* here?" I cock my head to the left as much as the pain will allow. "And what the hell are you staring at?"

Brian has been looking at some point above my right eye for about a minute. When he speaks, he's still calm and quiet. "You had an accident. The doctor came because of the accident. You're in my flat because you drove here earlier today. I'm staring at your forehead because you have a nasty cut, and I think it's time to change the dressing."

I take a minute to process the precise information. "But I still don't know what happened."

"That's because it's a head wound. You'll remember it soon. Right now, I need you to be still and relax."

Brian stands up and walks out of my view. I'm left alone to think. I can't remember what happened. Why did I come to the flat? I remember being at Mickey's condo but not here. The last time I was here I made a complete mess of things. I hadn't had any contact with Brian since that night. I wish I could remember why I came back. Why did I—

Scotland! Yes! Mickey said Brian was going back to Scotland, and I wanted to see him. No, I didn't want to see him. I wanted to apologize to him in a note—a card—left at the concierge counter. And then Brenda said I should go up and leave it in the flat because Brian wasn't in. So I came up to the flat and decided to leave it on the piano and—

Now I know what people mean when they say a memory came flooding back like a tidal wave. I feel hot and sick. My pulse is racing and I can't catch my breath. I remember that horrendous, never-ending chord that resonated through the flat when the legs gave way and the body of that heavy piano slammed to the floor. The crescendo was deafening. It scared the holy shit out of me. Brian comes into my field of vision again. He's carrying something—a tray, I think. As he sits down beside me, I just start blabbering. My chest expands and my breathing starts to go haywire as I gasp, "I broke the piano. Oh, my God! I broke the piano. I'm *so* sorry, Brian! I broke your piano. I didn't mean to! I *swear* I didn't—"

"Calm down. Just calm down. Take a deep breath. Listen to me. I want you to relax, okay?"

The tone of his voice is soothing, but firm. He's rubbing his palm on my chest in a slow, circular motion. I try to do as he says. I close my eyes and concentrate on his sensuous touch. God, his hand is big and warm! I regain my composure.

"That's it. That's good. Just relax. It's true. The piano isn't in top form right now, but it wasn't your fault. You didn't know the legs were unscrewed."

My eyes pop open. "Unscrewed? Why?"

"It was going today. They were finally going to haul the body out over the balcony with a crane. They prepped it by unscrewing the leg bracings. You were startled by Joe coming out of the bedroom and stumbled back into it. It could have happened to anyone, right?"

I nod in agreement. I'm feeling better about the piano, but who the hell is Joe? Brian stops rubbing my chest. It feels empty and cold without his hand there.

"Now, in a minute I'll need you to hold still, okay?"

"Okay." The word comes out sounding distracted because I'm still trying to figure out who Joe is. I don't remember anyone named Joe, and why was he coming out of the bedroom? Brian is messing with something. I can't see what he's doing with his hands. I'm focused on his face—and on some guy named Joe. "Who's Joe?"

Brian isn't paying attention to me. "Hmm?"

"Who is Joe? What was he doing in the bedroom?"

Brian gives me a puzzled look. "Fixing the clothes rail, finally. It only took him two and a half bloody months."

I sigh with relief. Joe is only the maintenance guy. "So, what happened after I... stumbled into the piano?" I pause. "Oh, my God! Did I faint? Please tell me I didn't faint!" I used to faint a lot as a kid. I stupidly disclosed that embarrassing tidbit to Brian the first night I came to the flat. On stage, you make it look dramatic and fall sideways in a graceful arc, but in reality, you always land flat on your face. Martin did at his brother's wedding. He was standing there as the best man, swayed a bit as the vows were being recited, and then just pitched forward, right next to the minister's podium. He fell flat on his face in front of one hundred and fifty guests, broke his nose and lost two teeth when he hit the altar steps. The videographer caught the whole thing on tape and his sister-in-law still won't speak to him.

"Well," Brian begins, holding up a length of gauze and a pair of scissors in my view, "technically—according to the doctor—you had a significant, fright-induced panic attack." He snips the length of gauze and puts down the scissors. "That caused you to hyperventilate." He's now folding the gauze into a small patch. "And that led you to pass out from lack of oxygen." He finishes his task, drops his hands into his lap and gives me a long, forlorn look. "Then you fell—face first—into my glass coffee table and smashed it to bits, along with my urn."

"*Oh, God,*" I groan, closing my eyes. "Brian, I am so sorry."

He sighs. "Yeah, losing that urn was a bummer." He lowers his head and he's on to his next task, cutting small lengths of adhesive.

I reach up to touch the wound.

Without looking up he says, "No, John."

I drop my hand to my side. I watch him, head down, engrossed in what he's doing. I see no anger, no bitterness, no hatred. He's calm and quiet. He's got those lovely, long brown eyelashes and the smoothest skin on his forehead. "Brian?"

"Hmm?"

"Aren't you mad at me… just a little?"

He shakes his head.

"But I've made such a mess of things. I've caused so much damage and I've—"

"It's not important." He looks up to survey the dressing on my forehead. "Now, I need to get this bloody thing off and it may hurt a bit."

Carefully, Brian peels off the adhesive strips. He's wrong. It hurts… a lot. I've always claimed a low threshold for pain. Over the years—to gain sympathy—I've kept it hovering around two-point-five. Anything lower just pegs me as an attention-seeking sissy and turns a sympathetic caregiver into a resentful bastard who inflicts even more pain. But this pain—in the range of five to six—is real. The adhesive is so strong it feels as if he's ripping off my skin with every pull. I can't help but wince and cringe.

"I'm sorry, love. I know it hurts but give me a minute," he coos in that beautiful, deep Scottish accent, trying hard to be gentle.

The sound of his voice makes it bearable. I close my eyes and concentrate on the faint clean smell of his soap and the undeniable fact that he just called me "love." He lifts a corner of the gauze pad and… it's stuck. God, I don't even want to imagine the crusty, bloody goop that's plastered it onto my forehead. Again, I have to wince.

"I know, I know. It's almost over," he quietly soothes, as if I were a child getting stitches.

Why would he do this? Why would he sit here and patiently clean this disgusting crap off my forehead? He could have the doctor do it, or a nurse. I bet he could even ask Brenda or Charles to do it. He finally peels off the caked gauze patch and turns away from me to put it—somewhere. Without thinking, I raise my hand again to touch the wound.

"No, John," he admonishes.

My hand goes back down.

He turns back to me and holds up a small brown bottle. "Now, I have to put this on it. Doctor's orders to prevent infection. It's definitely going to hurt."

I squint at the sinister-looking bottle. "What is it?"

Brian examines the label. "I'm not quite sure, but it's got a lot of iodine in it so I know it's going to hurt like hell. You ready?"

I take a deep breath and brace for the pain. "Yes."

He's right this time. It hurts. It hurts like blinding hell. It hurts so much that I pass out—again.

Brian

I watch as his eyes flutter open. I've been checking on him for the last half hour, ever since he passed out—again. I had no idea he'd be out that long but Alex thought he was suffering from exhaustion and trauma long before today's panic attack. I don't know what caused that, but Mickey may know.

"Did I pass out again?"

"You're fine now. The dressing is changed."

Again, he lifts his hand to touch it. This time, since it's not oozing and caked with blood, I let him. I stand over him and watch as he gingerly explores the edges with his fingertips, feels the adhesive strips, and checks the size of the gauze pad. And as I look down on him, I ask myself: What the hell am I going to do with him? He's made me so unbalanced and unsure of myself. He's caused so much emotional chaos in my life and an unbelievable amount of monetary damage, yet I'm not angry with him. I can't even pretend to be angry with him. I sit down on the edge of the sectional and look into his eyes. God, I want to kiss him—badly. My entire body aches to crush him hard against me, to feel what I felt once before. I want to love him and protect him. I desperately want to take care of him and make him happy. I just don't think I can tell him all of that.

"Can I have some water?"

"Can you sit up?"

"I think so."

I go to the kitchen for a glass of water. I watch from behind the counter as he struggles to sit up. At first, he'll be dizzy. I hope he doesn't have another panic attack and pass out once he sees the state of the piano over the back of the sectional.

John

Who would think just sitting up could make your head spin in circles? I'm dizzy but I'm determined to remain conscious. I don't want Brian to think I pass out every time I move. I close my eyes and let the swimming feeling subside. I take a deep breath. Opening my eyes again, I feel better. My head is clearer. I focus on different items as I pan the flat: the painting of the bus on the far wall; Brian off in the distant kitchen; another painting; a pile of suitcases abandoned near the entryway; the hallway entrance; a large stain of (I'm assuming my) blood with glistening chards of glass and pottery on what was once a pristine white carpet; and a humongous, flattened grand piano. It looks like a morbidly obese, three-legged spider that collapsed under its own weight. The legs are splayed out in all directions and there's a gaping horizontal crack running along its side. I feel so bad about that beautiful, expensive piano. Brian returns with my water and sits down beside me. He hands me two tiny, red pills. "What are these?"

"Just take them."

I sip some water and swallow my pills. "I came here to apologize. When Mickey told me you were leaving…" It's too hard to finish the sentence without choking up, so I concentrate on drinking the rest of my water. When I'm through, Brian takes the glass, sets it on the table and then brushes a lock of hair off my forehead. He's looking into my eyes but I can't tell what he's thinking. I whisper, "You were going back to Scotland?"

He nods.

"Without telling me?"

He nods again. "I needed to clear my head. I wanted to get out of England and—I'm sorry—far away from you for good."

Oh, that makes me feel *really* great—like a million bucks! The man I love more than anything; the man I can't stop thinking about day and night, needs to leave the country to get away from me—*far* away from me. Oh, yeah. That's just a hoot! "Then why didn't you leave?" My voice is shaking as the anger quickly builds.

"You'd passed out and gashed your head, John. What was I supposed to do?"

The level of my voice is rising. I'm not hiding my anger now. I'm working myself up to a small explosion. "Call an ambulance, have me carted out, pay the housekeeper to clean up this mess and be on your way!"

"It wasn't that easy…"

"Sure it was, if you were so *desperate* to get away from me—excuse me, *far* away from me! If you couldn't *stand* to be anywhere near me! If I *disgust* you that much—"

He lowers his head. "You don't disgust me."

"Sure I do!"

"No you don't."

"Then what is it, Brian? What is *so* terrible about me that you can't even be in the same country as me? *Huh?* Is it the kiss, Brian? Are you afraid I'm gonna tell all your straight friends that you *kissed* a man— that you kissed a *gay* man? *Huh?* IS THAT IT?" I'm waiting for an answer. I'm shaking with anger, my face steaming. And the fact that this patient, gentle man isn't angry with me for entering his home uninvited and causing well over a million dollars worth of damage will not lessen my fury because I'm too busy acting like a spoiled, selfish brat to care about that right now.

Brian

With my head hanging down, I rub my eyes with thumb and finger. This is hard for me. I've never discussed my feelings with anyone except Simon. I'm so uncomfortable I can't even look at him as I speak. I stare at my big feet. "The first night you came to the flat I was dumbfounded. There you were, in full fig, ready to go to a party, sitting out on my balcony. You were so nervous. I can't stand nervous people, but once you relaxed, I just wanted to spend the whole night talking to you. I didn't want you to leave. I *really* didn't want you to leave, and I don't know why." I wait for a response, but there's nothing, so I go on. "At the theater, I felt terrible about what Carol said. I was responsible for putting you in that uncomfortable position." My throat tightens with nervousness. My forehead is hot, and I still can't look up at him.

"It's okay. You can take your time."

A few minutes pass before I continue as I try to gather my racing thoughts. "After, when we kissed...." I close my eyes, reliving the wild passion I felt, remembering how I wanted him and how sensational he smelled and tasted. Now I can barely speak and my words come out as a whisper. "I can't begin to describe what was happening to me. I don't know what was going on inside me. I've never felt like that before in my life. I couldn't get enough of your unbelievable scent. I wanted you so badly and I think.... Jesus, this is hard. I think I love you. I just.... I just don't know how it happened... or why... or what to do about it." I'm rubbing my temples now, trying to ease the extreme tension across my forehead. I don't have any more words. That's it. That's all he's getting.

John

I'm staring at him as he stares at the floor. I can't believe this is real—that this isn't a dream. I'm afraid to move. I'm afraid if I do, I'll wake up alone in my bed, the same way I've awakened after so many countless dreams I've had of him. I swallow hard. I lean forward and press my lips to his forehead. I gently kiss it and let my lips linger there, soaking up the intense heat of his soft skin. This heat doesn't feel like a dream. This heat feels real. I whisper his name. He lifts his head and for a moment, our mouths hover near without touching. I slowly lean in, tilt my head to the side so we don't bump noses, and just barely touch his lips with my open mouth. He quickly pulls back, confused and unsure, eyes blinking rapidly, breath quickening. I give him a moment. It's all new to him and I have to be careful. I love him so much, and I don't want to spoil this. I lean in again, slowly—once more, just barely brushing his lips with mine. I can almost feel his fear, but hesitantly he returns the touch and then presses in a little more. After a few seconds, I feel his tongue opening my mouth wider, and then I'm completely his. Under his weight, I fall back on the sectional and submit to every thrust of his tongue and every bite of his teeth. His kiss is voracious, fierce and unbelievably powerful, as if he's releasing weeks of frustrated desire as he bears down on me. I groan. I moan. I pull my mouth away only to whisper his beautiful name over and over. I'm breathing hard in his ear and gently biting his neck. Then my fingers are in his hair, pulling his head down and crushing his lips on mine again. I'm jamming my tongue in his mouth, digging deeply, tasting as much of him as I can and still it's not enough. This all-consuming arousal is so intense. I'm sweating like crazy, my body heat is out of this world and I need to feel more of his weight pressing down on me. I *desperately* want to have sex with him. I want it so much. I've never, ever wanted it this much. I reach down and grope for the waistband of his jeans, searching for the buttons. He pulls back a little. His voice is thick and lusty—almost a grunt—as he gasps into my ear, "John?"

"Yes, Brian," I gasp back breathlessly, still fumbling for the buttons.

"If I help you, can you make it into the bedroom?"

Oh, hell yes! I'd prefer to have him blast my fine ass to heaven right here, sprawled across the sectional like a hedonistic sacrifice, but if he's dead keen on prudish formalities—that's fine. I'd slither across that pile of broken glass on my naked belly if I had to. "Yes, Brian! I can make it into the bedroom." I'm still wildly groping for those elusive buttons with sweaty fingers. Screw Levi Strauss and his goddamned button flies!

"Good." He's kissing the left side of my forehead now, being careful not to touch my gauze patch, still breathing hard. "I've got some board members coming in less than half an hour."

It takes a few seconds for my brain to process that last sentence and for my fingers to stop fumbling at his waist and realize we've left the subject of extreme horniness and impending hot sex behind and have moved on to... board members? "What?"

"They'll be here in less than thirty minutes. I can explain the piano well enough, and I can pull a chair over the stain, but you lying here on the sectional.... Well, I don't want it to look like a convalescent ward, do I?"

A convalescent ward! "Wha— Wait a minute. What the— What the hell are you saying?"

He looks over at the conference room's wall of glass. "The curtains. They were sent out for cleaning when I thought I was going back to Scotland." He looks back down at me. "You can see straight through from here."

I'm staring up at him, half-stunned and quickly ramping up to half-furious, as he hovers over my face. Is he *serious?* He scheduled a meeting—*here? Now?* And he expects me to listen to some lame crap about *curtains?* I explode. "BRIAN! *What the—* You've just professed your love for me, we're in the middle of getting all hot and horny, I'm *definitely* expecting some mind-blowing sex here, and you want me to get lost because you've scheduled a *damned meeting?*"

He's scrambling to clean up around me. "Look, it's an important kick-off conference with eight of my VPs from Glasgow. It's one I've already rescheduled twice before. When I cancelled my flight, I just thought: Why not fly them out here? I didn't plan to.... I wasn't thinking of.... I had no idea we'd...." He stops what he's doing, looks at me with spooked-rodent eyes, and then grabs the tray of gauze and adhesive and bolts for the safety of the kitchen. I'm propped up on my elbows, and my mouth is hanging open. This is unbelievable! In my stunned state, I have no idea what to say, and on top of everything, I'm feeling dizzy again.

He comes back to me and looks here and there for any stray first-aid supplies he might have missed. "It shouldn't take long. Probably just a few hours to go over the key issues and milestones. Ready?"

"Wha—"

Before I know it, he's got me hitched up under my armpits with my arms flapping, and my lethargic ass is being dragged backward around the flattened piano, down the hallway, and into the master bedroom with my lead feet and noodle legs frantically trying to keep up with my fast-moving torso. This is no way for a theatrical star and television celebrity to be transported! It's embarrassing! Brian, strong as an ox, unceremoniously heaves me up, dumps me on the bed like a slab of beef and hurls a blanket in my face. God, I'm pissed! I'm fuming! And I am *really* questioning my undying love for this man! "*Stop it!* JUST STOP IT!" I wildly flail my arms, trying to throw off the damned blanket and struggle to my knees. I need to overcome this ever-increasing dizziness and show him some true bitch-fury. As I pinwheel my arms to keep from pitching forward off the edge of the bed, I realize I'm not accomplishing either feat.

"Look, I know you're angry with me and I am *so* sorry, but they've already landed and they're on their way."

Attempting to hone in on his voice, I apprehensively scan the bedroom like a disoriented drunk trying to track an elusive bumblebee. Where the *hell* is he now? His words are faint, trailing in from the dressing room, I think. To me, they sound muffled and warped. I shake my head a few times, trying to get my brain and eyes to focus, but it's no use. Everything is fuzzy. He appears around the corner in dark gray slacks, a bright white shirt and a smoky blue silk tie dangling loose around his neck. He throws the matching suit jacket over the back of a chair, stands in front of the lowboy mirror and runs his fingers through his hair. Et voila! Each strand is coiffed to perfection. How in the world can he do that? My mousse-and-spike routine takes twenty minutes. I shake my head again, trying to clear it. I can't fret about comparative grooming regimens right now. I need to concentrate on being furiously angry and super pissed off... but I'm so damned groggy. I try to make my trembling voice sound serious as my head swims. "Brian, do *not* do this to me."

He's looking at my reflection in the mirror as he fumbles with his tie. "It's important to me, John."

Still acting like a spoiled brat and thinking only of myself, it's my sacred duty and my God-given right to remind him of his only priority. "No, *I'm* important to you."

"I have to keep this meeting. It's important."

He's calmly holding my gaze. He can see I'm seething with anger but it's having no effect on him. So then, because I'm so frustrated and I'm used to getting what I want, and there's nothing heavy to throw at him and nothing (within arm's reach) that I can break, and I don't know what else to do, the shit hits the fan in a mighty big way: "NO! I'M MORE IMPORTANT THAN THE GODDAMNED MEETING! I MATTER—THE MEETING DOESN'T! I DON'T WANT YOU TO HAVE THE MEETING! I WANT YOU TO CALL THESE...THESE STUPID VPs AND TELL THEM TO TURN AROUND, GET THEIR FAT ASSES BACK ON THE PLANE, AND...*AND BUGGER OFF BACK TO SCOTLAND!*"

I can't believe how loudly I've just shouted or how much I'm shaking and wheezing. Right now, I probably look like an hysterical, detoxing drug addict who's having an asthma attack and desperately needs a fix. I clutch at my heaving chest, fearing a heart attack. Brian stopped fumbling with his tie the second my tantrum started. Now, with it still hanging loose around his neck, he turns and walks toward me as I'm kneeling, shaking, wheezing and dangerously swaying on the edge of the bed. I have this horrible feeling he's just going to haul off and smack the living shit out of me. I'm not sure my gorgeous face could survive a third busted lip. He stands right in front of me without speaking. Then his phone buzzes. He pulls it out of his pocket. "Yup?" His eyes are glued to mine. "Okay, give me a minute." He pushes a button on the phone without taking his eyes off me and calmly says, "They're in the lobby. If you want me to tell them to leave, I will."

I can't detect any hatred or anger in his voice—not an ounce. "I don't want them here." I try to say it with authoritative conviction, but it dribbles out as a pathetic whimper.

"I know you don't. You'll never want them here. You'll never want anyone here, and you'll always expect to get your way. You'll shout at me and throw tantrums, and I'll never be angry with you. I've told you how I feel about you. Nothing will change that. No one will change that. This meeting won't change that. I really need to have this meeting."

If I tell him to cancel the meeting, he will. As I look into his eyes, I know he'll do whatever I say, and he won't be angry with me. If I tell him to put them back on the plane, he'll do it without resentment. I've won. I sit back on my heels, exhausted. "Okay."

He pushes the button. "Edward, come on up." He steps closer to the bed and without hesitation, I reach out and set his tie in a lovely knot, gently cinched up to his neck—the luxurious silk running through my fingers like melted butter. I turn down the collar of his crisp shirt. He looks so handsome and so beautiful. I gently pull on the tie and he bends to kiss me—soft and tender. He moans. I run my lips over his face, exploring its contours. I whisper his name over and over, and breathe "I love you" into his ear half a dozen times. I look into his mesmerizing eyes and unglamorously yawn. I'm so tired. My heavy head is lolling on my shoulders and I can't keep my eyes open. I yawn again—nice and loud, presenting him with a mouthful of teeth. I don't know why I'm so dizzy and sleepy. Then I remember my two, tiny red pills. And then I remember nothing… for a long time.

Brian

The meeting goes as well as can be expected with my mind focused solely on John asleep in the bedroom. If Charles were here, I could have him playing nurse but I sent him back to Scotland. I thought I should put him in charge of the mansion, and he missed his extended family. I'm not sure how obvious my lack of concentration is as I glance at everyone around the conference table. I thought they would have tired by now, but they want to go over everything—every little detail of the new venture. Normally, that would impress me. Tonight, it just irritates me. I've got other things on my mind. An hour and a half into the financial report I suggest a twenty-minute break. The smokers are dying to get outside to feed their addictions. Others want to call home or check messages. I need to change John's dressing again.

As I walk into the bedroom, I see he's rolled onto his right side, even though I had rolled him onto his back twice before. His mouth is open, his face is relaxed and his breathing is slow and deep. Gently, I roll him onto his back, sit on the edge of the bed, turn on the light and set up my tray of gauze and adhesive. I peel off the strips from his forehead and remove the dressing. The cut looks much better. It's a healthy shade of pink with little discharge, no swelling and no more blood. This next patch might be the last one he needs. Alex said he wanted the cut exposed to air as soon as the risk of infection was gone to help it heal faster and scar less. I dab on the iodine and quickly dress the wound, making sure to keep any stray wisps of hair away from the adhesive strips. I take the tray into the bathroom and wash my hands. By the time I come back into the bedroom, he's rolled back onto his right side. I sit down for a minute and watch him sleep. His mouth is closed now, and every time he exhales, I hear a clear, high-pitched whistle. It's odd, but cute. I stroke his stubbly cheek with the back of my hand. I have to touch him to make sure he's really here, really a part of my life — and really mine. I turn off the light.

I barely last the final two hours of the meeting. My concentration is so bad I record the remainder of it on my mobile. I'll listen to what was said later. By the time I get everyone down to the lobby and shuttled back to the airport in cabs, it's half past midnight and I'm exhausted. It's been a long, emotional day. Ordinary things that were supposed to happen didn't happen, extraordinary things I never imagined would happen have turned my calm, quiet world upside down, and I don't know what to do. I pour some scotch, step out onto the balcony, and pace as I call Simon. It's late but he's never kept regular hours since Robert went into hospital. I hope he's available now because I really need to talk. He answers on the first ring. "Brian, how are you?" He sounds tired.

"Simon, is it too late to call?"

"Never too late, good man. Never too late. What can I do for you?"

"How are things? How is Robert?"

Simon sighs and his voice drops a level. "Don't ask. At this point, it's not worth mentioning." Then he livens up. "Tell me something interesting; take my mind off it."

"John is here."

"Where? At the flat?"

"Aye."

He pauses. "You didn't go to Scotland."

"No. I had every intention of being there tonight but things just kind of…"

"Backfired. What happened?"

"I told him. I told him I loved him."

"Really? How did that work out?"

"I don't know yet. He's asleep."

"*Asleep?* You tell a guy you love him and he falls asleep? That's not a good sign, Brian. Your delivery needs some work."

"I drugged him."

"*You what?*"

"It's a long story. I don't know where to begin."

"You can begin by sitting down. I can't stand it when you pace and talk."

"Sorry." I collapse into a chair, set down my scotch and stare across the river.

"All right. Now, slowly — explain everything that happened… slowly."

I tell Simon about the day's events: the movers coming for the piano, the unbelievable accident, and finally giving the sleeping pills to John under Alex's instructions and hauling him into the bedroom. I omit the details of the lovely tantrum. He's silent for a long time.

"So now you've got John Kaiser sleeping naked in your bed."

"No, he's got his clothes on."

"You didn't even *undress him?*"

"No."

"Why not?"

"There's no way I'm undressing a bloke who's virtually unconscious. That's just *not* going to happen."

Simon lets out a painful "arrggghhh" as if he's disappointed in me and frustrated with me. At this point, he's either rubbing his temples or pulling out his hair. "Okay, so now he's lying fully clothed in your bed."

"Yes. What do I do?"

"Well, you sound tired. Are you tired?"

"Absolutely knackered. It's been a long day."

"Then go to bed, Brian."

"In the spare bedroom?"

"No, in your bedroom. Go into your bedroom, take off your clothes and climb into bed with John."

"I can't."

"Yes, you can."

"Simon, really. I...I don't think I can."

"You can do this. It's not a big deal. You told him you loved him. He's in your bed. You've seen enough cheesy romance movies. This is the next step."

"I'm just.... It's not something I've ever.... I mean, what if he wakes up?"

"If you haven't killed him with the drugs, he probably will."

"And what if...? What if he wants sex?"

Simon is thoughtful. "Well, Brian, like any other young, healthy, horny, virile, sex-starved, head-over-heels-in-love gay man, he probably will. And it'll be okay."

"But I've never.... I don't know how to...."

"But he does. He'll know what to do. Christ, he's gay! And I think you'll find it's not that different from what you're used to. Hell, from what I know of your current sex life, you'll probably think it's better. Ultimately, it's just a different view—a wider perspective. Things are quite simplified. You find the target—there's only one and it's deceptively accommodating—aim the battering ram in the right direction and give it a gentle shove."

I run my fingers through my hair. "Bloody hell."

"Brian, what are you so afraid of? It's not that hard. It's...it's—How can I put this so you'll stop over-analyzing everything? It is what it is. Just get undressed, climb into bed and see what happens. It's a new experience. Don't freak out about him, don't pull away from him and don't worry about him." He pauses for emphasis. "And above all, *don't* judge him."

"Oh, God." This pep talk isn't making me feel any better about the situation.

"Look, remember the kiss? Remember how hard it was at first because you fought it?"

"Aye."

"Then remember how good it felt once you accepted it—once you accepted him?"

"Aye, I do."

"This is the same thing. You're off balance because you're used to being in control—and you will be again, eventually—but right now, there's nothing to control. It's got to take its own natural course. No planning, no scheduling, no arranging. Just don't fight it, okay?"

"But—"

"No! For once, just let it go and see what happens. You've lived the straight life for forty-one years. Along comes John and you fall in love. Now it's time to lean a little. Okay? *Okay?*"

It takes a while for me to answer. "Okay."

"So go to bed."

"I will."

"Goodnight, Brian."

"Goodnight, Simon, and thanks."

"Don't mention it. Call again if you need to, anytime. I'm always here for you."

"I know." I end the call, finish my scotch and go back into the flat. I turn out the lights and head for the bedroom. There's John, still fast asleep on his right side. I walk into the bathroom, strip off my clothes and step into the shower. The jets pound against my skin as I turn slowly, head down and eyes closed. I'm remembering Simon's advice. I'm not going to analyze everything that might happen, that could happen, that probably will happen. I'm just going to let it happen. I'll get through this first night with John.

I turn off the jets and pat myself dry. Stepping out of the shower, I take a good look at myself in the mirror. I don't flex my muscles. I don't pose. I just stand there and critique my body. I'm trim, fit and muscular. I have some chest hair, but not a significant amount. I don't think he'll have a problem with it, but if he does—tough. I'm not going to wax it off. I'm not saggy anywhere. My abdominal muscles are tight, and I don't have love handles. All in all, I'm not worried about those parts. What worries me is dangling between my legs, limp and foreboding. I'm a tall man. Proportionately, I'm a big man. And because

I'm a big man, I've got big hands, big feet and big tackle. Right now, that's my only concern. I've done all right with women, but what about John? He's the one in the bedroom, and if I remember the human anatomy correctly, even though it's been almost twenty years since medical school, I think it could be a problem. I should have asked Simon what he meant by "deceptively accommodating." I mumble the words aloud, "Deceptively accommodating." It sounds like an asinine sales pitch touting the spacious interior of a Mini Cooper. Those aren't reassuring words to a man who can't even fit in a Volkswagen Beetle.

I wrap a towel around my waist, collect my clothes into the hamper and turn off the light as I head back into the dark bedroom. I walk to the left side of the bed, drop my towel and climb in. Pulling the sheet up to my navel, I lie down and stare at the ceiling. Through the skylight, I watch wispy clouds stream by as I listen to John's slow, rhythmic breathing. I can easily accept his little whistle; I'm just glad he doesn't snore—or fart. I turn my head to look at his back and then stare out the skylight again. In my mind, I go over all of the significant events of the day as my eyelids grow heavy. I am physically and mentally spent. I am truly wiped out. Tonight, for the first time in eleven years, I relish sleep. Eventually, my eyes close and my head falls to the side. The last sensation I have before I drift off into a deep, exhausted sleep is the feel of warm mist coming in off the river and settling on my face.

19
The Puppet Master

John – April 11

Of all the things Brian told me he disliked the first time I came to the flat, I wish air conditioning wasn't one of them. It's stifling, and I'm beyond hot. There's a faint breeze rolling in off the river, but it's warm and misty – like a summer fog. I don't know how long I've been sleeping. Brian took off my watch. I don't see a clock on the nightstand, but it's dark. I'm lying on my right side, facing the dresser and the bathroom doorway. I sit up slowly and swing my legs over the edge of the bed. I wait for the dizziness to engulf my senses, but my noggin feels pretty good, just a little lightheaded. I finger the gauze patch. It's different in shape than the first time I felt it. Brian must have taken time out of his meeting to apply a new dressing. I don't even know what the cut looks like, and Mickey will have a heart attack once he finds out. My whole body is clammy with a new epidermis of sweat – dried and fresh. I carefully stand up. I can make it to the bathroom if I keep my right hand on the nightstand for balance and then switch to my left hand on the dresser when I cross to the bathroom doorway. Once I'm in the bathroom, I'll have the long sink counter to get me to the urinal on the far wall and the toilet next to it.

I love this bathroom with its cool slate floor, thick blue-glass sinks and pristine vitreous china urinal – obviously mounted for Brian's height, not mine. I'd like to take a cooling shower but the last thing I need is for Brian to come out of his meeting and find me in it, sprawled out on my ass. Besides, I don't have any idea how to work the elaborate controls. I turn on one of the sink taps and pat cold water on my face and neck with a washcloth, being careful to avoid my dressing and my bruised cheek. I peel off my shirt and rub the washcloth all over my torso and down my arms. I drop my pants, step out of my damp briefs and run the washcloth over my lower body, spending extra time on those significant areas—front and back—because when Brian comes out of that meeting, I intend to get me some sex. With the sticky layer of sweat now gone, I feel cleaner and cooler. I leave the washcloth and clothes in a heap on the floor (one of my more irritating habits), turn off the bathroom light and head back into the dark bedroom, again using the dresser for balance.

I pull open the nearest drawer and find dozens of socks, fastidiously rolled and lined up in rows. I move down the length of the dresser and pull open the next drawer, only to find two stacks of soft cotton t-shirts, folded to anal perfection. Finally, the third drawer has what I'm looking for: boxers. Even in the dark, I see they're sorted by color. I choose a dark pair. They're either blue or black; I'm not sure. Hopping around like a crazed pogo stick, I nearly land on my ass trying to pull them on with my balance still off. They're too big, but they are oh, so soft. I wish I had thirty pairs of these luxurious silk beauties. As my eyes adjust to the darkness, I check out myself in the mirror. The color looks good with my pasty-white skin (I'll admit, I could use a tan). If it weren't for the gauze patch above my right eye, the bruise on my cheek, and my bedhead hair, I could pass for a hot-looking underwear model in a photo shoot. That's what they do: Find someone with a killer-view penthouse and pay him shitloads of money to use it for a four-day shoot. Of course, in this shot I'd be standing more to the left so the cameraman could take the picture with the reflection of a sexy vixen spread out on the bed behind me. I set my face with a smoldering "come hither" stare and move to the left as if I'm setting up for the shot. And that's when I finally see Brian lying in the bed behind me.

I whip around, stunned. I thought he was still a hundred feet away in a meeting on the other side of the flat. I realize I have no concept of time and I'd slept much longer than I'd thought. I run my fingers through my hair. What do I do? Now that my dream guy is laid out before me like a pagan offering, I'm in a state of confusion. He's close to the left edge of the bed, bare-chested, with the sheet pulled up to his waist. It's certainly not what I expected. I thought I'd have to chase him down to jump his bones. But he obviously had no problem getting into bed with me, so I walk back to the right side and climb in under the sheet. This is a palatial bed. With me on one side and Brian on the other, there's still a good six feet of space between us. I scoot across the expanse and stop just before our bodies touch. He's in a relaxed deep sleep, and looking at him this closely, I don't think he's wearing anything under the sheet—again unexpected, but highly appreciated. I take a long moment to study his exposed body.

He's lying on his back with his head turned away from me toward the open sliders. His left arm is bent at the elbow and his left hand is about five inches from his face, palm upward and fingers curled. His right arm is folded across his ribcage. With each breath, I watch his arm rise and fall, along with his chest and unbelievably flat stomach. Physically, he's nothing short of perfection, possessing every masculine feature that excites me. He is truly a beefcafe, with so much well-defined muscle mass it's no wonder he was able to haul me back onto the landing with only one hand at the mansion. He's ripped beyond your average gym rat, but not to the point of a frenzied, egotistical bodybuilder. These formidable muscles aren't from steroids. They're from lifting weights—*big* weights. And because he's so tall, his tight muscles are long and lean. He doesn't have that puffer-fish look so many short guys have. He's got robust pectoral mounds (but not man-breasts, thank God!), and lovely dark, taut nipples. The mass of fine hair on his chest is light brown and curly. Shaped like a V, it trickles to the thinnest line as it travels down his torso to his sexy, cavernous navel. I can't believe he hides this phenomenal physique in business suits and long-sleeved dress shirts. Just looking at him, lying here in a deep sleep, causes my body to heat up—fast. I want to touch him. I want to grope him. God, I want to smell him! I carefully re-position and lean in closely to the sheet with my nose hovering over his crotch, hoping he doesn't wake up to find me sniffing his privates. There's the faint smell of soap but if I concentrate, there's that wonderful man-scent, too: Musky, leathery, warm male genitals. I inhale deeply. That unique aroma—Brian's soft scent—is an aphrodisiac for me, and my body heat intensifies. I'm out of his boxers in seconds.

"Brian?" I whisper.

No response.

"Brian?" I whisper again, with more intensity.

"Hmm."

"Move your arm."

There's a pause. Brian sighs and moves his arm to the left, further away from his face.

I roll my eyes. "No, Brian, your other arm. Move your *other* arm. Lift it up."

At first, I don't think he hears me because there's no immediate re-action. Then, he slowly lifts his right arm off his ribcage. I duck my head underneath it, squiggle my body up against his right side, and nestle my left shoulder into his armpit—a perfect fit. I press my cheek to his chest and drape my right arm across his stomach. I hold my breath. It's a bold move and I'm really excited. My heart is racing and my penis is pressed hard against his hip, ready for action. I'm as still as can be, unsure of what he'll do. With my head on his chest, I hear his heart pounding rhythmically. Strangely, he's still asleep. I count the beats and wait one minute, two minutes, three minutes… and then four minutes. How the hell can an insomniac still be asleep with a hot, naked body pressed up against him and an erection perforating his thigh? I wait another minute.

Finally, Brian sighs again, drops his right arm onto my shoulder and turns his head toward me. He buries his face in my hair. Several minutes pass without further movement and I just wait… because the love of my life is still fast asleep. Jeez! At this rate, it'll be dawn before I get any sex. I'm working on my next plan of action (something that might involve groping) when he begins to nuzzle my head in his sleep, moving his face back and forth in my hair. This oddness goes on for about five minutes, until his chest swells as he inhales a lungful of my scalp's scent. He moans as he exhales, and it sends a wave of excite-ment through me. I react by gripping his stomach and digging into his abdominals with my nails.

"Mmm," he groans in response. The rumbling sound comes from deep within his chest. It's the sound of pleasure, and I know he's not asleep now.

I raise my head and begin kissing his pectorals. The dense muscles twitch beneath my lips. I caress his nipples with my tongue and teeth — nibbling, sucking, and licking them tenderly. He moves his left hand to cup the back of my head and guides my face up to his. As he slides his tongue deeply into my mouth, I slide my hand under the sheet and down the shaft of his penis. Brian's reaction is immediate: His eyes open wide and he freezes. His body tenses under my touch. At first, I don't know what's happened. I'm afraid he just realized he's woken up from an erotic dream to find he's been kissing a man instead of a woman. Then it dawns on me: This is the first time he's ever had a man fondle his penis — not an everyday occurrence for a straight guy. It's got to be a shock. "It's okay," I whisper. "It's only me. It's John. I love you." I search his eyes, wanting him to trust me. I need to know he's not afraid of me. I exhale near his nose once, and then again. His nostrils quiver and he pulls my face closer.

"Again," he whispers.

I exhale once more — deeply, right over his nose — as he inhales. He lets out a long breath, his eyes close, and his body relaxes back into the mattress. "It's okay?"

"Aye."

I stroke his penis under the sheet. It's wet and it's long. It's really long. I feel it throbbing — literally undulating — against my palm. I watch his face intently. With his eyes closed, his brow is furrowed as he concentrates on my touch, on the feel of my hand — a man's hand. It's bigger and stronger and rougher than a woman's hand, but I'm very careful. I press down as I stroke it again, trying to create the friction that will blow his mind. His pelvis arches up against my palm, begging for more. I stroke it once more and he reaches down to place his hand on mine, pressing it down harder, showing me how much pressure he wants me to use — how much he needs to feel maximum stimulation. I comply, and a short gasp, followed by another deep groan, comes up through his chest as his body writhes in ecstasy. I've never seen a man's face filled with so much passion, sensuousness, and desperate desire. It's clear he needs sex as much as I do. I move my mouth to his ear and breathe his name. "Brian." I bend to nuzzle his neck. "Oh God, Brian, do you want me? Please say you want me. I'm begging you. I'm so desperate for you. Please...."

I look up into his face and his eyes open just a fraction. I stroke my hand up and down his penis, again and again. I keep telling him I love him and want him and need him, over and over. As I stare into his eyes, I humbly beg him for sex—something I've never done before—with tears streaming down my face. Finally, he nods.

I eagerly pull the sheet away from his waist. I've smelled his intoxicating genitals. Now I'm dying to see them, and... I'm in a slight state of shock. This moment has now become a unique situation for me. Brian's penis is like the mega roller coaster at Mason Holloway amusement park back in Chicago: The Silver Bullet. Up close, it's a lot bigger than I thought it was, which scares the crap out of me and it seems to go on forever. But I'm determined to ride it because I've been looking forward to it and I want that powerful thrill. And once I get on it, I just know I'm gonna scream my ass off. The heavily veined kielbasa, emanating from a wild thicket of dark brown hair and glistening with precum, is backed by two monstrous testicles. This man is amazingly hung!

"John, obviously I've never...."

I'm trying to recover from the shock of finding the pony I'd always wanted (and was told I'd never get) under the Christmas tree. "I know. Um, it's okay. I can show you. We just.... I mean, it's.... Uh, you can't just...." Ultimately, there's no tactful way of saying it. He needs to know his size is an issue. "Um, you're really big, Brian."

"I'm so sorry."

"Oh, no. Don't be sorry. It's good. Really. It's fine. I think eventually you can... you know, go for it. But at first, you just have to be slow, okay?"

"Okay."

I kiss him long and hard, tasting him as deeply as I can. Then I pull back. "The best position to start would be on your knees behind me but you really, *really* need to be super slow. Okay?"

He solemnly repeats the words as if they were a sacred utterance. "Right. Super slow."

I'm nervous. I have no idea if I can do this. I haven't had many partners, no one in the last two years, and his size has me concerned. I sit back on my knees. Brian sits up, gets on his knees and positions himself behind me. As he moves, I take another look at that unbeliev- able tool jutting out at a perfect right angle to his body and beg my anus to step up to the challenge and perform a small miracle. I tuck two pillows under my legs to give me more height and then bend for- ward, dog style, with my head hanging down. I spread my legs apart and wait. My nervousness goes up two levels, and I start to sweat. I have no idea what he's thinking as he kneels behind me and looks down at my anemic rear end. This is when I'm vulnerable. Right now, he could decide this isn't for him—that no matter how much he loves me, it's something he doesn't want any part of. His rejection would devastate me. It would just kill me.

It's disturbingly quiet in the room, and my heart is beating faster than a hummingbird's wings. With my head hanging down and my eyes closed, I silently beg him not to reject me. For the longest time, there's no movement behind me and I'm worried—and sweating even more.

Suddenly, Brian's big warm hands are on my upper back, near my armpits. He runs them down over my ribs, the sides of my damp torso, and lets them rest on my hips. Again I wait, not knowing what's going on in his mind. My chest is expanding and contracting fast. I open my eyes in anticipation. I look down at my hands braced on the foam mat- tress, fingers pale and spread wide, miniscule beads of perspiration at the base of each nail. I hear my breathing and my heartbeat—nothing else. He carefully spreads my cheeks with his thumbs and I feel him against my skin. I close my eyes and as he gently presses forward, I open my mouth wide and let out a long, low gasp. I can't remember the last time I experienced this sensation, but I've missed it, and it feels so good. Brian's own lubricant helps, despite his size. I swallow hard and dig my fingers down into the mattress as his penetration slowly increases. My heart is racing. Fresh sweat is dripping from my fore- head and chin onto the sheet, and more sweat is pooling along my spine. My armpits are sweating profusely, and that's making me more nervous. I shouldn't be sweating this much. It's not attractive to sweat like this. Women don't sweat like this. I'm trying to stay calm and keep my muscles relaxed but at this point, I'm way beyond normal nervousness — because of all the sweating — and Brian has stopped all forward progression. I can't concentrate. I can't think. And now, to my horror, as I assume this unflattering position in front of the man I love more than anything in this world, I know why he isn't moving. My muscles have just constricted. They've seized up, clamping down on him like a blood pressure cuff. Oh, God! I can't believe this is happening! I'm afraid I'll freak out and panic. I have no idea what to do... so I cry. Oh, God! I don't want to cry in front of him. A woman wouldn't cry. I'm humiliated, and I can't imagine what he must think of me. "Brian, I'm so sorry," I blubber through my tears, trying to look back at him. "I can't.... It isn't.... It won't...."

He rubs my wet back. "Shh."

My breathing becomes wheezy and the panic starts to set in. "I'm so embarrassed. God, I'm so ashamed!"

"John, take it easy. It's all right. Everything is fine. We'll figure this out." As always, his voice is reassuring and gentle. "You're getting too excited and you're tensing up. Don't panic. You need to calm down and relax, okay?"

Calm down and relax? How can I calm down and relax? Brian has been with so many beautiful women — like Carol — who give him 'normal' sex and here I am — a crying, sweating, neurotic, emotional wreck on the verge of a panic attack with my glowing white ass in the air, and my muscles throttling his penis. I've made such a mess of things again, and I'm too tensed up to do a damned thing about it. And with my back to him it's even worse, because he cannot think this cumbersome position is, in any way, romantic or sexy.

But within seconds, I realize I have to get a grip on my emotional state or I *will* have a panic attack and pass out. And the last thing I want to experience is the horror of passing out with Brian's penis stuck halfway up my rear end. God, I would just *die* if that happened! I put my head down, focus on my hands, and collect my thoughts. I'm determined to do as he says: calm down and relax. And I may cry my ass off, but I will *not* pass out. "Okay," I sob, trying to steady my nerves. I need to forget about the awkwardness of the situation and how much I'm sweating, the fact that I'm crying, visions of perfect Carol, my lovely anal death grip and all of my other paranoid thoughts, and instead concentrate on slowing down my breathing. It takes me a few minutes to reel it all in and get everything under control. Brian, still rubbing my back, waits patiently. I finally stop crying. And then, as my breathing returns to normal and my muscles start to loosen up, he begins...

It's hard to describe how smoothly and methodically he works, positioning my body one way, and then moving it another way, rotating his pelvis and my hips—sometimes in unison, sometimes in opposing directions—massaging my muscles so they'll relax even more. And as they do, I feel him tenderly guiding me back toward him. I close my eyes tighter and concentrate on what I feel as he probes into my body. With my mouth hanging open, I gasp with every move—my torso hot and tingling and dripping with sweat.

"Does it hurt, John? Should I stop?"

Even with my mouth wide open, I can't speak. I can't answer him with words. All I can do is shake my head vigorously, and grunt a few unintelligible syllables. "Ungnahug ungna."

"Are you sure?"

I nod several times and grip the mattress even tighter. There's no way I want him to stop. This feeling is too incredible. Brian focuses on what he senses from my body and adjusts his actions, waiting patiently when he knows I've tensed up. He's letting me take my time adapting to what's happening, and that's important because my organs seem to be moving around a bit. I'm surprised when I realize my buttocks are resting firmly against his pelvis. It's the strangest feeling I've ever had: I'm a pig on a spit—solidly jammed on him like a great big penis puppet and he's the Puppet Master. I gaze back between my spread legs. I'm greeted with the curious sight of Brian's humungous scrotum (the left sac bigger than the right) dangling like a swollen pendulum behind my more-compact version, and I flash back to that stud bull in Rittersby. It's as if I'm sporting a cool set of jumbo backup balls—that truly envious pair I'd haul out on special occasions (like fine bone china) when I really wanted to impress someone. I'm so hot; every inch of my skin is on fire. Brian is breathing hard, and his thigh and groin muscles have tightened up in anticipation of what's to come. He's waiting for sex. He wants it, and he needs it.

I breathe deeply. My muscles are relaxed and I'm calm. At this precise moment, with his body right up against mine, everything is aligned and it all feels right. "Okay. Now just... move in and out... carefully... just a little... really slow, at first."

Holding my hips, Brian moves his pelvis backward and forward—working a slow, steady rhythm, creating a little friction between our bodies. His low groans sound primitive and painful. I'm in heaven, experiencing sensations I've never felt before. Then the words come, in between my gasps and moans. I don't have control over what I'm saying. I just know I have to say it—all of it, to him. I tell him how much I love him, trust him and need him. I tell him how I've never felt like this before about anyone. I beg him not to stop loving me because he means everything to me. I pour out my heart to him without reservation.

Several minutes pass, and he's still pressing forward and pulling back. With my eyes closed, my attention is devoted to every contraction I experience as he glides against my flesh. The feeling is indescribable. It burns, it tingles and it excites me. I clench my teeth and groan. Brian's muscles tense and relax behind me. His deep gasps tell me the friction is satisfying his needs. I'm moaning loudly, and I've reached that point where my muscles are starting to throb. I feel tears running down my face and I taste their salt. "A little faster, Brian. Please. I love you... so much."

My own rhythm engages as Brian bores deep, countering my movements precisely, matching my speed. Again, my mouth is open and I'm gasping hard while the sweat pours off me. My body heat is almost unbearable. Within minutes, as my muscles begin to pulse, I realize I need our pace to be more vigorous. I swallow hard, forcing the words out between grunts and gasps. "Brian! Faster... and just a...a little harder. Please!"

I increase my rhythm as I feel him pull me into his body with every thrust. We're pounding against each other intensely and I can't help myself as I shout his name, over and over. I need him to hear me say it, to hear that I love him—that I want him and crave him—more than anything. Brian doesn't say a word, but his groans are guttural and loud. Our pace increases and I can't counter his forward drilling. He grips my hips tighter to help me slam back against him, making each penetration as deep as possible for maximum intensity. I feel ecstasy as he hits my prostate. I have no control over my words or my movements now. I'm screaming something that started out as, *"Oh, my God! Oh, my God! Oh, my God!,"* then quickly digressed to, *"Oh, my! Oh, my! Oh, my!,"* and finally ended up as a desperate, high-pitched chant: *"Ohm! Ohm! Ohm!"* I'm digging my fingernails down into the mattress — the titillation is that unbelievable. My back arches, my head turns up toward the ceiling and then slumps down, dripping with sweat. Our pace is intense as we crash against each other. I feel Brian tuck his pelvis and raise my hips as he tries to hit my pubic bone at a sharper angle in his quest for more friction. He also zaps my prostate again. *"Ohm! Ohm! Ohm!,"* I scream. I'm a panting demon, clenching my teeth hard. The whole bed is lurching as he throws back his head and his heavy grunts suddenly turn into sharp, loud exclamations of euphoria. I can't keep up with his momentum. It takes all my strength just to keep my skull from slamming into the headboard with every intense thrust he hits me with, even as he grips my hips. This big Scotsman is just hammering me with serious sex! The power of his thigh muscles astounds me and so does his stamina. He's been plunging me for what seems like half an hour, but I know he's about to explode. His body is starting to tremble and I hear the urgency in his cries.

Finally, he speaks. "John, I can't—"

"Wait! Please!" I'm barely able to get the words out. I need more of this excitement. The sensation is unreal and I don't ever want it to end.

Still teasing my prostrate, he gasps, "John! I need to—"

"Ohm! Ohm! Ohm! Almost…almost—not yet! Brian, please!" I'm pleading with him. I'm begging him. I'm screaming and crying so hard, but he's done all he can. He's exhausted and nearly spent as he grabs my hips and starts pushing me forward. *"No!"* I force myself back into his pelvis and then suddenly realize I'm about to come. I straighten up until my sweaty torso is vertical and my back is against his hot chest. I execute one gigantic full-body jerk and watch in dreamy amazement as the watery *Mark of Zorro* sails out of my engorged penis

and splats across the headboard in three rapid-fire pulses. Brian's body arches back and convulses in violent spasms. He digs his fingers into my hips and crushes me against him as he growls like a deranged animal and hurls our bodies across the bed. I clench my teeth as I feel a titanic burst of semen surge within me. The explosion sends a searing shockwave through my body. I can't see a damned thing. My vision is gone as my eyeballs roll back in their sockets and the last memory I have is a tingling sensation in my arms and legs—right before I pass out.

Brian

I think I'm in shock. I can't see anything and my body is numb. If someone were to cut off an arm or leg right now, I wouldn't know it was happening. My heart is pounding out of control and I can't catch my breath, so I'm wheezing. John, face down in the mattress, clearly is passed out. I'm sprawled across his slippery body like a mortally wounded heifer twitching in its death throes with my groin muscles still convulsively shooting bullets of semen into him. I'm like a bloody petrol pump that just won't shut off. I blink my eyes, trying to get back my vision. I give myself a moment to regain feeling in my limbs and then work my arms under John's chest and roll our torsos onto our sides so he doesn't suffocate. I need to relax and gain control of my senses. I close my eyes and concentrate on slowing down my heart rate and calming my muscles, which are still frantically pumping away. A few more minutes pass before I can breathe normally and reclaim ownership of my pelvis. When I open my eyes, I can finally see. Still holding onto John with one arm, I reach down and painfully extricate my spent (yet surprisingly still semi-erect) cork from his backside. There's some blood, but not as much as I thought there would be. I let go of him and roll onto my back. I close my eyes and analyze my present condition.

Every muscle in my body is now relaxed, except for my bionic penis, which seems to think a second round of bum fun is in the cards. I'm weak, yet I'm unbelievably excited and agitated, as if my veins are surging with adrenalin. I am so damned tired. I'm sore, hot and exhausted. I've got to cool off with a shower. I roll John out of the wet-ness and over to the right side of the bed. I take a few minutes to clean up his anal tear using the iodine and a length of gauze, wadded up and stuck between his cheeks. I strap it down with a length of adhesive across his butt. I sit back on my knees and survey my masterpiece like Picasso critically examining one of his sculptures. I'll admit a bouquet of fluffy, white gauze shoved in a butt crack is not the most attractive look for England's Sexiest and Most Desirable Gay Man, but I'm not going to enter it in a bloody Florence Nightingale competition, so what the hell? I cover him with a blanket. It's hot in the room, but his skin is cold and clammy as the sweat begins to dry. I climb out of bed and head for the bathroom.

I stand in the shower with my back to the controls and my head hanging down. I've got the jets aimed at my torso, blasting me with warm water. Everything between my navel and my knees aches. I close my eyes and turn around. I lift my face up to the showerhead and stand still, letting the spray pound my face and run down my chest. I feel it flow into my crotch and trickle down my legs. As I experience the calming sensation of water cascading over me, my mind is busy digesting the amazing event that happened in the bedroom. I just had sex with a man. No. I just had the most supreme sex of my life with a man — with John. It started out awkward and clumsy, and it ended up awkward and clumsy. In between, it was unbelievably erotic, primitive and fierce. At times it hurt like hell, but it was so satisfying, stimulat-ing, and passionate — like nothing I've ever experienced. I remember everything he said — every single word. I can't believe how much I wanted to hear him say those things. All my emotional needs were met with just those words. I grab the soap and lather myself from head to toe. I wash my hair and brush my teeth. By the time I've finished, I feel pretty good. I'm sore as hell and exhausted beyond belief, but I'm looking forward to climbing back into bed, holding John closely and getting some sleep.

John

My body is twitching and I'm sensing my surroundings as I regain consciousness. This time, I'm not confused or disoriented. This time, it wasn't a head injury. I know exactly where I passed out, when I passed out and why I passed out. I don't want to open my eyes yet. I want to concentrate on all of my other senses and enjoy the experience. I'm lying tightly against Brian's right side, my head is on his chest, my left shoulder is in his armpit and my right arm is draped across his ribcage. My body is exposed—no blankets or sheets. My left leg is straight, my right leg is flung across Brian's hips and his hand is resting on my thigh. My ass is sore, but considering the extensive activity it recently engaged in and the lack of lube, it doesn't feel as bad as I thought it would. There's something wedged between my cheeks. It feels like cloth. For lack of a better candidate, I'm assuming Brian put it there. Given his size, I'm sure I bled and I appreciate his thoughtfulness, but it must look ridiculous. I feel his heartbeat through my cheek. The slow, steady rhythm is familiar to me now. He's in a deep sleep. My arm rises and falls with each breath he takes and he's softly inhaling and exhaling into my hair. I smell his clean body, lightly scented with soap, which tells me I was unconscious long enough for him to shower. I smell my own body odor, foul and irritating, coupled with the itchy tackiness of dried sweat on my back, my forehead, and in my armpits. My stomach is growling. I haven't eaten since Sunday morning. Now, I open my eyes.

Across Brian's chest, I see the dark sky outside the open sliders and there's finally a cool breeze coming through. I take a deep breath and run my fingertips back and forth over his left nipple. His pectoral quivers beneath my touch. I can't believe this is happening to me, that I'm here with him. It's a wonderful dream come true. I close my eyes again, remembering the phenomenal sex. It was truly amazing. Who am I kidding? *I* was truly amazing. I was brilliant. I never thought I could be so fantastic. I should get an award for having the most talented rectum in London.

I snuggle up closer along his side, molding my body to his contours. I wiggle my toes. To me, being here with him is perfect. It feels right, as if it was meant to be. He's asleep, but I need to know how he feels—if it was okay for him. It didn't start out well. I sweated too much, I nearly panicked, I cried, and in the end, I passed out. Now I'm sticky and smelly—and worried. My stomach growls as I whisper, "Brian?"

No response.

"Brian?"

"Hmm," he mumbles into my hair.

"Was it okay? Was it all right? I mean, was I—"

"Hmm."

I think that means yes. It was fine. I was okay and he enjoyed it. I wait a minute. Again, my stomach lets out a rumble. "Brian?"

There's a long pause. "Hmm."

"Is it okay that I sweated so much, and panicked, and cried a lot… and passed out?"

There's another pause and then a sigh. "Hmm."

That must mean it's okay. He's thought about it, what happened didn't bother him, and all is well. I wait another minute, truly concerned about how bad I smell. "Brian?"

"John," he drowsily croaks. With his face buried in my hair, his deep voice is muffled, but understandable. "I love you to death, but I'm so damned tired. I've had a long day and I'm worn out. I really need to sleep." The words are soft and low.

"Okay. You go back to sleep. I love you, too." I squeeze his chest and close my eyes as my stomach churns.

Brian

I love him more than anything and the sex was beyond phenomenal, but he's such a pain in the ass right now. He smells bad, his stomach is growling, and he's stuck to my side like a barnacle clinging to a boat, but it's the blasted questions that are driving me crazy. I know he's wired up, but I'm so tired. If he'd just lie still and be quiet for an hour, I'd be happy. I give it a few minutes more and then I can't stand it anymore. "John."

His head eagerly pops up. "Yes, Brian?"

I let out a long sigh. "Go get something to eat, love."

"It's okay. I'm fine."

"But I'm not. Go." I lift my arm, and he crawls out of bed, padding off naked to the kitchen, sporting what looks like a pathetic, home-made fart silencer taped to his ass. Now, maybe I can get some sleep—or not. Within minutes, I hear clattering pots and pans, running water, and clinking glass bottles. A refrigerator full of ready-made food, well stocked by Charles on Sunday afternoon when it was apparent I wouldn't be going back to Scotland—and John has to cook. I try to doze off, even amid all the racket. The sound of shattering glass pierces the air and my eyes fly open.

"It's okay! I'm all right! There's no blood," John's voice quickly re-assures me. And then, as an afterthought, "Um... I don't think it was that expensive."

After ten minutes more of various loud, unfamiliar noises, it's alarmingly quiet. It's too quiet, and it worries me. I imagine he's probably hit his head on an upper cabinet door and knocked himself out. I'm just about to climb out of bed to check on him when I hear him happily singing to himself. God, he has a beautiful clear voice! I could listen to him sing for hours. And as he sings, I realize the side of my body is cold without him stuck to it. I turn my face to the right, but his head isn't there. I can't breathe in his scent. With my eyes closed, but unable to sleep, I wait for my love to come back to me. And as I wait, I spend my time thinking of all the things I'll have to do now that he's in my life. I'll have to get him a parking stall and a set of keys for the flat. He'll need credit cards and closet space. I know he'll want to change the furniture... and he probably likes to take baths.... I'll need the con-tractor in for that... and the eye doctor. He squints a lot, so he must have... an eye exam... and a nice... dressing gown....

■ ■ ■

Whoever invented this horrendously expensive, motionless mat-tress never encountered John. He's like a baby elephant thrashing about on a waterbed as he clumsily crawls back to me. Without open-ing my eyes, I lift my arm and he easily slides in along my side. His body is cold and clammy. He doesn't smell anymore. He must have wiped himself down with a washcloth at the sink. I give him a minute to settle in as he painstakingly fuses his body to my side, wedging his limbs into crevices I didn't even know I had, determined not to leave any air gaps. Then I bury my face in his messy hair. All I want to do is smell him. I take in a deep breath. Everything is as it should be and now I can sleep. Minutes later, John has other plans. He hasn't moved a centimeter, but his body is heating up fast, and I mean *amazingly* fast. "Brian...?"

"No. I need to sleep."

He's quiet for a bit, but he's already sweating as he rubs his hand on my stomach. "Please, Brian. *Please.*" His voice is impassioned as he begs me.

He turns his face up to mine and I bend to kiss him. I don't know what elaborate meal he cooked, but now I know he smothered it in tons of garlic and a shitload of onions. I gently pull away. "No, John. I'm exhausted. Let me sleep awhile."

He opens his deep blue eyes and gives me a pleading look as he whispers, "But I really want you. I need you—again. Now. Please?" His hand slides down past my navel.

Within seconds, I'm back on my knees, drilling into him. It hurts like hell and I growl like an enraged bear trying to pry open a camper's ice chest. He sweats like a fat bastard in a sauna and screams as if a blind man is stabbing him to death with a dull ice pick. I finally figure out why he keeps shouting "Ohm!" The piercing war cry seems to be his orgasm indicator. The sex is just as frenzied as the first time. Unbelievably, it lasts even longer and again he cries, but this time, he's only passed out for about ten minutes.

John

I'm wide awake. I'm excited to start this day—my first full day—with Brian. I wiggle my toes. I'm lying in bed on my right side, Brian is spooning me with his face in my hair and his arms are wrapped around me. My arms are on top of his and he's breathing slowly. He's still asleep but I want him to wake up. "Brian?"

"No!"

Okay, that definitely means no. We're not getting up yet, and we are *not* going to have sex again. It means I have to wait, but I'm so eager for this day to start! I want to be out in public with him. I need to show him off. I wait five minutes and then tense my body and press back into his pelvis with my butt. Brian's arms clamp down on my chest like a vice. That means no sex, stop fidgeting and let him sleep. I lie quietly for a few more minutes, but I have no intention of letting up. I want to be outside. I want everyone in London to know we're together. "I JUST GOT LAID" is written all over my face and my fans need to see it. Just as I'm about to try again to get my way, Brian's phone buzzes on the nightstand. I pick it up and stare at the illuminated touch screen and dozens of buttons. I've never seen a phone like this. I'm sure it's custom. I'm focusing my fuzzy vision on the buttons with my thumb hovering over the upper left one. I press it at the precise moment Brian mumbles, "Lower left."

The screen goes dark. "I'm sorry."

"She'll call back."

I continue holding the phone, thumb poised above the lower left button, waiting for the call. When it buzzes, I punch the button and hand it to Brian, who pulls his arm from around me to take it. Since he labeled her a "she," I eagerly listen in, which (I believe) is my God-given right.

"Yup. That's right. Yes. All of my appointments. Wednesday is fine. I will, I promise. No. Saturday should work. I understand and I appreciate it. I really do. Fine. Goodbye, Edna."

Brian hands back the phone. I try sliding it onto the nightstand but end up dropping it on the floor. Brian stretches, pulls me in tightly, smashes his face into my hair and settles back down for more sleep. His muffled voice pierces the silence. "John?"

"Yes, Brian?"

"When you get out of bed—"

"I promise I won't step on the phone."

He yawns. "Good boy. I don't want to replace it... again."

He thinks he's going back to sleep, but that's not happening. I've dubbed his phone call the official start of our day and I wait just thirty seconds before I start asking questions. "Brian?"

"Hmm."

"Am I your boyfriend?"

There's a pause. "Hmm."

Good! That means yes. We're a couple. We're exclusive, and he's all mine. "Brian?"

"Hmm."

"Can I move in with you?"

"Hmm."

Excellent! That mean yes, too. This is my new home. I can change the furniture, get most of his clothes out of that gargantuan dressing room, and fill it with my stuff. Next question. "Brian?"

"Hmm."

"Can we get a dog?"

"No."

Okay. I've encountered my first unacceptable answer. "Brian?"

"Hmm."

"Was that your secretary in Scotland?"

"Hmm."

"Will you have to fly out there on Wednesday?"

"Hmm." Within seconds, his body tenses up as I'm sure he remembers last night's star-performance tantrum. He pulls his face from my hair. "Are you going to have a problem with that, John?"

"I don't know. Can we get a dog?"

Brian

I groan and bury my face in his hair. He's manipulative just as Martin said, but that's okay. If I didn't kill him over the piano, the urn or the table, he knows I won't deny him a dog. "Aye, but not until I get back. I need to make sure the bloody thing goes with the artwork and isn't an embarrassment."

"Okay. That's fine. I can wait. We'll go to the shelter and pick her out together."

I'm not keen on a dog but if it makes him happy, we'll get a dog. I squeeze him and start to doze off, desperate for a few more minutes of sleep. Then I remember something important—something *very* important. I pull my face from his hair again. "John, do you need to call David? Do you need to tell him about this—about us?"

His body tenses and there's a long pause. "No."

"Are you sure?"

There's another long pause. "We broke up."

"When?"

And yet another long pause. "A while ago."

His voice is too quiet. Something isn't right. I press my lips to the back of his head. I'm not sure what's going on but he's uneasy and I don't like it. "Do you want to talk about it?"

No response.

I nudge him a little. "John?" I wait and still no response. His body is rigid and he won't say a word, so I'm really concerned. Something serious happened. I have no idea what, but I know he'll tell me eventually. I kiss the back of his head and squeeze him again. "Okay, we'll leave it for now, love. If that's what you want." We sleep for another half an hour.

■ ■ ■

Showering with John is a unique experience. He turns a normally mundane task into something very sensual. It's apparent he hasn't had physical attention in a long time, and it's apparent he requires it. He's a tactile person, needing to touch and be touched — everywhere. With his eyes closed, he stands there: head back, a smile on his face, arms outstretched and legs spread wide — waiting to be touched. I'm hesitant. It's the first time I've ever been offered a man's body in the shower with its significantly large bits and bobs dangling in front of me like a fat pork sausage and cheese balls strung up in a shop window. It's not going to be the same as fondling a woman. A woman has more up top and a lot less below. And there's another issue: I'm not physically attracted to men. I don't know how to start or where to start, but because he's expecting something, I quickly decide to approach this mission from the safest position. I turn him around so I'm facing his back, soap up my hands, reach around to his front and just start groping. One great thing about John is he doesn't care what the hell I fondle, as long as it's attached to his torso — preferably his sizable genitals that slip and slide out of my soapy hands like a squirming puppy. That makes him happy. Another great thing about John is that he's a thirty-one-year-old man who's extremely ticklish, so I can make him jump and squeal, and giggle like an idiot. That makes me happy.

Eventually he turns around and we press our bodies together with his lips on my neck and me whispering that I love him into his ear. We hold each other and turn slowly under the spray as if we're dancing. We kiss long and passionately, unable to satisfy our desire for each other. We wash our hair together. I carefully peel off his gauze patch and decide he doesn't need another one. He begs me to let him shave my face. I'm wary at first, but he's meticulously careful and does a better job of it than I do. He shaves his own face, and then he does the oddest thing: He sits down and shaves his legs. "You shave your legs?"

"Sometimes."

I sit down next to him on the shower bench. "Why?"

"A lot of dancers shave their legs. Some dancers wax 'em. I thought you'd like it."

"Why would you think that?"

"I don't know. I just thought it might make you think you were with a woman."

I lean into his hair and nuzzle him. "I know I'm not with a woman. I'm with you. If you do it because you want to, that's fine. You don't need to shave your legs for me because I'm bloody well not going to shave mine for you. No hair on this man gets cut, waxed, shaved or plucked—unless it's on his head. Whatever is hairy stays hairy, okay?"

He gives me a smile and kisses me. "Okay." He kisses me again, more intensely, and his smile fades. "Brian, can we—"

"No, we can't." I stand up, grab one of our discarded washcloths and step out of the shower. "Housekeeping will be here in twenty minutes and we need to be out, so hurry up and shave those legs."

"Where are you going?"

"To wipe your groin graffiti off our headboard, love."

20
This Is Love

John – April 11

Our first day outside is exhilarating. Walking along the avenue with Brian (a prominent, just-been-laid bounce in my step) is like being the only kid on the block with a shiny new bike. Everyone is ogling it, everyone wants to ride it, and no one can have it. It's all mine. Of course, my looks have always turned heads, but it's the combination that's causing jaws to drop—and that's what I really like. We are two handsome, sexy men, and we look hot together. I'm wearing my jeans and one of Brian's soft, cotton button-down shirts, which is so big I have to roll the cuffs, but I love the way it feels. He isn't holding my hand yet. I'll give him a bit longer before I expect that of him because holding a man's hand in public is something he's not used to. It becomes another action item on my mental list of 'Brian's Introduction to Desirable Gay Activities,' right below oral sex, frottage and shopping. We stroll down the street for breakfast at a trendy café. I blush through our entire meal as he gazes at me across the table. I am so giddy and happy! It's the perfect opportunity to stand up in front of everyone and just burst into a boisterous song. I stifle that urge, and instead channel Dame Kiri Te Kanawa and quietly hum *I'm In Love With A Wonderful Guy*. Afterward, we head to the drug store for various toiletries no man should ever be without: a firm toothbrush, coated razor blades, a non-greasy facial moisturizer rich in hyaluronic acids to restore elasticity while maintaining firmness, and four big tubes of lipid-based lubricant. There's another item I wish I could get but not while I'm with Brian. After some unobtrusive searching, I realize the small store doesn't have it anyway. Brian is embarrassed when I stand super close to him as he's paying the cashier, but she's pretty, he knows her by name, and I must convey my subtle hint that he's no longer available. Now that I have this gorgeous new boyfriend, I'm a tiny bit possessive. And even though I'm a really nice guy, I swear I'll rip the head off any shrew who tries to steal him from me with my bare hands.

We stop to get various newspapers, fresh flowers, and fruits and veggies at the local market. As we walk around, I learn about all the things Brian will and will not tolerate in his home and in his life. He won't lower the urinal or get a stepping stool, so I either use it as is, or stick with the toilet. He will have his contractor install a bathtub. He'd prefer less mousse and gel on the weekends, but he understands the image I have to maintain. No naked trips through the flat because we're not exhibitionists. No groping in public without permission because we're not desperate. Don't feed pigeons that land on the balcony because pigeon poop is unsanitary and housekeeping won't touch it. I can replace any furniture in the flat but I can't touch the artwork (and because I broke the Grecian urn, he means that literally). If we get a dog, we also get a groomer. He doesn't care what we get as long as it's fixed, won't eat shoes, and isn't tall enough to drink from the toilets. He'll order a custom cell phone for me, but I can't put irritating ringtones on it. I can order whatever I want in a restaurant, but no meat is allowed in the flat, so plan my doggy bags accordingly. If I want to read *The Wall Street Journal* (yeah, right!), I can do so only after he's read it or order my own copy. I'll have a parking spot in the garage for my Boxster once his mechanic has fixed the oil leak and the electrical short—and it's already in the shop. Unequivocally, there will be no pissing in the atrium bamboo. That wasn't high up on my list of things to do, but Mickey thought it was a brilliant idea after a night of heavy drinking and killed thirteen stalks (death by urine), so Brian thought he'd better mention it—just in case. His rules might be off-putting to some. He probably sounds like a tyrant, but I've got him wrapped around my little finger tight enough to break any of them if I want to— and he knows it.

Heading back home, we have an awkward moment when I ask him for money. My wallet is somewhere in the flat (probably with my watch and phone), but I need something from the over-priced culinary shop now. The moment becomes even more awkward when I ask Brian to wait for me outside while I make my purchase. He uses the time to respond to email and isn't fazed by my request or interested in what I buy (typical hetero male). When we get back to the flat, he unpacks the food. We've spent our morning in the neighborhood, walking and shopping, and now he's making fresh pasta for lunch. He loves pasta. Most everything he eats, he eats with pasta. "Brian?"

He's busy sorting his ingredients. "Hmm?"

"I need to use one of the guest bathrooms. I want to take a quick bath."

Chrome pasta machine in one hand and a carton of eggs in the other, the consummate chef is absorbed in his prep work. "That's fine, love. Be careful, don't slip," he mumbles.

"I won't be long." I grab my package and hastily walk down the hallway, past the library, and into the first guest bedroom. I cross to the bathroom, walk in and lock the door behind me. I start for the tub... and stop. It's oceanic! It's not a bathtub; it's a damned wading pool. Loch Ness Nellie could get lost in that thing! I certainly can't take the time to fill it. I unlock the door, walk back through the bedroom and out into the hallway. I pass the second kitchen, the theater and the home gym. I enter the second guest bedroom, cross to the bathroom and open the door. I don't believe it! It's the same. It's the exact same-sized tub! I'm screwed. I'll just have to fill it. There's nothing else I can do. I close the door, walk to the tub and turn on the taps full blast. I flip the drain lever, quickly strip off my clothes and open my package.

I pull out a red-bulbed, stainless steel turkey baster. I need to deal with the remnants of Brian's semen and that means an enema. It was a spur of the moment thing, something I wanted to feel more than anything in the heat of passion, but I know — for health reasons — I've got to clean out my canal. The sensation of that momentous event was unbelievable. I wouldn't change it for the world. And if I can pull this off without Brian finding out, it will have been worth it. I've never done this before, but Ben — Mister Know-It-All — swears it works. He tried to explain the technique during lunch one day, but I cut him off. Highly descriptive anal cleansing and three-bean chili do not mix well.

I peer down into the tub. Even with the taps running full blast, there's barely two inches of water. I'm getting nervous. I can't wait for this thing to fill up. Frustrated, I run my fingers through my hair and pace the floor, wondering what to do. I'm not coming up with any brilliant ideas. I'm not coming up with anything. Finally, because time is wasting, I just grab the baster and climb over the edge. Not knowing how I should position myself, I get down on my hands and knees with my head facing away from the drain and taps. I fill the baster with water and take a deep, calming breath because I know I need to be relaxed for this to work. I try inserting the baster, but it's really long and I have to twist my torso at an odd angle. I jab myself. My muscles tighten up as the nervousness creeps in. I take another deep breath and try again. Again, I jab myself. I try again, and again — and yet again. By the fifth jab, my nerves are shot and I've only worked the baster in a few inches. My heart is racing and I'm sweating. My free hand, the one that's holding the baster, is shaking and the blood has drained from it. My other arm is exhausted and about to buckle under my weight, and my knees (grinding into the floor of the tub) are killing me. The water level is only at about three inches and I've been in here too long. I told Brian it would be a quick bath. In a minute, he'll come back here, afraid I've slipped and hit my head. I need to get this process going, but the baster isn't even halfway —

Knock, knock. My head shoots up, eyes wide.

"John? Are you okay?"

I take a second to slow my breathing before answering because I can't sound nervous or panicky. I raise my voice to be heard over the noise of the running taps. "I'm fine, Brian. I'll just be another minute or two." I hang my head, close my eyes and wait for him to leave — hoping he bought my lie. With my eyes closed, I'm also trying to remember if I locked the door. I think I did. Yes! I remember coming into the bathroom and locking the door behind me. A second later, my eyes pop open. I locked the door in the first bathroom but not in this one! I yank my head up to see Brian standing a few feet inside the open door. He's staring down at me as I kneel in this tremendous bathtub with a red-bulbed, stainless steel turkey baster sticking out of my ass.

Nothing can top this humiliation. This is the worst moment of my life. I hang my head and cry. There's nothing else I can do. I just stay in this embarrassing position and bawl my head off. Within seconds, and still with my head down, I see Brian's big feet—in socks—stepping into the tub in front of my face. He sits down on the wide edge and hauls me up so my chest is lying across his thighs. "It's okay, John. It's okay. Shh. Shh. Just rest a minute. Just give yourself a rest." He should be laughing, but (unbelievably) he's not. Still bawling like a big baby, I reach behind me, trying to pull out the embarrassing baster. Brian grabs my hand. "Leave it for now. We'll deal with it in a minute." His voice is calm and reassuring. He's rubbing my back with long, slow strokes as I continue to cry. "Shh. Shh. Everything is okay. Everything is fine."

When the heavy crying lets up enough for me to speak, I don't even know what to say. How do I own up to this? How do I explain such a God-awful, humiliating position? I just want to die. "Brian, I was…. I was trying to…."

He leans sideways to better analyze my ass's predicament. "Obviously, we're trying to do some sort of flushing back here, right?"

I nod and keep on crying.

"Okay. We'll deal with that thing in a minute. It can wait. Apparently, it's not going anywhere, anyway. First, we calm you down. First, we take care of John, right?"

I nod again and still keep on crying.

"Just breathe deeply. It's going to be all right. I promise everything will be fine."

I take three or four deep breaths, and the crying eventually turns into great big sobs and a runny nose. Brian strokes my back for a long time, not saying a word. Finally, I readjust my chest on his thighs and turn my head to the side. A few minutes pass and my sobs are reduced to snotty sniffles.

"All right. Are you relaxed?"

I nod.

"Good." He leans over to flip the drain lever. "I think we'll use fresh water and just leave the taps running. Now, I haven't done anything like this before, but I understand the basic concept, and I'm sure I'll get the hang of it once we get started. You need to hold very still,

John. I'll go slowly, but you tell me if I poke you or if it hurts, all right?"

I nod again.

Brian works gingerly with the baster as I lie across his thighs. For a while, the only sounds in the room are the running bath taps and whatever he's flushing out of me. He doesn't jab me at all. I probably have three years of medical school to thank for that. As I'm facing the back wall of the tub, I stare at the fantastic grout job someone did on these tiny iridescent glass tiles, and as I stare, I contemplate my present situation: Here I am—England's Sexiest and Most Desirable Gay Man—on my knees in a bathtub, having my rectum flushed. An embarrassing task compassionately executed by my beautiful, multi-millionaire boyfriend of less than twelve hours. Even with the great sex, he must be having second thoughts about me. "This is horrible, isn't it, Brian?" I finally manage to say.

"No, John. This is love. This is what it all boils down to at the end of the day." He continues to work the baster. "It's not glamorous. It's not exciting. It's just the normal stuff you do because you really care about someone."

"But it's disgusting to you, isn't it?"

"Disgusting? Not at all." He concentrates on his work at hand. "You should hear what Simon does for Robert—day in and day out—week after week. He never complains. He never whines, and he doesn't think it's disgusting."

I close my eyes and let out a satisfying moan.

"Ah, you're really enjoying this now, aren't you?"

"Hmm." I smile. I am enjoying it. I feel so relaxed lying across his thighs with the warm water running out of me and his big, strong hands touching my body. "Is it AIDS?"

"Excuse me?"

"Robert's illness. Is it the virus?"

"No, it's lung cancer. Well, it started out as lung cancer from a twenty-year, two-pack-a-day habit he just couldn't break. Now it's everywhere: in his organs, his glands, his bones." From the ensuing silence, I can tell just talking about it pains him. "It's in his brain."

We're both a bit melancholy and my eyes are still closed. "I wish I could meet Simon," I eventually say.

"I'm sure you will, love. He's important to me, and I know you'll like him." He reaches over and turns off the taps. "Okay, that's good. I think we've done the best we can."

I sit back on my knees in the tub and face him. "Brian?"

"Hmm?"

"I'm sorry I cry so much. I'm not normally like this. Since meeting you, I've become really emotional. I know it's...it's not very manly."

"No. It's not. And I'll admit I'm not used to it." He gives me a smile. "But it lets me know you're upset and you're hurting... and you need me."

I spread his legs wide so I can come in closely and get right up in his face. I've got crusty snot around my stuffy nose. I'm sure my face is blotchy and my eyes are swollen and probably red. At this point, I don't care what I look like. He's seeing me at my worst but I know it's okay. I gaze into his eyes. He didn't make fun of me and he didn't judge me. He just took care of me. I love this wonderful man with all my heart.

"So, are you okay?"

I nod.

"That's good. That's all that matters. John needs to be okay." He reaches up to brush a lock of hair off my forehead. "And... we don't try to do things like this alone ever again. Do we?"

I gently kiss him. "No."

"Because we have each other and there's nothing to be ashamed of — ever. Okay?"

I kiss him again. "Okay."

"Now, do you know what this means?"

"That you love me unconditionally more than anything else in this whole wide world," I proudly proclaim.

He rolls his eyes and shakes his head. "No, John. It means from now on, we use condoms."

21
That Amazing Eurostar Chunnel

Brian — April 11

My first day with John has been eventful, for sure. I hadn't planned on performing an enema before lunch. But surprisingly, the day has also been enjoyable because he's so lovable and easy to be with. We're in the library, lying on the big sofa. He's curled up along my left side, head on my chest and the baster fiasco cleared from his mind. My nose is buried in his hair, as usual. I have my evening newspapers, and he has his e-reader. Well, it was my e-reader until he wiped out everything I had stored on it trying to download his own selections. Fortunately, the e-reader seems to hold his interest long enough for me to read my papers. Unfortunately, he's downloaded *Learn Welsh in Thirty Days*. The ensuing dialogue goes something like this:

"Brian?"

"Hmm."

He holds up the e-reader so I can see it. "What's that word?"

"Aeroplane."

"How do you say it?"

"Awyren."

He repeats my pronunciation. I continue reading my paper. Five minutes later…

"Brian?"

"Hmm."

He holds up the e-reader. "What's that word?"

"Seamstress."

"How do you say it?"

"Gwniadwraig."

Again, he repeats my pronunciation. Again, I continue reading my paper. Five minutes later...

"Brian?"

"Hmm."

He holds up the e-reader. "What's that word?"

"Kitchen."

"How do you say it?"

"You know a dictionary comes with that book."

"I know."

"Why don't you use it?"

"I want to hear how it sounds, and I want to hear *you* say it."

I nuzzle his hair and enjoy my paper for another five minutes.

"Brian?"

"Hmm."

He holds up the e-reader. "What's that word?"

"Aeroplane. You've already asked that."

He stares at the screen. "Have I?"

I take the e-reader from him and back the screen two pages to show him the same word. I hand it back to him.

He squints hard at the screen. "Oh, yeah. You're right."

I pull out my mobile and scroll to a number. "Hello, Cecilia? It's Brian. I'm great. How are you? Good. Is Lydia in tomorrow? I need an appointment. Yes, a full exam. No, it's not for me. The name is Kaiser. Yes, K-A-I-S-E-R. First name is John. That's right. Yes, it's *that* John Kaiser. Um, yes. I'm sure he'll sign an autograph. Hang on." I pull the mobile away. "What time, John?"

"Hmm? It doesn't matter," he mumbles, still squinting at his e-reader.

I pull the mobile back. "How about three? Is that okay? Fine. He'll be there. Thank you, Cecilia. Goodbye." I text Jack regarding the appointment time and add it to my calendar. Before I can even turn off the phone, John grabs it. He sets down his e-reader — any interest in learning Welsh now gone — and settles down into my side with his new toy. He busily punches buttons and thumbs the touch screen, working through menus and options fast. Still breathing in his scent, I watch his progress over his head, one eye on my news article and the other on his furiously moving thumbs. He's found my stock market reports and periodical subscriptions that are about as interesting to him as the theory of plate tectonics. Now he's moved on to the home security menu. His body stiffens as his interest is peeked.

"You can unlock the door with this?"

"I can unlock the door, turn on the shower and boil water for tea."

"And I get one of these?"

"If you want."

"Oh, I *definitely* want." He spends time turning the library lights off and on, opening the skylights, and raising and lowering the plasma screen. I continue to watch his moves. All the while, I'm rubbing my face back and forth in his soft hair and his scent is beginning to excite me. Again, he's off searching for more menus. "No games?"

"No games."

"I'll need games."

"You'll have games."

More furious punching and scrolling. I know what he's looking for. I know exactly what he's looking for. I continue reading my article until his body stiffens again. I look over his head to see the screen. He's found the business end of things (accounts, ledgers, and spreadsheets that will show him what I'm worth, but I know they won't interest him) and my address book. It's what he's been searching for all along. He's staring at the screen now, unable to go any further. I watch as he tentatively punches one or two buttons. "Brian?"

"Hmm."

"What's your secondary access code?"

"That's private."

Silence. Again, I watch as he backs out of the menu and selects a few different options. He's trying to bypass the code. He never will. He's back to the access code screen. He enters some number sequences but he just causes a white screen with black text to become a black screen with flashing red text: Access Locked. "Brian?"

"Hmm." I rub my face in his hair and stroke his arm with my fingertips. I love the feel of his skin. It's so soft. I know I need to have sex with him soon. My body aches for him and that's an unfamiliar (but quite enjoyable) sensation for me.

"I need to know your code."

"No you don't."

"Yes I do."

"Why?"

"Well, what if you forget your phone at home and I'm here? I can tell you an important phone number."

"I don't need my mobile to access it. I can get information from it remotely when I'm anywhere in the world." I can do several things without having the mobile. If I forget it somewhere, I can lock it until I'm able to retrieve it. If I lose it, I can wipe out its memory or, if necessary, fry the circuits, rendering it useless. But that doesn't interest John. All he wants is the code. He lays the mobile on my stomach, sighs, and hugs me. He's trying to think of something—anything he can say or do—to get that code.

"I love you," he declares.

"I know you do."

"We shouldn't keep secrets from each other."

"You're right."

"Your code is a secret."

"My code is private."

"It's the same thing."

"No. A secret means I'm trying to keep something from you. Private means I'm trying to keep *you* from something." He lifts his head off my chest, giving that nonsensical gibberish more thought than it deserves. I stroke his hair, wondering how long he'll bug me for the code. The fact is, it's more important to him that he has it than it is to me that he doesn't have it, and he's almost realized that. He lays his head back on my chest and picks up the mobile.

"I really want the code."

"I know you do, love."

"If I had it, I wouldn't tell anyone."

"I know you wouldn't."

"Please, Brian. May I have the code?"

I lean forward and place my cheek against his head. "Hit that red button. Now, punch in one-zero-zero-eight-four-nine-four. Wait a minute. Let the screen advance. There's a second sequence. Okay, now punch in three-five-five-eight-eight-one." A thumbprint authentication screen appears.

"Will that happen every time I use the code?"

"No, it's just come up this time because you tried some wrong numbers." I press my right thumb to the screen and a scan bar descends from top to bottom.

"Fabulous! I want that! Will I get that?"

"Aye." The screen clears and John has his access. He's fully absorbed now, his fingers flying across the touch screen, scrolling through hundreds of names. It takes him a minute to realize he's in my business directory and not my personal one. He corrects his path in seconds. I take a deep breath as I watch him scroll to the first female name.

"Who's Angelica?"

"A friend."

John's thumb moves to the delete option. "Did you date her?"

"Yes."

"Did you sleep with her?"

"Yes."

Angelica is deleted. John continues scrolling. "Who's Anna?"

"A friend."

John's thumb moves to the delete option. "Did you date her?"

"Yes."

"Did you sleep with her?"

"No." His thumb hesitates over the delete option. I rub my face in his hair, wondering if Anna will join Angelica. And... she does. For the next five minutes, John furiously wipes out any woman he thinks I've dated, which is every female he finds in the directory including Edna, my sixty-three-year-old executive secretary, and Wanda. I haven't the heart to tell him I can retrieve the deleted entries with the push of one button. He'll find that out when he gets his own custom mobile. For now, he gets his way. It makes him happy, and I've come to realize if John is happy, I'm happy. I stretch my legs and adjust my back to relieve cramp. I check my watch. My body craves him in the worst way, but I don't know how to ask him for sex. As stupid as it sounds, I've never had to ask anyone for sex, and I don't know what to say. "I'm tired." It's the best I can come up with… and it's enough.

John stops scrolling. He bends forward and sets the mobile on the coffee table. He leans back and turns his face up to mine. I kiss him, cupping the back of his head with my hand while I press gently against his lips and dig in with my tongue. His taste is so incredibly unique. Within seconds, he's sweating. I pull away and look into his eyes. I brush away a lock of his messy hair. His poor backside has been through so much today, and he needs a rest. "Do you want to make love to me?" I'm not sure if that phrase is acceptable among gays. Maybe I should have said, "screw me." His eyes are searching mine, puzzled by my question. Yes, I probably should have said, "screw me."

"You mean we could…? We could change it around?"

I sigh with relief. "Aye. That's what I mean."

He's nervous. "We could. If that's what you want. If you think that's something you want to try. But we don't have to, if you don't want to—just yet. We don't have to do it so soon… if it might bother you, but if you—"

I cut off his babbling with another deep kiss because it's obvious we're both desperate for sex—any kind of sex—and he's wasting time. "Do you want to?"

His head bobs up and down. "Oh, *hell* yes! Please. More than anything!"

I pull back my head and study him. "This is going to hurt, isn't it?"

"Well, it's going to hurt a little. Or, maybe more than a little—at first. It could hurt a lot, depending on… how relaxed you are and the size of, you know… 'it.'"

Okay, this should be an interesting jam session. Never needing that important bit of information until now, I have no idea how big my 'it' is. I can't even say I've ever seen my 'it.' The damned thing has been moving the mail back there just fine for the last forty-one years without fail, so I've pretty much ignored it. But John is well endowed and he's eager—a little too eager—so no matter the size of my 'it,' I think I'm going to be in for a lot of pain. I stand and pull him up by his arms. "Yeah, I kind of figured that." I grab his clammy hand and head off to the bedroom, pulling him along behind me. "Just remember: My 'it' isn't the Eurostar Chunnel, so don't spend the next three hours trying to pound your way to Calais. The only action my backside has ever seen has been in a doctor's office. You be careful messing about back there and mind what you're doing. And I don't care how excited you get, don't you dare use those bloody nails!"

22
Commitment

Brian — April 12

We're sitting in the sun outside a small bistro, just a few blocks from the flat. I know John will enjoy coming here on a regular basis. He's watching hundreds of people walk by and dozens ask for his autograph and want to take a picture with him. They're thrilled with his stitches and his bruised cheek. They think he got the injuries filming one of his own stunts for the series. Even the show's producers, who've given him a few days off, are happy with that story. They claim it will bring in more viewers because it adds a touch of reality to the show, and reality is so popular right now, they were disappointed I didn't think to memorialize John plowing his face into the table with my mobile. A few of John's bolder fans—men and women alike—ask him for a kiss. He loves the attention. He thrives on it. He has the greatest personality and extreme patience when he deals with these nice, but intrusive, strangers.

I'm sitting about a foot back from the small table, reading my paper. At first, John was offended by my position in relation to him. He's made it clear: As an open couple, we're to sit close together when we're in public. I had to explain that with my height I can't cross my legs unless I'm well away from the table. And right now, sitting here with my legs crossed is the only tolerable position my poor ass can bear. It seems the size of my 'it' doesn't quite match up to the rest of my two-meter frame. And although they were very flattering, John's numerous questions about whether I use a loofah or exfoliate my bum with a scrub to get it so smooth didn't relax my muscles one bit. I am anally retentive (literally), and it's clear he's going to have to saddle up this tight-assed draught horse a few more times before it's even mildly comfortable with a rear mount. Ultimately though, he had a blast. Truth be told, he had two fairly decent blasts before he got way too excited and passed out in the middle of blast number three—and that made him happy, so I'm happy. My big butt is on fire and having his dead weight draped across my back for nearly fifteen minutes was irritating... but I'm happy.

From behind my newspaper and sunglasses, I watch as a decent-looking young bloke in tight jeans saunters by and smiles down at John. As he passes, John turns to glance at his ass and then turns back around and sips his coffee. He looks at me when he sees me staring at him. "What?"

"What the bloody hell was that?"

"What was what?"

"Did you just check out his backside, John?"

He takes another sip of coffee. "Habit. It doesn't mean anything."

I look at him for a few seconds and then continue reading my paper. I won't say I'm jealous, but I'm certainly not happy about it. After all, he's supposed to be *my* boyfriend. My jaw is tense as I lower my paper. "What about...? I mean, have you ever—"

"Of course." He smiles at the people walking by.

"When?"

"Early on."

I slit my eyes. *"How* early on?"

"At the pub in Rittersby."

Again, I look at him for a few long seconds before I go back to my paper. I'm agitated and he knows it. He knows I want an answer. I yank down my paper. "Look, if you think I'm going to—"

"You have a great ass, Brian. You have a sexy, hot ass," he quietly assures me. "Every time I see it, I just want to grab it and bite it—hard. It really turns me on."

I lift my paper and clear my throat. "Well... all right then. I suppose that's fine." We return to silence as John watches the people and I read. Twenty minutes later the barista delivers his second coffee and my second tea.

"Brian, do you love me?"

I don't look up from my paper. "Aye."

He tears open a packet of sugar and pours it into his cup. "Tell me."

"I always tell you."

"Tell me again. I need to hear you say it."

I stifle a yawn. "I love you."

He stirs his coffee. "And promise you'll never leave me."

"I can't promise that."

"What?" He stops stirring. "Of course you can. You need to. You need to promise me you'll never leave me."

I turn the page. "John, eventually I'll leave you. I'm nearly eleven years older than you. Chances are I'll buy the farm and the wheat field long before you." The barista brings his second pastry and my second plain toast.

"I mean, for someone else. You won't leave me for someone else, will you?"

"No."

"I'm your life partner, right?"

"Aye." I still haven't looked up from my paper.

"I mean, you wouldn't want me to leave you, would you?"

"No, but—"

He turns toward me now, his voice full of concern. "But what? What do you mean? What are you saying?"

"If you met someone else, if you really wanted to be with someone else—"

"What? You'd let me go? Just like that?"

"Well, if you really wanted—"

"You're not supposed to just *let me go!* You're not supposed to do that! You're supposed to *fight* for me! You're supposed to win me back!" He's getting himself all worked up.

I drop my paper, take off my sunglasses and give him an exasperated look. "Are you planning on leaving me for another bloke?"

"Of course not!"

"Then why are we even discussing this?"

"Because it's important! It's important that I know you'll always want to be with me!"

"I'll always want to be with you."

"And you'll...you'll win me back if I ever leave you—which I won't, but I need you to say you will!"

"I will. I promise. I'll win you back, okay?"

He stares at me while he contemplates my sincerity. "Okay." Satisfied, he spreads his napkin on his lap, picks up his pastry and calmly bites into it. He resumes gazing at the people.

I watch him until I'm convinced he's gotten that rant out of his system. His emotions baffle me. I don't know what gets into him. One minute things are fine, and the next minute I'm dealing with Raging Hormonal Hanna from Hell. I don't understand a single thing about him, and I doubt I ever will. I put on my sunglasses and raise my paper.

"You think I'm silly."

"No, John," I say from behind my paper. "I don't think you're silly. I think you're very needy, highly emotional, and sometimes—just sometimes—a little bloody paranoid."

"But that's okay, right?"

I turn the page. "Aye, love. It's fine." Two months ago, I wouldn't have committed to a three-day getaway with a woman, but over the last three days I've told a man I love him, have had sex with him, have allowed him to move in with me, have flushed his rectum, and have committed the rest of my life to him—willingly. The most shocking thing about the situation is that I'm okay with all of it, and I have no idea why. After another hour, we walk back to the flat and have insatiable marathon sex (with no mention of loofahs or exfoliating scrub) until John has to get ready for his eye appointment.

23
Claiming What Is Rightfully Mine

Brian – April 12

I have to tell Mickey what's happened. If I let it go too long he'll never forgive me, and worse, he'll find out from someone else. The few die-hard paparazzi who hang around here have already snapped some obvious pictures so it's only a matter of time. With John at his appointment and Mickey straight off the plane and undistracted, this is my best opportunity. I'm apprehensive because I don't think he'll take it well. He sees John as a son and he's very protective of him. Unfortunately, I'm becoming very protective of him too *and* very possessive, so we may have a problem — a big problem.

He stomps into the flat. "Brian! How's it going?"

"Fine, Mickey. How was your flight?"

"Horrible as usual: lots of turbulence, screaming babies, corny chick flicks and tasteless food. Had a really hot flight attendant, though. Man, was he sexy! He had the tightest buns, Brian and these long, slender fingers. He kept winking at me. I think he wanted my number but you know, he was on the job — had to keep it professional, right?" Mickey shakes his head and whistles low. Then he sees the defeated piano. "Lord of the Dance! What happened?"

"There was a small accident. It's hard to explain."

"I'll bet! Is it a total loss?"

"Definitely."

"Wow! That's a real shame. I bet Moyra had a big fat cow, huh?"

I smile without answering. Oh, yes. She certainly did. And even though it was heavily insured, I still had to write out a big fat check to appease Moyra and make that big fat cow disappear. I must *really* love John. "Let's grab a drink and go into the library. I'm sorting some things back there." I walk to the bar and pour two drinks; straight scotch for me and a scotch and soda for him. "Mickey?"

"Oh, yeah." He tears his eyes off the slain piano to take the drink and then trails behind me as I head to the library. "Well, anyway, I was glad to get your call. Surprised though. I thought you'd be in Scotland. I'm glad you're here because I need your advice about that nightclub contract. What'ya think? Do I need that disclaimer in there? I figure it can't hurt, but I don't want it to break the deal."

"Leave it in. If they don't like it, let them walk. If something goes wrong and you don't have it—"

"I know, I know. I'll lose my freckled ass. Damn!" He shakes his head. "If it's not one thing, it's another." He flops down into one of the chairs. "So, what's up?"

"It's about John."

"Yeah? Hey, he called me yesterday and said he had a little accident. He cut his head open and had to get stitches! God, I went ballistic! He says he's okay, though. I told him 'okay' means nothing. I want to see him. I need to see what he's done to that million-dollar face of his! They've still got lots of scenes to shoot to finish up the season. No facial scars. It's in his contract."

I sit across from him on the sofa. "Mickey, we need to talk."

"I know what you're going to say: The cancer research benefit has stalled. Brian, with all these trips to LA I've let it fall behind, but I'm on it now, one hundred percent."

"That's not what I want to talk about."

"No? Okay, what then? Have I let something else slide? If I have, I'm really—"

"I said, it's about John."

"Johnny? What about him?"

"He had his accident here in the flat on Sunday."

"Here? He cut his head here?" Mickey is surprised and confused. He obviously doesn't know about any of John's previous visits. "What was he doing here?"

"He came to see me—well, to leave something for me. Look, that part really doesn't matter."

"He's okay, though, right? I mean, he's fine, isn't he?"

"Yes, he's fine. Alex said—"

"*Alex?* You had to get Alex? Brian, what happened? Are you sure he's okay?"

"He's fine. Believe me, he's okay." This is not going well.

"So, what? He cuts his head open, sees a doctor, and you just send him on his merry way—all without telling me?"

"I didn't send him anywhere. He stayed here... with me."

Mickey sighs. "Well, thank God for that! I'm glad you kept an eye on him. You hear all these stories of people just having a little head injury and a day later—boom! They're as dead as Disco. So, is he at the condo now?"

"The condo? *Your* condo?"

Mickey's eyes start darting back and forth, and he nervously licks his lips. He looks as if he's been caught in a lie, and I don't think he's even told one... yet. "Uh, yeah, he's staying with me for a while."

Something is going on here and I know it has to do with John breaking up with David. "Why?"

"Um, he's having some work done on his brownstone— remodeling stuff, I think. It's no big deal. It's only temporary. You know, just for a while."

He's uneasy, and now he's flat-out lying. I want to press him on it. I want to know more because he's hiding something important, but I have to deal with this situation first. I have to tell him about John and me.

"I'll give him a call to let him know I'm back." Mickey pulls out his mobile.

"Mickey, he's not at your condo. He spent last night here, too... with me."

"Oh. Where is he now?"

"The optometrist's. He's getting an eye exam."

"An eye exam? Fabulous, Brian! I've been hounding him to get his eyes checked for years. How'd you do it?"

"I just made the appointment and sent him."

"Wow! Pretty good job. You ought to be a manager." He sips his drink. "Hey, I'm sorry to hear Carol didn't work out. Shame about that, but what are you gonna do, huh? Are you seeing anyone new? Did you meet anyone while I was back in the states? Maybe line up a date for the cancer benefit?"

He's in a really good mood. I can't get him to belt up or stay on track.

"Hey! I have this lovely gal. Brian, you have *got* to meet her: sophisticated, high profile. She's got some good connections, too. Let's see.... Where's her number?"

Mickey is fiddling with his mobile. I need to get his attention back and fast, before John gets home. "Mickey, I'm already seeing someone."

"Huh? Well, that's fabulous! That's excellent! Who is she? Do I know her? What's she like? Any connections?" He's on the edge of his chair, poised like a gossip queen, ready to pounce on any juicy tidbit I'll throw his way.

"It's not a she." I look down into my drink. "It's a he."

"What? What do you mean, a 'he?' What are we talking about here? I was talking about a date for the benefit. What are you talking about?"

I take in a deep breath, exhale, and close my eyes for a moment. "I'm seeing a bloke." I look up.

For once, Mickey doesn't have a response. He's quiet. His mouth is closed and he's looking at me with unblinking eyes. I'm waiting for reality to sink in. He can be a bit of a scatterbrain, but he's not stupid. If he paid attention to what I told him in the last ten minutes, he'll get it. He's thinking hard now, mulling something over. He's remembering what I said, and his face is turning red. Now I see beads of sweat. He's got it. He finally understands what I've been trying to say. "But I don't.... That doesn't make.... You're not...." Confusion is all over his face. He licks his lips, looks around the room bewildered, and looks back at me. "He's been *here* the last two nights?"

I nod.

"In your flat?"

I nod again.

He swallows hard. When he speaks, his voice is barely audible.

"In… your bed?"

I nod once more and watch him carefully, waiting for a full reaction. His face is expressionless, which is unusual for Mickey.

"Why, Brian? How could you…? Why would you…? You're not even…." He can't finish the sentences. He sinks back in the chair and stares down into his drink. "You've got all that money. You're tall and handsome. You could have any woman you want—*any* woman. How could you take Johnny?"

"Look, I know this is a big surprise—"

"How could you do this when you *knew* how I felt about him?"

"What?" Felt about him? What is he talking about? What the hell just happened here? Did someone change the channel?

"Ten years, Brian. I waited ten long years. You planned this all along, didn't you?"

"*What?*"

Mickey stands up now and points his finger at me. "You told me to stay away from him! You told me to keep my hands off him and then you do *this* to me! You *steal* him from me!"

"*Steal him?*" Christ, I had no idea Mickey fancied John! I can't believe my tight ass has had the pleasure of entertaining my oblivious fat head for the last three months.

"Ten years! I waited ten years and you'd planned to take him all along! *Backstabber!*"

Backstabber? Now I'm angry. "Oh, come off it, Mickey! Ten years ago, John was nothing more to me than a name on a piece of paper you shoved under my nose asking for advice on how to make it into a legal contract! I didn't even know him!"

"Yeah, right, Brian! *Let me hear your pathetic excuses!*"

I stand up and take a step toward him. "*Pathetic excuses?* Listen, you stupid jackass! I told you to lay off him because he was only twenty years old and you were his damned manager!" I'm fuming now and nearly shouting. "And he wasn't the only one, was he, Mickey? Half a dozen times I told you not to try to screw around with your clients, you bloody fool! Look what it got you! Three lawsuits and you asked me to bail your lousy ass out *every time!*"

"*Aha! But you didn't, did you?*"

"Damned right, I didn't! You *never* should have gone after them. They didn't want you, Mickey."

"Yeah, right," he snorts in a nasty, dismissive tone.

"I'm serious. They didn't want you. They *never* wanted you." Thinking back to the exhaustive rounds of bruise-inflicting, heart-stopping sex John and I had earlier today, it almost pains me to tell him this last bit of information: "And neither does John."

Mickey is stunned by my words. He wasn't expecting that. Not from me—his good old mate. He collapses back into the chair and looks up at me. "But I wanted *him*, Brian. I really wanted *him*."

I look down at him with exasperation. "Aye. You wanted all of them."

"But he's so...so special. He's so beautiful and precious. It should have been me, Brian. It should have been *me*, not you. I was there for him, not you. Every time David hurt him it was *me* he turned to."

I run my fingers through my hair and sit down on the sofa. "Bloody hell. Is that why you never wanted John to break up with David—just so you could always rescue him?" I'm appalled. "How could you do that to him? How could you let him suffer through that? You convinced him to keep living that miserable life just so you could...?" I'm so disgusted with his selfishness I can't even finish the sentence.

"He would have wanted me eventually, Brian. He would have seen I was exactly what he wanted and needed."

All I can do is shake my head at this pathetic, demented louse because he's obviously left the reality planet far behind to live in his own twisted dream world of misguided, pining adoration. Then, within seconds, his demeanor changes from demented louse to demonic bastard.

"What did you do, Brian? Huh? What did you promise him if he slept with you?"

"What?"

"What did you hound him with? What was the bribe? Was it money? Did you promise to throw your money at him if he had *sex* with you? How did you harass him into letting you *screw* him?"

Again, I feel the anger welling up inside me fast. "Mickey, I didn't

304

promise him anything, and I didn't harass him."

He springs to his feet again. *"Liar!"*

I stand up too, full of rage. *"Look, I didn't go after John! I didn't want to be anywhere near him! I didn't bribe him with money and I didn't harass him for sex!"*

His crazy eyes are wide with hatred and bitter resentment. *"THEN WHY THE HELL IS HE EVEN WITH YOU?"*

"Because I love him." John's quiet voice startles us. He's standing in the doorway with a small bag from the eye doctor in one hand and my evening papers in the other.

"Johnny!" Mickey gasps.

John comes into the room and sets the bag and papers on the coffee table. He walks over to me, stands in front of me with his back against my chest, reaches down for my arms and pulls them up across his rib-cage. He crosses his arms over mine and relaxes his weight back against my body. It's the same position he demands in bed when I spoon him, even though it cramps the hell out of my shoulder and causes one of my ass cheeks to go numb. He says it makes him feel safe. He's staring at Mickey. When he speaks, his voice is calm. "Brian didn't harass me and he didn't bribe me for sex. He was going back to Scotland to get away from me. I only found out he was leaving when you mentioned it on Saturday. I came here on Sunday to apologize for things I'd said and done that made him feel... uncomfortable. I had an accident and cut my head so Brian didn't go to Scotland. He stayed here... because of me. And yes, I've had sex with him — willingly. That's all you need to know. The rest is private. It's between us."

There's a heavy silence in the room. Mickey doesn't know what to say, and I don't have anything more to say. I just keep a tight hold on John, my only concern in this whole fiasco. I press my nose into his hair and watch Mickey over the top of his head.

"Is it true you wanted me to stay with David so I'd keep running to you every time he hurt me?"

I realize John was standing in the doorway for some time, and now I'm wondering what else he heard. It wasn't my intention to expose Mickey's old indiscretions.

"Johnny, you know I was only thinking of your career. A breakup.

Well, that would have been—"

"Really bad press, I know. It could have damaged my career and the tabloids would have had a field day." John substantially tightens his grip on my arms as if he's bracing for something he knows is about to happen. "But then again, if I had ended it earlier, maybe I wouldn't have been beaten, and raped... and sodomized."

Instinctively, I try to move my arms. John digs in his nails, hard enough to draw blood that drips onto the carpet. I've felt a powerful sense of anger only once before in my life just like the absolute blinding rage that's boiling up inside me right now. If John didn't have his arms clamped down across mine, I'd lunge at Mickey and rip his damned head off. My voice is low, shaking with fury, and my body is hot and tense. "Someone had better explain—*now!*"

Mickey stares at the floor. "It shouldn't have happened. I thought he'd be on the photo shoot for weeks. At least, that was the plan. He was fired for assaulting one of the other models—Lars' boyfriend. When he was sent back to London, well... Lars didn't call me until it was too late. He was already here, already drunk and out of control. He'd already..."

Mickey can't finish the sentence. He doesn't have to. Every piece of the horrific puzzle falls into place.

"I made everyone promise they wouldn't tell," John adds.

This is unbelievable! "Everyone? Who else knew about it?"

"Martin, Jeff, Ben, Prissy, one doctor and the police."

I'm stunned. "Why didn't you tell me?"

He turns his head to the side and whispers, "It was right after the birthday... thing." It's obvious he doesn't want Mickey to know about the kiss. "I had made such a mess of everything. I didn't think.... I mean, we weren't speaking and...."

I close my eyes and press my lips to the back of his head as I squeeze him. I feel so sick that I wasn't there for him. Right now, the only person I want to kill more than Mickey is David. "I understand. I'm so sorry," I whisper down into his ear.

"I know. It wasn't your fault. Anyway, I agreed not to press charges if he went back to LA and never came here again. That's the only positive thing that came out of it. I finally got rid of him, for good." He turns back to Mickey and raises his voice. "Mickey, you can either accept our relationship or not. At this point, I don't care. You're still my manager under contract, but we can terminate it if that's what you want."

"No. I still want to be your manager, and I'm sure I'll be okay with... your relationship eventually. It's just going to take a while to get used to. It came as a shock—a really big shock. Brian, I guess we've hit a brick wall, huh?" He tries to muster a smile for John's sake, but it's just a menacing sneer, and there's venom in his eyes. He truly loathes me, and my status has gone from good old mate to number one enemy. That's fine with me. I feel the same way about him. I hold him personally responsible for every second of pain John suffered at David's hands, and I will *never* forgive him for that. I don't say a word. He sets his glass on the table and walks out of the library. I slip one bloody arm out of John's grasp, take out my mobile and punch in a few numbers. John pulls my hand lower so he can see the screen, too. We watch Mickey walk out of the flat and around the atrium. He hesitates at the lift, starts to turn back toward the front door, changes his mind and continues on into the lift. I lock the front door, toss the mobile on the sofa and tightly hold what has rightfully become *my* precious John.

John

The confrontation with Mickey puts a damper on the rest of the evening, our last night together before Brian flies to Scotland. He waits until we're eating dinner to tell me he'll be gone for more than a week—that when he said he'd return on Saturday, he meant Saturday, one week out. That's ten days. I want to complain. I want to argue and throw a tantrum and demand he come back earlier, but he's moody, quiet and distracted. His present state of mind would siphon off the potency of a tantrum, rendering it ineffective—even if I could break something expensive. At least we'll have a night of great sex... without sweat.

I finally find the panel that controls the air conditioning for the bedroom. It's in the dressing room (of all places!). I crank it up while

Brian is out on the balcony making a quick phone call to Simon to get an update on Robert. Since the weather is still stiflingly humid, my goal is to make sure I don't sweat like a garden soaker hose during sex. That much sweat isn't attractive, and I want to stop it before Brian complains. Half an hour later, we're lying naked on the bed. I'm on my back, arms folded behind my head. Brian is beside me, propped up on his elbow, looking down at me. He's studying my features and his forehead is wrinkled. He looks concerned, as though global warming was weighing heavily on his mind. "What?"

"Hmm?"

"What's wrong?"

"Nothing."

I watch as his eyes pass over my face with curiosity, as if seeing me for the first time.

"Today, Mickey said you were beautiful. Why is it I don't notice that about you? Why don't I see your beauty?"

His question catches me off guard.

He reaches out to stroke my cheek. His expression is so troubled. "I can't understand why I don't notice that—why someone else has to tell me you're beautiful."

Now that I think about it, he's never complimented me on my looks. He's never said anything about my looks, and everyone I meet—at some point in time (usually right away)—says something about my looks because I'm damned good looking.

"How could you deal with that?"

"With what?"

"With me never saying anything, never noticing?"

"I just thought you loved me for other reasons."

"I do, but...." He shakes his head. "Still, I should have noticed something so obvious to everyone else."

I stare into his eyes. "What *do* you love about me?"

He sighs. "You're honest. You never try to be someone you're not, and you don't try to impress me." He rolls over on top of me and places his forearms on either side of my head, propping himself up above my face. When he speaks again it's in a whisper. "You have the most phenomenal scent. I've never experienced anything like it before.

You try so hard to do well, John, even when you bugger up, and you've really buggered up a lot. But most of all, your emotions—good and bad—are so real. I truly love that about you." He bends his head and kisses me. It's a fantastic kiss, but I can tell he doesn't want sex yet. "Now I understand Mickey's reaction. I understand his anger."

I give him a puzzled look. "What do you mean?"

"If he's been in love with you for the past ten years, and then I come along—someone who can't even appreciate the beauty he sees day after day—and take you away from him in just a couple of months..."

"You didn't take me away from him. There never would have been anything between Mickey and me."

"I know that, but in his warped mind it was going to happen. It must kill him inside to know I've been making love to you." Again he kisses me. This time more intensely. But still, somehow I can tell he doesn't want sex yet.

"Did you really refuse to bail him out three times?"

He sighs again. "You heard a lot more than you should have. Mickey had a tendency to misread the signs: a simple peck on the cheek given as a thank you, a tight hug when someone greeted him, a wink or a compliment on something he was wearing." Brian shakes his head. "He thought every gesture from one of those young lads was an invitation to intimacy. He saw flirting where no one else did, and he thought they all fancied him."

"Because he wanted to believe it so badly?"

"I think so. I watched him do the same thing with Lars. Obviously, he still wants to believe it."

"You met Lars?"

"Aye, and I knew Vidal was his boyfriend. Mickey didn't have a clue."

I remember the sad scene at the airport. "No, he didn't. What happened to the lawsuits?"

"The lads weren't stupid. They didn't want to go through the court system. I'm sure none of them could afford a solicitor. They were just starting out and they had their future careers to think about. What other manager would touch them if they knew there was always the possibility of being sued? They just wanted money, pure and simple. Mickey paid them off."

We lay together in silence, looking into each other's love-struck eyes. Eventually, Brian lifts his pelvis and reaches down to adjust his genitals, which have been crushed against my hipbone for the last ten minutes. I spread my legs wide to give him more room and make him feel comfortable. I have a cute phrase I thought up to describe his enormous tackle. Of course, I'd never tell him, or anyone else, what it is. He'd kill me if he knew I had a pet name for his penis. It's just my little secret, never to be revealed. I run my hands up and down his muscular back and his tight buttocks, letting my fingertips gently probe between his velvety smooth cheeks. I'm trying to make an arousing gesture — something that might get him horny — but there's still no indication of sex. We just continue to lie together, gazing at each other.

"Is the air on?"

"Hmm. It was so warm and I thought it might help you sleep better before your early flight tomorrow morning."

He hesitates before answering. "You know, you're probably right. I think it will. Thank you, love."

I look into his troubled eyes. He must still be upset about Mickey. "He'll get over it in time."

"You think so?"

"Of course." I give him a big smile and lightly pinch his ass. "It's Mickey."

24
Goodbye, John

John – April 13

It's four-fifteen and Brian is in the shower. I should roll my coma-tose body out of bed and join him – if only to beg him to fondle me, but it's too early and I'm dead tired, which is odd. I woke up with unbe-lievable energy after two nights of rowdy, loss-of-vision (and loss of consciousness) sex. Last night, I didn't get any sex and I can barely open my eyes. I don't even want to wiggle my toes. I clutch at the blanket, pull it over my head, and wait until he comes into the bed-room fifteen minutes later – showered, shaved, blow-dried, and im-maculately groomed with a towel around his waist.

"Are you coming to the airport with me?"

"Hmmpfumpf," I mumble from my dark hovel.

"Then get up, love."

Acting upon that command is going to require super-human physical strength this cowpoke may not be able to rustle up, even though he didn't ride the big, bucking bronco last night. I pull the blanket off my face, stiffly sit up and yawn. My puffy eyes are mere slits, and someone appears to have flocked the inside of my mouth. I don't know it yet, but a scrap of gauze is also stuck to my cheek, en-hancing my outer beauty. I throw off the blanket and pull my legs over the side of the bed. I stand up, lean my full weight against his chest, scratch my numb butt seductively and pucker up for a kiss. I've got blotchy skin, crusty eyes, killer morning breath, dark stubble, and bed-head (oh, and that proud scrap of gauze). I look like shit, but I still ex-pect a kiss.

He surveys the luminescent glow of my early-morning radiance from his superior height. "Wash up first."

"No," I croak. "I want a kiss."

"You look like crap, John." His words are blunt, but true.

I aim a big sour yawn up into his face, my wrath for the unkind observation. "I know, but I still want a kiss—now." I get a lovely kiss from my stud muffin, soft and slow. I reach down, pull the towel from his waist and happily fumble around in his hairy crotch like a kid in a sandbox searching for his favorite Hot Wheels. He closes his eyes, moans, and presses his lips to my forehead. I reach around, grab his ass and crush his body against mine.

He pulls away. "Not now. Go wash up."

■ ■ ■

Getting to the airport takes over half an hour. There's a lot of traffic on the roads. I sleep on Brian's shoulder while he makes phone calls and rifles through his briefcase. At Heathrow, even with four active terminals, it's a zoo. With construction going on all over the M-25, Jack dumps us off at terminal three and we take the Express to terminal five. I've never been here this early at this time of year. It seems as if every Londoner is catching a flight somewhere, and it's not just business commuters with carry-ons. There are a ton of families: parents trudging through the concourse with mountains of luggage, sulking teenagers buoyed along by earbuds tethered to MP3 devices on their hips, hyper toddlers playing tag among the kiosks, and crying babies (many needing a diaper change) in strollers. Apparently, pilots of four major airlines are threatening a sympathy strike in honor of the taxi drivers, and everyone here is trying to beat an unknown doomsday deadline. With his briefcase and carry-on, Brian leads the way through the sea of bodies. I schlep along behind him, lugging his laptop. As we make our way through the mass like spawning Chinook braving the powerful Russian River, he frequently looks back to make sure he doesn't lose me. Now and then, when things get thick, he reaches back for my hand so we stick together. Eventually, as we head to the far end of the terminal, the crowds thin out. We're on our way to the outlying gates where the private and chartered jets are waiting. Finally, I'm able to walk beside him.

"Now look, I've left you three credit cards and a set of keys on the kitchen counter. If you lose any of them, just call Charles. You've got his number. He'll know what to do. When you go out clubbing with your mates—"

"I'm not going to the clubs while you're gone."

He gives me a dubious look and starts again. "When you go out clubbing, use the limo. It's easier to fix than the Rolls if it gets dinged or scratched, and it's easier to clean if someone's been sick in it. Your car is out of commission for a while. It needs parts ordered. You really should maintain a sports car like that, John."

"But I like driving my Boxster."

"I know you do. But you can drive the Reventón or the GranTurismo, if you want. You can drive or ride anything in the garage, except the 848 and the mc-12. Be careful in the shower. I've set your controls so you shouldn't scald yourself, and remember to take your contacts out at night. Harry will call you about the bathtub. He's at the East River Street condo working on some renovations, but he'll come over whenever you say. Just tell him what you want and where you want it. It doesn't matter to me." Brian stops walking, looks me up and down, and then starts walking again. "He'll probably try to set you up with his daughter. Tell him you're seeing someone. If he won't let up—and he probably won't—tell him we're sleeping together. He'll find out anyway." He stops walking again, and intensely stares down at me. "Look, while we're on that subject; I know you tell your mates everything, but what goes on in our bedroom...."

"I know. That's private."

"It's just that some things we do... and some physical attributes about me... I'd rather not...."

"I understand. That's only between us, right?"

"Right. And I'd really prefer no one find out you call it 'Papa Brian's Massive Rear Spear Gear.'" He gives me a sly wink and starts walking again. "And remember, Alex is going to stop by next Friday to look at your stitches," he calls out over his shoulder.

I stand there with my mouth hanging open as he walks on toward the gate. *Oh, my God!* How did he find out? How the *hell* did he know about my pet name? It takes a minute before I start walking again. I'm beet red, out of breath, and his laptop is banging against my thigh when I finally catch up to him. "Brian, I didn't.... I mean, I haven't told that to *anyone!* I swear!"

"Good. I'm glad to hear that. It's flattering, but it's also really embarrassing."

"No, it's...it's certainly not something I would *ever* tell—anyone. I promise." I catch my breath and swallow hard. "But how did you find out?"

"You talk in your sleep."

I stop dead in my tracks. "I what?"

He stops and turns back to look at me. "You talk in your sleep, John. Most of it's just a bunch of gibberish, but you're quite chatty and you giggle a lot." He turns and starts walking again.

I giggle? In front of my boyfriend? When I'm asleep? How embarrassing! I haul ass to catch up to him again. "Jesus! What else did I say?"

Brian is studying his boarding slip as he's walking. "Hmm? Oh, you prattled on with some crap about wanting to be a puppet and not a garden hose. Now look, they'll come to hang the curtains next Thursday. Don't leave those buggers alone in the flat. The last time they were there, they convinced Charles to get a second ladder from the basement and then helped themselves to my best scotch while he was gone. Keep an eye on them, or better yet, have Joe up there when they come. Okay? John? John?"

"Oh, yeah. I will. I promise, I will. Brian, do I always talk in my sleep?"

"No. Just last night."

■ ■ ■

We finally arrive at the gate and Brian turns to take the laptop off my shoulder. A few dozen people are milling around. Most of them are fat, balding men in ill-fitting business suits, waddling back and forth and talking loudly on their phones in a silly display of self-importance: bloated-faced, thick-necked He-Men who absentmindedly scratch their balls and spit without thinking twice. I know we have to say goodbye in front of them. I'm just wondering how we'll say it. I have no idea how comfortable Brian will be showing affection toward

314

me in this type of atmosphere, but I'm pretty sure I'm about to find out.

"Goodbye, John," he formally says, untwisting the tangled strap of the laptop case.

"Goodbye… Brian." I gaze up at him with a small smile, trying to lasso his attention, hoping for just a little more. It certainly doesn't feel right to say goodbye like this to someone I love—someone I've been sleeping with for the last three days. I'm mortified when he turns and walks down the gateway and around the corner. My God, he could've at least hugged me! None of these pompous twits would have reacted to a simple hug. I feel like an idiot just standing here staring at the empty gateway. I finally turn around to head back through the busy terminal, shocked by (and very disappointed in) my new boyfriend.

"John!"

I stop and turn to see Brian walking back up the gateway without his luggage. If he's just coming back to remind me to pick up his phone messages at the concierge counter, I'll pinch him. He strides right up to me, cups the back of my skull, bends his head and kisses me like nobody's goddamned business—working his tongue deeply into my mouth. His other hand is in the small of my back, fingers spread wide, grinding me hard against him for one last major jolt of Papa Brian's primo penis erectus. He moans softly. My body heats up instantly and I'm sweating. I'm ready for sex—right here, right now. He pulls away from my mouth and whispers in my ear, "I'm sorry."

"It's okay," I whisper back.

"No, it's not. I know this is important to you, but it's all new to me and it's going to take me some time. You may have to remind me, okay?"

I nod, nuzzle his neck and press even harder against him. I can't speak, and I'm oblivious to the stares of everyone around us. My arms are clutching his back. I don't want him to leave me. I don't want him to go away.

He pulls back again and looks down into my eyes. "Normally, I wouldn't do this with so many people around. I wouldn't be so openly intimate in public. I guess by now, you know that's not my style. But I don't know any of these silly buggers, and I won't see you again for ten days, so what the hell, huh?" He gives me a smile.

I smile back and then my smile fades as my eyes travel all over his face, trying to take in every beautiful feature I'll be deprived of. "I'll miss you so much."

"I'll miss you, too." He kisses my forehead, pulls away and turns to walk down the gateway.

I watch him leave and let out a long, slow sigh. Now I'm well aware of all these men—and a few women—staring at me. I look at some of their faces. Mouths are hanging open. Some were offended by it. A few were stunned by it. One or two were okay with it. I'm used to the looks. I've been dealing with them for years. I turn, walk back through terminal five and take the Express to terminal three. I climb into the limo, lie down and sleep until Jack arrives at the flat. I'll need my energy if I'm going to help Joe get rid of that piano and rip out the bloodstained carpet. Then, I'll figure out how to get my stuff out of Mickey's condo.

■ ■ ■

Revealing what's happened to the nincompoops starts out as a fiasco. At first, when I explain how I got my head injury, they don't believe me. They just think it's some fantastic lie I've conjured up to cover up the fact that I whacked my skull on the corner of the medicine cabinet in Mickey's guest bathroom—because I've whacked my head in the same way on numerous other things in the past. I'm a bit accident-prone and my head usually takes the hit. In the end, I go through the whole story—except for the sex parts—and drag them back to the flat to see the piano, now in several pieces out on the balcony.

Prissy looks down with wide eyes on the mountain of splintered wood, entangled wires, brass mechanics and cast-iron plate. He reaches back to pick his panties out of his butt. "You busted this?"

"It was an accident."

Jeff whistles low and shakes his head. He sticks out his toe and gives the pinblock a hesitant nudge. "A Bösendorfer. Honey, that must have been worth a fortune."

Ben adjusts his glasses and leans in closely to give my stitches a skeptical look. "And you're sure he didn't clock you one when you busted it?"

I pull away from his looming face. "Yes, I'm sure. I fell. I passed out and fell into the glass table. That's how I cut my head."

Martin crosses his arms and looks down at the piano. "This is freaky, man. I mean, this mate must have some loose screws if you can cause this much damage and he doesn't kill you. Either that, or he's in love with you, Johnny."

I can't help but produce a monumental smile as I fantasize about my sexy new boyfriend and his wicked, manly attributes. "He's in love with me. He told me so."

They all look at each other and then turn toward me en masse.

"So you two have had sex," Prissy accuses, his eyes narrowing.

"Um..." My face is getting hot and I know it's turning red. I'd forgotten about Prissy's hyperactive sex detector and his irritating persistence once he's activated it.

"You have! You *have* had sex!" Prissy insists. He moves in closer and inspects my face, as if the telltale signs of being tossed around like a rag doll on the receiving end of Brian's truncheon are embedded in the pores on my nose. "You've had a *lot* of sex." He gasps, his eyes fly wide open, and he points as if a scarlet "SM" (for Sex Maniac) has magically appeared on my forehead. "And it's *hot* sex, isn't it, Johnny? You've had some massive, hot Scream-Your-Ass-Off sex with Brian, haven't you?"

At this point, my face is fire-engine red. "We...we've been intimate. Yes."

"Wait a minute. Does this mean he fancies men now?" Martin asks.

"No."

"Not at all?" Jeff asks.

I shake my head.

"So it's just you?" Martin says.

I nod.

"And does he still fancy women?" Ben asks.

I don't have an answer. It's a question that's been on my mind, too—and one I wanted to ask Brian before he left. "I'm not sure."

Ben, Jeff and Martin contemplate that revelation for a minute. They're now on a mission to classify Brian's orientation, and I'm wondering what they'll come up with.

"Let's get back to the sex," Prissy says.

Jeff gives Ben a puzzled look. "So… what does that make him? Is he bi?"

"Hell if I know," Ben mutters.

Martin shakes his head. "Right now, he's just one strange mate."

"Brian is not strange," I insist. "He's just…. He's not attracted to men."

"So… he's not gay because he doesn't fancy men," Martin says.

"I want to hear more about the sex," Prissy interjects, crossing his arms.

"And if he doesn't fancy men, he can't be bi," Ben says.

"No, the sex — talk about the *sex*," Prissy insists.

"But honey, he fancies one man; he fancies Johnny," Jeff says.

"Okay, maybe he's just a little bi," Ben says.

"What about the *sex*?" Prissy demands.

"You twonk! You can't be a little bi. You're either bi, or you're not bi."

"Well, he's bi, then. I guess…" Ben is clearly confused.

"Ah! But he's not bi if he stops sleeping with women now that he's with Johnny. Then he's been turned… I think," Jeff says.

"Yeah, but if he still doesn't fancy men, what's he been turned into?" Ben says.

"I want to hear more about the *sex*!" Prissy demands.

I need to shut Prissy up because his voice is getting screechy. "You're not hearing anything about it. It's private. It's just between us."

He excitedly grabs at my shirt with tiny, shaking fingers. "But he's good, isn't he, Johnny? I mean, he's tall, right? He's got long legs. And he's got those great big humongous hands with super-long fingers, so that means he's gotta have a great big long — "

"*Look*, just let it go." I pry his fingers off me and slap his hands down. If Brian finds out this horny urchin is fishing for the size of his penis, he'll kill him.

"Why don't you want to tell me if he's hung like an elephant?"

Martin is getting irritated with Prissy, which rarely happens. "Oh, for Christ's sake, Prissy! Leave him alone. He said it's private."

"But we always tell each other stuff like that. Silly willy chat has never been off limits."

"Well, it is now," I insist.

"Why?"

Martin sighs and rolls his eyes. "Because Brian isn't really gay-man gay. He's just sort of..."

"Semi-bi?" Ben suggests.

"Or quarter-turned?" Jeff offers.

"I don't know. I guess he's sort of... straight-man gay. And that makes it off limits," Martin says, glancing at Jeff.

Prissy shakes his head. "That doesn't even make sense."

"Well it's the best I can do so stick a sock in your cakehole, shove it way down and give it a good hard twist."

Prissy pouts and picks at his panties.

Ben watches his diminutive, admonished princess diligently digging for gold in his itty-bitty butt crack. "So, what do we do now?" he asks as we all stand around the butchered piano, looking a bit lost.

"Well, honey, we could go out to dinner and hit a few clubs," Jeff suggests.

"We could take a credit card and use the limo," I add with a big smile.

■ ■ ■

With Jack and Prissy's help (Jack because he's strong and Prissy because he's not working right now — and fancies Jack), I collect my things from Mickey's condo when he's in LA. Even though I've seen him and I've been cordial to him on the set and at my rehearsals, the brief conversations have been strained, and I avoid him in private.

I've spent a lot of Brian's money on the flat. I started out with intentions of restraint, but most gays love to shop, and whipping out those black cards got easier as the days went by. With a skilled installation crew (decent eye candy, too), the Brazilian ebony floors were laid down in a day and a half and stained the next day. I chose spice-toned furniture for the living room, banishing his off-whites and creams to the basement storage rooms — all in preparation for our future dog. The balconies gained Herculean copper fire pits and tall privets surrounded by geraniums in brightly colored ceramic pots. I had the white awnings pulled down and dyed in soft shades of umber, sienna and olive green. I hung up bird feeders and birdbaths even though Brian is going to make me get rid of them the minute he sees one speck of pigeon poop. The chunks of piano were given to my friend, Alfie—a local progressive artist—as raw material. If he can create some modern artwork out of it that Brian likes, he might just buy it back. In the kitchen, the stark white walls and cabinets got a fresh coat of burnt umber to warm them up and the granite countertops and stainless cooktop were pulled out and hauled over to the East River Street condo. My big surprise for Brian, a dark red Aga cooker, was hooked up, test fired, and deemed ready for use, and the poured-concrete countertops are still curing under plastic sheeting. Harry came over to talk about installing a bathtub, and he did try to set me up with his daughter. He was persistent, as I guess most fathers trying to offload their thirty-seven-year-old, single daughters would be. I finally told him Brian and I were sleeping together thinking that would shut him up. He countered with the fact that she looks like a guy, sporting thick sideburns and a bushy uni-brow, and attends the same fundraisers Brian does. Since I'm one hundred percent gay and she sounds like a cross between Elvis and Frida Kahlo, I told him I'd stick with Brian. His final words to me, said with a wink: "I don't blame you. I'd stick with him, too."

As the flat's transformation winds down, delivery men parade an endless array of beautiful accessories into the lobby and up the elevator: glorious, thick-pile rugs, plush throw pillows, and eclectic, whimsical do-nothings whose only purpose in life is to sit proudly on tables and shelves in tasteful groupings of odd numbers and attract dust. Prissy helps me by signing for deliveries when I'm at work, and two days before Brian's return, as the final pieces are being brought in, I'm ready to unveil to the poops everything I've accomplished so far.

I spin around in the center of the living room and then fall in a dramatic défaillir pose on a cinnamon sofa. "Well, what do you think?"

Ben gives me a thumbs up as he cuddles with Prissy on a complimentary nutmeg loveseat. "It's fab, Johnny!"

Jeff nods his approval at various items and sinks into a curry club chair. "Honey, it's *très chic*, just marvelous."

Martin picks up a silk saffron-gold accent pillow and fingers the fringe. "It's a little... colorful, isn't it?"

"Of course it's colorful." I wave my hands around in an all-encompassing sweep. "It's full of life. It breathes. It pulsates. It's vibrant and vivacious!" I take a good look at Martin's concerned face. "You don't like it."

"I'm just thinking..." He scratches his head and tries his best to admire two large Maplethorpe and Hockney coffee table books (not really his style). He clears his throat. "Won't Brian be stunned to see his penthouse...? Well, to *not* see his penthouse?"

I flip over onto my belly and prop myself up on my elbows. "Marty, you're looking at a guy who hums show tunes all day long, moisturizes every chance he gets, and shaves his legs. Leaving me alone for ten days with three no-limit credit cards and a blank canvas could only have produced this outcome. It was inevitable."

Jeff tosses a fennel pillow at Martin. "He's right. It was inevitable."

Martin catches it and throws it back. "Okay, if you say so."

"Yes, I do," I confidently surmise. "Brian has had enough of calm and boring and beige on vanilla with ivory-piped accents. It's time for him to get a great big dose of *me*."

■ ■ ■

I miss Brian immensely. And while transforming the flat takes up countless hours of my day that aren't spent on the set or at rehearsals, and I go out to dinner and clubbing with the nincompoops on the nights I don't have a performance (and sometimes, even after a performance), I still have a hard time lasting ten days without him. I call him numerous times a day—every day—and the lengthy phone calls always end with me crying and begging him to drop everything and rush home to me. It's not just that I miss him, but I'm paranoid he's going to meet a woman who'll steal him away from me. I've decided that in the future, I'll make damned sure Papa doesn't go anywhere for such a long time unless he takes his spoiled, self-centered boyfriend with him.

25
An Ass By Any Other Name

John — April 22

Today, I'm more than ready for Alex's visit. My cut is itching like crazy and I want these stitches out so I can scratch the hell out of my forehead. Ben told me to slap the cut every time it started to itch. Supposedly, the "stinging" sensation of the slap makes it stop itching. So I spent an entire day slapping myself silly. It didn't stop the itch. It just made me look like a slaphappy moron in front of Joe and the guys who came to hang the curtains, and gave me a severe headache. Why I always follow his asinine instructions like a gullible idiot, I will never know.

Alex arrives at eleven, and when I open the door, I'm without words. He's good looking. He's *unbelievably* good looking, and young—about my age and about two inches shorter than me. Even though he's of Asian descent, he's got blue-green eyes, high cheekbones, and a strong square chin. His short reddish-brown hair is immaculately trimmed at his neckline and around his ears. It's the type of haircut I often see on—Jesus Christ, he's gay! Brian has a gay doctor! I'm not without words because I'm attracted to him. I'm not attracted to him at all. I'm without words because he's really good looking... and he's young... and he's Brian's doctor—*and he's gay!* I was expecting a gruff English guy in his late fifties, balding with a paunchy belly, yellow teeth and arthritic hands, not a hot, young gay Asian who looks as though he should be on the cover of *Attitude*. He makes me uneasy, even before he steps into the flat. "Your name is John, right?"

Damn! He's got a Scottish accent, too. I nod once. Stunned out of my skull, it's the best I can do for the moment.

"Hi. I'm Alexander Pham. Everyone calls me Alex. You're looking a lot better than the last time I saw you. Much more color, other than red, and you're vertical. May I come in?"

I hesitate to move. I want him to go away and never come back—ever. I finally stand aside and let him walk into the entryway. He's holding a small bag. Without any prompting from me, he takes off his coat, pushes the button that opens the closet, and hangs it up. He acts as if he's right at home and I don't like it one bit. He proudly walks into the flat with the mute idiot (that would be me) trailing along behind him. His jeans are so tight I can't imagine he'll be able to sit down. And of course, he has a round compact ass and doesn't hesitate to swing it back and forth in my face, either. Still holding his small bag, he sweeps the living room with wide eyes. "Wow! It looks like you've made a lot of changes in here."

I'm not sure why, but I don't like the tone of his voice. It's as if he's saying, "So, I see you've made yourself feel right at home by spending Brian's money, you little gay gold digger!" I finally find my voice and attempt a defensive tone, which unfortunately, comes out sounding petulant instead of bitchy. "We have to make the changes because we're getting a dog."

"Oh, really?" He nods gravely. "Yes, a white carpet wouldn't hold up long with a dog in the flat, would it? Of course your blood didn't look too great on it, either, huh?" His grin flashes two rows of glowing white teeth.

If he was trying to be humorous, he missed the mark, and I let him know it by not reacting to his comment. That makes him a little uneasy, and oddly, his uneasiness makes me feel better, more smug and superior.

He turns toward the kitchen. "I'll just wash up and we'll—Oh!" He stops when he sees the curing countertops covered in plastic.

"You'll have to use the bathroom. It's just—"

"That's okay. I know where it is." He waves his hand at me and heads off down the hallway. "I've been here dozens of times."

Dozens of times? Just *who* does he think he is? He's trying to push my buttons, exactly like Carol. He wants to rattle me by insinuating he spends a lot of time here, giving Brian private consultations and exams. Well, I won't stand for it! I had a problem challenging Carol when she was sinking her claws into Brian, but that's because she was a woman. I didn't know how to deal with a woman as a rival. This is a man. This is a *gay* man. I don't have a problem telling a gay man to stay away from my boyfriend. If he even *thinks* he's gonna get close to Brian, I've got big news for him. Brian is mine and I'm here to make sure he knows it. I bite my thumbnail and pace the floor until he comes back. My face is hot. I need to get myself worked up into a Snotty Bitch Queen frenzy. I've seen Ben do it (in crowded restaurants when we've stupidly shown up without reservations) with fabulous results, and even though it's a role I'm not used to playing, you can be damned sure my catty ass is gonna try to win an Oscar.

"Okay. Let's take a look at that cut." Again, he's got that gorgeous smile on his face. It's unnerving. "How about over here in the light? Natural light is always better."

To me, his words sound condescending even though he's only asking me to sit where the sun is coming in through the sliders. He's being too nice. He's trying to gain my trust and put me off my guard, but I am *so* on to his game. I know how conniving a guy can be when he's trying to steal another guy's guy. As I sit down, he comes right up to me so his face is inches from mine when he examines my cut. He has the smoothest, flawless light-brown skin (microscopic pores, damn it!), and I don't smell any cologne. A hot gay who's not wearing cologne? That really curdles my blood. That means he was hoping Brian would be here so he could flirt with him. My claws come out. It's time to set him straight. I watch him open his bag. "You know, I'm not just his friend," I quip, probably a bit too loudly and too abruptly.

He seems a little perplexed. "Okay…"

I feel my pulse increasing. "I live here. I live here *with* him."

"I'm glad to hear that." He leans closer to me, intent on examining my stitches. Then he turns to his bag.

"And I'm…I'm not some guy he just picked up off the street."

He turns back to my forehead. "Hold still for me, John. So I take it you two practice monogamous sex, then?"

How *dare* he insinuate we sleep around! I'm outraged and my face is burning. "Of course we do! We're not seeing other people! We're exclusive!"

"I'm really glad to hear that."

I can tell by his tone he doesn't believe me. "I mean it. I'm not just a weekend fling."

"I'm glad to hear that, too."

"I'm his life partner. He's not looking for anyone else. And he's *not* attracted to other men."

"I'm glad to hear that, too."

"Would you please stop saying that?" I blurt out with frustration.

He sits back and looks at me. "Stop saying what?"

"That you're glad to hear everything I have to say. It's *really* irritating."

He smiles. "But I am. I'm really happy to hear it."

I cross my arms and glare at him, now in an all-encompassing Snotty Bitch Queen state of mind that could smote Hera, as I sarcastically say, *"Really?"*

"Aye, really." He puts whatever he used on my forehead back into his bag.

"You're happy that I'm telling you he's *my* boyfriend, and we're exclusive, and no one is going to take him away from me."

"Well… yeah."

It's time to let him know that I know what's going on. I'm not as dumb as he thinks I am, and there is no way I'll let him steal Brian. I level my poisoned-dagger-eyed gaze at him, set my jaw and lower my voice. "Look, I know you're after him. I know you want him. Why would everything I've just said make you happy?"

He smiles and cocks his head. "Because he's my brother, John."

To call me a horse's ass at this moment would be an outrageous insult to the horse—and to his ass. I close my eyes and hang my head. God, how could I have been so stupid? I can't begin to redeem myself after that classless act of unrelenting bitchiness. Humiliating shame begins to ooze from my pores as I search for my meek voice. "So… you're not trying to take him from me." It's a statement more than a question.

"No, John."

"And I'm guessing… (Jeez, this is *really* embarrassing) you're not gay, either."

"Uh… no, John."

Now I hear the similarity in his voice. He sounds so much like Brian I can't believe I missed it. "God, I'm an ass!"

He gives a small laugh. "Oh, I wouldn't say that. You're quite refreshing."

I lift my head in amazement. "Refreshing?"

"Well, yeah. It's nice to see you're so serious about him. He's certainly dead serious about you. If you hadn't reacted so strongly I might have had my doubts. I might have passed you off as—what did you call it?—a weekend fling."

I give him a weak smile. "I'm sorry I thought you were gay."

"No harm done. Coming from you, it's a compliment."

He takes my wrist with his thumb and finger and studies his watch for about thirty seconds. It gives me a chance to really examine his features. In a way, he looks like Brian and in a way, he doesn't. He lowers my hand. "It was the haircut and the tight pants more than anything else."

"Oh. Well, I always look like this right before I go to Kenya. I get a really close trim and fatten myself up as much as I can. Believe me, in six months I'll be a skinny hippy." He winks. "My awesome ass is always the first thing to go."

"Kenya?"

"Aye. I go every other year. Brian schedules a cargo plane to deliver tons of medical supplies and equipment, and then a bunch of doctors fly over and put it all to use."

"Wow. That's amazing! He's never said anything."

"Give him time. You haven't known him that long. He's a pretty interesting guy if you can tolerate the arrogance, but you have to pull a lot out of him."

Now I'm uncomfortable. I've just made it blatantly clear to a guy that I'm sleeping with his brother, and I feel as if I need his approval. "Are you okay? I mean, with me being with Brian?"

He studies me a minute. "It floored me when he told me—a major shock to the system. It's not every day my big brother calls me to his penthouse to staunch a head wound and tells me to be extra careful because he's in love with the bleeder—who just happens to be a gay television star. But I think you're really good for him, John. You're a bit paranoid and overly possessive, if you don't mind me saying so, and I'd tone down that bitchy attitude just a little. But for Brian, who spent a long time not giving a shit about anyone and tried to get by without anything that might upset his dull, perfect world, you're probably the best thing that could have happened to him. He's had some... dark years. But why did you think I was after him?"

"Excuse me?"

"Well, I knew he wasn't going to be here and I obviously know who you are. If you thought I was gay, why didn't you think I might walk through that door and be interested in you? You're really good looking, and no disrespect, but I've heard you're pretty conceited."

"I am. I mean, I have been. At least, I usually am."

"But you never once thought I might be interested in you?"

"No. That never occurred to me."

He stands up. "Hmm. Maybe you're both good for each other. Well, I have to go. My flight leaves in eight hours and I've still got a lot to do."

I stand up, too. "What about my stitches? When will they come out?"

Again, he smiles, and now that I really look at it, his smile is Brian's smile. "I just took them out, John."

I reach up to touch my forehead. "Oh."

He hands me a tube of ointment. "Here. Use this daily. Try not to scratch it for a few days. I know you want to, but just let it heal a bit more so it doesn't leave a great big scar, okay?"

"Okay."

He walks to the entryway and takes his coat out of the closet. Again, I trail along behind him. "Goodbye, John. Tell Brian I'll call him in about six months." He reaches for the door handle.

Suddenly, I realize having access to Alex right now—while Brian isn't here—is the perfect opportunity to deal with my big problem. "Alex, wait! There's...there's something else I, um...."

"Yes?"

"I tend to…. I sweat a lot."

He looks me up and down, confused.

"No, I mean… when we… when we're… uh…."

"Oh, you mean when you're having sex?"

I nod as I feel my face getting hot, yet again. "It's embarrassing. It just pours off me, especially when the weather is muggy. Is there something I can take for it—a prescription that might make it stop, or tone it down a little?"

"Aye. There's a pretty good prescription on the market, but has this ever happened before, with other people?"

"No. This has never happened to me—ever. It's like the more, um, intense things get, the more I sweat. And even though it's not really body odor sweat, with Brian's sense of smell I'm worried that it's a turn off."

Alex sets his bag down, leans against the entryway wall, crosses his arms and gives me that familiar Mallory smile. "Have you ever thought it might be the other way around?"

"Pardon?"

"Have you ever thought the sex gets more intense *because* you sweat so much?"

I jerk my head back like I do right before I walk into a spider's web (but I don't flap my arms, scream, and do the funny little "Oh, my God, a spider!" dance). "No, I hadn't thought of that."

"And that maybe Brian is okay with the sweat; maybe he's *very* okay with it?"

"No, that never occurred to me."

He looks at me thoughtfully. "Tell me something, John. Why is Brian with you?"

I'm not sure what he's asking so I just shrug my shoulders and give him a questioning look.

"You know it's not because you're good looking. Brian doesn't react to looks. He's never reacted to looks. Brian only reacts to…"

"Scent." Jeez! Again, how could I be so stupid? It's what he said the night before he left.

Alex smiles. "Why don't you try an experiment? Since it's worse when it's so muggy, turn on the air one night and see what happens."

I squeeze my eyes closed, wince and hang my head.

"Okay. I guess you've tried that?"

I nod.

"And what result did you get?"

I raise my head and look at him. "Nothing. Not a damned thing."

"Do you still want that prescription?"

I shake my head.

"Bang on!" He picks up his bag. "I gotta go. Goodbye, John. You take care and stop worrying. He's with you because you're who he wants. You're exactly who he wants."

The minute the door closes behind him, I slump against the wall. How could I have been such a dumb ass? I missed an entire night of sex because of my stupid decision to turn on the air conditioning. I can't get that night back, but I can promise Brian two things: The second he walks through that door tomorrow I'm going to charge him like a wild boar, and I'm going to sweat my ass off like the winner of a bhut jolokai pepper-eating contest!

26
Ten

Brian – April 23

"Hey, I'm—" It's all I get out on the first try. "John, can I— John, let me— Christ! Can I at least take off my—"

I can't even pull my arms out of my coat sleeves. His sweaty body is all over me—lips, arms, legs—and he won't let up. Within seconds, I'm obsessed and slam him against the wall, crushing his body hard with mine. We're kissing, biting, grabbing, squeezing, pulling, pushing and grinding on each other like sandpaper on wood. I've missed him so much and it's clear this carnal frenzy won't make it to the bedroom. We're ripping each other's clothes off with my briefcase, carry-on, trench coat and laptop under our feet. The scene in the entryway is utter chaos. I can't imagine what it looks like from the atrium through the frosted glass door. At one point, I'm slammed up against it, panting and moaning. At another point, he's slammed up against it, crying and gasping.

Shirts discarded and pants and boxers bunched around our ankles, we quickly make our way to the floor by ungracefully tripping over the carry-on and landing in one big naked heap—his ass up, my ass down. We're like two inept college wrestlers vying for the prime position—groping and grappling with arms and legs, bracing against the walls and the entryway table, trying to gain leverage. Eventually, the table (and everything on it) crashes onto its side and gets kicked and shoved further into the flat just to get the ungainly thing out of our way. Finally free of clothing (and any sense of modesty), we scramble about the floor on our bellies like two horny lizards, banging our elbows and knees on everything in sight. Our pricks are swollen to comical proportions and our balls are slapping against our thighs like giant chicken wattles as we struggle to pin each other down, trying to satisfy needs that haven't been met in ten long days — and we're both determined to be on top first.

We pant and grunt as we strategize every move — both of us too paranoid to release whatever appendage we're clutching for fear of losing the upper hand. I'm the stronger and the heavier one by almost two stone, but the sweat pouring off John's body and his fantastic dexterity make it impossible to hold onto any part of him for more than a second. It's as if I'm wrestling with a greased piglet. He's just squirming all over the place. He also has the advantage because he kicks, scratches, and pinches — hard. And because he was raped, I won't do anything too rough that could bring back that horrible memory. It takes some effort, but I finally get his sopping-wet body pinned flat on the floor. Unfortunately, he's stomach up, ass down, and panting in my face with a devil's grin and wild eyes. It's not the position I was going for, but I make the best of it by trying to lift his legs up and onto my shoulders. It's not the wisest decision. John has powerful dancer's legs, and when he kicks, it hurts.

He aims for my shin and hits it with deadly precision. *"Bugger!"*

"Oh, sexy Papa, I plan to!" he wickedly hisses, stretching up and kissing me roughly. Within seconds, he's twisted free and pinned me to the floor: stomach down, ass up, legs forced open. I'm gasping as he rams me hard, fast, and deep, slamming down on me with a vengeance that fills me with ecstasy as he sinks his fingernails into my lat muscles.

"Ow! The nails, John! Bloody Hell! Mind your damned nails!"

He's telling me he loves me, over and over, but I can tell by his force that he's really pissed because I wouldn't come home early and this is my punishment. I grit my teeth, silently apologize to my shocked sphincter and let him pound away as I concentrate on the weight of his wet body slamming against me and do my best to match his fast rhythm. His passion lets me know he missed me, and wants me… and needs me. During this powerful drilling, his stamina runs out pretty fast. John is forceful and thorough, but he can also be impatient, and when he's excited he doesn't set the pace to make it last. He quickly grunts himself into a frenzied orgasm, his body trembling uncontrollably before he falls limp on top of me. Once I realize he hasn't passed out, I let him straddle my back for a while to calm down and relax his muscles. I feel his warm breath as he moans into the back of my neck. He knows what's coming. He knows what he's in for. It's my turn now, and Papa Brian is about to ream him bloody senseless.

I start slowly — rubbing his back with long strokes the way he likes — determined to make this last as long as I can. With his legs spread wide, I work carefully, listening to his moans to gauge my force. I want him to enjoy every minute of this and I don't want him to feel any pain. He knows I have the stamina to keep it going as long as he wants, and as long as he needs, so I don't need to rush. I slide my arms under his chest and roll our bodies onto our sides, allowing him to arch his back against my pressure. His eyes are closed. He closes them to heighten his other senses — to intensify the experience. He's whispering that he loves me and needs me. I continue to pulse into him with a slow rhythm as his fingers claw at the floor — as if they were digging into a mattress. I bend to nuzzle his glistening neck. I need to inhale the intensity of his sweat and the sweetness of his scent as we make love. With the tip of my tongue, I taste the salt excreted from his body. It thrills me beyond belief, and I groan into his ear. I reach down and press my fingers into his hip as I control the pace of our rolling rhythm, making sure our movements counter each other perfectly. I maneuver his body gently, determined to find that one spot he really responds to. It's like twisting and turning a rabbit-ear aerial on an ancient black-and-white television, trying to get optimum reception. I finally hit the jackpot and he starts to pant with excitement. He's almost at that point where he wants it faster and needs more force. I wait for his words. I wait for him to beg me, and when he does, all I want to do — my only desire — is to give him supreme pleasure and satisfy his needs. As I thrust harder, he becomes euphoric, gasping in short bursts with his mouth open and his eyes still closed. He starts chanting his mantra, *"Ohm! Ohm! Ohm!"* I hold onto his hips tightly to keep his sweat-drenched body from sliding across the floor as I vigorously pound him.

Faster and faster, I drive into him until I know he can't take any more. His face is bright red, dripping with sweat and tears. He's screaming that he loves me and shaking uncontrollably. I'm a wailing ox whose gonads are being crushed by a steamroller. Like a pump-action water pistol, he fires off two rounds of hot juice straight across the entryway, scoring two direct hits on the doorknob almost a meter away. My own release is monumental. The ensuing blindness is gratifying, and I collapse—exhausted—onto his body as I wait for it to pass.

In the end, we're smashed up in the corner next to the hall closet—sticky, sweaty, and spent. It takes twenty minutes to clean up the luggage, the wet mess and clothes, and deal with his lifeless body. How a healthy, adult male can cry and scream his head off during sex and still manage to hyperventilate himself into unconsciousness every time he climaxes is beyond me. And as I carry him off to bed, I notice two significant things: The flat has hardwood floors, and John has packed on some extra weight in the last ten days.

27
Accepting The Reality Of Our Situation

John – April 23

I open my eyes to see Brian's big hands holding an open book. I yawn, stretch my arms and wiggle my toes. We're lying in bed. He's propped up by pillows and I'm in front of him, leaning against his chest. His body is generating a wonderful deep heat against my back and along my thighs. I turn to look out the sliders. They're open a few inches for some fresh air. It's raining hard and the sky is a dismal gray; everything looks gloomy, drab and faded. I feel Brian's heartbeat, strong and slow. "I hit the doorknob?"

"Nailed it twice."

I smile to myself and wiggle my toes again. That's a personal best for me and I'm so glad I had a witness. "You cleaned me up."

"Aye."

"Thank you."

He kisses the back of my head and turns the page. It's so nice to have a caring boyfriend who wipes down your unconscious, sweaty body and hauls you off to bed after welcome-home sex, instead of leaving you sprawled out on the entryway floor like a smutty doormat. I turn to look at the book. Nothing of interest for me there—it's in Welsh. I have dozens of questions. I want to know more about Alex and Kenya. I want to know what Brian thinks of the flat—if he likes the changes. I want to know when we'll get our dog. I want to know if he's brought me a present… and I want to know one other thing. I open my mouth.

"Just let me finish the chapter, okay?"

I close my mouth—for a minute. "Read out loud," I blurt out before he can say anything.

"Fe ddechreuodd y gwŷr ar faes y gad flino."

"Wait, wait. Where are you on the page? I want to follow along."

He points. "There, okay?"

With my contacts floating in solution on the bathroom counter (as usual), I squint hard at the fuzzy lines of long and short dark dashes. "Okay."

Brian reads on while I listen to his deep voice. I'm not following along as he reads. I close my eyes and turn my head to the side to feel each syllable come up through his chest as his curly hair tickles my cheek. I open my eyes and stare at the downpour for a while. Whatever he's reading sounds sad, as if it was meant to be read with this oppressive weather. I close my eyes again and continue listening to his mesmerizing, unintelligible words. Eventually, he finishes the chapter and sets the book aside. His arms envelope me and he nuzzles my hair.

Without opening my eyes or turning my head I say, "I'm so glad you came back to me."

"Did you think I wouldn't?"

"Ten days apart is a long time. It's a long time for second thoughts. You could have stayed in Scotland and just left me here. I was afraid you might think I was wrong for you—that this... was wrong for you."

He's silent for a long time. It makes me uncomfortable and it worries me. "It's not wrong for me."

I open my eyes and turn my head forward. I place my arms on top of his and trace a bulging blue vein running along the back of his hand with my finger. I love his hands: enormous, strong masculine hands with neatly trimmed nails and big, wrinkled knuckles. My hands look small, almost delicate compared to his. It's amazing how little hair he has on his hands and his arms. I swallow hard, preparing to ask the painful question. "Are you still attracted to women?"

There's a long pause. "Aye."

I clench my teeth and pinch the skin on the back of his hand hard. His body flinches a little, but he doesn't say a word. I hurt him, and he knows I did it out of frustration. I feel terrible and start rubbing the red welt I've caused. A few tears run down my cheeks and I sniff back some snot. He nuzzles my hair as the rain pelts down on the skylights above.

"I'll always be attracted to women, John. It's the way my brain is wired. You'll always be attracted to men. It's the way your brain is wired. That's the reality of our situation. There's nothing we can do about it. You have to accept it. You know that."

"But…"

"What?"

"Brian, you're not attracted to men, so I don't have to worry about you wanting to be with another guy. And even if you did like men, I'm sexier than anyone else so I still wouldn't have to worry." I feel him laughing a little, but we both know it's true. I'm the best he'll ever find and no one could ever love him or cherish him the way I do. I rub his hand, still trying to make that welt disappear. Again, I have a hard time saying what I have to say and the words come out in a whisper. "I can't compete with women."

There's another long, uncomfortable span of silence. This time he doesn't say a word.

"When you're away on your trips and I'm not there with you… I'm afraid you'll meet a woman and…." I close my eyes as tears stream down my face, momentarily unable to finish the sentence but not the horrible thoughts racing through my brain. Without the burdensome (yet moderately reassuring) noose of a marriage vow, some gays practice fidelity when they can see the whites of their lover's eyes and a screw fest when they can't. Those screw fests are what quickly generated the force field between David and me once I realized that was his idea of commitment after we arrived in London. Now, realizing how passionate Brian and I are together, I can't bear the thought of him making love to someone else, especially a woman, when we're apart. More tears cascade down my cheeks. "You'll forget all about me here."

He hugs me and nuzzles my hair. Then his mouth is at my ear. "How can I forget a bloke who sends me text messages saying, 'I love you, Papa. I need sex. Please come home now,' a hundred times a day?"

I give a faint smile, even though he can't see it. "You know what I mean."

He sighs deeply and squeezes me even tighter. "I'm attracted to women. I always have been and I always will be. But I'm hopelessly, happily, and desperately in love with John. He is the soul in my heart, the air in my lungs, and the blood in my veins. No woman anywhere in the world could ever compete with him or take me away from him. I will never forsake him."

"You swear?"

"I swear." He kisses my head. "Are you always going to need this?"

I wipe my wet face with the back of my hand. "Need what?"

"Shitloads of bloody reassurance."

"Oh, yes. This is going to come up all the time."

"Well, I have something for you. I was going to wait until after dinner but since you're determined to feel insecure at the moment..."

I'm excited when he holds out a small package. He remembered to bring me a present! "What's this?"

"Open it."

I rip open the wrapping paper and find my new cell phone. "My phone! It's custom?"

"Aye."

I notice it's bigger than Brian's phone. "But it doesn't look like yours."

"You wanted more features. See, if you push that—now you can put in your own access code."

"Fabulous! I'll let you know what it is."

"I don't want to know it."

"Well, I want you to know it."

"Here. Touch that."

"What's this?"

"What does it look like?"

"Your address book?"

"Hmm."

"So I can get in here? I have access from my phone?"

"Aye."

"And I can delete people?"

"Aye."

"Oh, that's perfect!"

"And… there."

"GPS?"

"Hmm. And if you touch that button — that's me."

"I can track you?"

"Wherever I go."

"That is brilliant!" I'm busy pushing buttons and scrolling the screen menus on my new phone, so excited I can stalk my boyfriend to my heart's content and wipe out every woman in his address book.

He holds out another package. "Here."

"What's this?"

"Open it."

"But what is it?"

"Just open it, love."

I rip open the wrapping and find a rectangular dark blue velvet box, imprinted with the gold mirrored and overlapping double C of Cartier. Immediately I think he's bought me a watch. When I flip open the lid, I see two exquisite platinum and diamond rings, one larger than the other. "Oh, wow! These are beautiful." I take out the smaller one (knowing it must be for me) and hold it up so it catches the light. "What is it?"

"My family crest."

"Really?"

"Aye."

I study the ring closely. Everything is so precise, so perfect. The detail is sharp and distinctive. I turn it around to read the gold-inlaid engraving rimming the outside of the band: MALLORY, with a diamond on either side. I tilt it and see there's more gold-inlaid engraving on the inside of the band: My True Love, Brian. I hand the ring to him. "Put it on, please." I hold out my hand and he tries to slip it on my finger. It fits… eventually, but he has to give it a good shove. "It's a little snug," I admit, trying to make light of the awkward moment. I've gained noticeable weight over the last ten days, especially in my stomach and my butt. We both know it. My fragile self-esteem is just praying he won't say he knows it.

"I must have miscalculated," he says tactfully. "We'll get it stretched."

I breathe a sigh of relief and take out the second ring. "What's this?"

"That's your family crest."

"It is?" I've never seen my family crest before. Dumber than dirt regarding the ancient art of heraldic symbolism and my own German-Italian heritage, I didn't even know I had one. Again, I carefully examine the ring and again, the intricate detail and craftsmanship amazes me. I can't believe he had these made in just ten days. He must have paid a fortune. The word KAISER is etched and inlaid in gold around the outside of the band, flanked by diamonds—just like the first ring. I tilt it to see the inside engraving. "Where's the engraving?"

"It doesn't have any yet. You think of something, and we'll add it."

"I want the same thing you wrote."

"No, John. Think of something you want to say."

"I want to say what you said."

"No, love. You'll think of something eventually. Be patient."

I grab his hand and slide the ring onto his wedding finger with shaking, clammy fingers. I can't describe how excited I am. This is an unbelievable moment for me. I bring his hand to my mouth and hold it there, pressing his fingers against my lips. Tears run down my cheeks. "These rings mean you'll never leave me, right?"

"Aye."

"You promise, Brian?"

He kisses my head. "I promise."

Brian — May 8

Over the next few weeks, through trial and error (mostly error on my part) and several small but highly effective tantrums, John and I fall into a normal, functional workday routine, acted out in the roles of an exasperated parent and a spoiled child. I get up early to watch the morning news undisturbed while I shower and shave. Then, I run his bath in the double-walled, hammered-copper behemoth he had Harry install. While I dress, I do everything in my power to coax his grumpy ass out of bed, sometimes resorting to pulling him out from under the covers and dragging him (naked and bitching all the way) into the bathroom, where he looks like a cannibal's simmering dinner as he splashes about in his bubbling, steamy cauldron. I fix our breakfast while he dresses, and we discuss our daily schedules as we eat. If I can keep him from getting too gropey and horny during our goodbye kiss, I can usually get him out the door and shuttled off to the studio by six-thirty. My business meetings, appointments and workouts take place during his studio work schedule, afternoon rehearsals, evening performances, and late-night clubbing.

On the days we don't work, we also have a routine. It might not be considered normal to most people, but it is quite functional—for us. Everything we do, whether it's a trip to the farmer's market, a walk through a museum, a country ride on one of the motorbikes or hours of shopping at Covent Gardens (God, John really loves to shop!), must all accommodate our unscheduled, very frequent and highly erotic lovemaking sessions—or, as John likes to call them, poker games.

Poker games are the number one priority on our free days and we take them very seriously. Our rounds are focused and exhausting. For hours, we are nothing more than a single, massive humping machine. We have sex, sharing the driving duties back and forth, until our backsides are aching. But we don't stop there, because there's good old, voracious oral sex, which got off to a rocky start because I didn't know what the hell I was doing. And John was too embarrassed to tell me I didn't know what the hell I was doing. Eventually, a little red wine and a lot of scotch calmed our anxieties, allowing the teacher to instruct and the pupil to learn—and that added a whole new dimension to my game, because if smelling John is like standing on the crumbling rim of an active volcano and deeply inhaling its torrid vapors, then performing fellatio on John is like plunging headfirst over the edge and happily disintegrating in its molten lava. He is exquisitely tasty. And we can easily follow up everything with a few rounds of mutual masturbation. While it never held my interest as a singles' sport, I enjoy partnering with John—a lot. Using plenty of lubricant, we fervently yank and wank each other's shank to the point of near blindness. Or, in John's case, to the point of near blindness immediately followed by the point of passing out. Between the two of us, we probably spurt enough semen to impregnate every woman currently residing in London—twice. We are the proud king and queen of masturbation ejaculation.

I'm assuming our sex frenzy will die down eventually, but considering John hadn't had sex in two years and I hadn't had anything remotely close to satisfying sex until now, it may take a while. Obviously, our sessions aren't all about sex. We use the rest periods to talk—to learn about and understand each other, filling in the blanks of our fledgling relationship to help it grow stronger. Sometimes our conversations are quite revealing. "How old were you the first time you kissed a bloke?"

"Nine."

"Nine? You kissed a bloke at nine?"

"Yup." He snuggles up along my side with his head on my chest and his clammy hand wedged down in my crotch. "Every day after school I went to the public library and stayed there until my mom picked me up on her way home from work. She was a seamstress at a bridal shop. I never had any friends. I was… a weirdo, I guess. The library was like my babysitter and I'd read books for hours. One Friday, they had this area roped off on the side of the building. When I came the next Monday, there was a bronze statue. It was a boy and a girl standing next to each other, holding books." He pauses as I stroke his messy hair. "Brian, they looked so lifelike. I thought that statue was the coolest thing I'd ever seen. One day, when no one was around, I went up to it and I kissed the girl. I just wanted to know what it would be like."

"How did it feel?"

"Cold, like I was kissing a pane of glass. But I kept kissing her, almost every day when no one was there. And then one day, I just moved to the left and kissed the boy."

"What happened?"

"I felt something warm inside—something familiar and safe. I liked that feeling. I started kissing him every day. I remember being at school, so eager to get out so I could run to kiss him. I named him Charlie. I really liked the way he made me feel. I liked kissing him… until some kids from school caught me. They laughed at me, chased me and beat me up. For weeks after that they just chased me and beat me up whenever they saw me."

"Didn't you tell anyone?"

"No."

"Why not?"

"I thought I deserved it."

"Why, love?"

"Because what I did was wrong," he softly confesses. "I knew I wasn't supposed to kiss a boy."

I nuzzle his head. I'd never realized—until now—how much he needs to be protected from the outside world.

"Brian?"

"Hmm."

"What were you thinking the first time we…? I mean, when you were behind me, just before…?"

"What was I thinking? Probably something like, 'Oh, shit! Oh, shit! Oh, shit!'" I say to lighten the mood.

"Be serious. I want to know. It's important."

"Why?"

"Because you took so long. You must have been thinking about something."

I close my eyes and let my mind wander back to that first night of wonderful sex—to the magic of it all. "I think my first thought was about how pale you looked. Your skin was so luminous in the dark, especially your butt: two glowing orbs that had never seen the light of day. When I ran my hands down your back I was surprised how soft it felt, how smooth your skin was—like worn silk or a woman's skin." I stroke his hair again. "I have to tell you, John, when I saw the size of your little anus, I didn't think it was going to happen. I looked down at that dot and thought, 'You've *got* to be kidding me.' I just couldn't figure out how I was going to make that work. It looked as if I was about to shove the trunk of a wooly mammoth up a gnat's bum."

He laughs at the comparison.

"God, I was scared. I mean, having sex with a man. It seemed… crazy, unreal, something you'd never imagine yourself doing—like robbing a bank or eating boiled tripe. But the sound you made when it did happen—that unbelievable gasp. That was… glorious. That whole spectacular event just stunned me. I was in awe of you. You were truly amazing. I hadn't felt like that since I watched the birth of my son."

John shoots up off my chest and stares down at me in surprise. *"Your son?* Brian, why didn't you tell me you have a son? Not telling me about Alex is one thing, but a son? Why would you keep something like that from me? I'm your life partner! I'm your lover! Oh, my God! Are you ashamed of me?" He's getting agitated and emotional… and it's unnecessary.

"No, of course not."

"Then why didn't you tell me about him?"

"He's dead, John." There's an uncomfortable silence as his shocked face hovers over mine, his hands braced on my chest as he props himself up. I can't remember the last time I spoke of Ayden — to anyone, although it was probably to Simon. It's a painful subject. I don't know when the right time would have come to tell John about him, so I guess now is good enough. "He died a long time ago. He was two. Moyra's mum dropped him down a flight of stairs on Christmas Eve — thirteen steps, I think. His neck broke in two places and that killed him, almost instantly. Almost…"

"My God, Brian. I'm so sorry," he whispers, palms still sinking into my chest.

I continue, remembering every minute detail of that horrific night. "He landed right at my feet. His eyes were staring up at me, but there was nothing I could do. It all happened so fast. It was over in just a few seconds. I couldn't save him. He was gone."

"Jesus. How did you cope?"

"I worked. I just kept scheduling meetings all day and all night — whenever and wherever I could, all over the world. I think that's what started the insomnia." I look into his deep blue eyes. "I loved him so much, John. I've never loved anyone or cared about anyone as much as him, until now — until you."

You would think our depressing disclosures might have dampened our libidos, but the revelation of John's need to be protected and taken care of and of my need to protect and take care of him only heightens our desire for ravenous lovemaking and so, the poker game continues.

"Brian?"

"Hmm," I mumble, dog-tired and ass-sore.

"What was his name?"

I yawn. "Ayden. Ayden Caine Mallory."

"Where is he buried?"

"He's not. His ashes are in a wooden box in a cupboard at the mansion."

He rubs my chest. "You should get him a nice urn."

I yawn again and pull his soft, warm body into mine as we get ready to sleep. "I did, John. It was Grecian."

"Oh, God, I'm so—"

"Don't say it, love. Let it go." I breathe a deep sigh of relief as an immense weight lifts off my chest and so many long years of pain and sorrow and bitterness rise up out of my heart and dissipate into the air. "I think we'll just spread his ashes somewhere in Scotland… together."

Brian — July 5

The *TruthFinder Murphy* studio isn't where I want to be right now, but I promised John I'd pick him up on the last day of shooting for the season. He wanted me to come earlier—to watch a few final scenes and sit down at their catered lunch, but he's lucky I'm here at all. I'm standing at the back of the main set, off to the side, practically in the dark, trying to stay out of Mickey's line of sight. He's glanced back a few times, and he's not pleased I'm here, either.

John's face lights up with a smile when he finally sees me. "You made it."

"I did."

"Will you come over and meet the cast and crew? A lot of them were at the birthday dinner."

"I don't think so." I shoot a glance at Mickey. "I'm pissing him off just by standing way back here."

John's smile fades as he briefly looks over his shoulder. "Sooner or later he has to get over it. He has to accept that we're together. It's been over two months."

"I know, but let's not rub it in his face, okay?"

"Okay." His smile creeps back. "Will you at least kiss me so the others will know?"

"John…"

"Just a little kiss, Papa. Just something—anything. I talk about you all the time and I've shown them my ring. It's important they know we're a serious, open couple. I want them to see we're really together." He lowers his voice and says, "I need everyone to know you're mine and no one else's. Please?"

He steps in closely and takes my hand. I bend my head, close my eyes and find his lips. I love kissing him—more than anything. Well, except sex. I know he wants a French kiss but there's no way I'll do that with Mickey here. I pull my head up (the advantage of being five inches taller) and end it. His eyes are half closed as he runs his tongue over his lips.

"I'm just going to say goodbye, all right?"

"Okay. Don't be too long." I watch him walk off. The kiss has got him excited. He's sweating, and he's going to want sex in the Rolls. He always wants sex in the Rolls, and in the limo, and in the Rover. Basically, he wants sex in anything that has wheels and the potential to move, but that's not something I'll do. I'm a prude and he knows it. Sex stays in the flat, and whenever possible, in the bedroom—period. That's my way. He doesn't like it one bit and we've argued about it, but he's had to accept it. Papa will not budge.

Mickey saw the kiss. John wanted him to see it more than anyone. Now he's glaring at me. So I glare right back at him, and I can't believe how much I enjoy glaring back at him. The disgust I feel toward him is profound. We both know I have something he wants—something precious he's pined for and lusted after for a long time, and something he will never have. He knows it's mine, and he thinks I stole it from him even though he never had it to begin with. He despises me absolutely, and the perfect words to describe the look in his eyes are seething, envious hatred.

Brian — July 6

It's late, the weather is balmy and we've just left a showing at a small popular art gallery three blocks from the flat. John knows the artist and I know the gallery owner who agreed to host the exhibit. To my surprise, it had an impressive turnout with positive feedback and numerous high-priced sales. A young Australian couple paid several hundred pounds for something entitled "Woodness." It resembled a warty penis rising up out of a jumble of pubic hair made from wire — piano wire. It looked as if the entire sculpture was made from a... Bösendorfer. Who knew you could create a two and a half meter warty penis — that someone would actually buy — from a busted piano? With John initiating the introductions, I also met some of my neighbors who aren't as terribly obnoxious as I thought they were. I still don't want to socialize with them and I'd never let them in the flat if they turned up at the door, but at least they're not complete assholes. I bought two pieces John wanted: a large oil painting he can showcase in the living room above the fireplace, and a smaller, highly erotic acrylic I won't allow outside our bedroom. We're walking hand in hand to the all-night convenience store that's a block from the flat. John wants a Spanish omelet, raspberry-and-cream-filled crepes, and fresh-squeezed orange juice in the morning, and whatever my love wants, my love gets, so I need a few ingredients.

He squeezes my hand and looks up at me. "Well? What did you think?"

"The king-sized crotch shots don't interest me."

"It's art, Brian."

I look down at him and roll my eyes.

He's silent as we walk and then eventually asks, "Is it because they were male?"

"Nope. I don't want six meters of gaping female genitalia hanging on my walls, either."

He smiles. "Okay. I can understand that. But you like the big painting for the fireplace, right?"

I hold open the door to the store. "Aye. I like that one. It's definitely my style."

"Good. I really like it, too. Thank you for getting it for me, Papa."

He stretches up to kiss my cheek and walks inside.

"You're welcome."

We meander down the aisles under the buzzing strip lights, listening to cheesy renditions of old pop music piped in on the overhead speakers. John carries the small plastic basket while I pitch in the ingredients as I find them. He's staying a few meters back because he likes to watch my ass when I walk. About a month ago, when I first realized he was doing this, it really bothered me. But then I figured: What the hell? Better to have him watching my ass than some other bloke's ass.

Eventually, we end up in the only open cashier line, queued behind a dozen other late-night customers. It's a strange reality for me because just a few months earlier, being a rather wealthy man, I would have had Charles do stuff like this or I'd have asked the store to deliver. Now, I enjoy doing this sort of activity with John, and I love being out in public with him. I like showing him off. I may not notice his good looks, but everyone else does—and that, I like.

I'm standing behind him, just off to the side, solidly pressed up against his back. My nose isn't in his hair. I won't do that here because that's private—just between us—and John has an image to maintain. He should never be seen in public with messy hair. I'm checking my phone messages with one hand. My other hand is shoved into the rear pocket of his jeans. Just recently, I've discovered blokes like to chat him up when we're making our rounds in the neighborhood. I've also discovered I'm a very jealous, overly possessive and highly protective boyfriend. So I stick closely to him, usually touch him in some way, and I'm wary of anyone who approaches him. He understands why I do it, and he keeps it professional when blokes ask him for an autograph, or a picture, or (sometimes) a kiss. In return, I never look at women. It's our unspoken agreement, and while it might not be the best arrangement for anyone else, it works just fine for us.

"We need lubricant," he quietly says.

"We still have some," I mumble without looking up.

"I know, but I want more. Ben told me about some new positions. They sound fun and I want to try them out. We need more."

I look down at him, pull my hand out of his pocket and roll my eyes. Every time we try these new positions John hears about from Ben, things don't go well. We are two uncoordinated, klutzy men who always end up looking like a great big mutated crab with our arms and legs flailing about, or a giant deformed pretzel with our limbs so hopelessly entangled and our bodies so overly contorted we can't tell our assholes from our navels. We are laughable. One of us usually gets whacked in the face with a knee, someone's balls get painfully squished and we *always* fall off the bed. The last time we attempted one of these embarrassing maneuvers, I scored a black eye, threw out my back and had to cancel two days of meetings. John got off easy with a bloody nose—and then promptly fainted at the sight of his own blood.

"Go. Now. Two tubes, please." He turns me around, pinches my butt and gives me a little shove.

Reluctantly, I put away my mobile and slog off toward aisle nine to get more lubricant.

John

I watch Brian walk off toward aisle nine—a familiar aisle to us both. I like to watch him walk. I like the way his butt makes his shirttail move with each step. He really does have an incredible ass—both in and out of clothes. He doesn't like trying new positions, but I do because it's hilarious. He's so terribly clumsy and stiff due to his tight muscles, and he swears up a storm the entire time (in that fantastic accent) because he gets frustrated with what I ask him to do. He's definitely a prude, but he's a good sport about it all, and in the end, we still have unbelievable sex—even after we fall off the bed. As a matter of fact, we have the best sex after he's been adequately frustrated and—

"Hey, John! How are you?"

I turn to see Strawberry Blond standing behind me with a big, fake smile. "Um, I'm fine." It takes a few seconds to recognize him outside the club atmosphere. He's rougher, not as clean cut as before. His hair has grown out and a three-day shadow of darker stubble covers his cheeks and jaw line—very George Michael-ish. "How are you, uh...?"

The smile waivers for a second. "Chris. My name is Chris. Remember?"

"Oh, yeah. Sorry. I just… I hadn't bumped into you in a while at any of the clubs."

He looks puzzled. "Well, I didn't know you were still going to the clubs. I haven't seen your Boxster in any of the car parks or at the meters in a long time."

"Oh, that's because I've been—" I cut myself off right before I tell him I've been going to the clubs in the limo. Now I understand why this guy was always at the same club. It wasn't just a coincidence. I'm a little freaked out.

"And what's up with your brownstone? I never see you there anymore, either. I see a couple of other guys. Did you sell it or lease it out?"

I don't know what to say. This guy is weird, and he's obviously a stalker. I take one backward step and position my small basket in front of my ribs like a shield.

His smile begins to fade. "So why didn't you call me, John?"

"I said I was still seeing someone."

He takes a forward step. "Well, are you *still* seeing him?"

I try inconspicuously to take another small backward step. "No, I'm…I'm seeing someone else."

"But you said you'd call *me,* John. You took *my* card. Remember? You said you'd call *me* when you weren't seeing someone." He takes another forward step, the smile now gone and his forehead wrinkled.

"I think… I think I said, 'maybe.'"

"No! No, you didn't. I *know* what you said! I waited for your call, John! I waited a long time, you know? That's no way to treat a guy!"

His agitation is making me nervous as I take one more backward step and bump into something very solid, very tall and very familiar.

Brian's voice is low and ominous. "Is there a problem here?"

Strawberry Blond looks up at him with his stubbly chin jutting out, as he defensively says, "No! We're just having a *private* conversation. It's none of your business."

My eyes bulge. I'm amazed by that response. He's certainly got some balls of steel. I wouldn't have the nerve to say that to this towering Scotsman if I'd just encountered him. Brian's big hand, clutching two tubes of lubricant, looms up in front of my face. He makes sure Strawberry Blond recognizes what he's holding and then lets them fall into my basket. "Oh, it *is* my business. It is *very much* my business."

Strawberry Blond finally looks as if he's about to shit a twenty-four-carat gold brick and swallows hard. I think his steel balls just went into hiding.

Fast as lightning, Brian pulls out his phone and snaps a picture of him, blinding him for a few seconds. "*This* is going to the authorities. I don't know *who* you are and I don't know what filthy septic pit your slimy ass crawled out of, but if I *ever* see you this close to him again I'll have you charged with predatory stalking. *Do you understand me?*"

Strawberry Blond nods his scruffy, pale-faced head and takes a huge backward step.

"And just in case you think I'm joking, I'll not only have *this,*" Brian raises his phone higher, "but I'll also have a copy of *that.*" He points to the store's ugly eyeball security camera. "And I swear I'll get my hands on any other surveillance video in this city that shows you anywhere near him. Have I made myself clear?"

"Yes, sir."

"Get out of here!"

Strawberry Blond nearly knocks over a display of Mushy Peas in his quest to find the exit. Right before he goes out the door though, he does a scary thing: He turns back, gives Brian an evil glare and holds up his hand like a mock gun aimed at him. He 'shoots,' turns, and quickly leaves.

Brian sounded dangerous and threatening. He was so masculine and protective, and caveman-like possessive. I liked it—a lot! My heart is racing and I'm sweating. With an erection happily throbbing away in my briefs, I'm steamed up and ready for sex. We've reached the cashier and Brian empties the basket. He gives me a puzzled look. "Are you okay?"

"No. Not really," I answer quietly and a bit breathlessly, my face flushed.

The cashier begins to total the items as he says, "Why? What's wrong?"

I turn into his body and lower my voice. "I got super excited just now with what happened. I need sex in a bad way."

He glances at the customers behind us and just as quietly says, "Well, you're bloody well not getting it here so just calm yourself down. Who was that bloke?"

"He's from one of the clubs. He's kind of creepy."

"You don't say?" Brian's words are said with mock astonishment as he hands over the cash for our purchases. "Did you pick him up?"

"No! Of course not! I met him a long time ago and only talked to him once."

Brian looks down at me with half-closed eyes. He thinks I'm lying.

"I didn't pick him up, Brian. I swear."

He grabs the bag. "Well, I don't trust him. I'm pretty sure he'll show up again. If you ever see him, you tell me. All right?"

"All right. Can we *please* go home now?" I press into his thigh so he can feel my immediate and urgent concern.

He's amazed. "Are you still…?"

"Yes. Yes, I am." I grab his free hand and haul his super-fine ass to the exit door. "And we really need to get home—*now!*"

28
Where I belong

John — July 9

We're in the kitchen. My big ass is spread wide on a bar stool at the counter and I'm nursing my wine. I've limited myself to just one glass a day as part of my effort to slow down my weight gain. I'm now wearing my ring on a platinum chain around my neck. The chain was another present from Brian because he grew tired of taking the ring every other week to get it stretched. I know what's causing the extra weight. It's going out to café lunches nearly every day with the nincompoops, restaurant dinners and clubbing several nights a week, not exercising the way I would if I were shooting the series, and Brian not saying one word about it. How he can still enjoy having sex with me sporting love handles, a great big butt and a walloping belly is beyond me — but he does and I'm so happy. I'm becoming his cute, little butterball, and my life is perfect.

Brian has his back to me, preparing our lunch: garlic pasta with sautéed vegetables and spinach salad with a lemon-dill vinaigrette. I'm rifling through his briefcase, sorting out the mess of loose papers, receipts, contracts, reports and notes. It's my self-appointed job, something I thought up to keep me involved in his business dealings. To be honest, I don't care about his business dealings. I do it because I'm nosey and it lets me ask him a ton of questions. I pull out a stack of photographs. "What's this? Is this another place you're thinking of buying?"

He glances over his shoulder and then continues slicing his mushrooms. "No. I already own that."

"Oh." I thumb through the photos. "It's nice."

"It's the mansion in Scotland."

"Is it?" I'm pleasantly surprised. This is the first time I've seen it. It's stupendous. It's bigger than the mansion in Rittersby. The Italianate architecture is impressive. The landscaping is immaculate. The tree-lined entry drive behind tall, wrought-iron gates is about three hundred feet long. It stinks of money as Evan would say.

"You like it, John?"

I pause before answering, sip my wine and continue to look at the photos. This is what a multi-millionaire can afford. This is the ultimate luxury Brian is used to. This is what he's missing. "It's big, isn't it?"

He goes to the fridge and pulls out onions. "Aye."

I flip to the next photo. "There's a swimming pool."

"Two, Olympic-sized — one indoor, one outdoor. Oh, and a lap pool off one of the ground-floor master suites."

"Really?" I flip through more photos. "And tennis courts."

"And stables and a range, too. You could learn to ride, John, and shoot clay."

"Hmm." I come to the end of the stack. I watch him as he chops more onions. He knows I like a lot of onions. "You really want to go back, don't you?"

He stops chopping, but he doesn't turn around. "Would you go, if you knew I really wanted to go back?"

I need to think about this. The mansion is stunning and it's grand. It's truly unbelievable. If we went to Scotland, I'd have servants waiting on me hand and foot, and it would raise me up to a lifestyle I've never experienced before. I'd want for nothing because Brian would make sure I had everything. I'd be a snotty, spoiled queen. But as I sip my wine, I know Brian and I belong here — in London, in the Docklands — in this beautiful flat, with him cooking our meals on his Aga and me still struggling to learn Welsh on my e-reader as he holds me on the big sofa in the library. This is where we should be with our outdoor cafés, the local farmer's market and our tiny, all-night convenience store. This spacious, opulent flat isn't one-tenth the size of that mansion, but I know this amazing flat is all we need to be happy. I take another sip of wine. Ultimately though, I want to be with Brian. I have to be with him and I need to be with him, no matter what, because he's my whole life. He's what I live for, and where he wants to be is where I belong. "Yes, Brian. I'll go to Scotland. It'll be great."

He turns around. "You're sure?"

I give him a big, genuine smile. "Yes, I'm sure."

"Good. That's settled." He turns back to the counter and finishes chopping his onions.

"So… when do we leave?"

He turns to add pasta to the boiling water. "We don't."

"We don't? We don't go to Scotland?"

"No. We don't go to Scotland." He dumps the vegetables into the hot skillet.

"But… why not?"

He glances at me. "John, you wouldn't last forty-eight hours. You'd be bitching your head off, throwing tantrums and pinching me. You'd be a right pain in the ass and make my life a bloody hell. You know it, and I know it."

At first, I'm incensed by his accuracy. "Okay, that's true, but at least I made the effort in saying I'd go… and it was sincere."

"Aye. You did, and it was. I'm impressed."

"So, we stay here?"

He stirs his vegetables. "We stay here."

I sigh with relief. "Fabulous. What about the mansion? You're not going to sell it, are you?"

"No. I'll convert it into a retirement home. They could use one out there."

"But then you'll have to spend a lot of time there to renovate." I'm starting to worry. I don't like him to be away from me and he knows it.

"No. It doesn't need that much work—just a bit of upgrading, like exterior ramps and bringing the rooms up to code for wheeled-chair access. I may have to add a few more bathrooms, upgrade the kitchens and widen some doorways. Charles can oversee it. He was in construction for years before he became my valet, and he can move his whole extended family into one of the wings, if he wants to. He'll be king and he'll love it."

Again, I'm relieved. "What about the mansion in Rittersby. Will you still buy that?"

"Aye. It'll be a good project for Simon. He wanted to be involved in it. It was his idea to begin with. I just hope it keeps his mind occupied after Robert is gone."

He stirs his boiling pasta while I sip my wine and summarize. "So... I'm happy, Charles is happy, Simon is happy, and a bunch of geriatric people in Glasgow and Rittersby will eventually be happy. What about you?"

"Hmm?"

"You wanted to go back to Scotland. It's the place you love the most and it's your home. It's where you belong. You don't get what you want."

He turns down the gas under his pasta and vegetables and walks around the counter to stand next to me. He looks at me thoughtfully before speaking. "You know, a long time ago this awkward, shy bloke told me you belong where your loved one is."

"Did he?"

"Aye, he did. At the time I thought he was an idiot."

I smile. "You did?"

"Aye. I thought he was bloody full of crap."

"And what do you think he's full of now?"

Brian takes in every feature of my face. "Everything that means anything to me."

With my monstrous butt swallowing the bar stool, I carefully lean sideways and kiss him. It turns into a beautiful, deep French kiss. Immediately, and as usual, I'm sweating. I want sex. "Brian, can we —"

"No." He quickly goes back to his vegetables and pasta on the cooker. "I'm hungry. I want to eat."

"After?"

"Nope. I have work to do."

"But I thought I'm full of everything that means anything to you?"

"You are, love. Just not right now and not later on. I have a lot of things to take care of today."

"But we could —" My phone buzzes, intruding on what was going to be some shameless begging for afternoon sex. I hit the speakerphone button. "Hey, Prissy. What's up?"

His squeaky voice is small and thin coming through the line. "Where's the Pierce building?"

"What?"

"The Pierce building. Didn't you go there about six months ago?"

"No. I've never been there."

"Yes, you have. It was on Gatling Road."

"No, that was the Price building on Gatling Way, not Gatling Road."

"Well I'm looking for a big building out here on Gatling Road, I think."

Brian turns and strains the pasta over the sink. "What's Prissy doing on Gatling Road? It's a rough neighborhood."

"Prissy, what are you doing out there? Brian says it's a bad area."

"I have an audition."

"An audition? Out there?" I watch Brian as he shakes his head. "No, you must have got it wrong. You need to get back on the bus."

"It's gone."

"Then get on the next one."

"It won't be here for ages."

"Okay, then call a cab."

Brian dries his hands on a dishtowel as he looks at me. "He can't. They're on a day strike."

"Johnny, I'm scared," Prissy whines. "This place.... It's like a slum and there're some guys — some really big guys up the street — watching me. Can you come get me?"

I look to Brian for an answer.

He takes out his phone. "It would take you more than half an hour to get to him, and I won't let you go out there. He needs to get out now."

"Police?"

"Even *they* won't venture into that area unless someone's been killed — and I doubt they'd get there any sooner."

"Prissy, just hang on a minute."

Brian now has his eyes closed.

"Brian?"

"Shh, John. Let me think."

"Johnny," Prissy pleads.

"Hang on, Prissy."

"But it's getting worse."

"In what way? What are they doing?" I watch Brian punch numbers into his phone.

"They're standing in a circle, talking, and looking at me."

"Okay, stay calm and try not to look—"

"What? *Gay?* Yeah, that's gonna be *real* easy for me, isn't it?"

"I was going to say scared. Try not to look *scared.*"

"Hi, Glenn, it's Brian. I know. I need a big favor, and I need it right now."

"Johnny, I gotta go," Prissy says in a panicked voice.

"No, Prissy. Stay on the line! Keep talking to me."

"No, I mean I gotta run. They're coming after me."

29
Guns And Roses

Prissy — July 9

I turn and run as fast as I can, and unfortunately, if they had any doubt I was gay just standing still, now that I'm running, it's obvious. I prance on my tippy toes and look like a dainty, little fairy cake. Even Benny has said so. And while I can run fairly fast, my problem is I have no idea where I'm running. I don't know this neighborhood at all. With my speed, I can outrun the two big fat ones, but I can't outrun the smaller guy. That must be why they gave him the pipe. I hear them behind me. I hear their pounding footsteps getting louder and louder. My mobile is ringing. It's probably Johnny. I'm panting hard and my heart is racing as I round another corner, and then another corner—and still another. This street looks just like the last one—dismal, with no one in sight. No cars, no people—nothing. It's deserted... and familiar. In my panicked state, I think I've just run my skinny, little ass once around the block. And now, even though my life depends on it, I'm slowing down. I'm exhausted and my lungs hurt. I still hear their footsteps, only now it sounds like more, and they sound closer. I look over my shoulder to see the initial three thugs have been joined by two more. They're yelling at me now—shouting horrible things and terrible names—names I've heard a thousand times before. My eyes are darting from doorway to doorway, desperately looking for an escape as I keep running. And then I hear it: A car—a big car—coming up behind me fast, just tearing down the street. If they've got mates after me in a car, I don't stand a chance. They'll drive me off to a deserted warehouse and beat my brains in... after they torture me. Someone will find my bones months later, picked clean by rats and mice. My God! I'm too adorably cute to die such a horrible death. I realize I should have called Benny to tell him I love him just as the car cuts me off at the corner. It comes to a screeching halt.

It's a big, black Jaguar with tinted windows and chromed spoke rims. The thickest, ugliest man I've ever seen, with a shiny baldhead and sleek wrap-around sunglasses, throws the driver's door wide open and steps out into the road. I rear up and stop a meter short of running into his barrel chest. He stands there expressionless with his arms behind his back, unmoving. I'm panting my ass off, staring up at him. I still hear the thugs running full speed behind me. They're almost at the corner, and because this big ugly man hasn't moved an inch to help me, I realize he must be one of their mates. Now I know I'm dead. I turn around and close my eyes. If I'm going to be beaten to death with a pipe, I'll face it, but I don't want to see it coming. I hear their footsteps almost on top of me, getting closer and closer. My heart is beating out of my chest. I'm thinking only of Benny as I squeeze my eyes tightly. I've accidentally peed just a tiny bit in my knickers and I'm bracing for the terrible impact of that pipe when I hear a loud 'click.'

The pounding footsteps stop. There's total silence except for the quiet idling of the Jaguar's powerful engine. I take a chance and open one eye just a fraction. Not three meters from me, I see five stunned faces, mouths open wide, bodies in quarter-bent position, seemingly unable to move. It's as if someone snapped a picture of these five clots in mid-run. The smaller guy drops the pipe and it rolls to the edge of the curb and falls into the dirty gutter. I open my eyes fully. Every miscreant is staring at something to the left of my head. I follow their gaze until my eyes land on the biggest gun I've ever seen in my life. I jerk back just a little and gasp. "Machine gun?" I whisper, not knowing what the hell I'm staring at.

"*A-K forty-seven assault rifle and her name is Fifi!*" Thick Ugly Man happily booms in a heavy, Scottish accent as he glares at the thugs. "Fully automatic, magazine loaded, safety off, and she's ready when you are, lads!"

No one moves a millimeter.

"No? Not today? That's too bad! Poor Fifi wants some fun; she wants some action!" He sounds truly disappointed as he gazes from one terrified face to another. "Well then, we'll be off down th' road, right?" With Fifi still leveled on the thugs, Thick Ugly Man bends to open the rear door and gestures me to climb in. I scramble all the way across the seat on my hands and knees. The heavy door slams closed behind me and within seconds, we're flying down the street like a jet-propelled rocket, the G-force pressing me back into the leather uphol-stery.

Thick Ugly Man is on his mobile. "Okay, boss. I've got him. Aye. Found him runnin' his tiny arse hell for leather straight down Gatling. Nah. The poor, sweet little poof had th' bloody shite scared outta him and he's fair-well knackered, but he's all right. Faced 'em down, too. Like a big man, he was. The wee boy has got some balls!" There's a pause. "Mallory Eight, West River, Docklands. Will do! Right on his posh doorstep. No problem. See ya' soon." He looks at me in his rear-view mirror. "Aye up! Yer a brave little 'un, aren't ya,' standin' up t' those bastards? Fix yer bonny bow and lie down on the seat, poppet. It's gonna be about a half hour drive. You've had it rough playin' with th' big boys, yeah? You rest up a bit."

I straighten my bow, yank my knickers out of my butt and gladly lie down as I'm told. I call Johnny to tell him I'm okay and then promptly fall asleep.

Brian

"Good. He's all right then." I finish plating the pasta and vegeta-bles and hand one to John.

"But Prissy said the guy had a gun—an assault rifle… named Fifi."

"Hmm. I figured that."

"You knew he'd have a gun named Fifi? Brian, who was he?"

I smile. "Angus. A driver for an old acquaintance of mine. He names all his guns. He says it gives him a better working relationship with his firepower. Fifi is a favorite. He's had her for a while." I'd like it to end there, on a humorous note, but John isn't satisfied with that answer as I dish the salad. "My acquaintance used to deal drugs and various other contraband, but he's been clean for a few years now—or

so he says. I remembered he has businesses in that area and his nego-
tiations usually require some highly persuasive safety measures. I
thought he'd have a driver somewhere close."

John is quiet as he eats. He's still bothered.

"What, love?"

"I just don't like guns and drugs and illegal things like that. That's
not common, right? I mean, in your businesses and the work you do?"

"No, John. This was a special circumstance—a *very* special circumstance. Prissy never should have been in that area. The unemployed
skinheads who live there are ignorant, racist, homophobic and violent.
It's a dangerous combination. He's lucky he got out alive. As for me,
I'm not into guns or drugs, and I don't routinely associate with people
who are. I won't do anything that puts me at risk of getting shot,
okay?"

He smiles and he's relieved. "Okay."

Brian — July 10

I pull out my mobile. "Hey, Simon. How are you? How is Robert?"

"I'm hanging in there and Robert has had a few good days, so I'm
not as stressed. We finally found a decent cocktail that's taking care of
the pain and has minimal side effects. It's turned him into a spaced-out
vegetable twenty-four hours a day and we can't have any intelligent
conversations, but at least he's not moaning." Simon hesitates. "I'm not
sure about the supplemental insurance, though. The drugs are expensive and they're considered experimental. They might kick back the
claim."

"Let them. Just use the money in the account. That's what it's there
for."

"Brian, I—"

"Simon, stop. I don't want to go through this again. Just use it
when you need to and change the subject, okay?"

"Okay. How's it going with you?"

"Great. Things are fantastic."

"Yeah? What's he like? What's it like to be with him?"

I realize Simon is a little envious of me and very intrigued with

John. "He's different. He's emotional and unpredictable. He's... sweet."

"Sweet?"

"I know. That sounds daft coming from me, doesn't it?"

"No, it sounds good, Brian. It really does. Tell me more."

"He's special and he's fun to be with. I really enjoy his company. He needs a lot of attention and a lot of reassuring. I have to tell him I love him all the time."

"Really?"

"Aye. Not that I don't, but I'm not used to saying it out loud."

"And he needs to hear it?"

"Often. Sometimes he's shy and moody."

"That's odd. He comes across as cocky and conceited and really full of himself on the show and in interviews."

"That's an image. It sells and it's made him popular. He's needy, Simon. And he's insecure about us — our situation."

"And that's okay with you?"

"It's okay with me. He's what I need. Emotionally, I don't work well with anyone but him. He understands me."

"And the other thing — the sex issue we discussed that first night? We didn't talk about it when we last spoke. I didn't feel it was my place to ask, and to be honest, when you didn't mention it, I was afraid you might have cocked it up."

"I didn't cock it up," I retort, mildly insulted. "My initial technique may have been a little... amateurish, but I think I did quite well in the end, considering."

"So, is it okay? Are you comfortable with it — with everything?"

My first thought is to tell him he should have warned me about that incredible urge to shit during sex, but eventually (Thank God!) it went away. "Aye, it's all fine. You were right, and it wasn't a big deal. We're a good match, so it works out well."

"Aha! So, is he it? Is he the one, Brian?"

"Yes, definitely. I don't want anyone else and I can't imagine being without him." I smile into the phone. "Today is our three-month anniversary."

"You remembered?"

"No, he's been sending text messages and leaving notes about the flat with suggestions of presents I should get him. He wants hives for the balcony—says we need to save the honeybees. I just picked up a dozen red roses and an assortment of his favorite chocolates. I'll take him out to dinner tonight, too." I give a small laugh. "Can you believe it—me buying flowers and chocolates for a bloke?"

"No, I can't. You really sound happy, though, Brian. It's been a long time since Ayden, and you finally sound happy. I guess it's okay to lean a little, huh?"

"Yeah, I guess it is. Look, I'm at the flat. I have to go. Give my best to Robert. I'll call you later." I return my mobile to my pocket as we turn the final corner on our way home.

"Are you sure you don't want me to pull into the garage, sir?" Jack asks over the comm.

"No, I'll just get out at the lobby. Please have the car detailed. I'd like it clean for tonight."

"Yes, sir."

As soon as the limo stops, I open the door and step out, holding the chocolates. I lean in to grab the flowers and my briefcase.

"Excuse me. Are you Brian?"

I straighten up to see a disheveled, smelly, heavily whiskered bloke in a filthy overcoat. His scent is... disturbing. "Yes, can I help—"

I see the flash off the small barrel a millisecond before I hear the discharge. I feel a terrible burning sensation in my lungs and a tingling tremor down my left arm as the bullet rips through my chest and explodes out my back. Immediately, I drop the flowers and my briefcase. When the second bullet hits me in the right shoulder, I drop the chocolates and begin to fall. I faintly hear more gunshots, and Jack shouting... and that's the last thing I remember.

John

I'm lunching with the nincompoops. It's a treat to have my days free so I can hang out, eat and chat. We've been meeting for lunch every other day for the past couple of weeks. A few reporters have dropped hints about my weight in their tabloids, and they've bolstered their borderline-unkind words with some unflattering photos. Physically, I'm not to a point that warrants blatant ridicule yet, but it's only a matter of days before I see the words 'tubby,' 'chunky,' and 'heifer' in the captions under those photos. If they did it to the Duchess of York, they'll have no problem doing it to me. So after tonight's anniversary dinner, I'll start a regimen to lose what I've gained since moving in with Brian. That's about twenty-five ample pounds spread generously across my midsection like an inner tube. I might try to work out with Brian at the flat, but our partnering efforts to date haven't been successful. I'm not a serious weight lifter to begin with. I'm easily distracted, easily bored and (with these extra pounds) easily winded. I whine and bitch ten minutes into my warm-up cardio. Besides, watching Brian lift those heavy weights, listening to him grunt, and seeing his glistening, sweaty body… Well, I just get way too horny. On a few occasions, he had to bonk me across the flat bench because I stripped down on the spot, kept shoving my ass in his face and wouldn't stop begging. Those weren't my finer moments and they certainly didn't please him. He takes his workouts seriously and Papa Prude has made it clear: Sex belongs in the bedroom.

We've all finished eating. Prissy just took us step-by-step through his ordeal on Gatling Road, and now he's telling us how he and Ben had car sex in a deserted car park later that day. It's a good thing the perky, little guy isn't easily traumatized. Of course, while listening to the car park story my mouth is hanging open. I'm so jealous. I've spent three months begging Brian for car sex and he won't give in, not even after some award-winning tantrums and heavy-duty pinching. My phone buzzes. "Hang on. Sorry, I have to get this. It's probably something about tonight. Hi, Jack. What? *WHAT?*" I stand up so fast I knock over my chair. The nincompoops are startled and other diners are looking at me. "When? Wha…? *No, no, say that again!* Is he okay? Where is he? *Where?* Um, yes…. No, I know where that is. No, I'll be there. You stay with him, Jack! *You stay right there with him!*" I look at everyone's stunned face as I start to sway. The room spins, my legs give out and I drop my phone. Ben and Martin grab me in my armpits just before I hit the floor. I can barely speak. "Brian was just shot," I whisper, and then I faint.

Brian

The pain is unbelievable! "AHHHHHHH!"

An unfamiliar face looks down on me. "I'm sorry, sir. I know it's painful. I know it really hurts. Can you tell me your name, sir?"

"Brian," I groan.

"Okay, Brian. Okay."

"AHHHHHHH!" I wail. Someone clamps a mask on my face as I try to look around. Where's John? I don't see... John. Right now... I really... need....

"I'm sorry but I've got to do this! I've got to stop this flow! Bear with me! Bear with us, Brian! Just hang in there, okay? Brian? *Brian?* We've got a problem! He's on his way out! *He's going!* Work faster, people! Get that oxygen ramped up and move him a little to the left! *Staunch that!* Now! Hurry! *We need to keep him conscious!*"

John

"BRIAN! *BRIAN!* No, no—let me—*let me go! Get off me!* BRIAN! BRIAN! Where is he going? *Where is he going?*" Martin is hanging onto me with all his strength. He's holding me back as I see Brian, covered in blood and yelling in agony, whiz by on a gurney. He's surrounded by medical personnel, tubing, wires, equipment. It's just one solid mass of shouting people and machinery flying by.

"Surgery prep, sir! He's being prepped for surgery!" a frazzled nurse yells as she runs past and blasts through a pair of metal, swinging doors with the rest of the entourage.

I try to break free of Martin's grasp so I can follow them. "*Let me in there!*"

"No, sir! You can't!" another nurse bellows as he sprints by, cradling bags of blood and slams through the same doors like a linebacker.

"I need to be with him! I need to.... I need to *see* him!"

"I'm sorry, sir. Please, just wait here. Just sit down and wait here," an overweight orderly demands, becoming an impenetrable blockade in front of the doors.

There's nothing I can do. I can't follow Brian through the big swinging doors. I can't be with him. We all sit down on a long bench across from the waiting room, frightened and confused. It takes a while for someone with any authority to even acknowledge us.

"Okay, how can I help you?" a doctor calmly asks, head down, diligently studying papers on a clipboard.

I quickly stand up. "I want to see Brian Mallory."

He looks up, bored. "And who are you?"

"I'm his partner. His...his domestic partner. I need to see him!"

"Domestic partner," he repeats, and then pinches up his face as if the words left a thin film of shit in his mouth. "What's your name?"

"John Kaiser. I really need to see him!"

"Calm down, Johnny," Martin says.

The pompous doctor takes a step back from whatever gay cooties he thinks I'm harboring. "I'd prefer to talk to a spouse... or at least a relative."

A spouse? Now I'm fuming and breathing hard. "There's no spouse! You have to talk to me! You tell me what's going on! I'm his boyfriend! *Why can't I see him?*"

Martin tries his best to calm me down. "Johnny, let's hold on, okay? You need to relax, man."

I snap at him like a wild dog. *"Don't tell me to relax! I don't want to relax!"*

He snaps right back. *"Okay, do you want to pass out? Huh? Because at this rate, that's all you're gonna do! Okay?"*

Martin is right, he's pissed, he can flatten my ass with one punch and he will if he has to. I need to get a grip. I take a deep breath. "Okay."

"It's going to be a while. I'm sure someone will come out to talk with you soon." The asshole doctor immediately turns to leave.

"Yes. Thank you," Martin says to his retreating back.

I sit down in a daze. I can't believe this is happening. My God! Who the hell would shoot Brian? I don't know what to do. I've never dealt with *anything* like this before. I open my phone and find Simon's number in his directory. We've never spoken and this is a terrible way to introduce myself. "Hello, Simon? It's John. Yes. Yes. Can you please come to London? Brian was shot. Just now. This afternoon. No, I'm serious. Then it must have happened right after he spoke with you. I don't know. No, I don't know. They haven't told me anything. Please come, Simon. I *really* need you here. I'm at Fenwick-Wright Memorial Hospital in Whitechapel. Thank you. Goodbye."

Two police officers appear around a far corner and walk down the hallway. We watch, as they first speak with the nurse at the reception desk and then turn toward us sitting on the bench. A feeling of dread creeps up my spine as I stare at their expressionless faces. "You're waiting here for Brian Mallory?"

"Yes," Ben says.

"Who's John Kaiser?" It's posed as a question but they're looking right at me. They know who I am.

"That's me."

"Mister Kaiser, I'm Constable Frank Cole and this is Constable Shelley Keenans. Jack Neiman is at the station providing us with a statement, but we're having trouble identifying the gunman. He wasn't carrying identification and Mister Neiman has never seen him before. At this point, all we know is that he was young and unshaven, with—I guess what most people would say—reddish-blond hair. I'd like to show you a picture of a guy. I just want you to take a good look at it and tell me if you recognize the person, okay?"

"Okay."

He holds out a photograph and I take it. Right away, I hone in on the hair color and the beard growth. It's Strawberry Blond. He was so angry with Brian that night at the store and he was such a weird bastard. He probably followed us home. I bet he stalked Brian for days, studying his daily routine and waiting for the perfect opportunity— just the right moment. I stare hard at the photograph. I'm looking at a dead man, stripped naked and laid out on a morgue gurney. He's the damned bastard who shot my boyfriend. I close my eyes and hand back the picture. "I recognize him."

"You know his name?" Officer Keenans asks.

I nod and open my eyes. "It's David Vector."

Prissy gasps. Ben, Martin and Jeff just stare at each other. I feel nothing but sick.

Both officers hit me with a barrage of questions. I can't answer them because I don't know why David came back to shoot Brian, except (maybe) out of jealousy. They don't tell me how he died—and to be honest, right now I don't care. They finally leave and it's an eternity before another doctor comes through the swinging doors. "Are you John Kaiser?"

I stand up. "Yes, yes. Is he okay? Can I see him now? Please, can I see him?"

"I'm sorry, not yet. He's just gone into surgery. What do you know about the shooting?"

I'm perplexed by the question. "Nothing. Just that he was shot."

"Were you there?"

"No. His driver called me. Will he be okay?"

"One bullet entered his chest in a critical area. It's done a lot of damage and it's still in there. We're having trouble finding it. That's one of the worst wounds and the first one we'll deal with."

"*Wounds?* How many times was he shot?" Jeff asks.

"We don't know yet. Several."

I grow faint and sit down, looking helplessly at the poops. They're all as shocked as I am. We assumed he'd only been shot once.

"We think five or six bullets may be lodged in his torso."

My head swims and I lean forward over my thighs as a wave of nausea passes over me and my skin turns clammy. Martin rubs my back as I try not to black out. I focus hard on the immaculately clean floor tiles. "I want.... I want to see him."

"That will have to wait. He's gone into surgery now." The doctor walks away.

Again, we sit and wait while various medical personnel rush in and out through the metal swinging doors, some heavily spotted with blood (Brian's blood?), some not. No one says a word to us. We're invisible. I can't figure out what's going on and it's frustrating. If I were his wife or even his girlfriend, I know they would treat me differently. I'm afraid Brian is going to die—and they won't let me see him. Finally, after what seems like numerous hours, another doctor comes out. She's tired and her words are a crushing blow to any optimism we might have had. "He's not doing well. He's in pretty bad shape. Keeping him stable has been a right chore."

I'm too emotionally drained to react with anything more than tears, but Prissy is furious and gets up in her face, even though she's six inches taller than he is. "Do you know who he is? He's got connections! He knows people with big guns and...and he's got lots of money!"

The exhausted doctor, staring down at this miniscule elf with yellow hair, flushed cheeks, and a pink bow, is not impressed. "I know who he is. We've had enough of guns for one day, and it's not down to money. It's got nothing to do with money. Sit down." He yanks hard at his panties and then does as he's told. She takes a moment to look at each of us as she rubs the back of her neck. Then she speaks. "Look, the gun wasn't that powerful but it was fired at least five times at close range and virtually all the shots went into his torso. One bullet went through his lung and straight out his back. Other bullets hit vital organs and several ribs. Two of his ribs shattered, causing even more damage — like shrapnel that exploded inside his body. It's a matter of finding the remaining bullets, stopping the blood loss and fixing the immense amount of damage. That takes time and skill, not money. We've sent in the second team, and I promise we'll work around the clock, but don't get your hopes up. It's touch and go. The only things working in his favor are that he's fit and he has a strong heart."

"Can I see him?"

"Absolutely not. Not while he's in surgery. But I'll try to keep you as informed as I can, all right?"

"Okay, thank you."

She gives me a hard look and glances at my chain. "Are you his boyfriend?"

"Yes." Tears well up in my eyes and I whisper, "Today was our anniversary."

She reaches into her pocket and pulls out Brian's ring. She smiles down at me. "When he first came in, he wouldn't let us take this off his finger. He put up quite a fight until we knocked him out. I was going to have reception put it in the safe with his other items. Why don't you keep it. We're short on beds in this area of the hospital, but I'll see if I can set aside a place for you to sleep here tonight. It's going to be a while."

"Thank you." I take the ring and stare at it while Martin unfastens my chain. I hand it to him; he places it on the chain, and hangs it back around my neck. I lay my head in his lap and cry.

■ ■ ■

At one-thirty in the morning, I tell the nincompoops to go home. They want to stay but there's nothing they can do. I promise to call if there's any news and give my keys to Martin. He'll come back later with clean clothes. I call Charles and tell him what I know, so far. He wants to fly out, but I convince him not to come. He has to cancel Brian's upcoming flights and meetings and help Edna with office matters. I don't know how to get in touch with Alex, but Charles says he'll do his best to get a message to him. Simon arrives at about two-thirty. I know it's him the moment he walks around the corner. He's a really tall, slightly balding man with a handsome, somber face, expressive Paul Newman eyes and a lanky build. I stand up, hug him tightly and cry. Right now, he's the closest connection I have to Brian.

"I'm sorry it took so long. It was hard to find a flight out and cabs are scarce here."

"I'm sorry. I couldn't send Jack to get you. He's too shaken up to drive."

"It's all right." He's talking softly and rubbing my back. "Let's sit down." He sits me down on the bench. "Okay now, John. Tell me what happened — everything you know."

While Simon holds my hands, I tell him about the call from Jack, the morgue photo and the vague updates from the doctors.

"Well then, it sounds like there's nothing we can do now, okay? The police are doing their work, and the doctors are certainly doing theirs. It's out of our hands, so we'll just wait. But we'll wait together, right?" He gives me a smile.

"Right." I lean against his shoulder and, finally feeling a small sense of security, fall into a dreamless sleep. When I awake, I'm lying along the bench with my head in Simon's lap. His coat is draped over me and his hand is resting on my shoulder. I sit up and yawn. "Any news yet?"

"No, nothing yet, John. I would have woken you. No one has come through those doors for hours. They're still working on him."

I yawn again and rub my eyes. Simon hands me a cup of water. I gulp it down, lean against his shoulder and stare at the swinging doors. "How did you meet him?"

"I met Brian Mallory fourteen years ago on a plane going from France to Scotland. I was supposed to be in economy, but I got bumped to first class because the steward spilt coffee in my crotch during a bit of turbulence." He gives a small laugh and a sigh at the memory. "I sat right behind him. He was on his phone, of course. I listened in on his call. He was telling his secretary about his old accountant who'd keeled over during a board meeting in Paris three days earlier."

I rise up off his shoulder to look at him in amazement.

"Oh yes, John. The corpse, in a body bag, was right there on the plane! Can you believe it?"

I relax back onto his shoulder.

"He told her he needed bank ledgers reviewed for some important meetings and didn't know what he was going to do. I interrupted him and introduced myself over the back of his seat. God, he thought I was cheeky! I said, 'Hello, my name is Simon. I'm an accountant and I'm sure I can help you. By the way, I'm gay. I hope that doesn't bother you.'"

"What'd he say?"

"He was pretty stunned. At the time, not too many of us were out, you know? He craned his head around to look at me and said, 'You listened in on my private call?' And I said, 'Yes, sir, I did. I'm an accountant. I can help you. Does it bother you that I'm gay?' And he said, 'It doesn't bother me one damned bit that you're gay. It bothers me that you're bloody nosey!'"

"That sounds just like Brian."

"Yes, it certainly does. Anyway, by the time we landed, I'd gone over five accounts for him and then followed him to three meetings in Glasgow after he bought me new pants."

"And you've been best friends ever since?"

"Friends don't come any closer than us."

"He tells you everything, doesn't he?"

"Well, I wouldn't say he tells me everything, but if he needs to confide in someone or wants personal advice, he comes to me. He doesn't always like what I have to say, but..." He's thoughtful for a moment. "I asked him out once, when Robert and I hit a bad patch. I knew he wasn't gay, but he was so handsome, so complicated, so damned arrogant, and he had those fabulous eyes, you know?"

I rise up off his shoulder and give him a smile and a knowing look.

"Yes. I guess you do know."

"Was he offended?"

"No, not at all. He said he was flattered, but not *that* flattered." Simon sighs, stretches out his legs and crosses his ankles. "Eventually, I smoothed things over with Robert and that was that. We've been together ever since."

"And how is Robert?"

"He's not well. I'm sure Brian told you about the cancer. It's advanced and it's spreading. It's faster to name the body parts that don't have it than the ones that do—and he still craves cigarettes. He's in the final stages. Now we just have to wait it out until the end and try to keep the pain at bay."

"I'm sorry I took you from him."

Simon lightly touches my cheek and smiles. "Pumpkin, don't worry about that. He's so drugged up with pain killers right now he doesn't even know I'm gone."

30
Bydda' I'n Aros Amdana' Ti Am Byth, Os Oes Angen, Cariad

John — August 4

I look around Brian's hospital room and I'm satisfied with what I've accomplished over the past few weeks. I hung deep burgundy curtains at the windows to frame the ugly, institutional blinds. I brought in a table for the foot of the bed and two tall vases that I keep filled with fresh flowers. I had hospital maintenance tack sheeting over the harsh, fluorescent ceiling fixtures and Martin set up floor lamps in each corner. He also brought two thick rugs from the library. On Brian's bedside table, next to an important blinking contraption that monitors his body temperature for first signs of fever and infection, I set up the only photograph I have of us: an impromptu, slightly out-of-focus snapshot Jeff took with my phone just a few days before the shooting. In it, we're out on the balcony on a beautiful, sunny day. Brian is leaning back against the railing and I'm standing in front of him. His arms are around me and my arms are on top of his. We're smiling into the camera and Tower Bridge is in the background. I remember that day vividly because Prissy nearly fell off the railing and into the river trying to moon a sightseeing barge with his tiny ass, and Martin had convinced Brian to buy a billiard table and put it where the piano had been. Martin loves to play billiards and so does Brian.

There's nothing I can do about the three stainless steel carts holding equipment that beeps and buzzes and spits out lengths of cardio readings on thin strips of paper, or the endless number of tubes and wires that run from various parts of Brian's body to each of these units. Some tubes pump things into him, some tubes drain things out of him, and the electrodes just collect information. Lime-green compression socks (the only pair they could find to fit his feet) intermittently inflate and deflate, filling the room with a nonstop 'hiss-suck, hiss-suck' sound. They're the only things on the bed that show signs of life. When Brian was brought out of the induced coma, I thought he'd just open his eyes and everything would be okay. I had no idea he'd develop a raging blood infection (septicemia, they called it) and fall into a real coma—a coma that could last for weeks, or months... or years.

As I sit in my chair next to his bed, I'm careful not to disconnect anything tethered from machine to man. I open my book as I've done for the past three weeks and prepare to read. As usual, I fiddle with our rings on my chain while I look for the spot where I left off. My ring is on the chain because I've lost thirty pounds from the stress and now it slips off my finger. Brian's ring is on the chain because I need to keep it close until he can wear it again. I only took it off once—briefly—to have Jeff take it to an engraver. I'd finally decided what I wanted it to say: My Whole Life, John.

I'll be the first to admit my Welsh just sucks. After all this time, I still can't pronounce eighty percent of what I say and I understand less than two percent. It really is a cumbersome language, but I'll keep reading to Brian until I finish the book. And if I have to, I'll start another one. And that's not all I do. I sing love songs to him at night. I read his financial newspapers to him from front to back every morning. I cut out and save the crossword from every issue of the journal. I brush his hair, shave his face and clean his ears. I write love letters to him, pouring out my thoughts and feelings. I fold them up and set them aside for later. I play his favorite classical music for him. I clean and trim his fingernails and toenails, and every night, even though hospital staff can't stand it and threaten to throw me out, I sleep on the floor rugs so I can stay closely to him.

"Roedd y milwyr yn llwglyd ac yn oer. Ac roedd nifer ohonynt yn sâl." I struggle along, trying to maintain the flow of the story. "Roeddynt yn gwybod bod rhaid i'r pentref fod gerllaw...." It doesn't sound as rhythmic and soothing as when Brian reads out loud, but I keep going until the pronunciation for one particular word stumps me no matter how many times I say it. "Llanfairpwllgwyngyngyll. Llanfairpwllgwyngyngyll." I've said this word before and I know it's still not right. "Llanfairpwllgwyngyngyll, Llanfairpwllgwyngyngyll."

Brian

I hear him — faintly at first — and then more clearly as he thoroughly, methodically, and painstakingly obliterates the beautiful Celtic language I've cherished all my life. He's trying to say the name of the village. It's the short version, but even the short version is tough for beginners. He's doing pretty well, although his attempts at proper pronunciation are torturing me. He's just not seeing it right on the page because he's not wearing his contacts, as usual. That's why he can never say it correctly. I've spoken that word to him a dozen times. I don't think he'll ever get it right unless we set him up with proper lessons, and if I have to listen to him say it wrong just one more time, I swear I'll strangle him. "Llanfairpwllgwyngyll, John. The bloody word is Llanfairpwllgwyngyll."

John

At first, I sit motionless — dumbstruck. I know it was Brian's voice and he just spoke to me. I raise my head to look at him. His eyes are closed and his face is impassive — the way it's been for weeks. For a moment, I think I imagined it.

"Really look at the word, love. Try saying it again without that extra syllable at the end." His rough voice is deep and soothing but his eyes are still closed.

I swallow hard, look down at my book and repeat the word. "Llanfairpwllgwyngyll."

"That's better. That sounds much better."

Again, I look up at him and slowly — very slowly — after three long weeks, his eyes open. His beautiful, pale green eyes finally open. As soon as I'm sure they're focused on me, I hoarsely whisper, "I love you."

"I know you do, but please don't read Welsh to me anymore. It hurts."

I smile. "I've missed you so much." I want to say it louder but my constricting throat muscles won't let me.

"I've missed you, too."

"Have you?"

"Yes, love. Very much."

I carefully part the tubes and wires and pull my chair closer to his bed. I lean in and kiss his forehead and his nose and his cheek. My tears are falling all over his face and I'm sniffling back snot, trying to keep it from running out of my nose and dripping on him. Crying like a baby, I put my mouth over his and slide my tongue inside, even though there's a tube running into his nostril that's in the way. The staff haven't brushed his teeth yet today, but I haven't brushed mine either, so what the hell? His immense strength comes up through his body as he meets my kiss with passion. There's movement under the sheet, below his waist. I place my hand there and rub gently. He moans and jerks his head just a little. I moan too, dig in deeper with my tongue and rub just a little harder. His moan intensifies exponentially, his head jerks again and I feel him pushing back on my tongue with his. He's really feisty for just coming out of a coma—and I like it! I dig in just a little deeper and press a little harder. He violently jerks his head away from me and pants, "Catheter, John! There's a damned catheter!"

I yank my hand away. "Oh, my God! I'm so sorry." Shit! I can't imagine how much that must have hurt.

His eyes are wide as he tries to catch his breath. "Let's just kiss, okay?"

"Okay." I start again—just kissing him gently. He moans and two of the monitors beep faster. I keep kissing, pressing in deeper with my tongue, tasting him—tasting what I've missed for more than three long weeks. The monitors beep even faster until one gives out a shrill alarm and a dozen lights start flashing like a vintage pinball machine going haywire on a triple-bonus score. Within seconds, hospital staff members burst into the room. I'm hauled out of my seat and shoved aside as half a dozen nurses and doctors hoard over Brian. For the next few minutes, they think he's having a seizure. His obvious erection finally convinces them otherwise.

Two hours later, after the doctors have examined him and run various tests, half the tubes and wires are disconnected. Someone yanks out his catheter, which just makes him yell at the top of his lungs (and sends a chill up my spine), he pulls out his own nose hose (the sight of which causes me to faint like a sissy precisely four seconds after I declare to three doctors and a nurse that I will not faint like a sissy), and two of the carts are wheeled out of the room. While I regain consciousness on the floor, the nurse brings him some semi-solid food and lets him brush his teeth. He's propped up with a few pillows and I sheepishly crawl up into my chair. I lean in closely and stroke his hair, gazing at his lovely face. It's a little gaunt from dehydration, and he could use a good shave and some sun, but it's still the face I know and trust, and love more than anything in this world.

31
There's Only So Much A Bloke Can Take

John — August 4

"Tell me what happened. I remember I was talking to Simon. I was in the limo and... I had some flowers."

I nod. "You were shot about four weeks ago as you stepped out of the limo in front of the flat. You just finished your call with Simon, and you'd bought me roses and chocolates. It was our anniversary."

"It was, wasn't it? How many times?"

"Six times. You were shot six times at close range. One went into your shoulder and the rest went into your chest and stomach."

He nods and closes his eyes. "I remember now. The bloke was really close to me. I remember the sound of that gun. What happened to him?"

"Jack shot him — dead."

He nods again. "Of course he did. Jack always carries a gun."

"He's your bodyguard, isn't he?"

"Unofficially. He must feel terrible he killed someone."

"He does. You're paying for him to see a counselor twice a week."

He opens his eyes and smiles at me. "Am I? Good. That's good, John." His smile fades. "Does anyone know who the bloke was?"

I hesitate. "It was David."

"David? *Your* David?"

I nod.

"You saw him?"

"The police showed me a photograph taken at the morgue. He'd dyed his hair and he hadn't shaved in a while so he looked a little different, but it was him."

Brian shakes his head. "David," he quietly says, almost to himself. He looks puzzled.

"What's wrong?"

"Hmm? Nothing, love. Nothing at all. Tell me about you. How have you been?"

"I've been okay. It's been hard without you, but I've kept you company. I've been here the whole time. I wrote you a lot of letters. You can read them later."

"Thank you. I would really like to do that. It means a lot to me to know you were here. I'm so glad I woke up to your voice and your face."

He's in such a good mood. He's in a fantastic mood. And that should have me jumping for joy, but I have some news that's going to piss him off. He'll probably go ballistic and shout at me, but I don't have any idea how to sugar coat this pill—and it's got a nasty taste. "I've got Simon at the flat."

"Really? Simon is here?"

"Yes, and Robert."

"Robert is at the flat? What's he doing in London?"

"Things are pretty bad. He's under hospice care now. The day you were shot, I called Simon and asked him to come to London, and then asked him to stay. He didn't know what to do with Robert. The hospital in Germany said hospice was the only option for palliative care. He wasn't going to get better and they needed his bed. I had him flown out here on a medi-flight. He has three nurses who take care of him in shifts."

"So, he's in a spare bedroom?"

"No, he's in your bedroom—I mean, our bedroom—so he can look out across the river and get the cool breezes coming in through the big sliders and watch the sunrise."

"So… Simon and Robert are in our bedroom… at the flat."

"Yes, just for a while."

He takes some time to think about it and then nods. "Okay. That's okay. I like them a lot. They're good friends. That's fine." He's smiling, but that's not the worst of it. I've merely stuck my gunpowder into the cannon's breech.

"And..."

"And what?"

"Prissy and Ben flooded the first floor of the brownstone, so now there's a little mold to clean up and they're in one of the spare bedrooms... with Ben's two cats... and his budgie."

Brian is now staring down at his green-socked feet, and he's not smiling—because I've just added my cannon ball. "So... we've got Simon and Robert in our bedroom at the flat... and Prissy and Ben... and two cats and a budgie... in one of the spare bedrooms." His voice is getting quiet.

"Yes, Brian." I carefully study his face before I hit him with the final blow. "And..."

"And... what?" He's almost afraid to ask, and he's determined to keep his eyes on his feet.

"Angina kicked Martin out because she thought he was sleeping with Jeff—but he wasn't. At least, not when she kicked him out. So he was staying with Jeff because he didn't have anywhere else to go, and that's when they did start sleeping together. And then Jeff's building manager, who's Angina's uncle, found out they were sleeping together and kicked both of them out." I wince as I finish the sentence because I know I've just lit the fuse—and now all I can do is wait for the Boom! and duck when something flies out of that cannon.

Brian closes his eyes. His jaw is set hard and he's trying to control his breathing. A vein is pulsing at his temple. "Do not say it. Do not tell me we've got six blokes... living in the flat."

I swallow hard and bite my lip. "Yes, Brian. Six blokes... two cats... a budgie... and Jeff's little ferret living in the flat." I have no idea what he's thinking right now. For a man who can't stand *anyone* in his home, I've really put his patience (and his undying love for me) to the test. It's deathly quiet in the room—just ominously and eerily quiet except for the hiss-suck, hiss-suck of his lime-green socks. I'm afraid to move, so I sit perfectly still... and wait. After an eternity, Brian finally opens his eyes and gives me a thoughtful look. Then he smiles. My lit fuse appears to have fizzled. All seems well and calm and I smile back at him with relief.

"Come here."

I slide in my chair.

He's still smiling. "Come closer."

I slide in a little more, lean in next to his face, and lovingly gaze at him. He is *so* handsome.

He pans my facial features and sighs before whispering, "I love you."

"I love you, too," I whisper back.

"I miss you."

"I miss you, too. A lot."

"Do you? What do you miss the most?"

I'm turning embarrassingly red in the face. "You know what."

"Do I? Tell me. Tell me what you miss the most."

I press my lips to his cheek and feel my body heat rising. "I miss sex with you the most."

"Do you?"

I lower my head to nuzzle his neck. "Yes."

"You need that? You need sex?"

"Yes, Brian. I need it. I need sex with you." I'm horny now, sweating and breathing hard.

"Really? You want that? You want sex?"

"Yes, I really want sex. I really want *you*," I huskily whisper into his ear.

"What are you going to do if I give you sex, John?"

"I'm going to cry."

"Are you? Are you going to cry hard?"

He knows I'm way beyond horny. He knows I'm desperate for sex. I lick his jaw and bite his chin. "Oh, yes. Definitely yes!"

"And what else are you going to do, John? What else are you going to do if I give you sex?"

I'm panting in his ear now. I'd give *anything* to have him take me right here in this hospital room. "I'm going to scream."

"Are you?"

"Yes, I always scream. You always *make* me scream. I can't help it."

I've got a fierce erection and the sweat is trickling down my back as I bite his neck and run my fingers through his hair. I'm trying to figure out how to climb onto this hideous, institutional bed without pulling out the remaining tubes and wires. I've just *got* to have wild sex with him.

"So, if I give you sex, if I pound you hard with fantastic, hot sex, you'll scream for me, John?"

I stand up, grab his hand, smash it against my erection and grind on it like a cheese grater attacking a hunk of Parmigiano-Reggiano. "Yes, Brian! I promise I'll scream for you. I'll scream bloody murder for you!"

"Will you? Are you sure?"

"Oh, yes, Brian! Yes!" I loudly proclaim. "I will! I swear to God, I'll scream my damned *ass* off!"

"Really, John? With six blokes in the flat?"

As unbelievably hot and horny as I feel, as overcome with sweaty passion as I am, and as much as I'm panting and heaving, I can understand his point. Yes, he's made it very clear. My erection semi-deflates, I release his hand, and sit down. Still panting, I swallow hard. "I hadn't thought about that."

"*NO! I can tell you bloody well hadn't!*" he explodes. So much for that fizzled fuse.

"What am I going to do?"

Brian's voice starts out low as he strains to dampen its magnitude, but the volume and intensity quickly amp up as his self-control depletes. "I'll tell you what you're going to do. *You're going to get two actors, one model, one hairdresser, one accountant, one dying man, two cats, one damned budgie and one BLOODY ferret out of that flat before I get home!* THAT'S WHAT YOU'RE GOING TO DO!"

"But Brian, I—"

"*No, John! No excuses! There's only so much I can take and this is unacceptable!*" Papa Brian is adamant. He's going to have it his way and I can't sweet talk him around this one—not this time. "I haven't had sex with you in four weeks, and I'll be *damned* if I wait one minute longer when I get out of here! And don't even *think* about getting a hotel room! I'm going to have extremely loud sex in *my* flat, in *my* bed, and with *my* bloke—ALONE! UNDERSTOOD?"

I humbly hang my head. "Yes, Brian."

John

I don't know what to do. The doctors say Brian will come home in three days, after one more minor operation. How do I kick out six friends who have nowhere to go in three days? I step out of the elevator and walk around the atrium. I haven't been to the flat in weeks. I've relied on everyone living here to shuttle clothes and necessities to me every few days. I have no idea what the place will look like—or what it will smell like—and I'm worried. I open the door, afraid of what I'll see. I'm shocked when I see… nothing—nothing odd, at all. The place is beautiful. It's immaculately clean. It's quiet. I walk to the kitchen. Not a single item is out of place. The countertops and sinks are spotless, and so is the cooker. The fridge is well stocked and there's no meat. I walk on. The living room is dust free, with fresh flowers in all the vases. The arrangements aren't that spectacular, but someone certainly made the effort. Off in the corner, on a rubber mat near the billiard table, there's a tiny ferret scampering around in a cage. He's got beady, little eyes, a pointy nose and a long, scrawny neck. He looks an awful lot like Prissy. I hear voices in the master bedroom. As I get closer, I smell mild disinfectant but it's not too offensive. I walk in to find thin, frail Robert hooked up to oxygen and propped up in the bed—which has been moved closer to the sliders—gazing out at the skyline across the river. Simon is beside him on the bed, filing his fingernails, and Ben is reclining on the chaise with two obese calicos, reciting Wilde out loud. He looks up, obviously surprised to see me. "Hi, Johnny! What are you doing here?"

"Brian sent me home to get some stuff."

He sets down his book. "So Brian is awake? He's out of the coma?"

"Yeah, he's finally awake."

Simon's face lights up. "Excellent! Robert? Robert? Brian has pulled through! He's out of the coma. He's going to be okay! You should have called us right away, John. This is fantastic!"

"I'm sorry. It slipped my mind. When he woke up, they had to do all these tests and examine him and everything. And then I explained what happened to him because he didn't remember it, at first."

"But he's got all his faculties now? They've said he's all right?"

"He's fine. He'll probably be released in three days and he's eager to come home. So... how is everything here?"

"Great! Just great. We've got our routines down now, don't we, Benny?"

"Yup, we're one big happy family. We temporarily stopped the housekeeping service. We couldn't get everyone out of the flat at the same time for them to get in here and do their thing, so Simon sees that everyone does his share. We all have chores and we all get along."

"I'm impressed." I'm more than impressed. I'm surprised. The poops have always bickered and fought.

"Yeah, it's weird, but Simon keeps us in line. He doesn't put up with any bullshit. It's pretty fab. None of us fight—at all."

"Where is everyone else?"

"Well, Martin and Jeff are at work, and Prissy is out on the balcony looking at people," Simon says.

I feel my face drain of color. "He's what?"

"He's looking at people. I bought him some binoculars," Ben says.

"*Holy shit!*" I know exactly what that means. I march back into the living room and head for the sliders. Sure enough, there's Prissy out on the balcony, naked (and visible to every vessel sailing along the river) except for an enormous pair of pink cowboy boots and that stupid bow. He's got his skinny, little body perched on a bar stool at the railing with his yellow hair blowing in the breeze as he spies on the buildings across the river. I snatch the binoculars from his hands. "Prissy, stop that!"

"What? What's wrong?"

I lift him off the bar stool and he quickly bends his knees and tucks his scrawny matchstick legs—which look ridiculous sticking out of those big, girly boots—up into his chest. I look like I'm clutching a tiny, anemic turtle that's lost its shell. "Put your legs down!"

"No!"

"Prissy, you bratty little shit! Put your legs down and stand up!"

"*Sod off!*"

I lower my voice. "I'll pinch you."

Like two useless antennae shooting out of his body, his spindly legs drop down and I stand him up on the balcony and turn him around to face me. "Don't spy on people. It's rude."

"No, it's not," he whines. "I'm just curious. There's nothing wrong with that."

"Look, I don't want Brian getting complaints from people across the river saying he's got a naked pervert over here spying on them."

Prissy looks up at me with arms akimbo on his non-existent hips and his back swayed. "Oh, *really?*"

"Yes, *really.*"

"Well excuse me, Mister Head-Stuck-Up-Your-Extremely-Tight-Ass, but the only way they're gonna know that I'm spying on them is if *they're* spying on me."

"Wha—" I close my mouth and close my eyes. In a way, he's got a valid point, but I don't want to argue with him right now. I open my eyes. "Look, just go inside, okay? I need a few minutes alone. I have some things to think about."

"Can I have my binoculars?"

"No!"

"*Nasty bitch!*" he bitterly cries.

I watch him stomp off in a steamy little huff—his too big, femmy boots flapping around his bony shins and clomping loudly on the hardwood floors as his tiny, albino butt cheeks jiggle like two minis-cule bowls of gelatin. "And for God's sake, put some damned clothes on!"

I turn back to the river and take a long breath. I've got to clear my head. I have to figure out how to move six people and their various pets in three days. My biggest concern is Robert. I know I can carefully transport him, but I can't just put him up in a hotel—not with all his medical equipment and special needs. And since they all get along— which is unbelievable—I'd like to keep them together if I can. That means I need a big place, at least three bedrooms, that's pet friendly, available, not horrendously expensive, furnished, and preferably in London... in less than three days. An unbelievable goal to achieve. I lean on the railing and watch the activity going on up and down this peaceful river as a gentle breeze blows in my face. As Mickey once said, it's a beautiful view. Under less stressful circumstances I might be humming *Old Man River* right now, or even *Moon River*. My mind wanders back to my first visit with Brian at the flat, seemingly ages ago. I was so nervous that night. I was so enthralled with him, so impressed by him. I remember he asked me to stand right at this railing and look out across the Thames at his first conversion. I remember staring at his beautiful profile, not wanting to take my eyes off him, and I remember his gentle words put me right at ease. I gaze across the river now and something catches my eye. I raise Prissy's binoculars.

John – August 8

"Brian! What are you doing here?" With a ceramic vase of fresh-cut flowers in one arm, I stare down at my watch.

"I live here, John. What does it look like I'm doing here?" Well, his arrogance is healthy, and I've certainly missed it.

"But I was going to come for you. I was going to leave in just a few minutes." I set down the vase and rush to help him take off his coat.

"I know. I didn't want you to come so I took a cab. The press was snooping around and I thought it would be—Ow!"

"Oh God, I'm so sorry."

"It's okay. Just take it easy, all right?"

"All right." I gingerly pull the coat sleeves down his arms. "How's that?"

"That's fine. Thank you."

I hang the coat in the closet and turn to him. He's leaning up against the wall, tired and pale. Just the short trip from the hospital to the flat has drained him. I brush his hair off his forehead. I stretch up and kiss him gently on the cheek. I take his arm.

He winces. "Ow, John."

"Sorry. I...I don't know where the wounds are."

"I know, love. They're not in the best places, let me tell you. But you just lucked out and grabbed the spot where they had the damned IV."

I'm an idiot. After sitting with him for nearly four weeks in the hospital, I should know where he's been shot and poked and prodded, but I always went to take my shower and change my clothes when the nurses and orderlies came to dress his wounds, and they never let me lift his bed sheets for fear of another infection. Side-by-side, we walk into the living room. He pans the large space, examining everything with a keen eye.

"Is it okay?"

"It looks good, John. Everything looks really good."

"And the smell? Does it smell okay?" The cats were well behaved and budgies don't stink, but that cute little ferret had a thick, cheesy funk hanging on him, so I'm a bit worried.

He looks at me and smiles. "Smells great. Smells like home." I follow him as he stiffly walks down the hallway to the master bedroom. He stops dead still in the doorway. "You've got to be kidding me! There is *no* way I can put up with those. No! I will not have those in the flat."

"Oh, they're not so bad," I cheerfully say, coming up beside him. "I like them. I think they're gossamer."

"*Gossamer?* More like God awful." He turns to me with a pained look, one that says, "Please don't do this to me," and then laments, "I can't stand sheers, John."

"Just give them a little time, okay? Let's see if they grow on you."

His look turns dubious. Getting him to put up with them is a long shot, but I've got to sell him on those hideous sheers. I follow as he walks to the foot of the bed, which I've moved back away from the sliders to its proper place. "I don't mean to be morbid, but which side did Robert sleep on?"

I pull out a receipt from my pocket and hold it up. "Don't worry. It's a brand new mattress."

"Really?" He's happy.

"I ordered one that's a little firmer for better, um... for better, uh..."

"Thrust during sex?"

I nod vigorously.

He nods, too. "Yes. That's good. For us, that's really important. The bounce was irritating, wasn't it? Messed up our rhythm. Like trying to screw on a bloody trampoline."

I turn to him and press my lips to his neck. I've missed the warmth of his body so much and I desperately want this awkwardness between us to go away. His strong arms encircle my waist and I sigh, unbuttoning his shirt as he lowers his head to kiss me. I peel the sleeve off his right shoulder and see the first wound. It's certainly not pretty, but somehow, it's almost sexy. I touch it gently with my fingertips and smile.

"What?"

"Hmm?"

"Why are you smiling?"

"No reason. I just saw it for the first time and it looks.... It looks really sexy—bad-boy sexy."

"Bad-boy sexy?"

"Yeah, in a weird way."

Brian is baffled. "A gunshot wound looks bad-boy sexy in a weird way?"

"All right, I know that makes me sound like a whips-and-chains pervert, but—well, there it is. I think it looks bad-boy sexy."

He shakes his head as I continue peeling off his shirt to reveal a disturbing raw gouge in his chest, right below his left pectoral, still held closed with a few strips of tape. This wound isn't sexy at all. This wound is shocking—bright pink, swollen, and ragged edged. It's obvious the doctors had to dig extensively to fix the damage from the bullet. Nausea overwhelms me. I take a step back. Tears are welling up in my eyes as I put my hands in front of my mouth.

"What, John? What is it?"

"Oh, God. I can't believe he did this to you."

"No, no, no. Don't cry. None of this deserves crying. John, do not... cry." He's looking at me hard.

I calm myself down and take my hands away from my mouth. "This is my fault."

"It's not your fault. None of this is your fault." He reaches out to hold me, carefully. He kisses my forehead. "It's just something that happened. You don't know how everyone's mind works. Some people—they're just screwed up. You know them as a mate for years. They seem okay for a long time, but then something happens—something they don't like and can't accept—and they snap. They do crazy things. They do dangerous things and hurt people."

"But if I hadn't gone after you, if I'd left you alone. If you'd never met me—"

"I'd have been miserable." He turns my face up to his and looks into my eyes. "I'd have been absolutely miserable. John, meeting you—falling in love with you—has been the best thing that's ever... *ever* happened to me since Ayden. You are everything in this world to me. I love you so much. I don't want you to forget that, okay?"

I nod, and he kisses my forehead. He finishes undressing and then takes off my clothes while I stand perfectly still with my eyes closed. He runs his hands up and down my body, letting his fingertips explore every curve and crevice they find—tenderly caressing and fondling every inch of me, just the way I like. He kisses my face a dozen times, tells me how much he loves me again, and holds me. I press my lips to his neck to find his pulse. I feel safe and secure. He pulls away and, amazingly, lifts me up (with a painful grunt), carries me over, and places me on the bed. It takes us a while to find a few positions he can tolerate, but once we find them, we stick with them all afternoon and continue on long into the night. We don't even stop to eat dinner or answer phone calls. His stamina is strong. His drive is powerful. His thrust is deep. His need for sex is insatiable as he clings to my body like a jockey hell bent on winning the Kentucky Derby on his prized, thoroughbred filly. But the lovemaking is also sensuous and relaxed as we remember each other's preferences and nuances. I generate unbe-lievable amounts of heat and sweat. We spend hours touching, strok-ing, probing, smelling and tasting every square inch of each other's emaciated body. Time and time again, I beg him to love me. Over and over, he does—and over and over, I cry and scream and tell him how much I need him. I have no idea how many times I pass out.

In the morning I'm on my left side, facing the sliders with Brian spooned behind me. His arms are around my waist. He's holding me as tightly as he can with five healing wounds in his chest and stomach. I'm exhausted, hungry and sore. But that's okay because more than anything, I'm just glad he's home. I've missed him so much. I wiggle my toes.

"John?" With his face buried in my hair his low voice sounds just as it always has in the morning—muffled and groggy.

"Hmm."

"I really have a problem with those damned sheers."

I yawn. "I know you do."

"Is it a 'gay' thing?" he gently asks.

I crack a smile. This wonderful man has *so* much to learn. "No, Papa."

"They've got to come down, love."

I bring his hand up to my mouth and kiss his fingers. "I'm sorry, but they can't."

"Why not?"

"When I saw the 'Lease' sign Harry put up, I moved everyone into the East River Street condo."

"And?"

I yawn again. "And Ben bought Prissy some high-powered binoculars."

There's a long pause and a deep groan. He reaches down to my hips and pulls me in closer. "I guess they're not so bad."

32
The Simmering Comes To A Boil

Brian — August 19

I set down my mobile and look up into eager eyes.

"Was that him?" Sergeant Mitner asks.

"Aye. He's on his way — maybe four or five minutes out."

"Okay, everyone! He's coming! We've only got a few minutes. Let's do a final check." He strides to the dressing room doorway and positions himself so he has a full view of the bedroom and the dressing room. "Make sure that camera has a clean lens and no glare! I don't want any glare! Pull those ugly sheers a little if you have to. Check all the plugs. Make sure everything's connected... and for God's sake, *don't trip over anything!"* He yells at the lads, who are probably hovering over Simon's shoulder, "You lot, stay put way in the back. You shouldn't even be here so keep it buttoned tight, don't mess about with the equipment, and stay out of the way, right?" Then he turns his attention to Simon sitting at his laptop. "Simon, how's the sound?"

"I'll need a check," I hear Simon say.

Sergeant Mitner yells to me, "Brian! Say something. Just speak normally."

"How is this? How's my voice?"

"That's good for me," Simon responds.

"Brilliant, Brian! It's coming through just fine." He walks back into the bedroom, rubbing his hands and scrutinizing every little thing. "Okay, that's good. I like what I see." Simon says Ian Mitner is one of the best at surveillance and stings — and he'd better be right.

A constable enters from the hallway. "Sergeant? The tenants have been briefed. They'll stay put until the all clear."

"Bang on! That's perfect!" He turns to me as I sit on the bed, propped up with pillows. Another constable is leaning over me, adjusting the collar of my shirt as he tries to hide the wiring for the secondary mike. Just as he completes his task, the sergeant hastily shoos him away. "Now Brian, he's probably going to be standing about here, right? And we've got the sliders open for a bit of noise off the river — just as a precaution so he doesn't hear us in the back room. But here's the thing: It may create ambient noise on the tape, so if you can get him to speak a little louder than normal, that would help, okay?"

"Okay."

He looks down at me with concern. "You all right?"

"Aye. Just a bit..."

He smiles. "Nervous?"

"Just a little, but not too — excuse me." I pick up my buzzing mobile.

"*QUIET! Call coming through!*" the sergeant barks.

"Hey, Brenda. *What?*" I pull the phone away from my mouth. *"John is here!"*

The sergeant is stunned. *"He's what? SIMON, JOHN IS HERE!"*

Simon bellows from the dressing room, *"Jeff, get him — NOW!"*

John

I step into the elevator and the doors close. Brenda seemed surprised to see me, which is odd. It's not the first time I've come home early from rehearsal, and she's never given me that "Oh my God, did I just fart in church?" look before. I'm here now thanks to a domestic technicality. We can rehearse without air conditioning and we can rehearse without a proper orchestra, but we can't rehearse when the sixty-two-year-old director's portly fifty-three-year-old wife stands in the middle of the stage and at the top of her shrill, operatic voice accuses him of sleeping with a twenty-four-year-old understudy. Especially when the accusation is true. We wanted to hang around and hear all the juicy details (that apparently involve an unplanned pregnancy that may or may not be aborted) but that's just tacky, so everyone left.

Besides, one of the gaffers still hunkered down in the rafters said he'd give us the full scoop in the morning.

Brian has a lot of work to catch up on, but I'm sure he can do that with me here. I bet I can even help him. Well, no—I probably can't. He once said trying to work with me in the flat was like trying to knit a scarf with five kittens in his lap. That comment (which should have been taken as an insult) made me happy because he compared me to kittens (which are so adorable!). So my goal is to be a kitten and claw at him incessantly until he stops working and pays attention to me. And if this savvy (and horny) kitten can get some sex out of it, that's just a bonus. The elevator doors open.

"What the HELL are you doing here?" Jeff shouts in my face, scaring the crap out of me.

"Wha—what the—" He's hauled me out of the elevator, and now he's shoving me around the atrium with one hand clamped on my shoulder and one hand clamped on my ass.

"Come on, come on. Move, move, move, Johnny!"

"What are you— Why are you—" I'm inside the front door before I know it. "What's going on?" I finally manage to blurt out.

He slams the heavy door. "No time, honey! *Move!*"

"Can I at least take off my jacket?" I try to pull it off my shoulders.

"NO! Move, Johnny. *Move!*" He spins me around, hits me with the shoulder and ass clamp again and continues to propel me through the entryway, past the living room, down the hallway, and toward the master bedroom. At the entrance, he's still trying to shove me, but I rear up and stop in my tracks. I'm not going anywhere. I see people I don't know—police officers—hovering over Brian, who's getting out of bed and coming toward me. "What's…what's all this? What's going on? Brian?"

"Get in the back, John. I can't explain right now." He's trying to push me closer to the dressing room and I'm resisting.

My mouth drops open as more officers spill from the bathroom. "But what are all these—"

"No, John. No questions. Not now. Get in the back." He tries to push me again, and again I resist.

"But I don't—" I need to see what everyone is doing. I want to understand why they're all here.

"Look, John. Listen to me." Brian gently takes my face in his hands and turns it up to his. "No. Look at me, love. Ignore everything else. Look at me and listen, okay?"

I'm worried as I stare up into his eyes. I know all this has to be important. I just don't know why. "Okay."

"I need you to go with this constable and get in the back. I need you to be quiet—no matter what you see or hear. It's important that you're quiet. Okay?"

"Okay."

He releases my face and kisses my forehead. "I love you."

I let the police officer take me into the dressing room. Inside, it's like command central with seven uniformed officers standing around someone seated at a small table. I move closer to see it's Simon, wearing humongous earphones and hunched over his laptop. On the laptop screen, I see Brian climbing back into the bed. The view is from above the lowboy, looking out toward the sliders. There's a camera in our bedroom? When did we get a camera installed in our bedroom? And *why* did we get a camera installed in our bedroom? We're not investment bankers. An officer sticks a pair of earbuds into my ears. Another one peels off my jacket. I hear Brian's voice as I watch yet another officer bend over him and adjust papers on his lap. It all looks and sounds so surreal. I scope out the dressing room and see the nincompoops behind me, huddled in a circle. Martin gives me a thumbs up and winks. One of the beefier officers takes me by the shoulders and positions me behind Simon, a little to his left. Then he stands there—directly behind me—very closely. I open my mouth. I want to ask a million questions, but Brian told me to be quiet. I close my mouth, readjust the earbuds for better sound and watch the laptop screen.

Brian

My mobile buzzes. "Yup? The door is unlocked. Just come in. I'm in the bedroom." I was relaxed before, but now my heart is racing. The adrenalin is pounding in my ears and I'm sweating. John wasn't supposed to be here. That wasn't in the plan but there's nothing we can do about it now, so I need to look calm as I watch this worthless piece of shit creep into the bedroom. He moves right to the foot of the bed, exactly where we'd hoped he would stand.

"Brian." The word comes out sounding dead, void of any affectation or emotion.

"Mickey."

His shifty eyes dart around. "You're here alone?"

"Aye."

"How are you?" he asks with no enthusiasm.

"Not too bad."

"Still in a lot of pain?"

"No."

He seems disappointed with that answer. "I was surprised to hear you came out of the coma."

I don't say a word.

He gives me a wicked smile. "I was surprised to hear you survived at all."

"What do you want, Mickey?"

The smile disappears. I'd never noticed how eerily flaccid his jaw is without a smile, until now. "Just a chat." He walks over to the sliders, fingers the sheers and looks out across the river. "You know, like we used to. I'd come over here and we'd chat."

"About what?"

He turns and looks at me with an incredulous stare. "Well what do think, Brian? What do you think I want to chat about, huh?"

"I have no idea."

"Oh, yes you do. Yes indeed, you do." He walks back to the foot of the bed and freezes as his eyes lock onto John's small acrylic hanging above the chaise. It's an abstract rendered in vivid, swirling colors, but a knowing eye can easily tell it's a subtle view of two men having sex — and really enjoying it. One has dark hair, like John. The other has light brown hair, like me. After a few seconds, he turns and sits down on the chaise. His expression shows the painting has unsettled him, but he quickly gets back on track. "Let's chat about Johnny, okay? Let's chat about him."

I stay silent.

Mickey clasps his hands in his lap. "How is he, Brian? How's Johnny?"

"John is fine."

"Oh, yeah?" Mickey unclasps his hands and crosses his arms. Furrowing his brow, he gives me a serious stare. "How's the sex, Brian? How's the *sex* with Johnny? Is it good? Hmm? Is it *really* good?"

I glance at the painting above his head and let the hint of a smile start to curve my lips. I look down at him. I'm really enjoying this confrontation because I hate him so much. I know I could bring him to his boiling point within seconds by telling him how unbelievable it feels to have sex with John up to five times a day, and how we can never satisfy our need for it. I could infuriate him by telling him how John screams and cries and passes out because our lovemaking is so all consuming. But the camera is rolling and this is evidence. I won't allow *any* aspect of our sex life to be exposed to the public. I let the smile fade and I stay quiet.

He stands and walks to the sliders again. "I'm only asking because I wouldn't know." He quickly turns around. "You see, you stole him before I ever got the chance to find out, Brian. You stole him and then you *violated* him! Yes, Brian. Every time you touch my...my precious Johnny; every time you lay your *filthy* hands on his pure, clean body, you violate him!" He leans toward me and sneers, "So tell me, Brian: What's it like to *violate* my Johnny?"

I enjoy challenging his spiteful, vindictive stare because he can't stand the thought of me having sex with John. It's been eating him up inside for months, and it's turned him into a raging lunatic seething with bitterness, but I still stay quiet. I have to wait for the right moment and it should be coming up soon.

He walks back to the foot of the bed and paces the floor, highly agitated. "You know, I can't believe I've let you touch him this long. I don't think you deserve him. No, Brian. You certainly don't deserve him and you shouldn't be touching him."

"Is that why you brought David back and gave him the gun?"

He stops pacing, but he ignores my question—at first. He looks at the painting again and then stares at me. "Do you know what it's like for me every night, to know that you're SCREWING HIM? *To know that you're getting something I CAN'T HAVE?"* His face is crimson and he's breathing hard. He's almost apoplectic. I've never seen him in this state. He finally calms down and grows quiet as he runs his fingers through his frizzy hair. "Yeah, Brian. That's why I brought him back and gave him the gun. To do a little job for Mickey. One last little job for good, old uncle Mickey, *and he fucked that one up, too!* Six bullets — six chances to kill you and he *fucks... it... up.* He didn't even shoot you in your smug face the way I told him to. The worthless pile of..." Mickey stands rigid, eyes closed and fists clenched, just boiling with rage.

"So now what?"

His eyes shoot open. "Now what? *Now what?* Well, obviously I have to clean up after him — just like I always did — with the producers and the press and the police. Clean up David's mess, clean up David's mess. All for Johnny." He raises his arms and spreads them wide. "All this, for Johnny! It's amazing what love will make you do, isn't it, Brian?"

"That's not love. It's a sick, twisted obsession."

He plants his hands on his hips. "Oh, is it really? Well, thank you for that clarification, Mister Mega-Millionaire, Mister Filthy-Stinking-Rich. Thank you for taking time out of your *busy* day with all your *damned, important* meetings to set me straight on that!" He digs one hand into his coat pocket and pulls it back out. "And since you're so smart, why don't you tell me what this is, huh? Go on, go on and tell me!"

A tremor of fear runs through me. "A gun."

"What was that? *Speak up, man!*"

I clear my throat and swallow. "It's a gun."

"Yes, Brian. *Very, very good!* It's a gun! It's a *big* gun, isn't it? It's a lot bigger than that piece of crap I shot you with in LA, huh?" He gazes down at the gun and strokes it, almost lovingly. He's mesmerized by it. "This gun is the easiest way to make sure you never... *ever* touch my precious Johnny again."

"And you think he'll come running to you after you've killed me?"

His head jerks up as if he's just remembered I was still in the room, eyes wide and demented. "Oh no, Brian. I know I can't have him *now.* I know he'll never be mine *now*. I just want to make sure *you* don't ever have him again, that *you* never touch him again."

I watch as he raises the gun.

John

My mouth is open. It's been open for a long time due to shock, but now I need to say something. Now I need to yell. I take in a deep breath preparing to scream out, and immediately the beefy officer standing behind me clamps his big, fleshy hand over my mouth and nose. It's not a wise decision. I've just inhaled a lungful of air and I need to release it. I'm staring at a laptop screen, watching Mickey point a huge gun at Brian, and I'll pass out if I can't breathe.

"You need to give him some air, mate, or that pretty little queen is gonna faint," Martin whispers to the officer.

He slowly releases his hand.

As I exhale and then take in a silent, long breath, Martin leans forward, pulls out one earbud, and ominously whispers, "Johnny, for Brian's sake, you... cannot... scream."

I nod and close my mouth.

Brian

I see tears well up in Mickey's eyes. His hand is shaking. "Why, Brian? *Why?* When you had your pick of all those beautiful women — any of them — why did you go after Johnny?"

I keep my answer short. "It was meant to be."

He violently shakes his head. "No. No, I don't believe that."

I hold his gaze as I try to end this scene because I know John can't last much longer in the dressing room now that he's seen a gun. "Mickey, I was meant to be with John until the day I die."

His hand stops shaking. "I wish I could say I'm sorry, Brian. I really wish I could say I'm sorry for doing this, but I can't, because I'm not. You took my precious Johnny and my mind can't accept that. You deserve this. You truly deserve this."

The gun terrifies me. It takes every ounce of courage to keep my eyes open, unflinching and riveted on it, praying he doesn't hit my unprotected face. Mickey, being the pathetic chicken shit that he is, tightly closes his eyes just before he pulls the trigger. I hear the discharge: an exploding cherry bomb that nearly pops my eardrums. I see the flash. It blinds me, like the combined flash of a dozen cameras. The projectile slams into my sternum, pushing me back into the pillows and forcing the air out of my lungs. The brutal impact sends a lightning bolt of pain through my body, but the slug falls harmlessly into my lap. Except for a little river noise coming from the open sliders, the room is silent again. Mickey cautiously opens his eyes. He's in shock as he sees me staring back at him. Without lowering my gaze, I reach down and pick up the mutilated bullet. I hold it up between my thumb and index finger so he can see it clearly. His mouth falls open. He looks down at the gun and turns it sideways, dumbfounded. "But I don't—"

Sergeant Mitner dashes out of the dressing room. "Mister Spencer?"

Mickey swings around to face him, mouth still open, eyes wide with surprise. "What?"

"I'll take that, please." He pries the gun from Mickey's grasp. "Can you turn around for me, sir?"

Mickey, still in a state of shock as he sees several constables pouring out of doorways, doesn't move. Sergeant Mitner turns him around and places cuffs on his wrists. Now he's facing me again. His eyes are demented and wild as they lock onto mine.

"Michael Lloyd Spencer, I'm placing you under arrest for the attempted mur—"

"*I HATE YOU! I HATE YOU! I HATE YOU!*" he screams in a shrill, piercing voice I've never heard before, the words coming out with a spray of spittle. His face is vibrant red. The tendons in his neck and the veins at his temples are bulging as he strains forward, trying to lunge at me. Sergeant Mitner turns him around, and he sees John standing a few feet away, brought out from the dressing room by one of the constables. His contorted face relaxes into a soft, caring smile. "Oh, Johnny, Johnny," he coos.

John's face is ashen. When he speaks, his voice is quiet, almost a whisper. "You were my manager and one of my best friends. I...I don't understand. How could you...?"

"You should have been *mine*, Johnny. I waited ten years and he took you, but you should have been *mine*," Mickey tries to explain, leaning toward him.

"All right, Mister Spencer. Let's go. This way. That's it. Just a little to the left. Now watch your step. Don't trip over that. That's good."

I climb out of the bed and untangle myself from the mike wires. I reach out for John and wrap my arms around him. I hold him tightly as he cries into my neck and while everyone else trickles out of the dressing room and the bathroom. I am so relieved this is over. The constables eventually leave, taking Simon's laptop and the bulk of the camera equipment. Simon and the lads flop onto the bed, exhausted from the stress of the ordeal. I rub John's back and kiss his head, telling him I love him, over and over, while he sobs. I am *so* proud of him. He kept quiet. He held it together. He didn't panic, and he didn't pass out.

33
The Sober Realization Of What's
To Come

John — August 19

Emotionally spent and drained of energy, we're sprawled out on the massive bed in various semi-prostrate positions. Brian has stripped off the Kevlar vest and is propped against the headboard with pillows, holding me in front of him.

Sergeant Mitner appears in the bedroom doorway. "Brian?"

"Yes, Ian?"

"There was a guy in the lobby who wanted to see you. He looked a little shady so I said no." He walks over to the bed and holds out a large envelope. "He asked me to give you this. I'll be off now. It was a good sting. Everyone did his part. I'll call you and Simon in the morning. You can come down to the station and we'll review the tape then, okay?"

"Okay. Thank you, Ian, for everything." He looks at the envelope briefly, sets it aside and wraps his arm around me again.

I twist my head so I can look up at his face. "I don't understand. How did you know the bullets weren't real?"

"I switched them," Prissy proudly says.

"The police had Mickey under surveillance ever since Brian came out of the coma and told them his theory on who was behind the shooting," Simon explains. "When they found out he purchased a gun and ammunition in LA, they knew he was getting ready to try again."

"I remembered you still had Mickey's keys from when we moved your stuff so I nicked them and went in one day when he was out. I replaced the real bullets with rubber bullets the police gave me. I even remembered to replace the one in the chamber." Again, Prissy is proud of himself.

"The most important one," Ben reminds everyone with his arm wrapped protectively around his petite princess.

"Then we just waited until he called Brian and you were out of the flat," Martin says. "We'd set up the camera days before by drilling a hole through the back of the bathroom cabinet and scratching off the foil on the mirror. And no, we didn't film anything until today."

"But how did you know Mickey was behind this from the start?"

"The bloke that shot me was a bum, John. He was filthy. When you said it was David, I knew he couldn't have purchased a ticket from the States. He couldn't afford it. Someone bought it for him and someone provided the gun." Brian takes a moment to kiss my head. "When he shot me, I remembered the sound of that gun. I'd heard it once before—eleven years ago—when Mickey accidentally shot me in the leg."

"Through forensics, we compared the bullet from eleven years ago to the ones pulled out of Brian's chest and stomach. We had a dead match," Simon says.

I look up at Brian again. "You kept a bullet for eleven years?"

"In a way. I never had it taken out. It was the day before Christmas Eve and I didn't want to miss my flight back to Scotland. It had lodged in the leg muscle and it wasn't bothering me much. I know hospitals are required to investigate gunshot wounds and I didn't have time to deal with that so I just had a little backstreet clinic sew me up. I thought I'd have it removed when I had more time." Brian falls silent.

"Then came Ayden's death," Simon offers.

"I forgot all about it," Brian quietly adds.

"That was a pretty dangerous thing to do—leave a bullet in your leg," Jeff says.

Simon turns to him. "In this case, Jeff, it was the *best* thing to do. Back then, they'd have dug it out and tossed it. Who's going to believe a man who says he remembers how an unregistered gun sounded eleven years ago? That bullet was a big piece of evidence. We *had* to have it." He looks at me. "That was the minor operation they performed after he came out of the coma."

I look up at Brian again. "And you didn't tell me any of this. Why? Why didn't you trust me?"

"It had nothing to do with not trusting you, John. I trust you with my life. You're just a bit... emotional. You have a tendency to get excited... and panic... and pass out. Would you have let me sit here while Mickey pointed a gun at me?"

"No, of course not. But we could have thought up another plan, another way, together." I'm upset because I wasn't included — in any of it. If I hadn't come home unexpectedly, I wouldn't have even been here for the sting.

Simon explains everything to me while Brian opens the envelope and starts reading the documents. "With David dead, Mickey could have easily told the police that he did buy a ticket for him to come back here, but that David stole his gun and tried to kill Brian all on his own out of jealousy. We had to get him to admit he put David up to the first try and that he provided the gun so we could get him for one count of attempted murder. We also had to get him to pull the trigger on Brian, himself, so we could get the second count of attempted murder, *and* we had to get it all on tape to ensure our best chance of the maximum sentence."

"I'd like to know how he got that big gun into England," Martin says.

"Maybe he took it apart and sent the bits through the post," Jeff suggests.

"Well, if we can prove that, we could probably add a few more charges," Simon says.

"I had the most important job. I had to switch the bullets," Prissy reminds everyone — again.

"And I'm grateful you did, Prissy. I owe you," Brian mumbles distractedly, engrossed in the documents.

"Okay. How about giving me a million pounds?"

My eyes go wide. "Prissy! Don't you *dare* ask him for money. You're staying in that beautiful condo *and* he got you out of Gatling Road. Don't you even think of —"

"Why not? He said he owed me. He's got a lot more. It's not like he's gonna miss one lousy million," he defiantly whines.

I feel Brian laughing low in his chest. Then he starts to smile. "Sure, Prissy. I'll give you a million pounds."

He's amazed. "You will?"

"Better yet, I'll give you one-point-seven million, okay?"

Now Prissy is excited and clapping his hands. "One-point-seven? *Really?*"

"Really."

I'm appalled. "You're kidding, right? You are not giving this pale-assed Tinkerbell one-point-seven million pounds."

Brian beams at Prissy and winks. "Sure I am."

"Why?"

Brian holds up the documents. "Because that's what the East River Street Residence Consortium is suing me for. Apparently, a few weeks ago, someone on the east balcony of this penthouse was documented no less than five times spying on the residents living on East River Street with a pair of binoculars — bare-assed naked."

Prissy's face has turned a deathly white. "Well, that could have been anyone." His little hands are desperately clutching Ben's arm and his big eyes are darting between Simon, Jeff, and Martin, pleading for back up. "We...we were all staying here. Anyone could have done that."

"Not according to this. They give a *very* detailed description of the individual." Brian studies the pages for a few seconds. "Let's see here... Oh, yes, and I quote: 'a miniscule, flat-chested woman with yellow, spiky hair, sitting on a stool, wearing cowboy boots, using huge binoculars, whose ghostly white, shriveled, naked body resembled a novelty store rubber chicken.'"

Prissy is outraged, but nothing can stop our laughter. We see it in his impish face but we still can't stop laughing. Jeff is rolling around on the bed in convulsions and Simon is almost peeing his pants. Martin takes the documents from Brian. He's got tears streaming down his cheeks from laughing so hard as he's trying to read them.

"A FLAT-CHESTED WOMAN? SHRIVELED? A RUBBER CHICKEN?" Prissy shrieks in his tiny, high voice. *"Who the hell would compare me to a CHICKEN?"*

"The entire East River Street Residence Consortium Board of Elders and seven investigating constables," Martin says. "They reviewed surveillance footage from a closed-circuit video camera sixty meters away and that's the best description they could come up with. They also couldn't find any" —Martin squints hard at the page— "'distinguishable male genitalia.'" He tries to keep a straight face but loses it at the end.

It takes a while for the laughter to die down as Ben holds Prissy, who's crying inconsolably, and rubs his back.

Brian reassures him. "I'll take care of it, Prissy. Don't worry. I'll make it all go away."

Simon finally regains his composure and says, "I don't want to spoil all the fun we're having but I need to point out something significant, something pretty serious."

Jeff straightens up and leans hard against Martin. "What's that?"

"This sting and the impending inquisition—and everything that's going to come along with it—will hit the papers soon, probably tomorrow morning. It's going to be a big deal, Brian; especially because it involves John. It's going to generate a lot of publicity." He pauses. "I think John is going to come out of this with an unbelievable amount of increased popularity, being the object of desire in what might be considered a love triangle that never was." He smiles at me and then focuses on Brian. "Unfortunately, Brian, it's going to hit you like a high-speed train at full throttle. You've had some relative privacy from the general public just hanging around your posh West River Street neighborhood for the last four and a half months courting your handsome, new boyfriend. But your personal life is going to be revealed to everyone—and I mean *everyone*. It's not going to be easy. A whole lot of intolerant people are going to make sure you know exactly what they think of you and your... alternative lifestyle and they'll do it in the cruelest, nastiest ways you can imagine." He turns to Martin, who's holding Jeff's hand tightly. "And that goes for you too, Marty, just not as much as for Brian. Unfortunately, he's a bit more high profile and so is John."

Everyone is quiet. We all know what Simon is talking about. We've all been there, except Martin. But he's hung around us long enough to know what he's in for. He's heard it and he's seen it. The situation will test his commitment to Jeff and it's going to test Brian's commitment to me. I squeeze his hands.

Simon says with sincerity, "We'll all be there, right beside you, solidly supporting you every step of the way. You know that."

Everyone nods.

"I know," Brian quietly acknowledges. "I know."

There's a lull as we all contemplate the future.

"So," Simon says, clapping his hands, breaking the silence, and giving Brian a big smile. "Do you think you can handle living the exciting life of a gay man with a bunch of interesting and fun gay friends?"

He looks down at me. "Oh, I think so; as long as John stays with me."

"Of course I'm staying with you. I'm not going anywhere." I gaze up into his eyes. "Because we don't try to do things like this alone, do we?"

He smiles. He's surprised I remember his words. "No, we don't."

"Because we have each other, and there's nothing to be ashamed of, right?"

He nods. "You are absolutely right, love."

▪ ▪ ▪

I hope you enjoyed reading this story as much as I enjoyed writing it. Please visit www.straightmangay.com to leave a book review and to learn more about *Straight Man Gay Two*.

Lightning Source UK Ltd.
Milton Keynes UK
UKOW04f0903240315

248413UK00001B/151/P